ADVANCE PRAISE FOR

BLOOD OF PARADISE

"*Blood of Paradise* proves that David Corbett can do what so few others can: write a thought-provoking, intelligent thriller that never loses its edge for a minute. Gripping, powerful, and beautifully written, *Blood of Paradise* is a terrific read that will keep readers enthralled from start to finish."

—JAN BURKE, author of *Kidnapped*

"David Corbett has created a *Quiet American* for the new century. Angry and impassioned, *Blood of Paradise* is that rare beast: a _____ _____ _____ _____ _____ thrilling."

...ad Thing

...through

...abroad.

...bravura

...tánamo

...age, as

...a novel

...at one."

...his Rain

...ery bad

...dly into

...tion on

...Reader

...y, there

...it now,

...Highway

...Daughter

ALSO BY DAVID CORBETT

The Devil's Redhead

Done for a Dime

BLOOD OF PARADISE

BLOOD OF PARADISE

a novel

David Corbett

BALLANTINE BOOKS · NEW YORK

A Ballantine Books Trade Paperback Original

Copyright © 2007 by David Corbett
Map copyright © 2007 by David Lindroth

Published in the United States by Ballantine Books, an imprint of The Random House Publishing Group, a division of Random House, Inc., New York.

BALLANTINE and colophon are registered trademarks of Random House, Inc.

MORTALIS and colophon are trademarks of Random House, Inc.

ISBN 978-0-8129-7733-2

Printed in the United States of America

www.mortalis-books.com

9 8 7 6 5 4 3 2

THIS BOOK IS DEDICATED TO THE MEMORY OF

José Gilberto Soto,
an American citizen
and union organizer
murdered in El Salvador
on November 5, 2004.
The crime remains unsolved.

The template for Iraq today is not Vietnam, with which it has often been compared, but El Salvador.

—Peter Maass, "The Way of the Commandos,"
The New York Times Magazine, May 1, 2005

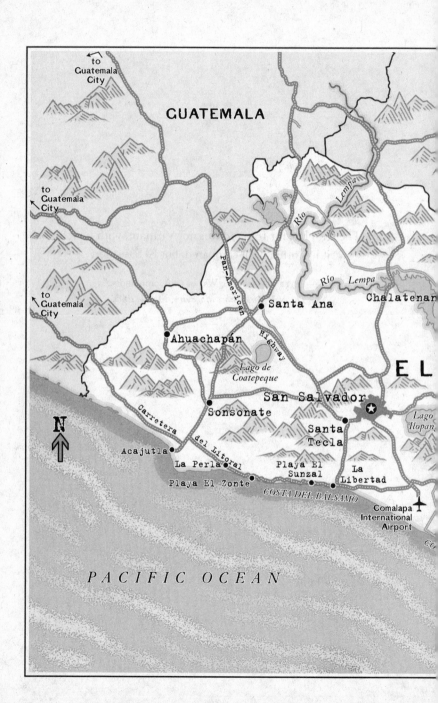

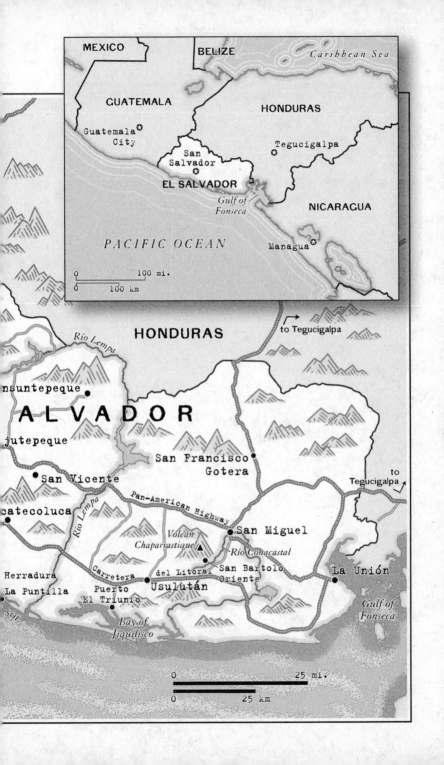

GLOSSARY OF TERMS

ARENA Alianza Republicana Nacionalista, the major right-wing political party in El Salvador

areneros supporters of ARENA

CAFTA Central American Free Trade Agreement

catorce familias the "fourteen families," an extended group of related Salvadoran families of particular wealth, power, and social prominence

caudillo a large property holder, military leader, or other "strongman"

Chávez, Hugo Leftist president of Venezuela; the current bête noir of American foreign policy in Latin America

efemelenistas supporters of the FMLN

FMLN Frente Farabundo Martí para la Liberación Nacional, the major left-wing political party in El Salvador, formerly the unified guerrilla opposition

Fuerza Aérea the Salvadoran air force

LEGAT legal attaché, the head of an overseas FBI office

Los Patrióticos a war-era death squad consisting of middle- and upper-class professionals operating out of the First Brigade's civil defense training program

Los Soldados de San Miguel a (fictional) death squad operating in eastern El Salvador

maquila a factory that assembles imported components for export

mara a Central American gang

Mara Dieciocho the smaller of the two main Salvadoran gangs, an outgrowth of the Eighteenth Street gang (Calle 18) in Los Angeles

Mara Salvatrucha the larger of the two main Salvadoran gangs, originally formed by Salvadoran refugees in Los Angeles as protection against Mexican gangs, specifically the Eighteenth Street Gang—members are called *salvatruchos*

marero a Salvadoran gang member

Mercado Nacional de Artesanías artisans' market, where native crafts can be purchased

ODIC the Overseas Development Insurance Corporation—a (fictional) export credit agency funding and insuring American investment in international development projects

placa a hand signal denoting gang affiliation

PNC Policía Nacional Civil, the national police force formed after the UN Peace Accords to supplant military involvement in routine police work

remesas remittances—i.e., money sent back to El Salvador from migrants abroad

SOUTHCOM Southern Command, the U.S. military's regional command structure for Latin America

PART I

WHATEVER BECAME OF THE LAUGH MASTERS?

It's only those who do nothing
that make no mistakes, I suppose.

—JOSEPH CONRAD, *An Outcast of the Islands*

1

Cocooned in a hammock at Playa El Zonte, Jude launched the siesta hour with a lusty tug from his beer, swaying beneath the thatched roof of a *glorieta*. Above, the sun was blistering; even the skirring wind off the ocean felt parched and hot. Below, the beach of black volcanic sand with its scatterings of smooth dark stone curled out to the point. He wondered what it would take to know—not suspect or hope or pretend but *know*—that the woman he spotted, out there on the rocks, was or wasn't the love of his life.

He knew her: Eileen Browning, fellow American. They'd bumped into each other here and there the past month at Santa María Mizata, Playa El Sunzal, most recently on the pier at La Libertad, browsing the fishmonger stalls. There, with the briny tang of ice-tubbed shrimp, mackerel, and *boca colorada* brewing all around them in the rippling heat, he'd almost convinced himself that Dr. Browning, as she hated to be called, had been coming on to him.

At this particular moment she walked the beach alone, sandals in hand, wearing a polka-dot halter and cutoffs and a wide-brimmed hat, eyes toward the water as she watched a stray dog take a crap in the shallows.

Mark that in your tourist guide, Jude thought, memorizing the spot where the dog crouched and guessing at the current so as to avoid an unpleasant step later. Meanwhile Eileen turned back and resumed her lazy march toward the *glorieta,* holding her hat atop her head against the scorching wind.

From their previous encounters, Jude had learned she was a marine's daughter turned scholar, down here for postdoctoral work in cultural anthropology. She was cataloging folk crafts—pottery, weaving, embroidery—before they disappeared forever. He liked that about her, the devotion to vanishing things. He liked a lot of things about her, actually. She'd grown up around strong men— raised by wolves, she put it—and was pretty in a smart-girl way, lanky and leggy with strawberry blond hair and gold-rimmed glasses. There were those, he supposed, who might find fault with her large teeth and big boyish hands, her long skinny feet, but he was at that stage when these things seemed the true test of her loveliness—the endearing flaws that made her unique. Her perfection.

As she came closer it became clear she intended to stop and visit, and his heart kicked a little. He roused himself from his torpor, thinking: Comport yourself, soldier.

It was the heart of the dry season, the beginning of Lent. The surf camp was otherwise empty of foreigners, just the two of them. The restaurant and bar remained open, though, for day-trippers like Jude, drop-ins like Eileen.

Entering the thatch shade of the *glorieta,* she dropped her sandals, removed her hat, and shook out her hair. Her halter was knotted at the neck, revealing bikini tan lines striping over her shoulders to her back. Jude pictured the triangles of white skin around her nipples, then nudged the thought away, not wanting to be unchivalrous.

"We meet again." She perched herself on the nearest table, took out a kerchief and mopped her face and neck, then dusted sand off her shins. "If I didn't know better, I'd think you were following me."

Her voice was a raspy alto, one more thing to like. Jude said, "If I was following you, I'd be behind you."

She cocked an eyebrow. "Point taken." Nodding at his beer, she said, "Mind if I . . . ?"

"No. No." He handed it to her and she knocked back a swig. He tried to picture her on campus, earthy babe of the brainy set. The bohemian broad.

"I'm going to want one of these." She handed back his beer and glanced over her shoulder. "Have you eaten yet?"

Behind her, two *indígena* women worked the kitchen attached to the bar. It was a rustic business: wood roasting pit, propane grill, a sand floor with a hen and several chicks dithering underfoot—plus the briny dog from the shallows earlier, watching as her two pups tumbled together, chasing each other around. The fried corn fragrance of *pupusas* wafted toward them, mingling with the smoky aroma of a roasting chicken.

"Just." Jude patted his midriff.

"Oh well." She made a lonesome-me face. "I saw the truck when I drove up—it's yours, right?—but there was nobody around. When did you get here?"

"Dawn." The best surfing came at daybreak and late afternoon, when the doldrums smoothed the chop from the ocean, the waves glassy. He'd stayed out longer than usual this morning, though, enjoying the solitude. Gypsies would show up the next few weeks, jamming the lineups. Come the rains, the ocean swelled. So did the crowds. "I was out beyond the break."

"I got here sometime around ten, I think, and—Oh." She took her glasses off. "Excuse me." She started working a speck of sand from her eye, blinking. It took only a second, but in the moment after, sitting there with her glasses in her hand, her face transformed. Unwary eyes. A helpless smile.

Jude marveled at that sometimes—the way a woman changed when all she'd done was remove a scarf, an earring. Her glasses. Maybe it was his little fetish, but he doubted that. He suspected the French even had a word for it.

"Anyhoo," the glasses went back on, "I got here hungry, then just decided to take a long walk down the beach before lunch."

Looking for me, Jude suspected. Hoped. Pretended.

"Now I'm famished." Instead of heading off to order food, though, she picked up her hat and started fanning herself with it. Wisecracking eyes, a rag-doll smile. "I didn't figure you for the type, by the way." She nodded at his board. "Given the work you do."

Suddenly, the air between them felt charged. "Figure me for what type?"

"You know." She affected dope-eyed hipdom and a blasted voice. "Jude McDude."

"Oh. Right. Me all over."

She nudged him with her foot. "I'm teasing." A new smile, half-impish, half-contrite. "My dad surfs. Big-time. So I'll grant you there isn't a type. And if an old leatherneck like Pop can hang with the waterheads, I don't see why a bodyguard can't."

He cringed. Bodyguard. It called to mind steroids for breakfast and cream corn for brains, all stuffed in a bad suit. But he guessed that if he reminded her the term of art was "executive protection specialist"—EP for short—it would hardly redeem her opinion of what he did. Or of him.

His cell phone trilled inside his ruck.

"I'll let you grab that," she said, getting up.

"No, it's okay." He reached down, pulled the phone out, and read the number on the digital display. He didn't recognize it. And he'd just begun his furlough, ten days off after twenty on, his usual work schedule. He was on his own time and didn't want intrusions. Especially now. "I can let it go."

"It's okay. I'll just grab some lunch and a cold one." She shot him another mischievous smile. "Let you deal with the captains of industry."

It's a wrong number, he wanted to say, but she was already ambling off. Jude stared at her back, exposed by her halter and crisscrossed with its misfit tan lines, and doubted he'd ever hated his cell phone more—at which point the ringer chirped again, the same numerals reappeared. He picked up simply to cut short the bother: "¿Quién es?"

It took a second for the voice on the other end to emerge from the static. "Hello? Yeah. Hello, Jude? ... My name's Bill. I was a friend of your dad's."

Ten years collapsed at the sound of the voice. And yet, in a way, Jude had been expecting this call. There were rumors.

The voice said: "Bill Malvasio. Not sure you remember me."

"Of course I remember."

"Kinda outta the blue, I realize."

"No. I mean, yeah, but it's not that. I was just ..." His voice trailed away. The static of the phone connection swelled then ebbed, a sound like sandpaper against skin. "I was just talking to somebody else. The shift, from that to this. To you, I mean. I dunno. Just sudden."

Jude had spent a good part of his boyhood watching his dad and Bill Malvasio head off together—cop weddings, cop funerals, drinking parties, poker marathons, or just another shift in the Eighteenth District. To call them best friends missed the thing by half. Malvasio was like family, but not the kind the women wanted around—more like a black sheep uncle, the fun uncle, the one with the wily mean streak. Jude hated admitting it, but he'd competed most of his life against Wild Bill, vying for his father's respect. And despised not Malvasio but himself for that.

"Listen, Jude. I realize this is a little late but, about your dad's passing, I'm sorry. Ray was still young."

Jude wrestled with a number of things to say, none of them particularly astute. His dad had drowned on Rend Lake—accident or suicide, no one knew for sure. A bad end to a lot of bad business.

"Proud man, your father. None of us were what they made us out to be. Certainly not Ray. I've got some stories in that regard, if you'd like to hear them."

Jude sat up in the hammock finally. Planting his feet in the rocky sand, he checked the incoming number again. Sure enough, Malvasio was in-country. "Run that by me again."

"We could get together. I mean, if you're up for it."

"When do you mean?"

"Now, you want."

Jude felt stunned by the offer, but refusing was out of the question. Hear a few stories about my dad? Sure. Add a few more collectibles to the museum of bullshit. But it wasn't just that. There were about a thousand questions he wanted to ask, starting with: "If you don't mind my asking, how'd you get my cell number?"

"I've got friends down here," Malvasio said. "If I didn't, I couldn't survive."

Jude was still sitting there, holding his phone, when Eileen walked back, a plate of chicken with *pupusas* and *curtido de repollo* in one hand, two cold beers in the other.

"Get whatever it was sorted out?" She sat down in the same spot as before, handing him one of the beers. Wiggling her hips to settle in, she set her plate in her lap and picked up a chicken thigh.

"I have to go," he told her.

Almost imperceptibly, her face fell. Then, recovering: "Anything wrong?"

"No, no. Just . . . an old family friend." Not knowing what to do with the beer, he just sat there, holding it like he was trying to figure it out. "He's over on the Costa del Sol. Wants to get together." It seemed unwise to say more.

"He's down here on vacation?"

She bit into the greasy crackling skin of the chicken. He caught himself staring at her mouth.

"Not exactly," he said.

2

EVERY KID GROWS UP KNOWING THERE'S A LINE BETWEEN THE LIFE he wants and the life he gets. Jude walked that line as long as he could, then crossed over for good one August afternoon before his senior year in high school.

He was sitting on his bed in the basement, icing an ankle he'd torn up during tackling drills the day before, when he heard a sudden clamor of men and cars just outside. The front door had a buzzer, not a bell, and someone jabbed the button hard three times. Jude listened as his mother droned "I'll get it" and clopped in her flats down the wood-floored hall. Then he heard her voice turn shrill and afraid as she argued with a man in the doorway.

It was just the two of them in the house. His sister, Colleen, had trundled off to her flute lesson. His dad had reported for duty.

He rose from the bed, tested his ankle, and hobbled upstairs. Turning the corner at the top, he came up behind his mother and found a half dozen FBI agents in their blue raid jackets clustered on the sunlit porch, with backup from Chicago PD. The lead agent loomed in the doorway, so eerily tall he had to stoop to make eye contact. The eyes were a milky green.

Holding out an envelope, he said, "We didn't come here to talk it over, Mrs. McManus. Here's your copy of the warrant. Now step aside, please."

They planted Jude and his mother in the living room and turned on the TV. There was breaking news, reported by a chesty moon-faced Asian woman in a bright red summer suit who'd chosen the Cabrini Green projects for her backdrop. Behind her, the skels were mobbing tall, draped in bling and pimped out in skullies or hats kicked right, Gangster Disciples, some of them throwing signs, stacking the Cobra Stones in contempt, the whole hand business, others crowing out, "All in one," or just bellowing names—Raymont, Stocker, Girl Dog, D.T.—like everybody was missing the show.

Jude noticed how the Asian newscaster pursed her lipsticked mouth around her vowels and cagily moved her microphone first to expose, then conceal, her cleavage. Looking back on it now, all these years later, he realized he'd focused on such things as a way to divert his attention from what she was saying. Regardless, whenever he dredged up the scene from memory, that's how he pictured it: sitting there next to his tight-lipped mother in the muggy August heat, watching as the plump Asian woman in her brassy red suit unmasked Sergeant Ray McManus as a rogue cop, complete with footage of him taken off in handcuffs from the Eighteenth District station house.

Jude's dad wasn't the only one named. His two best friends on the force, Bill Malvasio and Phil Strock, faced the same charges: jacking drug dealers, basically. Jude remembered thinking at the time (and on and off in the years since) that thousands if not millions in the greater Chicago area would shrug off such behavior as proof of a go-getter attitude, not guilt. And the accused seemed to know that only too well. According to the reports, they'd nicknamed themselves the Laugh Masters, mimicking rappers—Laugh Master Ray, Laugh Master Phil—to make it all sound like some crazy prank. Except the stories of street dealers dragged off, pummeled with batons, boot-stomped till they lay unconscious in their own blood—then robbed of cash, drugs, jewelry, weapons—didn't seem like such a stitch to the powers-that-be.

Strock, on disability leave, got arrested at his north-side flat. Malvasio, the reputed ringleader, was never found. He'd fled, rumors went, to El Salvador, where he had contacts from taking part in a police training program. And that, for those who cared, added the final ironic twist to the whole business: The man who got away vanished down a path paved with good intentions.

———

JUDE DROVE IN HIS PICKUP TO SAN MARCELINO, A FISHING VILLAGE at the western, shabbier limits of the Costa del Sol, barreling down the long dusty lane from the highway as he headed for the restaurant on the beach where Malvasio said he'd be waiting.

It was late afternoon, Jude delayed by a herd of intractable oxen on the road between La Libertad and Comalapa. He parked his truck in an alley beside the restaurant, hoisted his spare from the truck bed, and checked it with the bartender to make sure thieves didn't walk away with it. Finding only staff downstairs, gathered around a boom box playing a jaunty two-beat *cumbia,* he climbed to the second floor. No one was there except a lone American sitting at a wood-plank table along the outer wall. Beyond him, the beach extended eastward for miles, rimmed with Miami palms and broad-leaf almond trees. Fishing boats—*lanchas*—dotted the surf, heading out for a night of work as a hazy red sun perched low above the horizon.

Seeing Jude approach, the lone man rose and stuck out his hand. "My God. For a moment there I would've sworn it was Ray."

It wasn't the wisest opening but Jude let it go. Besides, Malvasio wasn't the only one startled by appearances. He was much thinner, still fit but wiry. The heat could do that. His once-handsome face looked drawn and weathered, rimmed with hair cut short and patched with gray, his skin tanned to the point he could pass for a local. Be a trick to match him with an old picture, Jude thought, wondering if that wasn't the point. Mostly, though, the change was in the eyes. They had a lifeless density to them now, like he'd walked back the long way from the worst imaginable.

"Sit," Malvasio said. "You want something to eat? Drink?"

Jude noticed that Malvasio was working on a bowl of *crema de camarones,* a cream chowder made with shrimp, and washing it down with Pilsener, the local lager. *Pilsener,* the ads went, *Es Cosa de Cheros.* It's a guy thing.

"Beer'd be nice," Jude said, taking a seat.

Malvasio turned his head and cupped a hand to his mouth, yelling to be heard over the boom box: "*¡Paulo, otra fría por favor!*" Turning back, he said, "Ironic, our both being here. In El Salvador, I mean."

Isn't it though, Jude thought. "You found out I was down here how exactly?"

Malvasio ducked behind a smile, picked up his spoon, and trailed it lazily through his soup. "Get right to the point."

"It's a fair question."

"Of course it is. But it came out sounding like you're sorry you came." Malvasio glanced up. "Are you?"

"Not yet."

That earned a laugh. "Well, long story short, like I told you, I've got friends down here."

"We talking about the guys you helped train, the ones who supposedly tucked you away?"

Their eyes met, and for an instant Jude saw the man he'd known growing up looking back at him. It felt gratifying. And unnerving.

Malvasio said, "Wasn't sure how much you knew."

"I'm just repeating what they said on the news," Jude said. "That a problem?"

"I don't know. You tell me."

Suddenly the waiter was there, prompting a truce as he set a small wet glass and another bottle of Pilsener on the table. Jude pushed the glass aside and wiped the tin taste off the lip of the beer bottle with his shirttail, waiting for the waiter to vanish downstairs again.

"I'd like to hear your side of it," Jude said, wincing a little at how earnest he sounded.

Malvasio tilted his bowl and spooned up the last portion of milky soup. "You're right. I met a guy down here through the training program, and when I needed a place to run I thought of him. He did me a good turn, stuck his neck out. And the FBI sent a fugitive team down here, they grilled my guy good but he held his mud—not that they could do anything to him, but still, I owe him for that. I've done what I can to keep my nose clean, not embarrass him, and he's referred me on to people he knows, a job here, job there. I've done okay."

"You work for who now?"

"I'd rather not get into names, if that's all right. Not yet. Let's just say I work for some people in business here."

That means less than nothing, Jude thought. "Doing?"

"Private security, same as you, though mostly I train. A lot of the guys down here are ex-military, which means their major talent is waiting to get paid."

He made a little snort at his own joke. Jude was still back at *same as you*.

"Any event, that's the long way around to how I found out you were down here. You're working for some guy who's involved in water issues, am I right?"

Jude's current principal was Axel Odelberg, a hydrologist working with Horizon Project Management, an American company lending expertise on aquifer drawdown and recharge rates for a soft drink company called Estrella. It had a bottling plant it hoped to expand near the town of San Bartolo Oriente.

Jude said, "How do you know that?"

"Saw your name and his on the checkout sheet at the archives at ANDA's headquarters in San Salvador."

ANDA was the national water agency, on the block to be privatized. Jude had accompanied Axel there more times than he could count.

"My people have land use and water rights stuff to arrange," Malvasio said. "That means they deal with ANDA all the time. Just luck of the draw, one day when I was on the travel squad, we showed up the same day as you, maybe couple hours after. I'd pick out McManus regardless, but with a first name Jude, I figured if it was just coincidence it earned some kind of prize. I asked my buddy—again, I'd like to leave out names for now, don't take that wrong—and he asked around and finally got back to me, gave me the bead on what you were doing here and how I might get in touch. I hope that's okay."

Too late if it isn't, Jude thought. It must have shown on his face, because Malvasio jumped right back in with, "Believe me, it's not like my guy's handing out your name and cell to the highest bidder. It's not like that."

"I'd like his name," Jude said, thinking: It's only fair. His information for mine.

"I'd really rather not do that."

"I'm not asking," Jude said. "I want his name."

Malvasio seemed taken aback by Jude's tone. He'd known a boy. "Listen, Jude, this guy, he can't afford trouble."

"How much did you pay him?"

"Nothing, it was a favor. Look—you know how things work here. The important stuff gets done on a handshake—people you know, people you trust. My buddy trusted me. The folks I work for would make things right if I crossed any lines, but I wasn't going to do that. I owe too many people and, really, all I wanted was to sit here, like this, with you. Ten years is a long time away from everything you ever knew. I saw a name I recognized, one that meant a lot to me once. Still does. It felt like a gift, I wanted to connect. If there's any blame to be had in that, it's mine."

Jude wasn't quite sure what to make of all that, but he felt moved. Again, the story was in the eyes. Malvasio could talk all he wanted about his "buddy"—that wasn't comradery, that was barter. Laugh Master Bill was a friendless man. Maybe he'd escaped his due in the States, but the past ten years had taken something out of him, like he'd served a kind of free-range solitary confinement. Not that lonesome excused anything. But if Jude really wanted to press the issue of the local cop digging up his private number, sneaking it to Malvasio, he'd also have to explain to somebody in officialdom that when a suspected felon, a fugitive—and, rumor had it, a killer—had used

Jude's number to get in touch, the upright American, young McManus, hadn't contacted the embassy, the FBI, the Policía Nacional Civil, or anyone else. On the contrary, he'd jumped in his truck and hustled right over. There were reasons for that, of course, but they wouldn't matter to anyone but him.

A pair of wispy spiders scurried across the tabletop. Watching them, Malvasio said, "Tell me what you'd like to do."

Jude made a show of his discontent but then just shrugged. "Nothing. Let's drop it."

Malvasio's smile started small, then grew. "Thank you, sir."

"These people you work for," Jude said, "what kind of business are we talking about?"

"They're old money," Malvasio said, "which down here means land. They grow sugar, bananas. Even found a way to expand their coffee production—no small trick, the way the Vietnamese have glutted the market the past couple years. There's a tale. You want a racket, try the international banks that funded that disaster."

"Your employers know what happened? Back in Chicago, I mean."

"It's a bit of an open secret and, well, it's interesting. What we did, me and your dad and Phil, I mean—it's a shrug and a wink down here. Somebody thinks you're out of line, he cuts out your heart and feeds it to the dogs. You find bodies along the road without heads or hands, they call it a haircut and a manicure. But hell, you know all that. You work here."

Jude owed his job to the explosion in gang violence since the end of the civil war, a circumstance that had prompted a resurgence of the death squads. Even the Policía Nacional Civil—the new, supposedly incorruptible national police force that Malvasio and other American cops had helped train—were implicated. No surprise, the few officers charged were always acquitted. What jury would convict them? The *escuadrones* went out at night in vans and SUVs with the windows tinted black, trolling for prey: gang members and garden variety criminals mostly, but prostitutes, too. Homosexuals. Transvestites. They called it *limpieza social*. Social cleansing.

"These people you work for," Jude said, "you get any read on
where they stand on things like that?"

"Things like what?"

"You know what I'm saying."

Malvasio waved him off. "I'm just the help. They don't share
their politics with me."

"What about *your* politics?"

"My what?"

"Your politics. Loyalties. Whatever."

Malvasio shooed a fly from his empty soup bowl. "Look, the point
I was making was just that the people who run things down here
are hard-core. To them, guy like me, I'm a prom princess."

"You may be selling yourself short there. I'm sure I'm not the
only one who might draw a parallel between what you and my dad
did back in Chicago and what happens here. Or have I got something wrong?"

The trilling of *chiquirines,* the local variety of cricket, crescendoed suddenly to such a pitch it nearly drowned out the *cumbia* music. Malvasio waited it out. "Is that really what you think?"

Jude began chewing his lip, a nervous tic he'd had for years and
seemed helpless to master. "You left behind some serious wreckage.
I'm sure you know that."

"Whoa. Whoa. Listen to me." For the first time, Malvasio's composure gave way. "Those stories that came out about slangers capped
by me or your dad? That's all crap. We killed nobody. Period."

"More from luck than intention. At least that's the way some of
the stories seemed to me."

"Whose stories, your dad's?"

"No." Jude and his father had talked about none of this before
he'd died.

"The news then," Malvasio said.

"Yeah."

"You believe the news?" Like it was the stupidest thing imaginable. "Look, we were wrong. What we did was wrong. Absolutely. But I'm gonna say this again—we smoked nobody. The body count they tried to lay on us was gang action, moes and hooks, doing what they do. Not us. You gotta believe that. For your father's sake."

Jude was of various minds as to what he should or shouldn't believe for his father's sake. "What about that guy they fished out of the Chicago River?"

It was one of the stories recounted on TV the night of his dad's arrest—some north-side banger claimed three men in coveralls and ski masks dragged him off his corner in a sleet storm, drove him down to the wharves, robbed him, stripped him naked, then gave him an impromptu back-flip lesson into the cold greasy river. Luckily, he'd found a ledge before going under one last time, and he'd stood there, screaming for help, till a warehouseman heard him.

Malvasio said, "You talking about Small Mickens?"

"I can't recall the name."

"I don't mean to sound glib, Jude, but if memory serves, he survived."

"He almost drowned."

"Small? Yeah. Water so deep he had to walk out."

"People die from exposure, too."

"It was a warm spell between cold fronts and he came out okay—I know, I was standing there. Besides which, Small had quite a little curb service, used eight-year-olds for touts—the news tell you *that*? A mouthy little wannabe always crowing about how he was in the mix with the Insane Vice Lord Killers, but he was from nowhere, a fat little freak who let any hubba pigeon with a wet spot between her legs work twists for rock." Malvasio sighed, dropped his head, and ran his hands across his cropped hair in a kind of private torment. After a few long seconds, he said quietly, "No. Cancel that. You're right. I said it before but it bears repeating: What we did was wrong. All of it." He looked up, eyes filled with: *How many times do you want me to say it?* "But we didn't kill people. We just . . . didn't."

Jude felt meager. It was, perhaps, a cheap shot, dragging in the death squad business. There'd been all sorts of rumors floating around back then, but nothing was ever proved. And yet: "Can I ask you a question?"

Malvasio chuckled. "There some way I could stop you?"

"That vice cop who was killed right before you disappeared. Winters?"

The mirth drained from Malvasio's face. "That."

"Yeah. That."

In the early morning hours before the Laugh Master arrests, a vice detective named Hank Winters was found on his back in an alley off Milwaukee Avenue, half his face ripped open from a point-blank gun blast. In the TV statements regarding Malvasio's disappearance, the police spokesmen took pains not to say too much about possible links between the two events. Malvasio wasn't a suspect, they said. They just wanted him to come in, surrender on the Laugh Master charges, help them sort out the Winters slaying if he could.

Malvasio looked off toward the darkening ocean, his eye twitching. Finally, in a soft, measured voice: "Lotta stuff got said about your dad and Phil and me. About how corrupt we were. Maybe so. But I've never, never known a cop more bent than Hank Winters. Guy had the conscience of a tapeworm. And plenty of enemies. Same deal with the other killings they tried to pin on us. You could fill a freight train with suspects for every single one. But when in doubt, blame the badge, right?"

"You saying you didn't do it?"

With his fingers, Malvasio pounded out a little rat-a-tat on the tabletop. "Okay. Fair enough. Let's deal with this." He took a longer pull from his beer this time, then settled in. The sadness in his eyes hardened into something else. "There was a pimp Winters was working as a CI and the guy needed a little arm-twisting. So Hank had a bench warrant issued on some failure-to-appear, just to drag the skank in, teach him a lesson. Thing he forgot to tell the two uniforms serving the warrant? This pimp was on a crack binge like the world was gonna end. Guys knocked on the door, the bag of crap opened up and shot the first cop in the head. Boom. That was it. Twenty-six years old, the cop who got bagged—your age, basically. With a wife and a kid and one on the way. I knew him, liked him. Thought he had, I dunno, promise. Winters got called in by IAD but he danced his way around the whole thing and that just got to me."

Good God, Jude thought. He's confessing.

"I knew Winters was seeing this call girl, had a crib off Milwaukee, and I waited for him. He got out of his car, I walked up and you should've seen his eyes. Like a couple golf balls. Must've thought I'd come there to grease him, but I just wanted to let him know—and let him know good—how I felt. About what went down with his stinking warrant. Didn't get a word out, though. He shoved a finger in my face, went off, said he had the drop on your dad and me and Phil. This proz he was about to see, she'd had a two-year thing with your old man and she knew all about Ray's business, our business, and she was gonna take us down if we didn't play smart. I don't know, it just twisted me up somehow and I decked him. I felt protective of your dad. He was the one with kids, you and your sister, which meant he had way more to lose than Phil or me. Any event, I clock Winters and he goes down to one knee. Then he draws his piece, the fuck. You work the streets, you know when a guy's gonna pull the trigger and when he's just waving the damn thing around. I didn't have a choice. I know that like I know I'm sitting here."

Malvasio's last few words, for all their import, sounded strangely far away. Jude found himself hung up on that one phrase: *She'd had a two-year thing with your old man.* The things you don't know, he thought. The things you should've been wise to all along.

"If it hadn't been for the Winters thing," Malvasio went on, "I'd have stuck around. Taken the heat like your dad. Like Phil. But there was no way I'd ever get an honest break on that, not with everything else. People want a hanging, they don't fuss much over details. And I figured, with me gone, your dad and Phil could point the blame my direction, say it was all my doing. And from what I heard about the deals they struck, I'd say that's pretty much what went down."

Jude had to admit this last part rang true. In their plea agreements, his dad and Strock made no admissions of wrongdoing beyond filing false incident reports and abusing overtime. All charges concerning abduction, robbery, and violence were decreed Not Sustained. The deals came with a price, though. The two men got drummed off the force, surrendered their pensions and benefits, after which they were expected to drift away shamefully into the unknown. And they did. Sure it wasn't prison, but even with whatever he'd been through down here the past ten years, would Malvasio really want to trade places?

"Tell me about this call girl," Jude said. "The one you said had a thing with my dad."

"You didn't know about that?"

"No." Strange, he thought, how pathetic that sounded.

"Look, Jude, let it go, okay? It's been ten years, your dad—"

"Is that why he tossed himself over the side of his boat?"

Malvasio looked stunned, even a little appalled. "Do you know for a fact that's what happened?"

"No," Jude admitted. "Nobody does."

"Then cut your old man some slack. Look, Ray made mistakes, some pretty serious ones."

"No fooling?"

"Okay. Okay. But that means what—you should hate him forever?"

"I didn't say I hated him."

"You should see the look on your face."

Jude felt the skin on his neck prickle with heat. "I don't hate him."

"Well, good. You shouldn't. I knew Ray better than anybody and there's still things I don't understand. But, just to tie up this one last thing, having a slice on the side isn't one of those things."

"How do you mean?"

"Come on, Jude." Malvasio looked off toward the ocean again, all scarlet and indigo with sunset. "It's not my place to say."

"Say what?"

"I didn't come here to make a case against anybody. I mean that. But your mother . . ." He let his voice trail off.

Jude knew perfectly well what he meant, but still said, "What about her?"

Malvasio's smile said, You don't fool me, but deferring to graciousness, he said, "Maybe it looked different inside the family, I dunno. But from where I stood it was pretty damn clear your dad was miserable. He hid it well—like I said, he was proud. But I don't begrudge him wanting a little company. A little affection."

Like I couldn't tell my parents' marriage was a disaster, Jude thought. "But a hooker?"

"Would it feel any less insulting if he'd taken up with a woman he could've actually started over with? Think about it."

Jude didn't need to. Besides, it wasn't really the who or the how bad of the infidelity troubling him. It just underscored how much, after all these years, he still didn't know, and how naked he felt having to rely on Malvasio to tell him—at which point he suffered one last twinge of distrust. It dawned on him that what he'd just sat through, all of it, might be nothing more than some kind of elaborate windup. He prepared himself for the pitch.

It didn't come. Instead, Malvasio stood up and, noticing Jude's beer was only half-gone, said, "I'm going down to kick the kidneys. You want to trade that for a cold one?"

Jude looked at his bottle. "I guess I'll finish this."

"Meaning no?"

"No. I mean, yeah, I'll take one. Thanks."

Jude watched Malvasio walk away, thinking: Sure. It must've been easy, blaming him for everything. And have I done anything much different? The meagerness came back, it felt wrong, and so, as Malvasio reached the stairway down, Jude called out, "Bill. I'm sorry if this . . . I'm sorry if I've made this here, between you and me, edgier than it needed to be. But you gotta understand, things went to hell for me and my sister and, yeah, even my mother, because of all this. And nobody, not one person, ever sat down and talked about what happened. Not so it ever made sense. So if I've come off a little half-cocked, whatever—like I said, I'm sorry."

Malvasio glanced over his shoulder with a look of puzzlement that softened into a pained smile. "You've got nothing to be sorry about," he said, then headed downstairs.

3

WITH SUNSET, SHADOWS GREW FAT IN THE OPEN-AIR DINING ROOM. Outside, the palm fronds and almond leaves whispered in a languid wind. Jude, sitting alone as he waited for Malvasio to return from downstairs, watched Paulo the waiter reappear, carrying a box of wood matches. Shortly the room was dotted with reddish pools of candlelight, shadows trembling up the whitewashed pillars, across the ceiling. It made Jude think of church and that just labored his mood all the more, until memory served up the ten-year-old recollection he'd been trying to keep at bay ever since he'd first heard Malvasio's voice on his cell phone.

It was the day before Thanksgiving and he was living with his aunt and uncle by then, to keep the family peace. His mother called, not to wish him well but to inform him that Fish and Game had telephoned to report they'd found his father's boat drifting out on Rend Lake—casting rod and tackle box aboard, a couple bass in the ice chest, plus two drained fifths of Early Times tossed under the seat. Mother opted out of further involvement—she'd hired a lawyer and filed for divorce by that point—so it was left to Jude and his uncle to respond when, four days later, a floater washed up. The body had gotten snarled, somehow, underwater.

They drove downstate for the identification. The morgue was in the basement of the county hospital, and the folksy staffer on duty led them to the fridge unit, slid the tray out, and unzipped the bag. The stench buckled Jude over and it took willpower to move closer. A faceless maw of waterlogged meat, scummy bone, and oddly pristine hair looked back. He knew if he retched he'd cry and vice versa so he battened down. In the end it was the personal effects, the wedding band and wristwatch in particular, that sealed the ID.

That night, back at his aunt and uncle's, Jude went to his room, unable to eat or even talk to anyone, until the exhaustion of the day took its toll and he drifted off into an edgy sleep. Around midnight, a nightmare woke him in which he was the one drowning and he shot up in bed, thinking: No. I am not my father. That thought stayed with him the rest of the night as the hours crawled past. And as he lay there, he realized he wasn't grieving just for the life lost but for the life that would never be, the day when his father stepped up, came clean, about all of it. Because you don't dive—or totter or slip or whatever—blind drunk into frigid water without a vest when all that's bothering your conscience is inflated overtime and some creative writing on incident reports. But the rest of the story disappeared with the old man himself, and that would never change, never get clearer, never come whole, and that drumbeat of *never* haunted everything.

Until tonight.

Jude still felt a little stunned at what he'd just sat   gh. There'd been enough admissions against self-interest and sufficient acceptance of guilt, as a lawyer might put it, to make Malvasio's story feel credible. Not that every detail could be taken to the bank, Jude supposed, but he had to admit he felt more convinced than not. Regardless, the man earned points for being willing to come here, square off across the table, and talk about it. It was something Jude's father had never done.

But something else was going on too. For lack of a better way to put it, Jude felt gratified. Some sort of psychological shift was taking place, the old rancor yielding to a new relief. The things that had happened all those years ago weren't, as it turned out, as unforgivable as he'd feared. It was the silence that had blown them out of all proportion, creating a darkness onto which every manner of sick deed and vicious impulse could be projected.

The thing about the call girl, even though it had come out of the blue, seemed not so startling with a little reflection. The old man had checked out of his marriage years before, going through the motions at best—at worst, tearing into his wife, and she ripping right back into him. Malvasio was right: a little company, a little affection, who didn't crave that? And where else would the old man meet somebody but on the job, and given he was a cop, who was he most likely to meet? He didn't walk out on his family, not until everything else came crashing down, at which point he was doing everybody a favor.

As for the Winters deal, even that seemed justified. Jude could imagine himself doing the exact same thing Malvasio had done—kill or be killed—knowing full well the self-defense was tinged with more than a little vengeful satisfaction. How could it not be? That didn't make it evil, just human. And why stick around if you knew it meant taking the fall for more than you'd actually done? Why martyr yourself for someone else's agenda?

All of which meant Jude had spent ten years indulging a righteous, bitchy monologue of grievance that now seemed largely beside the point. And now that the Laugh Masters seemed brought down to size, his resentments felt small as well.

As for the possible ramifications if anyone—his employer, for example, or the authorities—found out he'd agreed to meet like this? It would take some thinking, but there were ways around that. He knew it was dubious judgment, being there, but hardly illegal. He had a right to his private life, they couldn't begrudge him that. Nothing Malvasio had said suggested he was into anything wrong (though the line got blurry down here), and all the old stuff was exactly that: old. If push came to shove, he could always cook up a story, tell whoever was curious that Malvasio told him all the old charges against him were taken care of, a deal with the government. How am I supposed to know otherwise? There, Jude thought. Simple. Always a way to work things out if you just take time to think things through.

Malvasio returned with two cold Pilseners and sat back down, glancing around at the empty room dotted with shuddering candlelight. "Looks like somebody died." Before Jude could comment, Malvasio added, "I may not have said this yet, but even if I have, it bears repeating—I appreciate your being here. I can only imagine what's going through your skull, sitting with me like this. It takes some nerve and, I dunno, grace maybe. I just want you to know I'm grateful."

Jude could feel his face warming. Good Lord, he thought, don't blush. "Thanks," he said.

"Not a problem." Malvasio sipped his beer. His eyes warmed. "If you don't mind, I'm bored with me. What say we talk about you for a while?"

"Like how?"

"Like tell me how you ended up here."

Penetrating question, Jude thought. And it just stirred up other questions, like: Where to start? What to leave out?

After his father died, things went wrong in a way Jude couldn't make right. Skidding between numbness and blistering rage, he made it past the holidays through sheer force of will and a knack for hiding, but he could feel it, the ticking bomb inside. It drove him a little nuts—he lost sleep, lost weight. Even little things became torture. Every time he walked away from one more botched conversation, he could feel the eyes boring into his back.

But he saw no point telling Malvasio any of that.

"I came down here when I was in the army," he said.

"Army. Really. When'd you join up?"

"Senior year."

"You mean after graduation."

"No. I dropped out."

Malvasio looked at him as though he hadn't heard right. "Dropped out?"

"It's a long story."

"So bore me."

"No, I just—"

"You were scholarship material last I heard, full ride, Notre Dame, Big Ten."

"I didn't play football senior year."

He might as well have said he'd run away to be a dancer.

"Okay, stop the car." Malvasio sat back, looking like he was mentally counting to ten. "Tell me what happened."

Go ahead, Jude thought. But all the words he might have used to explain things felt just out of reach. He hid behind a shrug. "I don't know what to tell you."

Malvasio reached out suddenly and gripped Jude's arm. The touch was manly but not weird. And strangely welcome. Their glances met.

"I mean, if you don't want to, I understand. But I'd like to hear about it."

Another layer of resistance gave way, Jude felt it, but he still couldn't quite unscramble his words. He felt like he was handing up a puzzle.

"It was about two weeks after New Year's, I guess. Yeah. Freezing cold, I remember that. Walked into the recruitment center in Joliet and said, 'I'm ready. Sign me up.' The sergeant on duty smelled something wrong. I was a little bottled up, I guess. After I left he called the house, the sergeant I mean, found out what had happened, with Dad and all. I came back with my application all filled out the next day and he just put it aside. 'Son,' he says, 'you seem wound a little tight to me. I don't want to hear back in a few

months that something happened in BCT and there's two guys involved, one's in irons, the other's dead, and I get to guess which one
is you.'"

Malvasio lifted one eyebrow a notch. "And you said?"

"I told him, 'I'm not a hothead. I'm not a fool. And I can take
anything you or anybody else can dish out. Watch me.'"

The curiosity in Malvasio's expression dimmed a little, replaced
by an odd regret. He shook his head, repeating, "You dropped out."
Then: "Wait—why Joliet?"

"I was living with my aunt and uncle then."

Malvasio's face softened. "Why?"

Jude wondered, again, if there was much point getting into all
that. "I was the only one left. Dad moved out right after the arrests,
Colleen went off to Madison with her scholarship. And I didn't get
along with my mom too well."

"Nobody did," Malvasio said.

"Yeah. That seems to be the consensus."

"The original Midwestern shrew, that woman—unhappy in
marriage, indifferent in motherhood, with a daughter who reminded
her too much of herself and a son who reminded her too much of her
husband."

"You saw all that?"

"I'm a lot of things. Blind isn't one of them."

Jude flashed on the day his mother had told him he'd be living
elsewhere until things got "sorted out." It was clear from the way
she said it that she wouldn't mind terribly if he stayed away for
good. And for the first time, Jude worked up the nerve to say: "I can
understand why you're ashamed. But why are you ashamed of me?"

"So," Malvasio prompted, "you ran away and joined the army."

"Yeah, I chose carpentry and masonry specialist for my MOS, always liked that kind of work. I ended up with the 536th Engineer
Battalion out of Fort Kobbe in Panama. We did a joint training exercise with the Salvadoran army and that's how I ended up here.
First time, anyway. We put up some bridges, dug some wells, built a

few clinics." At the time, he'd puzzled over the coincidence of getting sent here, of all places, given the rumors about Malvasio. It seemed a kind of paradox: No matter how far or fast you run, the echoes are always right there behind you. "We got sent back in again after Hurricane Mitch, choppered in food and clothing, helped rebuild roads, handed out water purification kits. Did the same thing all over again when the earthquakes hit in 2001."

"Maybe I'm missing something," Malvasio said, "but that's a far cry from what you do now."

"I'm getting there," Jude said. "End of my second tour, while I was up here after the earthquakes, me and a couple guys in my unit went barhopping in the Zona Rosa. I met a guy at Los Rinconcitos named Jim Leonhard, an EP with Trenton Service Consortium, this security firm out of L.A.? We hit it off, Americans abroad, that whole thing, but when I told him I was the son of a cop—I didn't tell him everything, naturally—he damn near creamed. Boom, I got recruited. Hard. And after a few more beers on the company tab, I figured, Why not? I was tired of the army, bored with construction work, and I liked it here. I don't know how you feel about it, but there's an odd attraction to the place. It's beautiful in places and ugly as a slum in others, but the people are great by and large. I mean things are fucked up too. God knows. I wouldn't have a job if they weren't. Anyway, I signed up for training at Heckler and Koch, learned the basics, boned up on my Spanish, and earned a black belt in Krav Maga. Leonhard stuck in a good word and Trenton took me on. I still get sent around to here or there, but clients like it when they know you've got a handle on a particular place. By and large I've been here, in El Salvador, pretty steady the past two years. Feels like home."

They talked for another half hour, Jude confiding things he'd kept bottled up for years, wondering at that but glad to have someone to talk to who knew the family story and wouldn't judge. Malvasio chimed in, telling Jude things about his father that cast the whole Laugh Master debacle in a kinder light. Finally, the back-and-forth petered out and Malvasio sat back, drifting away into thought. His features sharpened in the candlelight, his dark eyes shone.

In time, he said, "I like hearing about your life. It's good to see you've done well, given how tough it was for you. Especially since I had no small part in it being that tough. I'm sorry. I haven't said that straight out yet, so there. Long overdue."

Again, Jude struggled for words. How long had he wanted someone to say no more than that? "Yeah," he said. "It's been interesting."

"We could do it again sometime," Malvasio said. "I mean, if you're up for that."

4

Jude had nine more days of free time before returning to work, and suddenly two new people in his life to spend it with. Or so he thought.

Hoping Eileen would materialize, he spent the first three days back at Playa El Zonte, surfing at dawn and in the late afternoon, lazing away the long, hot midday hours in the same hammock, struggling through Manlio Argueta's *Cuzcatlan,* and hoping he'd impress her if she caught him reading it. He would've liked a better plan than just sitting there waiting, but he had to hope that she'd felt what he'd felt, that spark, and would circle back again, wanting to reconnect the same way he did. After three days, though, he had to give that up and go on the hunt.

He ventured as far west as Punta Remedios and Playa Los Cabanos—hanging out with the off-season tourists and Eurotrash vagabonds, scouring the near-empty beaches, waiting—then back east to check in at Playa El Tunco, Playa Conchalio, plus all the places they'd bumped into each other before: Santa María Mizata, Playa El Sunzal, the pier at La Libertad. He practiced the nonchalant greeting he'd use if he actually did find her, even as he chided himself for not finding out where she was staying, getting a number where he could reach her. Ask questions, he thought. You want to hook up with someone, ask questions. Idiot.

He kept his hope alive by remembering the way she'd looked when he'd seen her last, the polka-dot halter and broad-rimmed hat, her tan-lined back, that moment of unwitting nakedness when she'd slipped off her glasses, while his thoughts became haunted by that smoky bedroom voice of hers. If she wasn't the love of his life, she'd at least become the focus of an ardent obsession. The harder he looked, the more intense the need to see her became and the worse it felt when he didn't, until the only solace he could muster was the irony that now he was the one with a devotion to vanishing things.

His newfound connection with Malvasio proved less problematic, logistically anyway. They met twice more over those same nine days, always in San Marcelino. Jude told no one about the meetings, and Malvasio came and went with a nonchalance that underscored how well-connected he'd become. Jude surmised it was likely they even knew some of the same people, the country being what it was, but they shied away from discussing that, preferring to reminisce, Malvasio increasingly open about his days as a street cop in Chicago. Jude couldn't help wondering at times what life might have been like had his father sat with him like this, opened up, but quickly he'd shoo the notion away, thinking it was as pointless as wishing he'd been born on a different planet.

At the end of his furlough Jude returned to work and the tunnel vision it required, shepherding his hydrologist, Axel Odelberg, from place to place: ANDA headquarters in the capital, the bottling plant out east near San Bartolo Oriente, the test wells along the Río Conacastal. Secretly, he prepared for an unforeseen encounter with Malvasio, wanting to make sure neither of them drew attention to the other, not wanting to have to come up with an explanation on the spot. But they never crossed paths, not until his twenty days were up, when his time was once again his own and he returned to the restaurant in San Marcelino for another get-together.

They dined on shrimp creole with *casamiento,* a rice and bean dish spiced with hot peppers, washing it down with cold Pilsener. The sunset drained its reds and golds into the ocean as they ate, the trilling of *chiquirines* and the muffled roar of the surf a steady background. After the waiter cleared their plates, Malvasio reached into his back pocket and withdrew a worn plastic envelope that he shook open. A dozen or so photographs tumbled out and he shuffled them into a stack. "Time for a little show-and-tell," he said.

He selected one from the group, spun it across the table. Picking it up, Jude saw Malvasio and Jude's father in waders with their fishing gear, standing to each side of a Latino man holding a pole of his own. They stood at the end of a dock somewhere, all sunglasses and smiles.

"That was up at Lake Darling," Malvasio said. "Fourth of July, year before the arrests. The man in the middle—his name is Ovidio Morales."

Jude caught the import instantly: a name. He studied the stranger's face more intently. "He's the man who helped you out when you ran down here." He felt puzzled—Malvasio had made such a point of protecting the man's identity before. He handed the picture back. "Why are you telling me this?"

"I feel I can trust you now." Malvasio gave Jude a disarming smile, then slipped the photo back into the stack. He took out another and handed it across the table. "I keep bringing up Candyman. You remember him, right? Phil Strock."

The picture was much the same as the first, three amigos, except the lineup was different and Soldier Field provided the backdrop. Jude's dad was in the middle this time, Strock to his left, Malvasio his right. All three in their blues, happy as coots, some kind of game-day duty. Three strapping cops. The Laugh Masters.

"I remember all you guys," Jude said. He tried to hand the picture back.

Malvasio didn't reach for it. "I've still got friends back in Chicago. Well, 'friends' might be a stretch. Guys who don't automatically slam down the phone when I call, which isn't often, I admit. Any event, I hear Candyman's dropped out of sight. And if somebody actually does cross his path, they say he looks awful."

Jude set the picture down, finally, on the table. "That surprise you?"

"What do you mean?"

"He got booted off the force and it's not like that was a secret. Who's gonna hire him? And he had that problem with his leg, the torn-up knee. Hear he's almost crippled. He gave up any claim to disability in the deal he struck with IAD. My guess is he's been on welfare or SSI or what-have-you for ten years, and the prospects there are pretty slim these days."

"Yeah." Malvasio nodded, staring at the picture. "You got a point." He seemed distracted. "But that kinda brings me around to something I was thinking about. Something that's come up. I've got a line on some work for Phil, if he's up for it."

Jude heard a commotion outside. Looking down, he saw an old man drawing a handcart with an oil drum lashed to its bed. Two stray dogs were nipping at his pant legs, and Jude watched as the old man fended the dogs off with a switch. Turning back to Malvasio, he shrugged. "That sounds good. Work, I mean."

Malvasio laughed. "Not that simple. If Phil ever got wind I so much as had a hand in doing him a favor, he'd hunt me down and set me on fire just so he could put me out with his piss."

"You think he blames you for what happened."

"Not think. Know."

"Lot of time's gone by. Maybe he's mellowed out."

"Mellow and the Candyman don't mix. The man knows how to milk a grudge. That ain't changed from what I hear. If anything, it's gotten worse if he's drinking the way they say."

Jude glanced down at the snapshot again. Strock wasn't the most handsome of the three, Malvasio was, Jude's dad a close second, but Strock had something about him. The slack smile, the sleepy eyelids. Lady-killer. "Why bother helping him then?"

"Because I owe him. I'd do the same for your dad if I could." Malvasio let that sink in for a moment, then: "Any event, that's why I need your help."

Jude glanced up. "Excuse me?"

"When's your next trip home?"

"I'm on the front end of ten days off. I wasn't planning—"

"I'll pay for your plane fare. I'm serious. Plus pocket money." He took a roll of bills from his pocket and started peeling off hundreds. He didn't stop till he reached fifty. Five thousand dollars.

"I'd like you to try and find him for me. Talk him into coming down, if you can. Ovidio has a friend with a construction company that needs to hire a man with Candyman's skills—he was one of the best snipers SWAT had, I don't know if you knew that. The work site's kinda remote and it's huge, hard to walk the perimeter. Thieves'll walk off with the barbed wire if you're not looking, let alone what's inside. The company wants to put a gunman with a scope in a tower, which is perfect for Phil. But like I said, no mention of me."

Jude eyed the money. "Tell me we're not talking about an airstrip."

Malvasio's expression went from puzzled to bemused. Then he laughed. "You serious?"

The U.S. Navy had one of the best radar installations in the hemisphere at Comalapa, but it did no good to track a plane and even pinpoint its landing coordinates if the local police couldn't get judicial authority to raid the property. Corruption being what it was here, that kind of authority was virtually unheard of if the location was owned by a prominent landholder. It raised the question, again, of who exactly Malvasio worked for.

"The way you described it—"

"It's a series of dormitories for the workers on a coffee plantation up in the highlands, near the Tecapa volcano."

The region, near the city of Berlín, was called the Valle Agua Caliente. It was known for its coffee production.

"Bill—"

"Here, I'll show you."

Malvasio flipped through the thin stack of pictures again and pulled out another for Jude to see. With the volcano looming darkly in the background, tidy rows of coffee trees, both *pacamara* and the smaller *bourbon* varieties, thick with berries, crosshatched a sun-swept valley. Only 2 percent of the rain forest remained, due to clear-cutting for plantations like this—coffee, sugar, cotton, rubber, bananas. But that didn't make it criminal. A sprawling array of concrete slabs—for housing, Jude supposed—lay in the foreground acreage, surrounded by a barbed wire fence.

Jude felt sheepish. "Okay. Sorry." He handed the photo back.

"No problem. I'd be skeptical too. I mean, I realize it's a lot to ask. Given the history, let's call it. You don't owe me a thing."

"I just—"

"There aren't many second chances in life, okay? Not when you've done what we did. I've been lucky. I'd like to share a little of that luck with Phil. If I can just get him down here."

Jude realized someone standing outside the situation might think saying no should be easy. He didn't have to be drastic about it, call the embassy, turn Malvasio in. Still, it took him several seconds to manage, "No hard feelings. But I think I'll pass."

Malvasio studied him a moment, as though his gaze might change Jude's mind. When that didn't happen, he collected his money and shuffled it back into a tidy stack. "Fair enough."

"I don't mean to be—"

Malvasio held up his hand. "No need to explain. Just an idea. Maybe I can work it out some other way."

"I'm sorry."

Malvasio sipped his beer and looked off. The silence, to Jude, felt excruciating. He wasn't sure why. "It's possible," he said, "I could call around next time I'm up in Chicago, ask around, let you know if—"

"Can I ask you something?" Malvasio's tone was cool but not hostile. "Your principal, you told me he's working on water usage for a soft drink plant out east somewhere?"

"San Bartolo Oriente. The plant's on the Río Conacastal."

"Do you know who the investors in that operation are?"

"Specifically?"

"Do you know," Malvasio repeated, "who they are?"

"That's not really my area," Jude said.

"So for all you know, the people involved in your hydrologist's project could be the worst of the worst down here. The oligarch goons who funded the death squads and all that hairy horseshit. Correct? Or am I missing something?"

Jude didn't care for the direction this was headed. "No," he said. "Probably not."

"It's the price you pay. Doing what we do. Here. You want innocent, move on."

"Yeah," Jude said. "There's always that chance."

Malvasio laced his fingers together, then tapped his thumbs against his chin. "You said you came down here while you were in the army. Built things—schools, clinics, bridges. Seem real proud of that. But the *salvadoreños* you worked with, helped train, who knows? If things take a turn down here, as they almost certainly will, those guys you helped train may end up building some things you want no part of. Places where people disappear, for instance."

"Bill—"

"What I'm saying is, the people who run the show have one thing on their minds and it ain't playing nice. They may wave the flag, talk democracy, pimp prosperity or whatever, but the bottom line's the bottom line: me first and money talks. Just how it is, how it's always been, always will be. And guys like you and me don't have a say in the matter. We just do what we can the best we can, stick up for the people we care about, and if we fuck up, as we invariably do, we try to make good for the people we've screwed, which is the best we can offer. Life in a nutshell. Same for cops and soldiers everywhere—you, me, everybody." Malvasio gathered up his money and put it away. He took a deep breath. "Look, sorry. I don't mean to put you on the spot."

Jude said, "It's okay."

"But let's say you—not me, you—had work for Phil. You brought him down here, lined it all up, got him something that paid him back for all he's gone through. In the final analysis, given who's who down here, you couldn't guarantee that whatever he did—or you did to help him—wouldn't have a taint to it, could you?"

"No, I couldn't."

"Would that stop you?"

Malvasio stared long and hard. Jude found himself wanting to look away.

"I didn't mean to—"

"Maybe it would. And there's no blame in that." Malvasio stood up. "Look, let's drop it. I'm gonna go down, get another beer. Want one?"

"Yeah. Sure."

Malvasio vanished and, in his absence, the excruciating silence returned. It felt worse than before, a punishment. And, in a way, a dare. For whatever reason, Jude flashed on something his father once said, near the end, during a particularly fierce bout of pre-shift drinking: "Guts and loyalty, that's what divides the great from the not-so-great." He threw back a shot for drama, then: "Which pretty much explains why nine tenths of humanity ain't so great."

Malvasio came back carrying two bottles of Pilsener and a greasy basket of *papas fritas*. "Still hungry, I guess." He dropped the fries onto the table and sat back down.

Jude glanced out again at the glassy ink-blue ocean, veins of amber and scarlet marbling the darkened sky. "Look, Bill. This thing with Strock. I can't make any promises. But let me see what I can do."

5

By the time Jude reached La Libertad and turned east toward the Costa del Bálsamo, night had fallen. He decreased speed, anticipating the switchbacks along the steep cliffs above the shoreline, Malvasio's five thousand dollars stuffed in his pocket. It wasn't the only thing he'd carried away. *The people who run the show have one thing on their minds. . . .* The phrase kept tracking in his brain, resonating in a way Malvasio couldn't have predicted.

In a perfect world, Jude supposed, everyone would be kind and selfless, abundance would be abundant, the snotty would share their toys, and the shepherd would lie down with the lamb or whatever. But in the here and now it was just a rule of the cosmos that more often than not the people who made things happen, the kind he was hired to protect, were rip-roaring assholes.

It was something that had been building over time. He'd taken the job on a lark, figuring if it didn't suit him he could always walk. But he'd liked the work, the demands on his mind, the calm required, the focus, the breadth of knowledge. And every now and then he got assigned a man like Axel, some hard-nosed pragmatist with not just his head on straight but a conscience in tow, which made things seem okay. But other times he felt like he'd taken a wrong turn somewhere and bungled his way into a kind of maze where around every corner there waited another prancing, self-infatuated gasbag who didn't give a rat's ass about anyone but himself—and came factory-equipped with a million excuses for why his smug little schemes were in fact the cornerstone of his virtue.

So tidy, the belief that everyone made out best if you slit their throats and raped their wives and sold their children into slavery on your way to the top. They'd do the same to you, or would if they had the spine, which made it all fair.

And stand back if some unthinking soul dared mention the tenant farmers evicted from their homes at gunpoint, their villages flooded by the latest pointless dam; the fisheries wiped out by a tourist haven slapped up on the beach; the teenagers hired for a *maquila* at a couple dollars a day, going home to their brothers and sisters in dirt-floor shacks for a dinner of cornmeal and bean paste and putrid water, while the men in charge made off like, well, bandits. You want the brass ring, you have to take risks, they'd tell you, though he'd never seen any of them risk so much as a bad tan. Poverty's a state of mind, they said, a victim mentality, a culture of blame—it's your own fucking fault if you're penniless, uneducated, screwed. Get some initiative. In the end, over time, beyond the rainbow, the system works. Look at me.

How many times had Jude sat in a car or at a restaurant table, listening to crap like that? And boy, those characters liked to talk. But over time, as he endured more and more monologues, he began to detect something else, something he felt sure they wanted kept hidden, if they even knew it was there. Basically, he saw a put-upon boy lingering behind the eyes, the kind of snot whose favorite phrase was "I don't care." Who grew up wanting nothing more than what he could get away with. Who only felt his manhood come to life when the one thing on his mind was himself.

And in the end, Jude knew, that's what it got down to—what kind of man you meant to be. Despite Malvasio's excellent point that anything you do, regardless how pure the motive, can be messed with, stolen from you, Jude had to admit he'd been happy in the army, building clinics and schools and bridges in the mountains, digging wells through granite and volcanic rock for people who had nothing. Not because he was making a bundle doing it, obviously, and not because he didn't recognize the military for what it was: a bureaucracy of roughnecks and good ol' boys beholden to men in suits. He'd just felt insanely gratified, even lucky, when at the end of each day the nearest villagers would gather around, offer gifts and food, then step back and applaud him and the other filthy, sweaty Americans like they were movie stars.

Not that it wasn't tricky, feeding off the thanks of others. That, too, was a kind of self-congratulation. Like money.

And there, of course, was the problem. Nothing bears up under scrutiny in the end. Every point of view has its blind spot. Every good deed has its rancid little secret.

And so the question became not *why* but *why not*. Why not do this thing, take the money, head back to Chicago? He could help Malvasio atone, give Strock back the life he'd thrown away, maybe even redeem his father's ghost. Could he honestly say for a fact that anything else he'd been part of the past few years had turned out better?

But there was something else too, something more personal. A lot more. These men he'd once looked up to so hard, his models for manhood, who'd sculpted his ambitions and taught him so much, then fallen so far—now, he thought, ten years later, disgraced and lost, they come to me. Me. The kid in the corner. Out of need, apparently. Guilt, perhaps. And? The world was an unforgiving place, living in it a rough business. Maybe happiness was virtue like the nuns had said, but survival required a little venom in the blood. Too much, you turned malicious. Too little, you were a sucker. It was why the cutthroats so often got the upper hand, he thought, because they could disguise themselves as practical, whereas their do-good naysayers came across as maudlin and shrill.

So here's your test, he realized. To fine-tune the poison in your heart, see if you're truly fit to walk the walk. Measure yourself against these misfits, these heroes gone wrong. These men.

And who knew, it might be fun. Mix it up a little, dog around on the wild side. Call it a good deed in a world fucked sideways. Call it an odd job during your week off. Call it whatever—it was the thing to do.

He pulled off the highway into the driveway of El Dorado Mar, the gated hillside community on the beach just west of Playa El Sunzal where he, his Trenton coworkers, and their principals bivouacked on weekends. A high chain-link fence marked off the compound near the highway, coiled with razor wire, over which sprawling thorny tendrils of *veranera* cascaded with their white and purple blossoms.

He waved to the guard on duty who carried a pistol grip shotgun slung from his shoulder. Recognizing Jude's pickup, the man rose from his stool and shuffled out to open the gate, fanning himself with his hat. Jude pulled through with a grateful wave, then drove down the winding lane toward Horizon House, as everyone called it, the darkness vaulted by white-barked eucalyptus trees and towering palms, illumined here and there by a lamplit window glowing beyond the feathery crown of a *mariscargo* tree.

Inside Horizon House, Axel sat hunched over the edge of the dining room table, engaged in an after-dinner round of euchre with two other Horizon consultants, Dillahunt and Pahlavi. A ceiling fan spun lazily overhead, but it only managed to push the heat around, so their skin shimmered from sweat in the lamplight.

The other EPs were outside in the back garden, downing beers and trading war stories from the sound of things, as they cleaned their weapons. Fitz—Mike Fitzhugh, the team's advance man—sat in his room, working the phones and Internet, tracking recent kidnaps, carjackings, murders, protests, so everyone could avoid the trouble spots in the coming days. In the kitchen, the only woman on the premises—Jolanda, the *servienta*—hummed to herself as she cleaned up the last of the dinner dishes, listening to an evangelical church service on her radio.

Spotting Jude, Axel threw down his cards with feigned disgust. "The prodigal!" He had a lanky, muscular build, searing blue eyes, a full head of blond hair blanching silvery white. He pulled up an empty chair. "Take a seat, my boy. Help me turn this god-awful luck around."

"Actually, I thought I'd head down to the beach for a swim." Jude tented his shirt, which clung to his damp skin. "Then I need to pack. I'm heading home for a few days. Check in on my mom."

He glanced around the table to see how the lie played. Pahlavi collected cards for the reshuffle. Dillahunt tallied points. Axel screwed up his face. "Nothing wrong, I hope. At home, I mean."

Remembering the bulge of cash in his pocket, Jude reached down, felt to make sure his shirt hung low enough to cover it. "No, Mom's fine. Just, you know, family."

Dillahunt glanced up at that. Lifting his froggish face with its wobble of chins to the ceiling, he intoned:

I do not like the family Stein.
Not Gert, not Ep, or even Ein.
Gert's writings are bunk.
Ep's statues are junk.
And no one can understand Ein.

Everyone stared at him as though he'd let rip with a honking belch.

"You have a dog act for a mind, Dilly." Axel picked up the beginnings of his new hand. He winced, then said to Jude, "Fine. Go. Swim. Leave me here with these insulting cards." To the dealer, he added, "You're a shameless cheat, Muldoon."

He meant Pahlavi. They called him Muldoon.

"Cheating is the last refuge of the unlucky," the man said, a hint of Oxford in his accent. He was plump, graying, Pakistani. He smiled, organizing his own hand.

Regaining Jude's eye, Axel nodded toward the kitchen. "There's leftovers from dinner, if you're hungry. Jolanda will fix you up a plate. Just ask."

"I'm fine," Jude said, rankling a little at the attention. Guilt, he realized. He liked Axel, the fondness was mutual, and lying felt cheap. But it would be insane even mentioning Malvasio. "Shouldn't eat right before a swim, anyway. Might get cramps."

Axel grinned. "That's superstition, you realize."

"'Fear is the main source of superstition!'" Dillahunt slapped down his first card. "'And one of the main sources of cruelty.'" He had a talent for stopping things cold. Glancing up: "I quote Bertrand Russell."

Axel rubbed the heels of his hands in his eye sockets. "Dilly, please. Rein it in." He blinked away some grit, then turned to Jude. "You're still here? Go on. Abandon me. Have a nice dip while these jackals rip me to pieces."

6

JUDE CHANGED INTO HIS TRUNKS AND A T-SHIRT AND BURIED MALvasio's cash in his duffel. The money felt strange in his hands, like it had a life of its own, stories to tell—but whose money didn't? He grabbed a towel and rushed out the door, thinking: All the more reason I do this thing, not someone else. I know the lay of the land, I can see these characters for who they are. More to the point, when the chore's done, I can cut the cord and walk away. Watch me.

He headed down the dark, winding path of volcanic sand that

led through a grove of broad-leafed almond trees to the water. As he came close to the beach, he picked out the voice—husky, womanly—struggling to be heard among several others amid the roar of the wind and surf.

Eileen.

He pulled up, thinking: Search up and down the whole Costa del Bálsamo, spend six days doing it—she turns up right here, under your nose.

As he broke into the clearing, his spirits dropped when he saw the crowd she was sitting with. He'd crossed paths with them before, a close-knit bunch, guests of an *efemelenista* professor with a vacation house here at El Dorado Mar. He hadn't realized they were friends with Eileen, and wasn't sure what to make of the fact that they were. Though there wasn't blatant ill will on either side, they weren't exactly Jude's kind, or vice versa. Don't read too much into things, he told himself. Wait and see.

They all sat gathered around a wood-plank table inside a thatched *glorieta,* the open hut lit by a single bare bulb. There was Waxman, an American reporter for a left-leaning Net zine, burly and freckled with thinning red hair. He was all right, Jude thought, but a little too earnest and wedded to the radical line. Beside him sat his photographer with the sneaky wit and sad eyes and impossible Italian name. He was an ex-con, the story went, a reformed pot smuggler, which made him the most interesting of the bunch for Jude's money. On Waxman's other side sat a young, slight Guatemalan woman named Aleris with waist-length hair and a badly scarred throat. According to the reporter, she'd been seventeen, trying to reach the States through Mexico, when the man she'd hired as a coyote raped and strangled her and left her for dead. Missionaries found her and nursed her back to health. She was connected now with the Stone Flower Association, an NGO doing outreach for prostitutes, and took every opportunity, whenever her path crossed Jude's, to make it as obvious as possible that she had no use for him or the men he worked for.

There were two other men at the table Jude didn't recognize. They were both shirtless and—this was the odd part—garishly tattooed. *Mareros,* he thought. Gang members. Somebody must have snuck them in. They'd never have made it past the gate otherwise.

Jude's work obliged a working knowledge of the local crime world: at the top, a virtually untouchable Mafia of ex-military officers and other prominent men; at the bottom, Mara Salvatrucha and Mara Dieciocho, named after the *marabunta,* a voracious ant. The gangs had roots in Los Angeles but had spread as far as Houston, Chicago, D.C., and Boston, while continuing to expand down here as well, especially since the Peace Accords in 1992, when America began deporting its *mareros* back to El Salvador. Some of them had come to the States as infants with parents fleeing the civil war. They'd grown up on the streets. Many could barely speak Spanish. Convicted on drug charges mostly but everything else too—car theft, burglary, rape, murder—they got shipped here en masse aboard weekly chartered flights under armed guard, courtesy of the U.S. Marshals Service. Several thousand a year got repatriated, sent to a homeland they'd never called home, America's latest export.

There were rumors that some of the Mafia syndicates were cherry-picking the *maras* for manpower, which, given the politics of the situation, meant that the command structure would remain intact while the foot soldiers filled the prisons. That's what they got paid for, Jude supposed, oldest story in the world. Meanwhile, cliques had taken over parts of whole cities in and around the capital, then spread to the smaller towns, muscling for turf and running protection rackets against gas stations, bars, buses, hair salons, any business that generated cash.

By the late nineties the gang wars had escalated to where El Salvador had the highest murder rate in Latin America, higher even than Colombia or Haiti. The death squads stepped in then—La Sombra Negra, Grupo Extermino—until the government got sick of the bad press and launched its own, more official crackdown.

La Mano Dura they called it—"The Firm Hand" or "The Iron Fist," depending on your slant. The police swept the streets and stopped buses, picking off any badass too dumb to hide his tattoos. You could get two to five years just for tagging, throwing up a *placa,* or being sleeved. And if they thought you were worth it, they'd stop you on your way from the prison on release, check for those telltale tattoos—or, if anybody in the car had them, pop you for criminal association—and throw you right back inside for another two-to-five.

The government knew the law was unconstitutional but it got renewed anyway as an emergency measure every three months. Human rights groups fought for its repeal. Some judges refused to enforce it, letting suspects go after just a few days in jail. But the sweeps kept coming. Some *mareros,* sick of the hassle, tried to leave the life and joined outreach groups for the purpose of proving to the authorities they'd left it all behind. Unless you had your tattoos removed, though—an expensive and sometimes fatal procedure: they used acid, white-hot machetes—the cops rounded you up regardless. Others headed north for their old home turf but if you got caught in the States things hardly got better; the Americans only had to prove you'd been deported before coming back and they could put you away for ten years. After which, they'd just ship you off all over again.

Thousands of *mareros* had fled the capital to hide in the smaller cities. Some had bagged up and headed off to Honduras or Guatemala or Nicaragua, picking up the gang life there. But others had drawn the line and decided to stand where they were, live proud, die young. Jude wondered which category could claim the two sitting there with Eileen.

Sensing it would be unwise to just barge in, he dipped back into the shadows, skirted the palms and almond trees rimming the beach, and headed toward the Comedor Erika, a surf shack serving food and drink on the beach till ten. He counted heads in the *glorieta,* then ordered another round for the crowd, thinking it might help with introductions. With an extra tip, he got Erika's ten-year-old daughter to help him carry the drinks through the trees.

The voices in the *glorieta* continued to swell. An argument—the two *mareros* were going at it. Jude gestured for the girl to wait a moment while he listened.

"We're trying hard as you, help *vatos* bang out. But now, *boom,* Uncle Sam says we're a terrorist organization. It's insane. Like we're fucking al Qaeda. Nobody can send us money from the States no more—so what can we do, who can we help?"

"I'll tell you the word on the street—guys in your group still ball on the side. It's all a scam."

"That's a goddamn lie."

"You got to change your life, *chero*. Your heart. Without Christ? No way."

Their English seemed largely free of accent, unless you considered the lilting cadences of East L.A. an accent. Jude strained for a better look. One of them, the one talking conversion, seemed almost normal in appearance: clean-shaven, barbered hair, glasses. Take away the garish inkwork sleeving up each arm and darkening his hairless chest and back, he could have passed for a software rep. The other had mournful eyes, an extravagantly sculpted goatee, slicked-back hair, and even wilder tats.

"Don't preach to me about Jesus," the slick one said. "Talk about scam."

"No, you listen." The devout one leaned in. "I was in the hole three months. Why? Some cat talking head in the metal shop came at me with a hammer. I messed him up, took his hammer and made him eat it, okay? So don't try to out-tough me, *chero*. But after, my whole face puffed up, I had infection everywhere. Cut on my head started leaking pus, feet turned moldy, skin started peeling off my legs. I was hideous, man. I smelled like death. Only thing they'd let me have was a Bible. Read it cover to cover three times. I turned to God and said, 'I give up. Help me.' It changed my life."

No one else spoke, the whole table enthralled or too polite to contradict him. Regardless, Jude relaxed. The *mareros* had handed up the flag from the sound of things, left the life, even joined groups to help the like-minded. It put the get-together in a different light. He leaned down, told Erika's daughter, *"Venga conmigo"*—Come with me—and led her out from beneath the trees.

Eileen spotted him first. She broke into a lovely smile that turned uneasy almost instantly and Jude's heart sank in a sadly familiar way. Coming up to the table, he said, "Thought everybody might need another," then started passing out drinks. Aleris, the Guatemalan woman, gestured to the two *mareros* to be still, then flashed Jude a vaguely hostile smile. The two *mareros* shrugged at each other across the table, aware something was up but otherwise lost, and Waxman and his photographer seemed confused too. Meanwhile, Eileen still looked torn.

Jude saw no point pushing it. "Go on back to what you were doing. I'm heading off for a swim."

"Don't forget this." It was Aleris, handing back the beer he'd just given her.

ON THE DARK BEACH JUDE STRIPPED OFF HIS T-SHIRT AND, A BEER IN each fist, headed for the water, dodging the smooth black rocks, feet sinking into the muckish sand as he splashed through the surf. He walked out maybe twenty yards, then just plopped down, facing shore. The water, at low tide, reached his shoulders—still warm from the day's sun—the waves gently nudging his neck, the back of his head.

He belted back half his beer in one go. It took away a little of the sting, being insulted like that, in front of everybody. Lifting his head, he took in the cloudless night, the spray of stars, a mist of tiny pinpoints of light smeared across the darkness. It made him feel lonely but not in a bad way. And that, he supposed, was as good as it was going to get.

He downed the last of the beer and tossed the empty toward the beach, then started in on Aleris's.

"Jude?"

The voice sent a shiver through him. He liked it so much, the gravelly lowness of it, like everything she said was a secret. Turning toward the sound, he spotted her silhouette against the darkness, mincing along the smooth rocks, arms extended for balance.

"Out here!"

He stood up and started back in. They met on the wet sand, just beyond the reach of the surf. The wind blew her hair across her face, the strands clinging to her throat or catching in the corner of her mouth.

"I came to apologize. What happened back there..." She looked off, unable to wrap it up.

"It's okay. Really."

"No. It was unnecessary."

Reaching down for his towel to dry himself off, he wondered what the others had thought when she'd excused herself, followed him out here. It took nerve on her part and he was grateful for the kindness. Then, fleetingly, he pictured the two of them entwined on the sand, all *From Here to Eternity*.

She said, "I don't know how much you caught of what they were saying. Jaime and Truco. They were both in Mara Salvatrucha. Now they run foundations here to help guys leave the life. Jaime's very Christian but Truco's got no use for any of that and they just lock horns whenever they're together. Meanwhile the anti-terrorist laws in the U.S. make it impossible for families to send money here to help guys turn themselves around. It's crazy, it's cynical—"

"I get all that," Jude said, not meaning to sound rude. "But I'm not sure what it has to do with me."

She looked away and, peeling a strand of hair off her face, said, "Look, I need a ride back to where I'm staying. Near La Perla. Give me a lift, we can talk."

7

Jude's truck shot down the dark coastal road, windows open, hot air blasting in. "I'm not trying to make excuses for Aleris or anybody else," Eileen said, her voice raised above the noise, "but it's the elections coming up. Everybody's on edge. No sooner did people think the FMLN might have a shot, the poor might actually have a real voice in the government for a change, than the Americans stepped in and said: 'Hold the phone.' This is their little fiefdom. They're all for free elections, just as long as they get to pick the winner."

Jude nodded mechanically. He hated politics—sanctimonious paranoids on one side, bleeding-heart incompetents on the other, that's how he saw it anyway. Sadism-Makes-The-Heart-Grow-Stronger versus All-You-Need-Is-Love: one side pimping freedom, when what they really meant was money, the other side screaming for justice, which translated into screwing the rich. Because what everybody really wanted was the upper hand—smack the crap out of your enemies, humiliate them, make them shut the fuck up. Forget consensus, bag compromise, to hell with logic or even getting much done except waxing indignant and milking the system. Which, as far as he was concerned, meant they were all nuts or crooked or both. Not that he'd actually say any of that. He doubted he could put it into words without it sounding like—how had Malvasio put it?—a load of hairy horseshit.

Meanwhile, Eileen rolled on. "There's a slow build going on a lot of people don't see. The Pentagon shut down the bases in Panama, so they need this as a staging ground when the time comes to turn up the heat in Colombia. The government there's made a big show of getting the right-wing paramilitaries to hand over their guns. None of them will ever get prosecuted for murder, robbery, or drug trafficking, of course, but that means the only irregulars are the leftist guerrillas and that simplifies the politics. If Venezuela provides a cross-border refuge, we can go after Chávez as well, kill two birds with one stone. If not for Iraq, it'd already be happening. There's oil down there, partner. Enough said."

A sudden bitterness crept into her voice at mention of Iraq. Jude shot a sidelong glance her direction, trying to read her eyes, but she just sat there with her feet perched on the dash, reaching out to etch a bit of flaking red polish from one of her toenails.

"Anyway, Washington's making threats about deportations and blocking *remesas* from the States if the FMLN wins. That's a third of the economy down here."

Jude scratched his cheek with his shoulder. "I've heard all sorts of numbers on that front, actually."

"Like what?"

"Like seventeen percent. Some as low as thirteen percent. You've got a huge black market down here—how do you factor that in?"

"You think I'm just pulling numbers out of thin air?"

"That's not what I said."

"It's almost three billion a year, can we agree on that? The economy tanks without it. Only country with worse growth in the whole hemisphere is Haiti."

"Recently, sure, since coffee prices went south. Doesn't mean it'll be like that forever." Jude couldn't pinpoint why, exactly, he was being so contrary. The thing with Aleris, maybe. Or the fact that, if he made too obvious a show of how much he agreed—and he did—it'd just look like he was trying to get laid.

Eileen said, "I heard that in California, the Salvadoran embassy started phoning people who've overstayed their visas—to 'remind them to vote.' You bet the message got through then. Election goes the wrong way, everything changes. You can't hide anymore. People up there called their relatives down here and lo and behold, Tony Casaca's poll numbers shot up."

She was referring to Tony Saca, mockingly called Tony Casaca by some. Tony Bullshit. He was the presidential candidate for ARENA, the right-wing party formed by Roberto D'Aubuisson and his ilk during the civil war as the political wing of their death squad network. D'Aubuisson proved a troublesome figurehead—labeled "mentally unstable" by the CIA, which was one of the kinder things he got called—and his henchlings in the White Warriors Union murdered Archbishop Romero, among several thousand others. So, over time, the finer minds inside ARENA nudged him into the background and reinvented themselves as a pro-business party, taking charge of the country when the Christian Democrats imploded. The CIA, thrilled at the face-lift, had been shelling out money through front companies ever since. Of course, the Chinese were rumored to be funneling money to the FMLN too, just not as productively.

"On top of that," Eileen said, "you've got the current pack of thieves siphoning government funds to their buddy Saca's election campaign."

"Accusations like that get tossed around every election."

"Because they're true."

"How come they never get proved?"

She shook her head, like he was hopeless. "That'll happen about the same time I give birth to a goat."

They entered one of the tunnels along the coastal road. Inside, the headlights rippled across a moonscape of rough-hewn rock. It was a good place for bats. And robberies. Jude juiced it a little until they came out again on the far side.

"Excuse me if I'm looking at this wrong," he said, "but unless I'm missing your drift, what you're trying to say is that Aleris and some of the other people you hang out with think I'm in with the thieves down here. Some sort of modern day Pinkerton. I dunno, maybe you do too."

"For God's sake—no, I don't. And what I'm trying to say is, even with the others, it's not personal."

Oh, it feels plenty personal, Jude thought.

"It's just—hear me out, okay?" She wrapped her arms around her legs and settled her chin on her knees. "Everybody's got this sick sense that the few good things that came out of the Peace Accords have come undone, and too much wasn't even started in the first place. There's forty percent poverty in the cities, sixty percent in the countryside. The big scare during the war was that if the guerrillas won you'd have mass migrations to the States. Well, a third of the country has emigrated anyway, with seven hundred a day trying to follow behind, and two thirds of those still here work in the underground economy, if they work at all. The water situation is awful—the rivers may as well be open sewers. Add the industrial waste and pesticide runoff from the plantations, presto—not a waterway in the country isn't polluted. You've got eight-year-olds with machetes in the sugar fields, thirteen-year-olds behind sewing machines in the *maquilas,* all of them making at best a couple bucks a day, millions of squatters crammed into *barrancas* in the city or stuck out in the country in their shoddy little *champas*. You've been to the dig at Joya de Cerén? Fifteen hundred years ago, the Indians ate better food and lived in better houses than any of the poor do now. That's progress for you. And the solution? Karaoke bars and burger joints. More sweatshops churning out crap sneakers and T-shirts."

She pounded her chin softly against her knee and made a moaning little sigh.

"Now you've got CAFTA coming, which manages to piss on the unions and just about everybody else except the same old cronies. But it makes such a great smoke screen. The *areneros* can carp about jobs, jobs, jobs, but it's just lip service. The system's rigged so the same folks at the top never suffer. There's a real tradition here of screw the losers."

"Lot of that everywhere," Jude said.

"Yeah, well it has a real nasty edge to it here. The rich aren't just snotty, they're vicious. The poor disgust them. Embarrass them. '*Qué grencho*,' ever hear that?"

"Sure. But they make fun of hillbillies back home, too."

"It's like poverty's a crime. The term 'vampire state'? It was made for a place like this."

Actually, Jude thought, it was made for a place like New York, thus the pun on Empire State, but before he could find a way to say that without sounding snide, she'd launched on.

"All the crap you hear about things getting better? Spare me. Economy's been flatlining for five years. Things are as bad as during the war, if not worse, and you don't have the guerrillas to blame it on. Country's still scraping the bottom of the UN's development index despite fifteen years of doing everything Washington wants. Debt load to international banks is obscene but they tax street vendors, not the wealthy. Meanwhile you've got generals at SOUTH-COM testifying to Congress about progressives down here as 'emerging terrorists.' That's creepy, Jude. Like calling the Maryknolls a terrorist cell—which happened during the war, by the way."

"Granted, things have ramped up since 9/11, and some of it's kinda off-the-wall."

"They're scared. Elections have swung left in Venezuela, Brazil, Ecuador, Argentina. Uruguay's next. Probably Bolivia after that. Maybe Mexico. People down here are sick of the corruption and the poverty. So what does the Pentagon do? Claim anybody who won't just shut up while the crooks cash in is on a jihad. You visited the embassy lately?"

"Sure."

"Then you know. The spooks have landed. Way too many trim fit guys in golf clothes wandering around the halls."

"Look, I've got beefs with the Pentagon too. Never met a guy in uniform who didn't."

"Jude, I know that. My dad's pure Corps. My brother's in Iraq. I've heard it all."

That was news, the bit about her brother. Jude tucked it away, then said, "Well, down here they're building roads. Schools. Clinics. I know. I helped."

"Not enough. Sorry. Not by a long shot. And not always for the best reasons."

"That's my fault?"

"The people you work for—"

"Axel's a hydrologist."

"For whom, Jude? The women lining up barefoot at the *pozos* every morning, carrying the jugs back home on their heads? Or the soft drink company pumping hundreds of gallons a minute, bleeding the aquifers dry, just so they can move on to the next place and do it again."

She'd done her homework. Jude hated this. God only knew what she'd think if he told her about Malvasio.

He said, "You don't know Axel. He's nobody's stooge."

"Then they'll bury his findings and hire somebody else. And what about the next guy they tell you to protect? What if he's not quite so noble?"

"I don't have control over that."

With one hand she gathered her windblown hair while the other reached out again for her toenail to etch away another scab of red polish. "Well, there's the two-buck question, Jude. That lack of control, who you work for—doesn't that mess with your head?"

Sure it does, he thought, and if I could manage a word in edgewise, I'd tell you about it. But before he could wring the piss out of that thought and say something reasonable, a figure tottered out of the darkness into the road. Spotting him in the headlights, Jude slammed his foot down on the brake. The tires squealed across the soft blacktop and Eileen turned white, gripping the dash as the truck fishtailed back and forth, then lurched to a dead stop. The engine sputtered and died, leaving as background only the tick of the radiator, the hush of the wind, the murmur of the distant surf.

Jude opened his door to get out. "Stay in the truck, okay?"

"It's just a *vagabundo*."

"I realize that."

"Don't hurt him, okay?"

Of all the things she'd said so far, that was the first that cut to the bone. It isn't personal, he thought. Sure. "I don't hurt people," he said. "It's not what I do."

He slid out and hailed the man, who swerved on his feet in his rags, clutching a bottle of *aguardiente,* the local white lightning. As Jude drew closer he could smell the filth on his body, the rotted teeth, and yet the man's eyes were feverish and sad. He looked ancient, though Jude guessed his age to be somewhere close to thirty. He asked if there was a problem, and tears welled in the drunk's eyes as he pointed to the roadbed. The carcass of a dog, hit by a passing car, lay in the dusty gravel. Jude went over, knelt beside the animal, and saw that the neck had been snapped—the dog, about the size and shape of a greyhound, lay at a violent angle, blood crusting its head, its eyes dull, chest still. *Aguacateros,* they were called, the stray mutts that slinked around everywhere, the males fully packaged, the females bearing swollen teats from nonstop litters. This one, he noticed, was a female. And apparently, somehow, somewhere, she'd found a friend. Or the friend had found her.

The *vagabundo* shuffled up behind, muttering a slur of heartbreak and anger. Jude said he was going to move the body a little farther off the road—out of respect, to spare it being crushed by another passing car—and the man mewled his thanks. Jude reached under the skeletal body, lifted the dead animal in his arms—so light, he thought, she would've died of starvation soon regardless—and carried her toward a bed of *chichipince* and set her down in the dense, dry vinery. The *vagabundo* followed and perched himself uneasily on a nearby stone, reaching down to stroke her cold flank.

Jude thought about asking her name, but didn't want to inherit her ghost, so he merely whispered, *"Lo lamento"*—I'm sorry—and squeezed the man's shoulder, his hand coming away with grimy dust that he wiped against his shirttail as he walked back to the truck.

He climbed behind the wheel and Eileen said, "I feel awful about what I said when you were getting out. What you did just now, it was . . ." She screwed up her face, trying to think of the one word that would absolve all the others. "I don't know. I'm just sorry."

The darkness remained still except for the wind shivering through the trees overhead, the waves throbbing at the bottom of the hill.

"You must think I'm terrible," she said.

"I think we're all terrible." He turned the key in the ignition and waited till the six-cylinder kicked back to life with an oily cough of black smoke out the tailpipe. "But only some of us are sorry, and that's the problem."

8

THEY CONTINUED ON IN SILENCE AND IN TIME PASSED AN EVANGELICAL church girded with whitewashed stone, the landmark Jude had been waiting for. He slowed for the steep turn into La Perla—a village of rustic-to-shabby homes made of brick or cinder block with barbed wire coiled around every yard, every rooftop, even the central pen housing the community's chickens. He'd driven right past it at least twice during his search for Eileen way back when, one of dozens of tiny coastal *pueblitos* along the Carretera del Litoral he hadn't given a second thought. No way he could've checked out every village, and yet he still felt unlucky. If you'd found her then, he thought, the spat you just had would've been over a month ago.

"Just follow this road back all the way to the beach," Eileen said, pointing the way. Then her hand reached across the seat and squeezed Jude's knee. "Look, I want to clear the air, make sure you realize how sorry I am for some of the things I said."

"It's not necessary. Really."

"I just wanted to explain where people's heads are at, mine included. I don't hold you personally responsible or anything for how things are down here, okay? I'm not that dense. And I shouldn't have gone on and on the way I did, either. I was just bothered by the way Aleris treated you and I get chatty when I'm nervous."

Jude liked the sound of that but he liked the feel of her hand more. He felt stirring in the bone zone and squirmed a little to squelch it as she added, "It's not like I don't know where you're coming from. Like I said, I've got a brother over in Iraq, First Marines. He got sent into Fallujah, after those . . . contractors . . . got strung up on the bridge."

She was referring to the detail of Blackwater Security ops, all former special forces types, who got ambushed in a Baathist stronghold a week after the marines took over for the Eighty-second Airborne. The marines got told to make things happen, and almost immediately they engaged insurgents in a thirty-six-hour firefight. Reports conflicted as to why Blackwater sent its men into that hornet's nest: Some said they were on CIA business. Others scoffed at that, saying it was a vanilla recon run for a private logistics convoy coming through the next day. Regardless, the insurgents were waiting. The images of jubilant crowds and the charred, smoldering bodies hung from the bridge girders were broadcast worldwide, America recoiling, Islam cheering, the rest of the world thinking: Get back to me later. Sent a shudder through the trade, that was for sure. Then the White House ordered the marines back in with a vengeance, to make a point: This ain't Mogadishu.

"You should thank God you're not over there," she said.

"I don't have the kind of experience they're after."

In truth, some firms were hiring anyone with a pulse and it was backfiring; ordinary Iraqis were growing weary of scruffy cowboys armed to the teeth strutting around. Now America was recruiting here for the job—the U.S. liked the Salvadorans, kidnappings were common here and war was nothing new. The local boys hardly lacked enthusiasm: "The Iraqi Dream," some called it. Guards could earn twelve hundred dollars a month in Iraq, compared to two hundred here, plus food, clothing, insurance for their families if they were killed or maimed. Hundreds of *veteranos* had shown up for the recruiters, and the ones not chosen almost rioted.

Noticing Eileen had fallen silent, Jude glanced her way and saw her with her head cocked, braced by her hand, her eyes blank. "Fallujah," she said. "God. You know how well that's gone, right? The town's been a haven for smugglers forever. Saddam used them for ripping off the oil-for-food program. They aren't insurgents, they're gangsters, with mortars and RPGs. They use women and kids as human shields, hide snipers and weapons inside mosques, hijack ambulances and load them with explosives, then send them barreling toward checkpoints, the whole deal. The marines knew what killing the contractors was all about: The insurgents wanted a massive retaliation, so they could get footage of dead women and kids on the news. The marines didn't want to fall for that, but the White House was scared of looking weak. You know what happened next. Six hundred civilian dead the first week alone, just what the bad guys wanted. Then the Iraqi units that were supposed to help out took fire before they even left Baghdad and just turned around, saying they hadn't signed up to fight other Iraqis. Our guys were on their own and things just got uglier. The press was awful, especially over there. The suits had to pull the marines out, turn it back over to the locals, which means pretty much the same hoods who'd been shooting back the day before. I'm not a knee-jerk peacenik, I couldn't go home for the holidays if I was. I'm glad Saddam's gone, I wish we could get rid of every asshole like him in the world, including some of the jerks who run things here—but, oh yeah, I forgot, this is a real democracy, our model for Iraq. Well, pity the poor Iraqis, you know?" She rubbed her eyes, moaned. "I'm wandering, sorry, but what I mean is the whole thing just feels like a hoax. My brother, he's alive but I haven't heard from him in way too long. I'm worried sick about him. For a lot of reasons. Something I don't talk about much."

She sounded frightened, angry. Jude could sympathize. And though he hadn't kept up with the news from Iraq too well, he did know marine commanders had studied tactics with LAPD, hoping to combat the urban insurgency the way the cops had suppressed the gangs. There it was again, he thought, that nexus, gangs and terror, like a self-fulfilling prophecy.

"I knew about your dad. Being in the Corps, I mean. Until you mentioned it tonight, though, I didn't realize your brother—"

"Yeah," she whispered, staring at nothing. "Yeah yeah yeah."

Giant mango trees and *ceibas* loomed overhead, interspersed with smaller, spindly *pacún* and *hicaco*. The thick sweet smell of corn broth came from a nearby *champa*.

"What's your brother think of your life down here?"

"You mean my politics?"

Jude sighed. "I mean whatever."

"He's a lot like my dad. And for an old leatherneck, my pop is pretty hip. Rides an Indian, reads Vonnegut, loves to surf. Shared a blunt with him once—UC Santa Cruz, my graduation party?" She shivered at the memory. "Never again, boy, let me tell you."

A goat tied to a *pepeto* tree foraged through low-lying *zacate* vines while scrawny cattle drifted like ghosts down the dusty lanes, which were pitted with large rocks. The truck lurched along, past a low plaster wall on which someone had spray-painted *Smok Weed* in fluorescent orange. Beyond the wall, two boys with sticks darted through the dark trees chasing a dog.

EILEEN LIVED IN A SMALL FOUR-ROOM HOUSE—THE USUAL, CONCRETE block and tin, garlanded with barbed wire, the windows barred—a few hundred yards from the beach. Locked up all day, inside it was stifling but clean, despite a hint of souring fruit rinds.

The main room was piled high with blouses, skirts, scarves, all hand-embroidered, plus handwoven mats and baskets. It looked a little like a vendor's stall at the Mercado de Artesanías. "Welcome to the home of Harriet Handicraft," she said, gesturing him in.

She struck a match, lit a kerosene lamp, then gave him a brief tutorial on her work: bright *camisetas* of orange and red cotton, with yokes of white lace shirring, sewn in Izalco; scarves with hand-knotted fringe made in Ahuachapán; wraparound tie-dyed skirts called *refajos* made in Nahuizalco; shallow brown baskets called *viroleños;* woven mats made from tule rushes planted under a new moon. Many items looked neglected, like they'd been tucked away somewhere for years.

"You see anything like this now, it's mostly for tourists," she said. "Seventy years ago, the *campesinos* used this kind of thing day-to-day. But in the thirties, after the rebellion under Martí got crushed in La Matanza, anyone so much as looking like an Indian got shot on sight. Interest resurfaced a little in the fifties, when the old women complained their daughters and granddaughters didn't care anymore. But things turned bloody again. Now those old women are dead. And the younger women who haven't forgotten the old traditions never knew them to begin with."

She leaned down to smooth the fabric of a handwoven tablecloth, then stood back, like the curator of a small, dingy, forgotten museum.

"I feel like a paleontologist sometimes. These are my sad old bones."

The next room was tiny, hardly more than a closet, with a narrow cot and a wood stool used as a bed table. Beyond it, toward the back, lay the equally minuscule kitchen and bath. To Jude's surprise, the house had running water, fed by a nearby well, and he went immediately to the kitchen's cast iron sink to wash the gritty sweat off his face and arms. When he was done he shook the water off, not wanting to towel dry. The moisture felt good on his skin.

Bringing the lamp with her, she came up behind him, touched

his arm. "Help me put the hammock up outside. I can't sleep in here tonight. And I've got a couple beers. They'll be warm but . . ." Her voice trailed away. She lifted her necklace and ran the chain back and forth below her bottom lip. "I'd like it if you stuck around for a while. Talk some more. I don't want to leave things the way they sit right now."

They hung the hammock between two four-by-fours supporting a sheet of tin that served as a roof out back. It covered a patch of broom-swept sand, rimmed with painted gourds, beyond which stood a patchy copse of *quebracho* trees, decimated for firewood.

They sat face-to-face in the hammock, legs dangling to either side of the webbing, rocking a little to feign a breeze, and sharing a warm Pilsener, passing the bottle back and forth. Eileen talked about her siblings: four sisters, three brothers. "You come from a big family," she said, "you see the world in a whole different light, trust me. Not just because Pop's a marine. Or he has five girls."

She was the sixth child out of the eight and by her account wasn't the wildest by far—that privilege belonging to the oldest, Bebe. She lived in a Paris squat, espoused unisex anarchism, sported elaborate Maori tattooing the length of her body, was pierced everywhere imaginable (a thought left hanging), and shaved her head. Their mother would not speak to her, nor Bebe to Mom. Dad the ex-marine once ventured off to Paris, to reconnoiter.

"Reportedly, they got blind on Bourgogne Rouge and Pop carried her home piggyback through the Sentier. I don't think Mom's quite forgiven him yet."

She pressed Jude now and then about his own family, but he knew better. It wasn't time for that. Always, after a quick, bland response, he turned the query back around to her. Luckily, she liked her family, liked talking about them.

Occasionally she lifted her foot, nudging his leg with it as though to prod him to say more. The fourth or fifth time she left it there awhile, her sandy, leathery sole lingering gently against his inner thigh. Then, suddenly, she rose from the hammock and grabbed the lamp. "I have *got* to take a shower." He caught something in her voice and, glancing up, saw she had her hand held out in invitation.

THE BATHROOM WAS HARDLY BIGGER THAN A PHONE BOOTH AND IT seemed even smaller in the lamplight. They had to stand face-to-face, one of them straddling the toilet. A gooseneck showerhead jutted out from the concrete wall, curving over the mirrorless sink then pointing straight down to a rusty drain in the floor. Given the arrangement, a shower meant the whole bathroom got wet.

They jockeyed for position, Jude dodging the showerhead as the small of his back parked against the sink while Eileen sat on the toilet and removed her denim shirt, her bra, then slipped her cutoffs down her legs. As he watched, Jude caught a hint of ammonia; the place was scrubbed clean. No off-putting odors for this girl. He wondered if that meant she had sex in here a lot.

She tossed her clothing out the door then took off her glasses, reaching to one side of him to drop them inside her travel kit on the sink. Her eyes swam a little as her focus adjusted, and he reflected again on that odd nakedness he loved so much, intensified now by her being, well, naked. She smiled up at him, two red ovals marking where the frames had rested on her nose.

Only then did it dawn on him the sneaky way she resembled his sister. He hadn't caught it before. Eileen was taller with less tortured hair but they shared the same freckled skin, the same warm brown eyes. And yet it wasn't just physical or even primarily so: They both had that brainy, strong-willed, don't-call-me-pretty sense of pride while remaining strikingly feminine. And their names: Colleen, Eileen. Christ, he thought, what a bonehead. He felt his arousal weaken and yet, just as quickly, it returned as she said, "So this is what a girl's gotta do to get your attention."

She reached up, took his T-shirt in her hand, and tugged, pulling his face, now in full blush, toward hers. She ran the tip of her tongue along his lips to moisten them first, then pressed her mouth to his, rubbing gently back and forth. She let go of his shirt, folded her arms behind his neck, and held him close, darting in and out with her tongue, the occasional bite, playful and gentle, her breath tasting yeasty from the beer. With her fingertips she gently traced circles on his nape till gooseflesh rippled across his shoulders and down each arm. His back began to ache from bending over but he feared breaking the spell if he straightened up.

She pulled back, uncurled her arms, and reached for his belt buckle. "I will confess to being turned on when I'm jaybird naked and you're not, but it's time to press on to the next phase, don't you think?"

She helped him out of his clothes and promptly took him into her mouth. She moved her lips and hand in unison, up and down, over and over, till he was slick with her spit and beet red. Meanwhile, her other hand reached up from underneath, faintly brushing the wispy hair on his scrotum, and it was right about then he stopped thinking about his sister.

She smiled, feeling him shiver. "Change places?"

He went to sit down as she stood but it took a couple moves to accomplish the change of positions. She laughed and kissed his ear and it felt like being forgiven for every stupid, clumsy thing he'd ever done.

Once he was seated and square she braced herself against the sink, lifted one leg and cocked her foot on his thigh, like she had out on the hammock, but now so he could reach her. She raised one arm behind her to hold on to the shower spigot for balance as he pressed his face to her bush, loving the briny musk of her smell and wondering if he should tell her that.

With one finger he reached inside, half expecting to encounter sand. You found sand damn near everywhere—in your hair, your ears, between your toes—why not here? But the flesh felt perfectly smooth. Slippery. Warm as a mouth.

He found the pebbly surface about two inches up and in and gently massaged in a circular, come-hither motion, reminding himself not to go at it like he was trying to flip a switch. It was something he'd learned from the mountains of smut on base in the service. Two things you never lacked on a military base: men with male authority issues, and jerk-off fodder. Lesbian porn, in particular, had always proved instructive. If you paid attention and could manage your inferiority complex, it was hard not to learn a trick or two. Still, he felt a little like a dance student, staring at his feet, counting his steps out loud.

Kissing her belly, he pressed closer, his free hand grabbing her hip for balance. She let him go on for a while, uttering warm little humming sounds, helpless sounds, then leaned back and moved her foot from his thigh to his shoulder. Removing his finger, he buried his face in her, licking her labia up one side then down the other, running his tongue in circles at the top, then repeating the circuit, varying up with long, slow movements all the way around. The hair of her muff tickled his nose so he quickened his pace, not wanting to lose his concentration, pressing a little more firmly, aiming high and staying there now—so she could plan on where his tongue would be. She sensed the change, found her own sweet spots and pressed in when she wanted it hard, eased back when she wanted it gentle, her hand at his nape, guiding him. His face got sloppy, his tongue began to ache, his breathing turned to a wheezy moan as the tang of her wetness soured in the back of his throat.

She let a little whimper leak out as a shiver launched up from the small of her back. She stopped him, lowering her leg. Reaching inside her travel kit, she pulled a foil package out and bit it open, then rolled the condom down his shaft, squatted on his lap, and slipped him inside.

She pulled him close and he buried his face in her chest, smelling the vinegary warmth of her armpits. He licked and bit her nipples or kissed her throat as she rode him, and she clutched him tight as she came, a soft, mewling, throaty cry—that voice, he thought, God how I love that voice—the sound like a long ghostly *no* but with a whimpering peal of surprise in it, too.

He felt good. He felt useful.

He began to slow his rhythm, but then she stood up and took his hand, urged him onto his feet as she turned her back and leaned over the sink, hands against the wall. For the first time he saw the tattoo on her right cheek, a red and black rose with *Smarty* written in a scroll underneath. Something she'd done for some other guy, he supposed, then drove the thought away as he entered her, pulled her back to him, the plump softness of her behind caressing his belly.

Grabbing her hips, he began easing her back and forth, gentle at first then stronger as he felt his own climax peaking. His pelvis began to smack against her rump and she turned her head toward him, murmuring into her shoulder, "It's okay, come on . . . give it to me. . . ." Barely a whisper, said to spur him on. And it did. He felt conflicted but too late. He pressed his face against her back, shuddered and, unwittingly, mimicked her own sound as he came.

As always, the guilt swam up from somewhere almost instantly. He should've lasted longer, should've pleased her more—these were the words banging around inside his head, but the guilt felt blacker than that, deeper. *Give it to me.* He wondered if she was the kind who liked to get hit, remembering their exchange from earlier: *I don't hurt people. It's not what I do.*

"Where did you go?"

He glanced up. She was smiling over her shoulder but with little darts of worry in her eyes. He wrapped her up in his arms, tight, to chase his thoughts away. With her fingertips she traced the hair on his forearms, his hands.

"I seem to remember something about a shower."

She reached for the spigot. Even knowing the water would be cold didn't prepare him. His spine locked, his knees buckled. She turned, clutched him to her, laughing, rubbing his skin hard: "Me too. Warm me up, warm me up!" He chafed her back as she reached for the soap cake on the sink and lathered up, washing herself, then him, then her again, back and forth, kissing him in between statements like, "You're a very attentive lover" and "Don't worry, okay?"

THEY SLEPT NAKED IN THE HAMMOCK WITHOUT MOSQUITO NETTING, a luxury only possible given the dry heat of the season. She lay curled on one side, entwined in his legs, her head on his stomach, breathing soundly and deep. Perspiration beaded on her forehead and upper lip. Whenever Jude wiped the moisture away, she'd twitch groggily and paw at her nose, eyes shut.

As he lay there watching her, the odd semblance to his sister prompted one of his favorite painful memories. It was after Colleen had left for college, Jude was living in Joliet. A box full of paperbacks arrived from Madison. They came with a note: *For when you need to get away and can't. And because loneliness gets boring. I know. Look after yourself.* As though that weren't odd enough, her choices revealed an uncanny sense of what he'd like—Kipling, Twain, Jack London, Graham Greene, plus a few trash paperbacks thrown in for no reason he could figure except they had a football or a swastika on the cover. He wrapped up the summer holed up alone and reading like mad, the way he'd always mocked her for doing. And she was right, the books gave him a welcome taste for escape to the far away. It was the most thoughtful thing she'd ever done for him. Years later he was still secretly thanking her—secretly, because after that summer no one in the family ever heard from her again.

In time he drifted off but never slept deeply, wandering in and out of quirky dreams. In one, a stray dog, limping from a fight, wandered down his old street in Chicago, and that woke him. The weight of Eileen's body and the sound of the ocean confused him momentarily. Doves cooed in the trees. It was near dawn, but still dark.

Remembering he had to get back to El Dorado Mar and pack, catch a flight to the States, he eased himself from under her. She groaned and stretched then curled up, snoring prettily. He fumbled around inside for his clothes, came back out for the sake of the moonlight and dressed in silence. He'd started the night thinking she disdained him, then pitied him, then kinda maybe put up with him because he reminded her of her brother—and how odd to feel the reciprocal connection there—and then *wham*. It put a whole new spin on getting lucky.

He was tugging on his shoes when she looked at him one-eyed through a whirlwind of hair. "You were just going to walk out, weren't you?"

He glanced up. "Not really." It sounded moronic so he leaned toward her, peeled the tangled strands of hair aside, and added, "I've got to run. I'm going away for a while."

That just came out sounding worse, but that was the story of his life.

Her other eye fluttered open, gluey with sleep. She struggled to get up in the dimness—groggy, naked, no glasses, ankles crossed, the chaos of hair. Beyond her, the moonlight cast the *quebracho* trees in a silvery glow. "I'm not going to see you again, am I?"

That one just about knocked him down. "Say that again?"

"You're the best-looking guy I've ever done the deed with, know that?" She rubbed her eyes then let out a long, wounded sigh. "Christ, what an incredibly dumb thing to say. Never know when to just shut up."

Jude felt stunned she could be so clueless about her own attractiveness—and yet hadn't he played the same trick on himself most of his life? As a teenager, when he'd begun to realize he wasn't too hard on the eyes, as he was told more than once, he'd never known what to say, and his clumsy silences tended to make girls think he was stupid or vain or screwed up or all three—to the point he'd come to believe that any compliment regarding his looks was a backhanded insult. Then came his father's scandal, the move to Joliet, his leap from high school to the service, from there to EP work: He'd never been in a situation that invited long-term anything, let alone intimacy. He'd taken his turns with prostitutes, but they invariably bored him or scared him and, in either event, hardly cured him of his suspicion that any compliment from a woman had a good chance of concealing a secret purpose.

And so it wasn't hard for him to turn Eileen's other statement around as well, transform her supposed concern that he didn't want to see her again into a secret admission that she hoped he'd take the hint and stay away—at which point the black mood that had descended after sex came back like a thunderclap. Even while a part of him felt an impulse to stop, look at her, read the cues more mindfully, he instead just glanced at his watch, said "I have to go," and left.

9

As Jude drove back through the tunnels and along the shoreline cliffs, headlights spraying the deserted two-lane highway, any lingering qualms he might have had about returning to Chicago vanished. Getting away now, however dubious the reason, felt welcome. He could use the trip to turn his mind away from what had just happened—how could something take off so brilliantly, he wondered, and crash to the ground so fast? Because you can't get the words out, he told himself, not the way you want. And then, when the thing starts turning to crap before your eyes, you act before you think. On the job it can be a plus, react fast, don't ponder the options. But not with women. Act on impulse, who knew what baggage you were dragging along? How many times had he done that? Whatever the number, add one.

He tried to muster a little hope that maybe, with his going away, they could gain some perspective. They'd get back on track when he returned, laugh it off, call it a misunderstanding—and yet it seemed cowardly to leave it like that. I should phone her now, he thought, straighten it out. He reached for the glove box to collect his cell, only then realizing he'd neglected to get her number. Though he knew where she lived now, he still had no clue how to reach her by phone. And she was in the same boat—she hadn't gotten his info, either. The international complications were irrelevant. There'd be nothing but silence between them the whole time he was gone. And maybe that's for the best, he thought. Even if it isn't, you're stuck.

HE ARRIVED AT EL DORADO MAR AS DAWN WAS HAZING THE SKY A grayish blue, and rousted the guard with a horn toot. Once the gate was drawn back, he drove down the winding tree-shaded lane to Horizon House, parked, punched in his code at the pass switch panel, and snuck inside.

Only Fitz was up—shorts and T-shirt, mussed hair, bloodshot eyes—sitting in the kitchen. He was the crew's early riser, a frequent insomniac, something he blamed on his demining work in Kuwait after the first Gulf War. It also explained the constant tremor in his hands: eighteen months of ten-hour days, spent beneath a brutal sun holding his breath, sticking carpenter nails into firing mechanisms and unscrewing detonators on Bouncing Bettys and Chinese T-72s. He said he'd seen other guys slip up—one second they're there, the next there's just a bloody spray of dust and that percussive *whoomph* you never forget. It was why he didn't take field assignments, just did the advance work for everyone else. He couldn't trust his body under stress anymore.

Even with Fitz's quirks, Jude felt relieved at having no one else to deal with. He didn't want his private life common knowledge, especially now.

Fitz had made the day's first pot of coffee and Jude poured himself a quick cup, needing a jolt to clear his mind before heading to his room to pack. He was taking his first sip when Fitz said quietly from behind, "Must feel good, get it out of your system."

Jude turned around. Fitz sat there, smiling. It didn't seem exactly a friendly smile.

"Excuse me?"

"The bone dance," Fitz said. "Poon platoon. Horizontal mambo." Something cold and a little vile slid around in his eyes, then stopped—that was the scary part—then slid around again. "No offense," he said, "but I kinda figured you as overdue. This job makes it hard. Hard to connect, I mean, with the ladies. Unless you pay for it."

Jude realized further silence at this point might seem overly fussy. "I guess you could say that."

"Word to the wise? Put it behind you." Fitz's eyes did their trick again. "Some fuckhead slips up through a crowd with a gun or a knife, your brain's wrapped around your dick? Don't think it can't happen."

Chances are good it's not an issue, Jude thought, thinking of where things stood with Eileen, but he'd be damned if he'd share that with Fitz. "Thanks for the advice." He managed a smile. Then, seeing a way to change the subject: "Mind if I ask you a question?"

Fitz dropped an unsteady hand into his lap. "Sure. Go ahead."

"I was shooting the breeze with some people down at the beach, and somebody mentioned a worker dormitory being built for a coffee plantation up around the Tecapa volcano. You heard anything about that?"

He'd had no time to do any independent digging into Malvasio's story. Not that he'd felt a pressing need, he'd resigned himself to the risk. Maybe that was rash but it was how he felt—and nothing that had happened since he'd agreed to go had changed that. He didn't want to call any more attention to his trip than he already had, but as long as he had Fitz at his disposal, why not one quick question? Just be careful, he told himself.

Fitz mulled it over. "Why do you think I'd hear about it?"

"No reason. I was just curious. It seemed odd, given the way coffee prices have been, that somebody'd be expanding."

"There's a whole lotta odd in the economy down here." Fitz drained the last of his coffee and it seemed a chore—closing his eyes to concentrate, holding the cup steady, putting it down slowly, like it might explode. "But if it's not a threat to anybody, I'm not going to pay much attention. I've got plenty to focus on as it is."

"Sure," Jude said. "Understood."

"You were thinking what—they were building an airfield? Drug labs?"

"I wasn't thinking anything, really. Like I said, I just wasn't sure it made sense."

"Some of the coffee producers have figured out how to turn a profit by growing a lower-grade bean, the *robusta* variety instead of *arabica*. I know that much."

"Okay. That explains it."

"I mean, I don't know for sure."

"But it makes sense." Come on, Jude thought. Let it go.

"If only making sense were the better part of normal down here." Fitz pushed out his chair and rose from the table to rinse his cup in the sink. "But I guess that's why guys like you and me have work." He glanced over his shoulder and smiled. "Have a safe trip home, by the way."

Two hours later, as Jude sat aboard the TACA airliner at Comalapa preparing for takeoff, that one word came back to him again and again: *home*. And as the moments ticked past, the things around him began to melt away—the other passengers gaggling about, the stewardesses slamming shut the overhead bins, the baggage handlers loading the hold below—and he found himself back on the living room couch beside his mother, listening as the FBI agents tore the old abode apart like it was a crack house.

He remembered the sound, like carpentry in reverse, the havoc punctuated with snide repartee and occasional laughter. The tall agent with the milky green eyes circled back from time to time, retaining an air of stoic calm, almost sympathy, but Jude saw through that. And the local cops, the ones who knew his dad, they just lumped around, unable to meet his eyes.

His mother sat there in a fierce stillness as the ransacking of her home dragged on. Jude, sitting beside her, made a show of complaining twice on her behalf, but all he earned for the bother was a phony promise the first time, a threat the next. He joined her in tight-lipped rage after that, feeling useless, and his torn-up ankle just made that worse.

The injury to his ankle, that was a story in itself, a kind of morality tale in miniature.

It was the day before, and right up to the moment he got hurt, things had been edging toward perfect: summer two-a-days, not too hot, first practice in full pads. Jude responded to the coaches' constant goad to *punish that man* by pasting some faceless sophomore on the hamburger squad during one-on-ones. Getting low and square, he drilled the kid so hard it turned heads—even the coaches flinched a little at the sound of the hit. But he wasn't done. He hoisted the kid clear off the ground, carried him back five yards, and, driving with his shoulder, planted him in the dirt with one of those fierce snot-gurgling thuds you dream about.

The showboating cost him. His ankle buckled under and almost snapped. He bolted up like it hadn't happened but he'd felt it, heard it even—the way you do, the loud clicking thunk in the joint, the echo up the bone. He tried to jog back to the tackling line but the thing turned to muck under his weight. Two managers had to help him off the field. Meanwhile, Mr. Faceless Sophomore Hamburger finally sat up and took a neck-snapping whiff of smelling salts.

And so, the day after, there Jude sat in the living room, next to his brooding mother, his ankle a fat, blue throbbing thing at the end of his leg, a testament to anybody who cared to notice what a hopeless case he was.

Finally, a cry went up from the basement, a sound so lusty you'd have thought they'd discovered Jimmy Hoffa mummified in the crawl space. The tall lead agent excused himself and followed the sound downstairs. Ten minutes passed before he came back, a clump of money in each hand, wrapped in cellophane like sandwiches—to contain the smell, Jude guessed. It looked ragged and soiled, street cash. The agent laid one stack beside the other on the coffee table, then stared right at Jude with those odd green eyes.

"Found these and more like them downstairs, behind a false wall panel, a matter of feet from where your bed is. About twenty thousand, we think. Just a rough guess. Mind telling me who it belongs to?"

Not a false panel, Jude thought, a loose one. He'd installed them all himself—he was good that way, working with his hands—knew the spot the agent meant, difficult to seal flush because of a bulging joint in a water pipe. He'd shown it to his dad once, asking advice. "Forget about it," the old man had said. "Hide it with something. A chair, some shelves." And Jude had done that: Hidden it. Forgotten.

Before he could say any of that, his mother reached out, grabbed his knee hard, and squeezed. "He's a minor. He's not answering questions till we speak to a lawyer."

Jude shot her a look but obeyed, saying nothing. The agent glanced from one to the other, waiting them out. Finally, he gave it up, collected the money, and said, "Very well," then returned downstairs.

Jude whispered, "He hid his—"

"Shut up!" In her lap she strangled one hand with the other. "For God's sake don't make things any worse than they are."

He waited but she wouldn't look at him. He wondered what she knew, what she was hiding. Or if she was simply trying to keep what remained of her life in one piece.

He sank into his own reckoning then, looking at the thing from every angle he could. He felt betrayed, the old man hiding all that money where it might be considered not his but his son's—*Cash ain't a crime,* he'd say, *and you're a juvie.* And yet Jude caught a backhanded compliment in it, too, a show of trust. *You'll know how to handle yourself,* his father seemed to be saying, *if it comes to that.* Did he ever intend to tell Jude about it? How did he think his son would react? Jude never learned the answers to those questions. By the time he got up the nerve to ask, the old man was dead.

It wasn't till some time later that he saw the other thing, the one that troubled him even more. There was an eerie parallel between what happened to the two of them separately, one day apart: proud and suited up one minute, humbled and taken away the next. Like it was meant to be, a lesson from on high to them both: Don't get cocky. The things you take for granted, rely on—the things that make you who you are—can vanish in a heartbeat.

And that's how you find out, Jude thought, what it feels like to be faceless.

10

MALVASIO SAT UP AND ROLLED THE STIFFNESS FROM HIS NECK. BESIDE him, the girl fidgeted beneath the sheets and drew away, sensing he'd woken. An unconscious impulse, her withdrawal, and unearned since he'd never touched her, not that way. He had his standards, after all. Some of these kids showed up already boiling with disease.

Her name was Anabella. She looked about twelve, scrawny and dark with a broad face and a stubby little nose. She had long straight hair that he foresaw getting cut short, molded into the pin-curled helmet the trashier local streetwalkers were famous for.

She was a reward, a bone tossed to him by the judge and the colonel, and only a fool would deny them their displays of macho largesse. She'd arrived last week from Honduras, one of thirty or so orphans and street kids on the *finca* at the moment, most of them due to move on today. Many had arrived with first degree malnutrition, endemic in the region—they didn't scream out at you with fly-coated eyes and bloated bellies like the haunting kids of Africa, they just withered away from diarrhea or slowly starved to death. Here on the *finca,* though, they'd been fed and treated for intestinal parasites to the point they were fit enough for work—proof, Malvasio supposed, that mercy took many forms.

Of the group, a precious few would get handed over to the nuns at a local orphanage, to see if they possessed a talent for obedient suffering indicative of a religious vocation. A few more, the most rugged and unappealing of the bunch, would get sent to the judge's cane fields. Others, boys and girls alike, would get shipped to brothels in Acajutla or the capital, where they would have the only encounters they would ever know with the rich and powerful. The rest—and this, Malvasio guessed, would be Anabella's fate—would get sent to Guatemala and then on to a ratty little suburb outside Mexico City. There, stashed in a guarded house run by *mamacitas* who would console them and beat them and tutor them in the tricks of survival, they would wait until the colonel's contacts arrived, pimps from a family of pimps who would dress them up in skimpy, hookerish things, pink and black, then parade them one by one in front of a crowd of nameless men until it was time to walk back into the catacomb of filthy rooms, armed with a condom and two sheets of toilet paper, where behind a drawn sheet they'd launch their new lives— fifty pesos for straight sex, clothes left on; fifty more pesos, the skirt comes up; fifty more, the bra comes off; fifty more on top of that for a blow job, with twenty more shelled out for every exotic position requested. Soon enough a wholesaler would step forward and pay for their transport to the border, and once across they'd get handed over to men waiting in vans that would carry them to the major hubs—New York, Los Angeles, Chicago, Atlanta—or anywhere else they could pay off their passage. For the next few years, maybe longer, they'd be at the mercy of men with wants that would make those days in the Mexican catacomb feel like Christmas, until they ran away or were killed for trying or died from an overdose or disease, the few survivors managing to soldier on with a steely, blank-eyed numbness that would be, from that point on, a lifelong companion—especially for those who graduated to the status of *mamacita* themselves.

For the past week the girls had helped clean the judge's hacienda, the boys joining the colonel's squad of *zacateros* clearing brush. It might well prove the last honest work many of them would ever know, just as they would look back at the *finca* itself as a sort of paradise.

Malvasio got up and drew the curtains open for the sake of a little air. He felt desperate for the rains, mosquitoes be damned. When he turned back around he found the girl watching him, the sheet pulled up to her chin, eyes dull as shirt buttons. Knowing what she wanted, he went to the room's one chair, dug inside his pant pocket, removed his cell phone, and tossed it onto the bed. It was one of five he owned, all bought from hustlers at the *mercado central*. The country was swimming with black-market cells and he made it a point never to use the same phone for longer than a week.

The girl gathered the thing up happily, instantly scrolling to the screen settings, holding the gizmo to her face like a tiny TV. Soon she'd be playing the various ringers over and over, fascinated by the dinky bing-bong melodies that, when loud enough, reminded Malvasio of Vegas slots. Bizet's "Toreador Song" seemed to hold a particular fascination for her.

When Malvasio fled the States, the man he sought out for help, Ovidio Morales, was a lieutenant in the national anti-narcotics squad, famous for breaking up a Colombian smuggling ring (while secretly shielding the local military officers involved). A man who understood loyalty and gratitude and the subtler nuances of the law, Ovidio proved an exceptional guardian angel, introducing Malvasio to men who could help him.

In time, with proper precautions, Malvasio ventured back to the States, stealing across the border with a new name each time—Richard Ferry his most recent incarnation. Up north he picked up odd jobs from men who could pay to see their seamier wants realized: landlords who had a gang or squatter problem, businessmen being shaken down by a poor choice in out-of-town company, drug dealers with runaway wives or accountants. It had worked out well for almost a decade, the work increasingly remunerative and complex, but the last job had backfired: A whole neighborhood had burned to the ground and a federal informant was among the casualties—through no fault of mine, Malvasio thought. Regardless, his situation in El Salvador went to hell. The U.S. embassy cranked up the heat, deploying an FBI fugitive unit in-country, just as they had when Malvasio first arrived. Fortunately, they enjoyed no more success this time than the last, but Ovidio couldn't risk protecting him anymore. And so Malvasio had to root around for another angel.

The man he found was Hector Torres, one of Ovidio's introductions. He owned the restaurant in San Marcelino where Malvasio met with Jude, plus other nightclubs and restaurants both around the capital and out east, in San Miguel, even one in San Bartolo Oriente named El Arriero. Great conduits for laundering money, restaurants, which was how Torres had insinuated his way into the graces of the powerful.

His uncle, the original owner of El Arriero, had been kidnapped by the guerrillas early in the war and then shot dead during an escape attempt. The body got dumped off in the restaurant's trash, at which point Hector stepped into his uncle's shoes and let it be known he would get his revenge. Soon members of the White Warriors Union came to call, and money started flowing from a group of exiled oligarchs in Miami and Guatemala City. The money arrived as investment capital for his expanding business interests, except those interests weren't expanding quite as much as the sums in question suggested. Instead he skimmed his take, then funneled the rest of the cash to the *especiales* from the National Guard or Treasury Police, who kidnapped suspected dissidents and handed them over to the Fuerza Aérea's infamous A-II unit.

That was how Hector came to know the colonel—Colonel Narciso Vides, a former intelligence officer with A-II, linked to the "night free-fall training" that consisted of dumping live, bound guerrillas from C-47s over the Pacific Ocean. A-II also had a knack for executing common criminals just so the bodies could get pitched from helicopters over the FMLN stronghold at Guazapa volcano.

With the Peace Accords in 1992, the colonel quietly surrendered his commission. He already had his future charted, thanks to Judge Saturnino Regalado.

The colonel and judge had forged their bond during the war, when the colonel introduced the judge to an Argentine military advisor who had a plan concerning the ever-expanding number of insurgent orphans in the countryside. The Argentines were old hands at this, the colonel said, and in short order the children were being collected and shipped off to other countries throughout Latin America for work or adoption, depending on their age, skills, or beauty. The scheme was originally conceived as a way to demoralize the resistance, but soon a method became a métier, even after the Argentine advisor slithered back to Buenos Aires in the wake of the Falklands disaster. And there was never a lack of children. The poor bred like cattle, the colonel was known to say—in a country the size of Massachusetts with a population density equal to India's, no problem loomed so large as the sexual liberality of the penniless. Who but themselves did they have to blame if their children became livestock, a point underscored by how freely some of them sold their kids outright—or, currying favor, handed them up for nothing—to the colonel's touts traveling village to village.

The blanket amnesty provided as part of the Peace Accords

shielded the judge and colonel from prosecution for crimes committed during the war, while simple corruption had protected them
since. Civil suits filed in the States had begun to blink on their liti-
gation radars, but locally the two men still had sheer political clout
and family connections to carry the day. The judge in particular was
untouchable, enjoying a social station having roots centuries deep in
colonial patronage and the *cafetero* system, a generous donor to the
church and its many orphanages. The man had powerful friends
everywhere—one might as well try to indict God's sidekick. And
the colonel had his *tanda,* military academy classmates, watching his
back, the ones still in uniform as well as those who'd already par-
layed their war service into private sector profit. He also took considerable care to champion war veterans, to the point many ex-soldiers
and their families saw him as a personal benefactor.

But the nexus of influence to which Malvasio was currently beholden remained incomplete without mention of Wenceslao Sola.

Sola, connected by marriage to one of the *catorce familias,* the infamous fourteen families, served as a secret *patrón* for several brothels about the country, which was how he went from being a mere
member of the colonel's and judge's social circle—everyone of a certain station knew everyone else in El Salvador—to the role of partner in their operation. In time, with contacts made during his travels,
Sola began not merely buying children for his bordellos but helping
to move them north.

There were other aspects of Sola's pedigree, though, that recom-
mended him to the colonel and judge. He'd come of age during the
last years of the war as a member of Los Patrióticos, a gang of
ARENA-linked professionals who matriculated through the First
Brigade's civil defense training program. Los Patrióticos embraced
the counterrevolutionary ethos with rabid gusto, forsaking firearms
(military ammunition might be traced) and preferring instead stran-
gulation, throat-slashing, and poisoning—but not before the captive
had been tortured, disfigured, and, if a woman, repeatedly raped. The

Grand Guignol sadism surprised some observers since, in the words of one atypically candid U.S. Department of Defense analyst, they were really nothing but "rich momma's boys and potbellied patriots."

This observation did not, of course, dissuade the U.S. Military Group from funding and training Los Patrióticos and others of their ilk. As one U.S. military commander on the ground confessed, "We're already a little pregnant."

After the war Sola did what everyone else in his circle did—milk his connections for plum business deals, aided by the privatization schemes of the American-sponsored neoliberal economic program, which basically handed back to the wealthy everything the Peace Accords had tried to redistribute. One such windfall was a seat on the board of Estrella in San Bartolo Oriente, which bought its sugar from cane fields owned by Judge Regalado, and which had Colonel Vides to vet its workforce for unionists and other *subversivos*.

In truth, the bottling plant's recent expansion concealed a hidden purpose: It was step one in the company's bid to move in as the regional water authority when the national water agency, ANDA, was privatized, something said to be in the works if ARENA could hold on to power in the upcoming election, a virtual lock given recent polls. And that scheme was green-lighted by the powers that be, both here and in Washington, as a way to pay back Estrella's board and executive committee for their help in furthering "hemispheric security." But then ODIC—the Overseas Development Insurance Corporation, an export credit agency based in Washington—butted in because an American conglomerate named Torkland Overby, tapped by the Estrella board to "invest," agreed to do so but didn't want to risk anything. Who could blame them? And even though the ODIC flacks were sympathetic—the bank was a way station for spooks, basically—their involvement triggered the bureaucracy and that meant scrutiny. So now you had pencil pushers kicking the tires and checking under the hood and sooner rather than later it dawned on somebody the thing was a loser. With the judge's irrigated cane fields and his sugar processing plant upstream already draining away over a thousand gallons a minute, the bottling plant, drawing off hundreds more, was sucking the aquifer dry.

But that wasn't the punch line. In the near term, the plant's expansion was geared toward increasing its production of bottled water, which Estrella intended to sell to all the poor schmucks whose domestic wells dried up or turned brackish from mineral intrusion because of the aquifer depletion. And if that wasn't cynical enough, they had a backup plan if the expansion proved unviable long-term: They'd close up shop, cadge another load of cash off whoever was willing, and build an even bigger plant in a better locale, claiming they wanted to conform to the new laws concerning wastewater treatment, which older plants like the one in place were allowed to ignore.

To their credit, the Torkland Overby wonks weren't entirely gullible, but they didn't want to sabotage the project either. In the long run, even if the old plant had to be shut down a few years out and this whole dog-and-pony show had to be repeated, Estrella was a major regional player with strong upside potential, and Torkland knew that. So what do they do? They hire a hydrologist to look into the matter, hoping to somehow confirm the aquifer drawdown is viable, or at least stumble onto some new, untapped groundwater sources in the area. But they don't have the good sense to retain a guy they can buy off. Instead, they bring on board somebody with a spine connected to his brain and guess what? The whole thing's about to go south, with upward of half a million dollars per director at stake, and you don't do that to someone connected by marriage to one of the fourteen families, especially when he has pull with the likes of Judge Saturnino Regalado and Colonel Narciso Vides. The calls will start and sooner or later the phone on the desk of Hector Torres is going to ring, and he'll turn to Malvasio and say, "This is why I pay you."

The hydrologist's name was Axel Odelberg—Jude's principal, imagine that. The whole thing felt haunted when Malvasio learned that. He started second-guessing himself, wondering if finally he'd managed to dig the hole he couldn't crawl out of. Then he shook off the hobgoblins and saw the possibilities. Take the initiative, he told himself, get in touch with Ray's kid and see what there is to see.

As things turned out it was a case of like father like son: The kid was the stalwart type, a little inward, more a follower than a leader, and almost embarrassingly easy to play. The trick was getting him to move fast, and Jude had obliged on that front like the good soldier he'd no doubt been. There are just some people who bite at sincerity and never see the next thing coming. The wounded ones—tell them you're sorry, sound like you mean it, then stand back and watch the miracles unfold.

The pictures had been a particularly inspired touch. Ovidio Morales certainly did exist, and thank his unlucky mother for that, but he bore no resemblance to the man in the photo Malvasio had shown Jude—that had been a deputy from the Cook County Sheriff's Department named Ike Ramona. And Ovidio had no connections to anyone working on the Tecapa volcano coffee plantation. Malvasio had taken that snapshot while driving through the region and had no idea who the land belonged to. So if things went sideways down the line and Jude tried to implicate Ovidio, all he'd have is a story concocted by that insufferable, elusive degenerate Bill Malvasio, who had been a plague to poor Lieutenant Morales for years, concocting self-serving tales of collusion and secret support that the good lieutenant had repeatedly and credibly denied to every law enforcement agency who'd ever questioned him on the matter, including the FBI.

There was a sad twist to the business, though. Malvasio felt for Jude, always had. He'd been raised in a family of bats—fussy wretch of a mother; headstrong old man who turned out, in the end, to be weak; a four-eyed frizzy-haired egghead sister. Malvasio figured Jude had been through enough and didn't want to see him disgraced. Or dead. And it was when he was racking his brain over that, trying to find a way out, that the thing had come together in his mind. Bring the Candyman down, let him be the final puzzle piece. It was beautiful, really, and almost felt like old times—in the good sense, not the gone-to-hell sense. And, for now, the powers-that-be still held out hope Mr. Odelberg might somehow prove a useful fool. As long as that held true—and as long as Malvasio kept thinking several moves ahead—everybody was safe.

A KNOCK CAME FROM OUTSIDE THE TWO-ROOM HUT. ANABELLA folded up the cell phone, padded into the bathroom, and shut the door. Malvasio called out, "*¡Momentito!*" and slipped on pants.

Opening the door, he found a gaunt, unsmiling man in a sweat-stained uniform with a shotgun slung over his shoulder. His head was shaved clean and he wore aviator sunglasses, resembling a giant bug. Beyond him, an old school bus—the kind called a chicken bus here—waited in the vast shade of several sprawling mango trees. Children filed out from the other huts under the watchful eye of the colonel's security squad.

Malvasio knocked on the bathroom door and told Anabella to come out. She opened up and stepped timidly into the main room, wearing the pale blue dress with the white collar and belt the judge's house staff had given her. She looked like a maid, except for the bare feet. Malvasio nudged her into the doorway, not intending to be rough but wanting it over with.

The bald guard gripped her arm and Anabella turned back, eyes flashing. Malvasio could imagine what she'd been thinking—that he was her guarantee. That's what Americans were for, it was how they ran the world—he'd taken her into his bed, hadn't he? And even though he'd proved unwilling or incapable of performing, it hadn't been her fault. But she caught on quick, none of that mattered. And it seemed to surprise her little.

Wordlessly, she shook off the guard's hand and tromped barefoot beneath the gaze of the judge's dragoons across the hard-packed dirt toward the shade of the mango trees. She glanced back just once with that same seething hatred in her eye, to let Malvasio know she thought he was pathetic. He couldn't help but smile; her rage seemed almost romantic. And what was romance without betrayal?

He consoled himself with the knowledge he had no more choice in the matter than she did. Neither of them was free. And without freedom there's no responsibility. Without responsibility, no guilt. He turned away and closed the door.

IN THE BATHROOM HE THREW WATER ON HIS FACE AND NECK. He wanted some coffee but realized he didn't have the girl to send up to the house to fetch it for him. She'd been around for a mere three days but as rapidly as that he'd grown dependent. It conjured thoughts of family, of all things, a notion he shrank from normally. Now it brought back all his heebie-jeebies about reconnecting with Ray's son, Jude. I watched that kid grow up, he thought, believed in him more than his own old man. Now Ray was dead but his faithless blood lived on. Malvasio wondered at that, how even the dreariest nobody, knocking a woman up, can achieve the only immortality we know.

He returned to the door and opened it just as the chicken bus, in an oily plume of black exhaust, departed for the Pan-American Highway. The windows glared from the sun so he couldn't see any faces, couldn't tell if the girl was looking back with that same impressive loathing in her eyes.

He remembered hearing from one of his sources in Chicago that even Strock, despite his other failings, had a child now. A daughter. Figure that one out, Malvasio thought. The Candyman, who chased skirt the way dogs chase cars, has a little girl—meaning, he supposed, that karma has a sense of humor.

He closed the door and sat on the bed. On the sheet, his cell phone lay open where the girl had tossed it aside. He picked it up and permitted himself one last rendition of the "Toreador Song."

PART II

CANDYMAN

It is always said that aggression begins in denial
and that violence originates in guilt.

—Michael Ignatieff, *Blood and Belonging*

11

Strock hadn't come to hurt anybody, least of all Peg. But the impulse started curdling up from someplace almost as soon as he parked at the bar.

The dancers came and went, prinked out in high heels and teddies, drifting through the murky radiance with bored eyes and forced smiles. They left behind clouds of soupy perfume while Trip Hop or whatever it was throbbed at bone-rattling levels like the sound track to a beating.

There were three bouncers.

They lazed in rumpled suits up near the private booths where the luckier girls sat with customers willing to pay for a little one-on-one. The largest of the bouncers stood six-six easy, with skillet-size hands and a shaved head. The next one seemed a poor imitation of the first, same shaved head but fleshy. The wild card was the third guy—a short, bony, long-haired hick with a fey cockiness about him, like he was some kind of hillbilly martial arts queen.

Strock picked at the wet gummy label on his beer bottle, trying to think through how he should handle this. All he wanted was a few words with Peg. She owed him that. She went by the name Celesta here and was taking her own good time in the dressing room.

Finally, in a pot-addled brogue meant to conjure Jamaica, the DJ boomed: "Takin' yo peeks, mons, will ya now, so slam those hands toge-thah for Stay-cee . . . and Cee-lest-aaaaah."

The two girls pranced through the tinsel curtain at the back of the stage, untying their tops as they walked and dropping them to the floor. Excess cargo. Meanwhile, the DJ cued up an eighties tune, remixed for dance: the Pet Shop Boys, "Yesterday, When I Was

Mad." Strock chuckled, it was all too perfect. You got him playin' our song, Peggers.

She grabbed the nearer pole and did a few routine swings, shaking out her long red hair. Her eyes were rimmed with eyeliner so thick she looked Egyptian, and glitter sparkled across her chest. She'd lipsticked her nipples too, an old trick.

As though on cue, the Pet Shop Boys chimed in:

Admitting, I don't believe
In anyone's sincerity, and that's what's really got to me

Strock collected his cane from the back of his bar stool, slipped down and began his limping approach toward the stage.

The crowd was scant, it was early. Men sat by themselves or in small clusters around the dim red room—frats, salesmen, off-duty cops. How many times, Strock wondered, when he'd still had his badge, had he sat there just like them? Every girl needs a pal in blue sometime. Not that he was bitter. He'd learned most of what he knew about music, food, and sex from strippers.

About fifteen feet from the stage he pulled up, still obscured by the dark, waiting as some frat in a Notre Dame sweatshirt tucked a bill into the elasticized crotch of Peg's bikini bottom. The guy got to rub his face against her sparkly chest for that and Strock hated him instantly. A whiff away from fall-down drunk, the boy spun around, cheeks dotted with glitter now, and pumped the air with his fists while his Greek buddies hooted or barked out goading obscenities.

Strock eased out of the dark toward the stage. He caught Peg's eye. "Seen a little girl around here?" He waved a bill at her, beckoning her closer. Come on, he thought. Play along. I'll say what I came to say and it'll all be over in no time.

Tottering backward out of the spotlight, Peg stared at him with those Egyptian eyes as though he were the one standing there naked. Even the lipsticked nipples looked stunned.

"You don't tell me where you moved, don't answer my calls, what did you think I'd do, huh? You know me better than that, Peg."

His voice had an edge to it. Scattered boos came from behind and a wadded-up napkin pelted his neck. From a nearby table a hand reached out and clutched his jacket. Unthinking, Strock spun around, whipped the cane high, then slammed it down so hard he heard bone give way beneath the wood. He pushed another hand away as the first man howled.

Strock turned back to the stage and hefted one knee onto the skirt. The DJ, dropping the Rastaman bit, growled through the PA: "Security—up front."

Strock got his balance, fended off the last of the grasping hands, then faced off with Peg. She backed up a little more but didn't run. The other dancer, Stacy, turned away and kept nodding to the beat, like it was no big deal. Just another night at the nude girl nuthouse.

Peg screamed, "Phil! What the—you're gonna—you—" Her Kentucky twang bent every vowel in two. She stamped her foot, wiggled her hands. "You got a serious *problem,* Phil, know that?"

"A free talk, okay?" It came out sounding shabby.

Her jaw dropped. "Here?"

"I wanna visit her. I got a right."

"Aw crap, Phil." Her eyes teared up. "You can't—you don't—"

He had no time to take heart from her pity. The cavalry arrived, Mr. Skillethands and Mr. Kung Fu Prissy-Hick Longhair vaulting onto the stage like a tumbling act, Son of Skillethands hanging back. In the melee that followed, Strock got in a few good licks with the cane, swinging it like an ax, but Skillethands parried the worst blows with his weight-room arms, and Longhair, true to Strock's suspicion, had a vicious scissor kick that landed once in the thigh, once in the chest, and finally in the midriff, robbing Strock of breath. They wrestled him down and punished him, tongues protruding through their teeth, lusty little gasps of fury. From behind, Peg shrieked, "Don't hurt him, okay? *Okay?*" But they got in their furtive stabs at his crotch and eyes, then trundled him off the stage, through the tables.

The front door slammed open, they heaved him outside, and the long-haired hilljack pitched the cane as far as he could into the dark. Mr. Skillethands, panting, told the two uniformed guards manning the parking lot, "Please escort this gentleman off the grounds." He cleared his throat and spat. "Now."

STROCK STRUGGLED TO HIS KNEES. BEHIND HIM, THE CLUB MUSIC soared briefly as the three bouncers trooped back in, then dimmed to a dull throb as the door closed behind them. His balls ached mercilessly from one particularly crushing squeeze. He ran his tongue along his teeth, checking for broken crowns.

Footsteps shuttled forward as the two outside guards approached. Strock lifted one hand above his head, face still brushing the pavement as he tried to catch his breath.

"A minute, fellas, all right? Just let me—"

A pair of musty desert boots entered his field of vision. Following the image upward, Strock discovered black polyester slacks tightening at a pudgy waist, a tattered black vinyl jacket. The face was triple-chinned. A shiny pate divided identical tufts of mousy brown hair.

It was the other one who spoke, though. "You're not gonna give us no more trouble now, are ya?"

Through the blur Strock saw a knobby man, tall as Lincoln, with a craggy face and slicked-back hair. Popcorn-knuckled hands gripped his knees as he leaned down.

"That was a question, fella. Round here questions go with answers."

"I just need a second." Strock coughed up blood. "Catch my wind."

"Plenty of wind up here." The wiry one slipped a hand into Strock's armpit and yanked upward. "See for yourself."

As soon as Strock had his balance he swung to rid himself of the man's grip. The elbow missed, but before Strock could regroup, the fat one aimed a cannister of pepper spray and let go, hitting Strock but the other guard, too. Both men grabbed at their eyes.

"Christ, Bursich, you tubby fuck, what the—"

"Sorry, shit, sorry, Jesus, sorry . . ."

"Anybody need some help here?"

It was a new voice, male, younger. Strock blinked and squinted but could see nothing through his scalding tears. Words sawed back and forth, ending with: "What say I take him off your hands?" Strock felt himself roughly pulled away. He coughed up a wad of caustic phlegm, then his bad leg buckled, lurching him sideways. The newcomer grabbed him up before he fell and kept them both moving. Kid's quick, Strock thought. Strong, too.

"Where'd you come from?" The words came out strangled with mucus.

"Let's get out of here. Then we'll talk."

The stranger let Strock rest against the side of a white sedan. Water chugged from a plastic bottle and spilled onto the asphalt, then Strock felt a wet handkerchief pressed into his hand. He spread the soaked hanky across his eyes, which felt like they were on fire.

"I need my cane."

"We'll get you another one."

"I'm lame. I can't—"

"We'll get you another one."

The stranger dropped Strock into the passenger seat, then slammed the door shut and hustled around and climbed in behind the wheel. Soon they were hurtling up the lakeside highway toward the toll road.

"Don't rub your eyes with that." The young man tugged at the corner of the wet handkerchief. "Just dab."

Strock opened his window. The air felt good on his face. "I know how to handle pepper spray."

The stranger turned off the highway before the toll road interchange and crossed some railroad tracks bordered by sparse woods. They were still in Indiana, somewhere between East Chicago and the Illinois line.

"You're name's Phil, right? Phil Strock. They called you Candyman."

Strock turned toward him, blinking, wincing. "I don't know you."

"You knew my old man."

"And he was who?"

"Ray McManus."

It took several seconds to focus and the effort hurt but Strock finally managed to keep his eyes open long enough to take the young man in. "You're Pop Gun's son?" Ray McManus had been the oldest man in the Eighteenth still working patrol, thus Pop Gun. "You used to hang around your dad's basement and watch us all cheat at poker."

"I watched a lot more than that."

They entered a neighborhood of nondescript one-story homes lined along curving potholed streets. It was dark and quiet. The air smelled of mud.

"Luke, right?"

"Jude."

"Jude. That's it. Sorry." Strock sat back a little, relaxed into the seat. "Well, Jude, let me tell you something. Your old man was a right cop."

That prompted a dreary chuckle. "Fat lot of good it did him."

"Fat lot of good it did any of us." Strock leaned out his window, still open, and spat. It tasted like he'd gargled with battery acid. "Pop Gun saved my life—know that?"

There was nothing but silence for several seconds. Then: "No. I never heard that."

"You bet your ass. I've got a crap leg and my life's a joke. But I'd be dead if not for your old man." Strock smiled ruefully. "Laugh Master Ray. Old Pop Gun."

Jude slowed for one last turn, then pulled into the driveway of a small ranch-style house with brick cladding to match the chimney.

"Weird coincidence," Strock said, "you of all people walking up like that when I'm getting my ass peeled."

12

Leaning in the doorway, Strock said, "Going through a divorce?"

The dining room was empty except for two mismatched chairs. The living room had a mattress on the floor near the fireplace. Pet stains and cigarette burns dotted the carpet.

"It's not my house. Rental agent knows my uncle." Jude checked Strock's eyes. "Let's run some cold water where they tagged you with the Mace."

"Lead the way." Strock hobbled behind Jude toward the kitchen, using the wall for balance. The burning had tapered off but not enough. His eyes and throat still itched with a scalding heat and his skin felt raw. Lurching over to the sink, he turned the rusty faucet handle and lathered up, gently washing his hands and face. Then he doused his eyes and put his lips to the spigot to slake his thirst.

"There's food in the fridge," Jude said from behind. "Help yourself." He stepped toward the door. "I've got one more errand to run."

Strock patted his cheeks with a towel. "I'll come with."

"I won't be long."

"I said I'll come with."

"It's personal, if you don't mind. I'll be back in a snap. Honest."

With that, Jude was gone. Strock stared after him, listening as the front door opened and closed. His leg throbbed from walking without his cane. Even if he'd wanted to chase after the kid, there'd be no way to catch up. If it weren't for your old man, Strock thought, no way I'd stay put in this hole. I'd find a way out if I had to crawl.

He checked the fridge; it was decades old, grimy white and humming in the corner like a little factory. He found a carton of eggs and a wealth of sandwich fixings inside. More to his liking, a twelve-pack of Rolling Rock sat there too. He grabbed two bottles, went searching for a church key, and in a cupboard found a fifth of Jack Daniel's and some giveaway tumblers bearing sports team logos. He took the bottle of Jack down, regarding it fondly. Kid wouldn't leave the stuff around, he thought, right where you could find it, if he didn't mean for you to have a taste.

MUSIC BLARED SO LOUD IT DISTORTED FROM THE TWO CHEAP SPEAKERS on the floor. The booth was made of frosted glass brick in which embedded neon tubes glimmered like little frozen thunderbolts. A plaster pedestal, the kind you see in a florist's shop, stood beside a squat armchair upholstered in fake velvet. An ashtray sat on the pedestal. A red felt curtain covered the doorway.

Jude pulled from his pocket the fifty dollars' worth of Babycake Bills he'd bought from the bartender and handed it to the dancer. "What's your name?"

"Heavenly." The girl was counting. She had straight sandy hair, violet fingernails, and muddy freckles head to toe. "Only thirty for a dance." She tried to hand him twenty back.

"Keep it. Peg go home?"

"Who?"

"Celesta."

Her eyes darted toward the red felt curtain. Two of the bouncers patrolled the mezzanine. "Listen—I can't let you talk to me. I gotta dance."

"She go home?"

"Come on. I asked nice. Please."

The seat cushion hissed as Jude sat down. Heavenly removed her top. Cupping her breasts, she pinched the nipples, which were oddly shaped, flaring out like little red stingers. Jude tried to convince himself this was merely different, not unattractive.

She started rocking her hips to the music, wagging her can and shaking her hair like a ten-year-old imitating a go-go dancer. Jude's mind began to drift. He'd been obsessing about Eileen the entire trip, envying the passion she brought to everything—her family, her work, politics, life. He could muster little of that kind of oomph—too wary, too shy, too glum—to the point he felt at times as though he were sealed up in a psychic cocoon, arm's length from everything and everyone. He wanted to believe Eileen could charm all that away, at which point his reverie circled back around to that night at her house in La Perla: the scent of her skin in the sticky darkness, the beery taste of her kiss, the moaning cry as she came and her dozy snore as she slept with him in the hammock. A perfect little movie, except for the end. He winced, picturing it one more time. How utterly you, he thought—take offense, get pissed, shut down, storm off. Make it right, he told himself. First thing you do once you get back, head to La Perla, talk to her. For once in your life let a woman know what she means to you.

Meanwhile, the robotic weirdness of the performance taking place before him brought his longing into high relief. God help us all if this is erotic, he thought, just as Heavenly, with the smile of a bored stewardess, minced closer. Reaching out her arms, she dropped her plump stinger-nippled breasts to either side of his face and did a little shoulder shimmy, pelting his cheeks, then leaned down to whisper in his ear: "We call that the Teaser."

Who's we, Jude wondered. "So, back to what I was saying—Peg, I mean Celesta, she go home?"

Heavenly shot another glance past the curtain. The fear, at least, gave her face some animation. "Yeah. You're not, like, a cop. Or one of Vince's guys."

"Go home, or sent home?"

"Really. Please. Don't cause me trouble, okay?"

PEGGY CHECK LIVED IN A WEATHER-WORN APARTMENT PROJECT NEAR Lake Michigan. In the parking lot, a handful of *chavos* loitered over smokes around a black Ford F-150 lowrider tricked out with flaming detail. Spotting a tattoo he recognized—MS 13, for Mara Salvatrucha—Jude suffered a momentary sense of whiplash. The Salvadoran community had grown considerably in the greater Chicago area since he'd left, shrinking the mental distance between there and here. Jude gave the group a wide berth—far enough to confer respect, not so far as to suggest fear—then climbed the pitted concrete stairs to the third floor.

Sidestepping a plastic trike and a headless doll, he made his way to Peg's door, then rapped gently, trying to peek in beyond the bedsheet at the window. Suddenly her face appeared—she'd pinned up her auburn hair, revealing a bruised cheek and smeared makeup.

"Let me in," he said. "Okay?"

The bedsheet fell back into place. Shortly a scrabble of deadbolts clicked open one by one and she cracked the door, speaking across the safety chain: "You lied."

Her voice, to Jude's ear, was pure coal country. He said, "He didn't find you through me."

"Like hell."

"Don't make me stand out here, okay?"

From below, one of the *chavos* whistled a tuneless melody while one of the others said, *"Llora a moco tendido, cabrito."* Cry your eyes out, sucker. Everybody laughed.

Peg said, "Loneliest place on earth, ain't it? Outside. When what you want is inside. Kinda like looking for work."

"I don't know how he found you, but it wasn't through me. I didn't even talk to him till after he was kicked out, I swear."

She stared at him a second longer then relented, closing the door to unbolt the chain and let him in. She wore ribbed black leggings beneath a white T-shirt that hung to her knees. "You said you'd have him outta town."

The heater blasted. A sour smell—curdled milk, fermenting in the rug—thickened the air. Coloring books littered the coffee table near the sofa.

"We'll be gone by tomorrow. I promise."

"Yeah, well." She tapped her dark puffy cheek. "Fat lotta good that does me now."

JUDE HAD DISCOVERED THE BIRTH CERTIFICATE FOR A CHELSEA CHECK in Cook County, tracking Strock's name in the paternity index. Malvasio had given him the idea, mentioning a possible daughter. The address on the birth certificate was years out of date, so Jude hired a private investigator to track down Peg. The man proved worthless finding Strock. "Deadbeats fall off the radar" was his excuse. In the end, thanks to information Peg supplied, Jude blundered his way to the right address on his own.

Strock lived on Broadway in downtown Gary; Jude had dropped by earlier that night. Deserted buildings lined the street and windblown trash ghosted down the sidewalks. The marquee of the abandoned Palace Theater read: COMING SOON — THE MICHAEL JACKSON PERFORMING ARTS CENTER.

He gained entrance to Strock's room courtesy of a woman across the hall who had a key for reasons she didn't share. She did share her name, though: Dixie. She had a weathered, pointy face lathered in makeup and rimmed with fried yellow hair. Her Chinese robe hung open over a white slip and her thin legs glistened from a fresh shave.

Inside the apartment, Jude wandered about, collecting Strock's passport and checkbook and other assorted personal effects that he stuffed inside a pillow case. Dixie made no effort to stop him or even comment, merely watching, cigarette tucked into the crook of her mouth. Before leaving, Jude checked the fridge—fireproof storage for the common man. He found only three cans of Pabst, a half-eaten potpie florid with mold, and a rank pair of waterlogged shoes. Recoiling from the stench, he slammed the door shut.

"Phil don't always keep track of what he's doing when he drinks," Dixie said, crushing out her cigarette on the linoleum floor with the toe of her mule. "And he eats out a lot."

Jude told Peg, "I'm sorry about whatever happened at the club. I mean that. I've got Phil put up where I've been staying. I'll have him far away by tomorrow."

She screwed up her mouth. It made her cheek look more swollen. "I don't know what to believe. I mean, okay, you seem legit and you've treated me nice enough, I admit, but I'm like way in the dark here and I just . . ." Her voice trailed away.

Jude studied her face more closely. The bruising had a deep scratch in it, most likely the swing had been a backhand and the guy had worn a ring. "Tell me who did that," he said.

"Just get Phil to where he can't fuck up, okay? I can't afford to lose me another job."

"I'm serious. Tell me who it was."

"I'm serious too. Drop it. They're assholes. So?"

Jude pulled out his money clip and counted out ten hundreds, from the money Malvasio had given him. "I realize this doesn't fix anything," he said, handing it out for her to take. "Maybe it'll help tide you over, though."

She eyed the cash, but before she could take it her daughter appeared. Rubbing a sleepy eye with the knuckles of her left hand, the little girl had the thumb of her right planted deep between her lips. She wore Pooh pajamas and mismatched socks, one blue, one white.

"Hey, Babyshines." Like that, Peggy Check's voice transformed. It was warm now, gentle. As though her bruised face, this strange visitor offering money, were all just part of the same bad dream. "It's late."

The little girl staggered up and attached herself to her mother's leg, thumping her head softly against the muscular thigh. Peg ran her fingers through the little girl's hair.

"Other day," Peg said, proud now, "we were out walking along the lake, you know? And this tree stands maybe fifty yards off the path. She looks up and points. 'See the birdy, Mommy?' I look and look, right? Can't see squat, and I'm twenty-twenty. I'm thinking, she's making this up, then sure enough, thing takes off, flies away. That's half a football field. Bird smaller than my hand, okay?"

Jude smiled but the little girl turned her head away, clutching her mother's leg still tighter. Kid's got sniper eyes, he thought. What's to wonder at? She's Phil Strock's kid.

A HALF HOUR LATER, he stole in quietly and found STROCK sprawled on the mattress in the living room with his limbs awry, a faint wheezy snore hissing through his teeth. Four empty beer bottles lay on the floor beside a Packers tumbler and the fifth of Jack, now half-gone.

How in God's name, he thought, are you going to get this drunken sack of tricks all the way to El Salvador? Punch line: one cocktail at a time.

He wondered what Eileen might make of him—or make of me, he thought, if I turned out like this. Was that possible? Only death had spared the old man, he supposed. How bad does it have to get before that's your choice—stay drunk or die?

In Strock's defense, Jude could see why Peg still found him attractive. Remembering the picture Malvasio had shown him, he saw the same strong lines in the face, the heavy-lidded eyes. His black hair remained full with just a brush of gray at the temples. A man with a fierce heart, Peg had called him, a good lover despite the drink. But he was haunted, too, got chased around by his demons and couldn't be trusted to hear a word you said. Worse, when he got mad, which was all too often, it was scorched earth—which brought Jude's parents to mind.

He'd stopped by the old house yesterday morning. Opening the door, his mother had greeted him with stunned dismay. Her graying hair clung to the side of her skull, fixed by bobby pins. Her blouse was old—Jude remembered it from his grade-school days—and she smelled of closed rooms and talcum powder. She was forty-six years old.

"Why didn't you call?" She sounded afraid. Then: "I was on my way to church."

She'd mentioned during his last visit she was attending services more. It didn't surprise him. She'd always been unforgiving; he could see her devout.

"This won't take long." He reached into his pocket for the cashier's check he'd bought, two thousand dollars, knowing better than to hand her cash, given the history. "I've had a little windfall. I know things aren't as good as they might be for you. Hope this helps."

She looked at the check like it might crawl out of his hand and bite. "What did you do to get this?"

Of course. He remained, after all, his father's son. The worst part was, she was right.

He considered asking her if it was true, what Malvasio had said, the old man's two-year thing with a call girl. He checked the impulse, sensing the question might seem needlessly cruel. It was possible his mother knew nothing about it. But two years—how could she not know?

"I'll get going." He turned to walk back down the steps, then something stopped him. He half pivoted, said over his shoulder, "Coll been in touch?"

While conducting his record searches for Strock, Jude had snuck in Colleen's name as well, wondering if by some off chance she'd migrated back to Chicago after college. At the main library, he'd even plugged her name into a website search engine—the only hit was five years out-of-date, Madison, no address or phone number. He found himself wanting to catch up, thank her for that lifesaving box of books, maybe even get some sisterly advice on how best to patch things up with Dr. Browning, who was or wasn't the love of his life.

His mother studied the cashier's check, flipping it over, front and back. "Like your sister would bother to call me," she said.

JUDE GENTLY KICKED STROCK'S LEG. THE MAN'S EYELIDS FLUTTERED and he sat up jerkily, shaking the grog from his mind.

"Back from the black lagoon," Jude said in greeting.

"You've got no idea." The words came out snarled and bleary. Strock tried to situate himself. "What time—"

"It's early. But we've got someplace to be." Don't tell him too much, Jude thought. Just enough to get him moving. "I've got a job for you. One that pays well. You can shower up in the bathroom down the hall. I'll make us some breakfast."

He went into the kitchen and gathered some eggs and bacon from the fridge.

From the living room, Strock called out, "What kind of job?"

13

"I'M GOING TO NEED SOMETHING COLD SOON," EILEEN SAID IN Spanish. "Just to rinse the dust off my teeth."

They'd started that morning in the cooler highlands to the north, but for at least an hour now they'd been driving along the scorched eastern plain. The volcano known as Chaparrastique loomed in the distance with its girdle of coffee and cotton planta-tions, a sky of blistering white for background.

The driver, a woman from the Casa de la Cultura named Lili

Recinos, remarked that there would be a place to pull over for drinks when the road split near San Miguel. She was part Ulua, part Lenca, with a broad dark face, arched cheekbones, obsidian eyes. "It's a shame you have to come all this way again so soon. But it was fortunate you could make the celebration, no?"

Originally, Eileen had come east from La Perla to help Waxman and Aleris monitor the national balloting for president. They'd made arrangements through the Election Observer Mission and the Junta Electoral Municipal in San Miguel, and she'd figured on a weekend trip, no more, needing to get back home to pack up her artifacts for storage and plan for a more extensive junket to Morazán in the coming week. Once she'd arrived in San Miguel, however, she'd connected with the Casa de la Cultura to finalize arrangements for the days ahead, and Lili, in a rush of excitement, had informed her that the villagers of Cacaopera intended to reenact the traditional selection of the village *alcalde* to coincide with the presidential vote.

Eileen had heard of the ceremony but never seen it, the kind of native ritual all but forgotten in the country except in the remotest villages—exactly the sort of thing she was here to study. She explained the situation to Waxman and he insisted she go, and so Lili had driven down to pick her up and take her into the henequen-covered hills to the same tiny village where, in another ritual two months before, she'd witnessed the villagers sacramentally washing the clothes of the Blessed Virgin at the junction of the Torola and Chiquito rivers.

This trip, she watched as a handful of men, candidates for the position of village mayor, or *alcalde,* lined up in the town square wearing white pants and shirts and broad palm-leaf hats. An equal number of men with bows and arrows stood before them. The candidates removed their shirts, hanging them on wood-framed yokes, then submitted their bare chests to a pinprick blow from an arrow, just hard enough to break the skin, after which the judges decided the winner on the basis of the purity of his tribal blood, assessed by taste.

All in all, Eileen found the procedure, not to mention the result, far more gratifying than that of the presidential election. Although the count had yet to be finalized, it was already clear that Tony Bullshit, former sportscaster, Washington's darling, and the right wing's new champion, had ridden a landslide to victory, earning nearly 60 percent of the vote.

She tried to be philosophical about it, put her own wishes aside. ARENA probably would have won regardless, given the country's often conservative peasantry, its reliance on America, its increasingly evangelical lean, its cynicism when it came to elections in general and its indifference in particular to Schafik Handal, the aging former guerrilla and FMLN candidate. Handal had hardly done himself any favors, kicking reporters from the largely right-leaning press out of his office when they tried to bait him into impossible positions—handing them a perfect opportunity to paint him as a Marxist hothead, an intractable tyrant, an old fool. And the *efemelenistas* were rumored to be going at each other pretty hard, the pragmatic progressives hammering at the hard-line *ortodoxos,* because it was the consensus that, had the party put up less of a throwback for a candidate, they might be in power now.

But there had been a considerable amount of shenanigans as well, beyond the usual fried-chicken handouts at local ARENA offices: busloads of Nicaraguans paid to cross the border and cast ballots in provincial towns; drunken *vagabundos* handed cash outside polling places; a sudden uptick in brutal murders the preceding week, blamed on gangs by the right, though just as likely the work of death squads hoping to toss a little raw meat to the law-and-order crowd; all that, plus the usual extortionate fear-mongering from Washington.

And so now she was returning to San Miguel to reconnect with Waxman and Aleris, who were understandably dispirited. They'd drive her back to La Perla where she'd pack up as quickly as possible, just so she could get right back here in her own car. For the next few weeks she'd wander the highlands, checking her notes and maps and dutifully recording the braiding of *plazón* hats in Chilanga, the weaving of ropes from *escobilla* in the village of Chirilagua, the manufacture of palm-leaf mats in Lolotiquillo.

How trivial all that seemed now. She was a chronicler of the quaint and all-but-forgotten in a country with a skyrocketing murder rate, institutionalized poverty, an environment in crisis, and a polarized political climate, where the rich plundered the economy and anyone with an eye to the future wanted nothing more than to get out. She'd have no more effect in changing things for the better here than she'd had trying to get her brother to rethink a second tour in the marines—or, more recently, getting Jude to ponder a bit more deeply who it was he was really protecting down here.

He'd been on her mind a lot the past week, and she wasn't quite sure what to make of that. She liked the dope, there you had it. She knew his type, maybe too well, and for all his knee-jerk male boneheadedness he was basically decent. And it wasn't just missionary instinct, thinking she could rattle his cage a little, make him see things differently—she saw something in him she couldn't quite put her finger on, the stuff of tarnished hearts and Steve Earle songs. But then there was all that other baggage—feeling wounded by his attempt to sneak away after making love, ashamed for reading too much into it, guilty for blurting out something entirely inappropriate at the time. *See you when I see you, stranger*—that's what she'd wanted to say, something glib and nonchalant. But pride took over her tongue, then her temper stepped in. Old story. She was, after all, the daughter of a man they called Colonel Tripwire.

Finally they came to where the highway split—south to San Miguel, southeast to San Bartolo Oriente—and Lili pulled off at a roadside *chalet,* a small thatched hut where an Indian woman sold drinks from a plastic cooler. They parked in the blinding sun beside a pair of dusty, sagging trucks, one loaded high with *plátanos*. The other was decked in blue and white bunting, the colors of ARENA, and in back the bed was littered with election posters and signs collected from along the road—not just their own, Eileen noticed, but everyone else's too. How thoughtful.

The *areneros* sat at a table in the feathery shade of several giant *ceiba* trees, sharing jokes with the truck driver, who looked like he could live without the badinage. Eileen and Lili ordered *agua cristal* and a tamarind *fresco* from the Indian woman, sauntered over to another spot of shade, and sipped their drinks as an old woman pushing a wheelbarrow full of *cocos* appeared from down the road, hoping to sell some to the woman who owned the *chalet*. A young girl trailed after the woman with the wheelbarrow, holding a towel over her head for shade from the sun.

Nodding to the *areneros,* Lili murmured, "Look at them. So full of themselves. They won. Like that's all that matters."

Eileen, steeling herself against the heartbreak in Lili's voice, said, "Admit it, if our side had come out on top, and by a twenty-point margin, we'd be crowing too."

"No. We'd be talking about what we intend to do. The things that will change."

"And slapping ourselves on the back just a little, no?"

Lili shook her head and looked away. "You don't understand."

No, Eileen thought, I do understand. But that was what Americans always said. The ones who came down, wrung their hands, pledged solidarity, then ran back home. "I'm still thirsty. Let me get us a couple more drinks." She excused herself, realizing this was but one more gesture of convenience—walk away from the hard part, spend a little money to smooth it over. It was impossible, knowing what to do.

Passing through a cloud of flies, she came up to the *chalet* just as the old woman with the wheelbarrow concluded her transaction— she'd sold five coconuts—and she and the little girl with the towel umbrella trudged off again, heading toward the turn in the road where Lili sat in the shade. Meanwhile, one of the *areneros* got up from the table, peeling away from his group to buy another round for the crew. Eileen was scouring her jean pocket for money as he came up behind her.

"You're an American." His English was melodic, the kind of accent you heard from Latino movie stars back home. Sensing her surprise: "I studied at San Diego State." He was fair-skinned, ginger-haired, with a lanky build and spaniel eyes. Smiling, he extended his hand. "My name is Armando."

It was one of those excruciating moments, not wanting to be rude but knowing Lili was watching. Manners won out—discretion and valor and all that, she thought, taking his hand. "Eileen."

He gestured expansively. "Let me buy the drinks for you and your friend. We're celebrating, as you can see."

"That's very kind," Eileen said, "but unnecessary."

His smile flagged as he glanced over at Lili, who was negotiating with the old woman and child for a few *cocos*. "And if I insist?"

Eileen handed a dollar to the Indian woman and gestured that the change was hers to keep. "You'll force me to be impolite, and that in itself would be discourteous. Then we'll both be to blame, won't we?" She turned to go. "Very nice to meet you, Armando."

He let her walk a few steps, then said, "We're not the devils they make us out to be, you know."

Pausing, she replied over her shoulder, "I certainly hope not."

She felt his gaze on her back like a scald but continued on, crossing the hard-packed dirt toward Lili, who waited in her oasis of shade, now in possession of three *cocos*. Attempting humor, Eileen said, "I'd say we have sufficient fluids now to last us to San Miguel." She handed the *fresco* to Lili, who plunged the pointed straw into the plastic sack and sipped, watching the old woman point her wheelbarrow toward San Bartolo Oriente. That was where, Eileen remembered, Jude and his hydrologist were doing whatever for whomever in the name of whatever—hard-nosed realism, maybe. Funny, she thought, how in a place like this—how did the World Bank put it: *catastrophic but improving*—everything began to feel either insidious or naïve, even pragmatism.

Lili said, "Do you know what that little girl told me?" She nodded down the road, where the youngster with the towel over her head plodded behind the old woman. "They live in a village ten miles or so down that road. A woman who lived in the next village over noticed the water in their well turning bad, so she complained to one of the citizen councils in San Miguel. Now the woman's gone. No one's seen her since yesterday."

Her voice was dull, her eyes impassive, as though this story wasn't something she'd just heard, but a tale from long ago, repeated so monotonously it no longer merited feeling.

Eileen said, "Gone as in how? Has anyone told the authorities?"

"I didn't get a chance to ask any of that," Lili said. "The old woman—the girl's grandmother, I think—told her to be quiet. Then she asked me to forget what I'd heard. She said the girl was wrong in the head, a liar, she makes things up. She apologized, and promised me the girl will get a beating when they get home."

14

JUDE AND STROCK SAT IN A SPORTS BAR AT O'HARE, WAITING FOR THEIR flight to Los Angeles. From there, they'd catch the red-eye to El Salvador.

All in all, Jude felt relieved—there'd been no need to ply Strock with half as much drink as he'd feared would be necessary. They'd gone to the clinic for his vaccinations and picked up a new cane, then bought a few beers at a package store to down with sliders over an early lunch. After that it was on to collect some clothes and a bag—not because any of it couldn't be had far cheaper where they were going, but only a jihadist or an imbecile shows up for his flight in this day and age without luggage—then a few more brews before leaving the car at the rental drop, and now a cold one or two before takeoff. On reflection, it did seem like a bucket of suds, but he'd never felt things skidding out of control.

Strock had been strangely open to the pitch. He found the prospect of work, regardless of where, appealing, and this would be tax-free, an extra bonus. "My little girl, a little money might help out," he'd said, something in his doghouse tone suggesting it might ease things with Peg, too, if she'd allow it. He'd go down to the tropics, get tan, dry out, come home flush with cash and in the pink. A changed man. His gaze turned inward when he talked about it. Beyond that, Strock stayed relatively mum and he seemed to take Jude's spiel at face value. At least until now.

"I haven't brought this up yet," Strock said, "but I've been wondering—you remember Bill Malvasio?"

They were watching college hoops on the TV over the bar. Despite himself, Jude flinched at the name.

"Sure. He worked with you and my dad."

"He and your dad were tight." Strock held up his hand, his fingers crossed.

"My dad was tight with you, too."

"Not like with Malvasio." Strock got the bartender's attention and signaled for another round. "Rumor has it Big Bad Bill ran south when the worm turned, down to where we're headed, actually. You ever hear that?"

It came out more like a prod than a question.

Jude said, "That was what, ten years ago?"

"I wasn't counting."

"You think he'd still be down there?"

"I didn't say he was down there. I said that was the rumor."

Jude checked the impulse to chew his lip. "Okay."

"You seen him?"

Jude laughed. "Okay, now you said it. Look, like I told you, it's been ten years. You don't really think—"

"That's not an answer."

Jude glanced up at the TV screen as a point guard in dreads nailed one from downtown. Groans and cheers and hand claps rose up among various clusters of men around the bar. Tell him, he thought. The truth, all of it.

And accomplish what?

"Seen him? No. The embassy hands out fugitive lists from time to time, I caught a peek once and saw his name."

"No fooling."

"It doesn't mean anything, except they're looking."

Strock sat there, puzzling him out. It took a while, then: "You're not the poker player your old man was."

Jude turned to face him square. Their eyes met. "You heading somewhere with this?"

"Wherever it goes."

"It's not going anywhere."

Strock grinned, like he wanted a fight. "Asshole gettin' a little twitchy there, Jude?"

"You're sounding like a drunk now."

"Malvasio put you up to this."

Jude glanced out into the terminal, the dull-eyed crowds chugging back and forth down the endless white corridor. "You're scaring me with this, know that?"

"Just tell me the truth."

"If you're gonna go off half-cocked, make stuff up, I'm not handing you over to the people I know. It's my reputation on the line. I vouched for you. And given what happened with you, my dad, and yeah, Malvasio, that took some doing."

It was a decent line of bullshit but Jude feared his voice had given him away. Strock sat there, a gnomish gleam in his eye.

"Remind me again, these people are who?"

"I can't believe this."

"There something more pressing you want to talk about?"

"I've told you already. A guy I know runs security for people who own a coffee plantation in the highlands. They're gearing up to build worker quarters and he's gonna need a man who knows how to use a rifle to protect the construction site."

"They couldn't find themselves somebody with the same skills down there?"

"Of course they could. We've been over this—my buddy asked me, I thought of you, remembered what my old man used to say about you. I thought maybe you could use the work. You don't want it, fine. But give me your ticket if you're not coming. I'll redeem it down there." Jude held out his hand. Not the poker player my dad was, he thought. We'll see.

Strock barely seemed to breathe. "You swear on your old man's grave Malvasio hasn't got a thing to do with this."

"My old man's grave is a shoe box with a plastic bag of ashes in it, stuffed somewhere in my mom's house, and I doubt even she could tell you exactly where it is. But yeah, I'm telling you the truth."

Strock studied him a little longer, then twitched from fatigue. A massive yawn convulsed his whole body. "Sorry, I just . . ." He shook his head to clear it. "Know what we used to call him? Bill, I mean." He gave Jude a second to guess. Then: "Streetlight. 'Cuz he wasn't gonna move till he saw green."

Jude wasn't sure what to make of that, but he welcomed the conversation's new tack. "And you and my dad were motivated by what—honor?"

"Ouch." Strock twiddled his cane with a sad, chesty laugh. "Fair enough. I'm an adult, I did what I did. Your old man, too. We knew what we were getting into. But listen—you bust the same mutts week in, week out, see them make bail in a heartbeat, worst of the bunch get right back out there, all cash and flash. Laughing at you. You can't do the job when the punks are mocking you."

"So you decided to make bank instead."

"Oh, yeah. Shoulda called ourselves the Scratch Masters."

"I'd call twenty grand an okay sum. And that was just my dad."

"You're joking, right? On the street, twenty, that's laugh-out-loud money."

"I didn't hear the FBI call it that when they found it hidden near my bed."

"Okay, yeah. We taxed them, sure. Same way the rat packers taxed their goddamn neighborhoods. Don't talk to me about money, junior. You weren't out there like we were. You put your life on the line, day in, day out, you deserve some respect at least. But cops? Politicians wipe their asses with us, judges think we're morons, lawyers think we're trolls. And the community? Get this—there is no 'community.' Just a pack of scamming loudmouths, make out like we're the problem. We're the crooks. That's the system. Well, we decided fuck the system. Fuck it all."

Jude let a moment pass, then said, "I watched my old man come home after his arrest like a bomb had gone off inside his head. Maybe not everybody had such a clear conscience."

"And what, you want me to feel sorry for you?"

"I'm not saying that."

"Pop Gun wasn't the daddy you thought he was. Pisser, ain't it?"

A woman's voice on the PA announced pre-boarding for their flight. Jude asked the bartender for the tab then settled up, using Malvasio's cash. He counted out two hundred dollars more from what was left and set it out on the bar in front of Strock.

"Know what? I've made a mistake. Here's your cab fare back to Gary or wherever. We'll go our separate ways."

Strock looked at the money like it was a trick. "Thought you wanted to do your old man proud."

"I wanted to help you out."

"I don't need your charity."

"Fine." Jude took the money back and stuffed it into his pocket. "I'll take that to mean you'll find your own way home." He picked up his carry-on and started to walk away.

Strock leapt after him, grabbing his sleeve. "Okay. Look, I'm sorry. I'm gonna need that cab fare."

Jude laughed. "Listen to you. Here's an idea, give Dixie a ring. You know, the old bottle job across the hall? Have her come save you. Won't be the first time—will it?"

Strock sat there like an invisible hand had reached up and grabbed his throat. "You mouthy little prick."

"I've got a plane to catch."

Jude turned to walk away again. This time he didn't feel Strock's hand on his arm. Instead, the wood cane whipped down hard on his shoulder. The pain lanced through his back, but he ignored it as, on instinct, he spun around and gripped the cane's wood shaft. He found Strock staring at him with vacant eyes—giving up the cane, swaying on his feet, then clutching the bar as he murmured something Jude couldn't make out. In the background, the bartender froze, everybody in the bar stared. From down the bustling white corridor, two security guards strode toward them.

Jude locked his arm around Strock's shoulder in a rough but chummy embrace and steered him back to his stool, pressing the cane into his hand. "I understand," he whispered. "I do. I understand. Let me handle this."

Within seconds three more guards joined the first two, all of them chunky or small. The battery part was easy—Jude told them it was his complaint to make and he didn't intend to make one. Just a misunderstanding. But he had to tap into a long neglected reservoir of wild Irish bullshit to get them to back off public drunkenness, and not just on Strock's account. The adrenaline racing through his bloodstream helped concoct a veneer of sobriety but his tongue refused to play along, here and there slurring a crucial word. And the guards weren't the most experienced bunch; they seemed terrified of thinking for themselves.

Jude showed his passport and work ID, spoke to them as one of the tribe, saying he understood their concerns. He promised to personally guarantee that none of them suffered for taking a little initiative, demonstrating some judgment and letting him and Strock catch their flight. On the other hand, if they were delayed, forced to miss their plane, there would be damages in the thousands of dollars, his employer would be obliged to recoup the loss. That meant lawyers, paperwork. Scrutiny.

From time to time he glanced sidelong at Strock, to see how he was holding up. Not well, and everybody could see it. Then the gate crew announced final boarding on the PA. Jude took Strock's arm, told the security team, "Appreciate your hearing me out," and dragged Strock with him toward the gate, whispering, "For the love of God, don't say a word."

They made it to the gate just in time. As they were lurching down the jetway, Strock suddenly stopped, grabbed Jude's arm, and spun him around. He had that same lost keen in his eyes. Then everything seemed to melt.

"I'm sorry," he murmured.

"Me too. I was out of line."

"That's not it." Strock licked his lips and glanced toward the waiting plane. "I mean, hey, you're right. Seriously, what kind of life have I made here that anybody but a crazy wouldn't walk away from in a heartbeat? It's just . . ." His voice grew thready.

"Look," Jude said, "give it a try. Two weeks. It doesn't work out, I'll pay your airfare back. How's that sound?"

15

THEY WERE AIRBORNE OVER THE GREAT PLAINS, HEADING WEST toward Los Angeles. Strock sat at the window, Jude on the aisle, the seat between them empty except for manhandled magazines.

Strock ordered two Michelobs when the service cart came around, downed one almost instantly, then nursed the second. Not wanting to seem a killjoy, Jude ordered one as well but just held it in his lap as he mulled things over. He felt lucky to have dodged a bullet back at O'Hare, and gave himself credit for some fast thinking. There was something empowering about getting away with a lie. And that's how things always started, right? A little deceit, crowned with a little success. Next thing you know: You're a Laugh Master.

Strock saw Jude wasn't watching the in-flight movie and leaned across the middle seat. Checking that no one was eavesdropping, headsets on all around, he said, "So, you want to hear the story?"

Jude met his eyes. "What story?"

"About how your old man saved my life."

Jude found it interesting the way both Strock and Malvasio felt a need to share redeeming stories about his dad. He shrugged. "Long flight."

"Exactly." Strock smiled. His eyes seemed clear again. "I mean, if you'd rather—"

"No. Tell me."

Strock undid his seatbelt, cleared away the dog-eared magazines, put his cane to one side, and hefted himself into the middle seat. The tight space cramped his bad knee but he'd yet to complain. By the same token, Jude's shoulder ached from where Strock had thwacked it; a knot the size of a plum congealed in the muscle.

Strock made another reconnoiter of the nearest seats. His breath had a warm, malty tang from the beer as he said quietly, "You remember a guy named Hank Winters, cop who got greased the night before your dad and me were arrested?"

Jude thought about Malvasio's confession and warned himself not to give anything away. "I remember the story. Don't think I ever met the guy."

"I doubt you did. Wasn't the social butterfly and thank God for that. Winters was filth."

"That seems to be the consensus. I mean, from what I heard on the news after the arrests."

"Don't get me started on the fucking news. Didn't tell half. Or even half of half."

"Okay."

"And the half of a half they did tell they didn't get right."

Strock went on to recount the same story Malvasio had told, the start of it anyway, about Winters with his crackhead snitch, the warrant that went bad, the murder of the much-liked young cop. "Winters and Bill were two of a kind, which meant they hated each other's guts. After Winters skates through IAD, he hunts up Bill, lets it drop that one of his contacts on the street—'a witness,' he says, the dick—knows what Bill and me and your dad have been up to. There were rumors of heat by then, we were all a little on edge. Winters says for a price he can suggest this witness take a vacation. For a little more, he hands us a name, we can do what we please."

Jude felt like stopping him, confirming that this witness was the working girl who'd had a two-year thing with his dad. But then he'd have to explain how he knew, and that could get tricky. Then it registered: *do what we please.*

"Bill figures Winters is wired, saying this. So he plays dumb. Tells Winters he hasn't got a clue what he's talking about. This so-called witness can't know squat because nothing's been going on, yack yack. But Bill knows, Winters knows, the whole fucking world knows that some woe-is-me loser crying crooked cop finds the right prosecutor? No way she won't get a hearing. On top of that—"

"How do you know it was a she?"

Strock blinked, straddling words. "What do you mean?"

"This witness who had the drop on you guys. You said 'she.' How do you know that?"

From somewhere behind them, a baby started crying. Strock turned at the sound, then said, "What's your point exactly?"

"No point. I just—"

"Tell you what—let me run through the story, then you can ask anything you want on the back end. That work for you?"

It seemed wise not to press. "Sorry."

"Not a problem. Okay. Bill reminds Winters that your dad has a family. He can't afford the legal bills that'd mount up, defending himself against the kind of things this 'witness' might 'allege.' Any event, Bill says, again just to protect your dad, he will personally pay off this sack of crap, through Winters."

Jude stepped in again. "Wait. Back up. I'm confused." He was having trouble making the two stories fit.

"It's like Shakedown 101. Winters says—"

"That's not the part I'm confused about."

"Bill—and I gotta give him credit for this—Bill played it smart. He denies everything but then offers to pay off Winters anyway."

"There—why would he do that?"

"Think about it. Winters has gone head-to-head with IAD and walked out clean as a cat's ass. Bill figures everything he tells Winters is getting said into a wire. So he denies it all."

"Yeah. Yeah. I get that part. But why offer to pay, then?"

"Where's that put Winters? He accepts, makes it look like he's extorting an innocent cop—who's trying to protect not just a buddy but his family. That'll be on tape. Jury won't like that."

"I'm sorry to sound dense—"

"If Winters was working for IAD, he'd refuse the money, say this supposed witness will just testify to what she knows and the chips'll fall wherever. Let Bill make the move after that. Otherwise it looks like entrapment. But none of that happened. Winters just wanted the cash."

Finally, it occurred to Jude what was bothering him. "When was this?"

"What do you mean?"

"Time-wise. This all happened the night before the arrests?"

It was Strock's turn to be baffled. "Who said that? No. This is, like, two months before."

It shouldn't have hit as hard as it did, but Jude realized only then that Malvasio hadn't just shaded things differently or left out a detail or two. He'd lied.

"So Bill sets up a meet with Winters, picks this alley between some run-down warehouses near the hooker strip over around

Rockwell Gardens. I climb up the fire escape to a roof nearby, see if Winters gets shadowed by a tac unit or a surveillance van. Turns out he comes alone, which was what we figured would happen."

"My dad wasn't there?"

Strock groaned, the interruptions. "We decided to leave your dad out."

"How come?"

"Reasons. All right? Let me finish. Winters gets out of his car, walks up, and Bill says he's only been able to come up with a third of what Winters wants. He needs another week to pony up the rest. Winters bitches but takes the cash. Boom, that's it. He's dirty. There was no wire. This was extortion, straight up, no frills."

The stewardess—thirty-ish, plump but pretty—came by, collecting empties. Strock downed the last of his second beer, passed her his two dead soldiers, and asked for another Michelob. Jude stood pat.

"Winters wants the rest of his money the following week. We meet the same place. I come along again but this time Bill brings a throwaway—this AK-47 bought from some gun monkey in the Robert Taylor projects. It's a crap weapon but untraceable so you make do. Besides, I'm a pretty good shot. Malvasio tells me to take up position at a window facing the street on the top floor of one of the warehouses along the street. When Winters gets out of his car . . ." Strock let the last word linger.

"Were you drinking as bad back then?" It came out cold and Jude regretted that but the thought had been hovering there for a while.

Strock looked stung, then outraged. The anger simmered a bit. "Yeah. Chipping the blow pretty hard, too. Touché. I was out of control. Which meant I didn't have a problem with one thing Bill suggested. Rob bangers? Lead the way. Take Hank Winters out of the box? Sounds like a good deed. And you'd be hard-pressed to find a cop in Chicago who wouldn't second that."

"Listen—"

"He let another cop walk into an ambush. Plus, on the personal front, he was squeezing us. Your dad as much as me and Bill. More, you want the truth."

"Yeah, I do. The truth would be a nice change of pace."

Strock made a face like that was just the funniest thing. "You think I'm lying?"

"I'm just saying—"

"You realize the problem with the truth, right? It's never really the truth. Specially in a thing like this."

"My point—"

"Way I looked at it? It was like chemo. You poison somebody to cure their cancer. Well, Winters was the cancer. We were the poison."

Jude's mind was whirling. "Wait. Go back a little. You said this was two months before the arrests."

"Right."

"But Winters wasn't killed until—"

"Exactly. Winters ended up dead and hooray for that, but I had nothing to do with it. I never made it into position that night. I got inside, started climbing to the top floor of the warehouse? The stairs—planks were rotted so bad they felt like cork. One gave way. I crashed clear through to the next stairway down. Damn near went through that flight too. Good thing I had the safety on or I might've blown my own head off. Not all the wood was rotted, though—too bad for me. This splinter, big fucking thing—right through my knee, tore the peroneal nerve. Felt like somebody slammed a screwdriver into the bone and left it there. I was choking on dust, tasted like rat poison, damn near blind from the pain, but I didn't want to call out or anything, might freak Winters, get Bill shot. That's what I was thinking. Thoughtful me."

"But you got out."

"Oh, there's a whole lot more to the story before *that* happens." Strock checked over his shoulder, wondering where his beer was. "Bill had no idea I was in trouble. He just knew Winters didn't take a bullet to the head as he sashayed up and demanded his money. Bill didn't have it, natch, because he expected Winters to be dead before it became an issue. He had to sorry up an excuse and beg more time. Winters wasn't the type to put up with that."

"So, what—he went to IAD?"

"I don't know for sure. I think Bill paid him a few more times, never everything, string him along. Till he killed him. You knew that, right?"

Jude froze. "Yeah. I mean, again, the news." He had no clue where to go from there.

"I don't remember the news ever saying up front Bill was the doer."

"No. They suggested. I just figured—"

"Your dad ever say anything?"

"Pop? No. Never. Anyway, back to this witness. What happened to her?"

Strock flopped his hands open. "Can't say. We never had to bother with her, I know that much. At least, not that me or my lawyer ever heard about. Maybe with Winters aced out she figured her point man was gone and she didn't want to risk coming forward alone. Any event, this is the story about how your dad saved my life, right? So let me get to that part."

The pretty plump stewardess arrived finally with Strock's Michelob. She was wearing fresh lipstick and framed her smile as she counted out his change. As she strolled off, Strock hoisted himself a little in his seat to steal a peek at her hip action.

"Bill figured I'd just lost my nerve. He came in expecting to rip me a new one. And even when he found out what really happened it didn't change his mood much. I'm lying there coughing up filth, my leg's all bloody and pinned beneath a tangle of crap. I took a beating, my back's twisted up, my hands are shredded from trying to break my fall. You name it. But Bill? To him it's, like, all my fault. Plus he figures I'm faking how bad I'm hurt because I fucked up the hit.

Know what he said? 'You got yourself into this. Now get yourself out.' Exit Bill."

"How long before—"

"Spent the whole night there. Freezing cold. Fending off rats. Hands and legs went numb, but the bleeding wasn't too bad, didn't fall completely into shock, thank God. About dawn, your dad shows up."

"How'd he know you were there?"

"Bill, I guess. Even lizards have a conscience." He said it like it pained him, then slugged back some beer.

"What did my dad say when he got there?"

"Nothing. He just came in, looked around till he found me, dug me out—I was loopy from dehydration and the pain. He hefted me up in a fireman's carry and got me out to his car. Had a thermos of coffee he poured down my throat. On the way to the ER we worked up a story about an accident fixing up your basement and that's what we told the intake nurse."

Strock sat back in his seat and stared out the window. The spine of the Rocky Mountains stitched through hardpack snow beneath an iron gray sky.

"Any event, that's the story. Bill left me for dead. By the time he told your dad where I was, dead's exactly what I should've been. And on some level I'm sure good ol' Bill was hoping I would be. You act like you don't know but I'm telling you, him and your old man were tighter than tight. Me, I was the third tit. And like I said, I had problems of my own. Bill saw that as just one more liability. Leave me there, turn his back, let me die—such a gift. But your dad didn't think that way. One big reason I'm on this plane, I remember that."

Jude couldn't escape the impression that something, again, remained unsaid. Before he could even begin to probe what that might be, though, Strock added, "The other big reason I'm tagging along? Okay, I get it, you haven't seen Bill down there. But I'm telling you, some stroke of luck, he crosses my path? I'll kill him.

Won't think about it, won't worry about it, won't lose a minute of sleep. He's a dead man, I get anywhere near him."

16

As they waited to change planes in Los Angeles for the red-eye to El Salvador, Jude realized this might be his last decent chance to call the whole thing off. But how would he do that, exactly—tell Strock the truth? Then everybody walks away empty-handed, and for what? Besides, the man said it himself: The problem with the truth is it's never the truth.

He tried to think things through: So Malvasio lied. Okay. Ask yourself why. To get you to do what he wanted, same reason you've been lying to Strock if you're willing to be up front about it. Which means, on that score, Malvasio's no worse than you.

As for the Winters deal, the original plan was cold-blooded, true—assuming Strock wasn't lying as well—but it never panned out that way and you don't know for a fact how the guy died. Malvasio could still be telling the truth about that, even with all he left out. He didn't want to tell you about the hush money because it would show how bad the old man had screwed up—shooting off his mouth to his hooker squeeze for two years, stringing her along, then needing his pals to bail him out when she called in her marker. Maybe Bill went for one last meet, to say he was through paying— he and Winters got into it, words turned to blows, and then boom. It was possible. It made sense out of both versions. Strock hadn't said anything about other murders—important—and Winters was crooked, a shakedown artist, missed by no one. Be honest: Have you really learned anything about these guys you didn't already know?

Of course, there was no telling what other lies Malvasio might've snuck into the story. The whole premise for bringing Strock down—that there was work waiting for him, that Malvasio wanted to make things up to him, he would've done the same thing for his good buddy Ray—it could all be a hoax. And the sympathy, the regret, the humility—all bullshit.

And yet the opposite was equally possible. Malvasio had plenty of good reasons to make amends to Strock—though, sure, that didn't mean it was his real intention or his only motive. And just because Strock had a love affair with his own hate didn't mean he wouldn't be better off coming down, doing whatever work Malvasio secretly found for him.

That was the problem—there was no way to tell. You've got no real proof, Jude thought, that things won't end up perfectly fine.

He tried to imagine what Eileen would think of all this, besides calling him nuts for getting involved in the first place. He went back mentally to their exchange on the road to La Perla: *We're all terrible. . . . But only some of us are sorry.* He'd felt an accord gel between them in that moment, one he'd squandered almost instantly, but it was one of the chief reasons he couldn't get her off his mind. She understood the blame you're born with, the nagging sense of fuck-up that never seems to lift—and the equal and opposite need to forgive, turn a blind eye once in a while. And so she more than anyone might understand why, in weighing Malvasio's story against Strock's, he remembered all the talks at the restaurant in San Marcelino, the first one in particular, when Malvasio apologized for all the harm he'd caused. Bullshit? Maybe. But it hadn't felt that way, and sooner or later you've got to trust your instincts or go crazy. And though Strock had his own glimmerings of regret, he also slid back way too easily into rage and self-pity. Ask yourself, he thought, who's come through these past ten years with a clearer sense of who he is and what went wrong. Who's the better man? Let that tell you who to trust.

Something else was at play, though. Secretly, he felt proud. Nine tenths of EP work was planning and keeping your eyes open, the rest was babysitting. This had been different—tracking Strock down, coaxing him along, it'd been no picnic. And the job wasn't done. He squirmed at the thought of needing to prove himself, but what was the alternative? Convincing yourself you had nothing to prove was just one more thing to prove and there you were, chasing your tail, round and round. Besides, if he just walked away now he'd feel like a punk, as though these men played rougher than he could handle. That wasn't something he intended to live with.

Maybe he wouldn't have to. The voice in his head that normally took him apart was cutting him some slack. Every now and then, it actually gave him some credit. No surprise, the voice sounded a little like Malvasio. But it sounded like the old man, too. And with that, deep down, an old wound seemed finally to close up a little. Now if he could only convince himself it was meant to.

They began calling seat assignments. Jude watched as the other passengers, returning émigrés mostly, queued up to board. He noticed that the wealthier the woman, the shorter the hair. The poorer passengers carried shopping bags stuffed to the breaking point with gifts for family back home. A few tourists were flying down as well (precious few, Jude noticed), plus at least six young missionaries— cheap suits, scrubbed smiles, martyred hair.

The gate crew called the final boarding group and Strock stood up, collected his cane, and headed for the end of the straggling line. Jude would remember later that, in the end, he decided by not deciding. He just gathered his carry-on and got in line himself. Follow through on what you started, he thought, mind yourself, and hope for the best. What else can you do?

LIKE MOST RESTAURANTS OUTSIDE THE CAPITAL, EL ARRIERO — despite its reputation as one of the best steak houses in the region— made little pretense of luxury: a bunker of whitewashed cinder block accented with brick and sheltered by giant *conacaste* trees, with a tar-paper roof coiled with barbed wire. The windows were small and dusty and blazoned with neon beer signs glowing blue and red in the sticky darkness.

Two burly guards in tan uniforms manned the brick archway, armed with MP5s. Through the entry, Malvasio spotted two more guards stationed in back beyond the large open-air courtyard. The customers were gone. The help ambled about busing tables, policing the gravel courtyard for cigarette butts, dousing the torches while *ranchera* music, the local equivalent of country-western, blared from tinny speakers.

At a table just inside the entrance, a young plump hostess with spit curls, her cleavage dotted with sweat, fanned herself with a menu, waiting for the others to finish their work so she could let them out and lock the doors. Malvasio ambled toward her and she smiled, revealing a gold tooth. Guessing his reason for being there, she pointed him toward the bar.

The metal door felt cool to the touch and swung open easily on its hinges. The room was empty and brightly lit and thick with the smells of spilled beer, fresh-cut pineapple, and ammonia, which the air-conditioning swirled around like soup. A cocktail waitress, barefoot now that they were closed, wiped down tables while Hector Torres, the owner, sat alone in the corner, tallying the night's receipts. He was a short man dressed in a *guayabera* and linen slacks, homely but strongly built, with a squarish, lumpy head and a boxy jaw. His hands and arms were matted in thick black hair, which set off his jewelry.

Malvasio pulled up a chair, glancing around the solemn wood-paneled room. Using Spanish, he said, "Feels nice, being out of the heat."

Hector whistled for the waitress's attention, letting her know with a glance that he and Malvasio needed privacy. With a dutiful smile she dropped her damp rag and slipped on her heels, then soldiered out the door into the gravel courtyard.

Looking weary, Hector massaged his eyes, taking a moment to collect his thoughts. The air conditioner rattled in its window mooring and dripped moisture into a pan on the floor. "Am I free to assume the matter we discussed is taken care of?"

Two days before, Hector had contacted Malvasio with news that a woman from one of the villages near San Bartolo Oriente had been complaining about the local well water. There were foreign church groups in the area, doling out school supplies and water purification kits with their Bibles, and the woman had shot off her mouth to them and God only knew who else. Naturally, she blamed Estrella—the wells had been fine before the bottling plant was built—and so Hector had received a call from Wenceslao Sola, telling him to shut her up before anyone of real consequence paid her any mind. Make an example. And, as always in circumstances like this, Hector no sooner put down the phone than he picked it up again, dialing Malvasio.

Given the notoriety the woman had created for herself, and fearing he might stand out if spotted, Malvasio hired the job out. With the economy in its perpetual funk you had *veteranos* from the uprising, both sides, freelancing any way they could, the local version of the Merry Men. Normally they just roamed the countryside, banding together in makeshift units and armed with war-vintage weapons— AK-47s the guerrillas had used, as well as the big German G3s or American M16s the government troops had carried—and jacking travelers or robbing banks or *tiendas* or anyplace else with ready cash. You could hire them out like day labor if you knew where to ask—the cathedral plaza in Usulután, for example. That was where Malvasio connected with four ex-soldiers he'd used before from the infamous First Brigade. He paid them half up front and gave them the details.

Later that same night, the four *veteranos* drove a stolen Jetta up the unpaved road to the woman's house. It was one of five *champas* in a rural hamlet tucked into the hills, all of the inhabitants too desperately poor to interfere with what happened or to even dare look out at the men who arrived so late. While two of them stood guard outside, the other two went in, snatched the woman from her bed, stuffed a *tapado* into her mouth to stifle her screams, and strangled her with an old-school garrote, made of piano wire and jump rope handles. Then they drove all night, reaching the hills of Ahuachapán in the west before daylight, and dumped the woman's remains along an isolated stretch of wooded road. They toasted their success with *aguardiente,* then headed back to Usulután where they torched the Jetta and went their separate ways. Come noon they regrouped in the cathedral plaza and waited for Malvasio to appear with the rest of their pay.

Hector sat back and frowned as he listened, eyes impassive, as though he were hearing the delivery schedule for the coming week's ice. "Thank you for the colorful story," he said finally, "but she was supposed to disappear."

Malvasio was thirsty, and wondered why he hadn't been offered a drink. "She did disappear."

"Dumping her by the side of the road?"

"My understanding is, they walked her back into the underbrush a good ways off the highway. And they cut off the head, the hands, and the feet, got rid of those elsewhere. I left that out, sorry. And you know how things work. Plenty of women missing at that end of the country. They'll think she's a runaway hooker from Acajutla, no one's going to link the body to here. Seriously, I don't see a problem."

"If they're telling you the truth."

"I've used them before. It worked out fine."

"It's a common mistake, thinking what happened before guarantees what happens next."

Malvasio rose from his chair. "If you're gonna start talking like that, I need a beer."

Hector waved his acquiescence and Malvasio ducked behind the bar, opened the cooler, and dredged up a Pilsener. "One for you?" Hector shook his head. Malvasio twisted off the cap and ambled back around, downing half the bottle before he dropped back into his chair. The interruption served its purpose. Hector seemed mollified, if not exactly pleased.

He said, "What about this other thing you're arranging?"

He meant the situation with Jude. The fact Malvasio actually knew one of the men working the hydrologist's security detail had lustered his reputation a bit. But they'd wanted him to turn Jude, make him a mole if not a full-blown accomplice. Malvasio had convinced them that was foolish, and risked ruining everything. His way was better—subtler, sure, with risks of its own, but more in keeping with what he knew of Ray's boy. Not to mention Strock. No one had any idea he was angling it all so that Jude, at least, came out alive.

He said, "The man I told you about, he arrives tomorrow."

"Your old companion."

"I'll have everything in place the next day or two. After that, it's wait and see."

"And this bodyguard has no idea what you're planning."

"Not that I know of."

"Is he stupid?"

Malvasio suffered a flash of protectiveness, which he hid with a shrug. "He's got a weakness, like we all do. I just happen to know what it is."

Hector finally found his smile. "And what might your weakness be, my friend?"

Malvasio knocked back the last of his beer and placed the bottle on the table. A drool of foam slithered down the neck. "You haven't figured it out by now?"

"If I had, would I tell you?"

"If you were trying to play me. Maybe."

Hector laughed unpleasantly. "How you love to complicate things. That's your weakness."

No, Malvasio thought, that's my protection. "In any event, I'd say things are in order. My operation's moving along nicely. And this thing with the woman and the wells, looks like it got nipped in the bud. Unless there's something you're not telling me." He waited a beat for Hector to respond, then pushed back his chair and got up to leave.

"As a matter of fact," Hector said, "there is something else I need to discuss with you."

Malvasio sagged. He wanted nothing more than bed. "It's not too difficult, I hope."

"But you have such a gift for the difficult, my friend." Using his pencil, Hector drummed a little accent on the table. "Why else would I bother with you?"

WORKING BY KEROSENE LAMPLIGHT, EILEEN FOLDED THE LAST OF HER *camisetas* and wrapped it in tissue, then laid it gingerly into its box with the others. She'd drive to La Libertad in the morning, store everything there, then continue on east to Morazán. She'd miss this little house so near the beach, cramped and stifling though it was. She envisioned telling her grandchildren about it when she was in her dotage, regaling them with tales of her adventures.

If she had grandchildren. If she reached her dotage.

She'd felt that kind of gloom hovering over everything the past few weeks. Blame the elections, she supposed, the lingering sense of defeat and menace. Not to mention her sad little misadventure with Mr. McDude. One more misstep with the menfolk, she thought, trying for a little sangfroid.

On the bright side, she reminded herself that everywhere she'd gone, from the cities to the beaches to the mountains, people had been unfailingly open and warm. Villagers with nothing had shown her the kind of generosity only those who rely on mercy comprehend. It was one of the most mystifying things about this country, how men and women who were so destitute could also be so selfless. Pretty soon you realized that though millions went hungry, you were the one who was starving.

It's late, she thought, and you're tired, and you can't indulge these kinds of thoughts right now.

She'd already packed her clothes and books, and so moved to her desk for the final push. Stuffing her field notes into her briefcase, she spotted a yellow pad on which she'd scrawled a poem the morning after Jude left. My God, she thought, tearing off the page and reading the first few lines—what a perfectly pissy twelve-year-old you can be when your feelings get hurt.

Walls with broken glass on top
protect the caudillo's garden.
You don't belong in there.
But handsome bruiser who guards the place?—

A noise outside interrupted her. It was far too late for anyone to be about. As though caught in a shameful act, she unthinkingly balled up the poem and tossed it into the corner, then grabbed her flashlight and went to the door, waiting a moment, cocking an ear. She couldn't afford to have anyone steal her distributor cap or spark plugs or tires. Waxman and Aleris had warned her about living here, but several families in La Perla had promised her she'd be safe, they'd see to it—one of those selfless acts she'd found so touching. And so she'd never feared for herself. The car, though, was something else.

A woman in the village had given her a whistle to blow should anything happen, and she removed it from its hook, placing the stem between her teeth. Switching on the flashlight, she swung the door open, ready to slam it shut again and throw the lock if she saw anything wrong. Fanning the light across her car, she saw no one was there. Trees shivered in the wind, the surf murmured in the darkness. Then a rustling came from her left. She spun the flashlight toward the sound and it came to rest on the same two boys from the village she so often saw out here.

As always, they were tormenting a dog, this time throwing stones.

Eileen ran them off, shouting at them to go home—it was late, she'd tell their fathers what they'd done. The dog fled as well at the sound of her voice, darting toward the ocean—all of which meant the boys would find the poor animal again, the scene would repeat as soon as the chance presented itself. There's a life lesson, she thought, switching off the flashlight. She thought of that night with Jude, driving along the coastal road. How tenderly he'd lifted the *vagabundo*'s dog and carried it away from the roadbed. Maybe that's what you have to do to save something down here, she thought, turning back into the house. Kill it first.

17

STROCK GAZED OUT THE WINDOW AS THEY BEGAN THEIR DESCENT INTO Comalapa. Dawn broke through the cloud cover in smears of cold light until at last the plane dipped below the misty layers of gray. A riot of blue-white hues erupted in the distance beyond a range of ancient volcanoes, the shadowy peaks giving way to sprawling valleys that continued down to a coastal plain where sugar cane fields, vast and green, divvied up the landscape into tidy shapes. The strangeness of the geography conjured both a bracing sense of welcome and a low-grade terror. What in the name of God have you gotten yourself into, he wondered.

Inside the terminal, uniformed troops patrolled everywhere—a variety of camouflage patterns, some the usual jungle greens, others ominously black and olive drab. Strock guessed the blackish fatigues belonged to some sort of special forces brigade. It was one of those things you learned among men—the more elite the calling, the more fetishistic the costume.

Police officers, a few of them women, patrolled everywhere too, wearing crisp uniforms of their own, dark blue drill with combat boots and forage caps, looking less like cops than just more soldiers. Jude had warned him there'd be tight security. Two groups with ties to al Qaeda had threatened terrorist attacks in-country unless El Salvador pulled its troops out of Iraq.

As he lined up behind Jude in the queue for their passport clearance, Strock took out the State Department notice he'd picked up at the vaccination clinic.

The criminal threat in El Salvador is critical. Random and organized violent crime is endemic throughout the country. . . .

Avoid travel outside of major metropolitan areas after dark and avoid travel on unpaved roads at all times. . . .

Many Salvadorans are armed, and shoot-outs are not uncommon. . . .

Jude, watching Strock stuff the traveler's advisory back into his pocket, said, "Don't believe everything you read."

"Wouldn't be work down here for a guy like you, let alone me, if some of it wasn't true."

"It was worse two years ago, trust me." Jude nudged his carry-on with his foot as the line edged forward. "You still have thieves everywhere, and only a fool would go into certain areas, especially at night. But Honduras has the real problem now. Guys over there climb on buses, pull out their nines, and rob everybody on board. That doesn't happen here so much anymore."

Strock said, "Gee, such a relief," glancing off to his left. Following his eyes, Jude spotted a small vestibule walled with glass where a priest and nun greeted some two dozen rough young men. The *vatos* looked scared, rolling down their sleeves and conferring in whispers as two PNC officers stood guard. Shortly, two more cops joined them. One read a name from a clipboard, and they collected a bulky burr-headed kid and took him away, leading him along a dim lowceilinged corridor of scuffed tile, then down a narrow stairway.

Jude guessed the detainees had just come from the States. They'd get taken away one by one for questioning, fingerprints, a tattoo check. Those tagged as *mareros* would get shipped straight to prison without a hearing, maybe stay there for years. The priest and nun were collecting those who could pass the screening but had no family here. The lucky ones. After a few nights on a bedroll at a shelter, they'd get kicked free with a little pocket money and a warning: Things are different here. Second chances are a lucky privilege and they don't come cheap.

A clamor erupted inside the glass-walled room. A pair of deportees—from opposing gangs, Jude guessed, Mara Salvatrucha, Mara Dieciocho—pugged off, throwing the odd wild punch, hurling insults back and forth. Others crowded around, teamed up. No sooner did the two cops at the door wade in, swinging their batons, than one kid spotted his chance.

He was small, trim, ghetto-handsome—exactly the kind to see prison, especially down here, as just a hellish, seamy, drawn-out way to die. He darted from the room, looked toward the doors beyond Customs, and bolted that direction.

He got thirty yards. He tried to hurdle the Customs desk but the agent on duty there snared him in a headlock till reinforcements arrived. Cops and soldiers materialized from nowhere and everywhere, summoned by whistle blasts, descending on the kid in a swarm. One of the dog handlers ran up late, and the German shepherd, straining at his leash, barked at the scrum of bodies with bared fangs, ready to lunge.

The officers hoisted the runner to his feet. He was a vision—eyes swollen shut, mouth dripping saliva and blood, broken hands hanging limp. His shirt was torn too, and the Gothic black lettering blazoned down his arm gave him away: *Dieciocho*. The police didn't bother to take him back to the waiting area. They dragged him away toward the dim corridor, down the narrow steps. He'd be in La Esperanza, the prison called Hope, by noon.

Things settled down but the air remained charged. People

minded their own business, avoided eye contact, shuffling forward as the line moved. Finally, with a cry of *"¡Pase!"* Jude got called forward. He told Strock to come with him.

The Delegado de Inmigración agent had a weak chin, tamped-down hair, and minuscule eyes trapped behind bifocals. Jude's paperwork was routine and easily cleared. Then the Candyman stepped up.

Strock was hardly the only traveler who'd yet to shave, but the grayish tinge to his stubble looked particularly mangy. He presented his passport and arrival questionnaire—Jude had filled the form out for him, identifying the reason for his travel as *vacation,* not *business,* to avoid the more probative questions. Under *Local Contact* Jude had written his own name and cell number. If anything happened to Strock down here, he'd want to know. And if that meant, in effect, he'd stepped into his father's old role—going along with Malvasio's play while backhandedly protecting Strock—so be it.

He watched as Strock braced himself for the inevitable questions and the lies he'd need to provide for answers. The homely agent merely stamped his passport, offered a tepid welcome from some bottomless reservoir of indifference, then once again bellowed *"¡Pase!"* for the next passenger in line.

OUTSIDE THE TERMINAL, DESPITE THE EARLY HOUR, THRONGS OF welcoming family and friends swarmed the sidewalk in the dense heat. *Bachata* music—ballads for the homesick, backed by cheesy synthesizers and drum kit beats—blasted from boom boxes as cab drivers milled through the crowd, touting forty-dollar fares to the capital.

Jude led the way to the parking lot, Strock lurching on his cane to keep up. They trudged across the spongy blacktop beneath a line of *almendra de rio* trees, moisture cloying their armpits and streaking the backs of their shirts, until finally Jude stopped behind his dusty, battered Toyota pickup.

Glancing around first to see if anyone was watching, he pulled a small telescoping mirror from his carry-on. "Set your bag down," he told Strock. "This is going to take a minute." He got down on his hands and knees to check the underside of his pickup, using the extended mirror and paying particular heed to the engine compartment, the transmission, the wheel assemblies. All was well. He got up from the ground, collapsed the mirror, and cupped his hand to peer through the driver-side window, studying the dash, the gear box, the ignition.

Strock, mopping his face with a handkerchief, looked over Jude's shoulder through the window. "You always keep your spare in the passenger seat?"

Taking a dollar bill from his wallet, Jude folded it in half and slid it along the door crack on the driver's side, all the way around. "Big trade in stolen tires down here. This is all just routine. Honest. Be done in a second."

It was half-true. Jude would have performed this little exercise regardless, having let the truck sit so long in a public place, but he had less habitual concerns in mind as well. There was just too much he didn't know, which meant it would pay to be a little extravigilant now that he was back in-country. If anything was going to go wrong, it would happen here.

He felt for the telltale, made of Scotch tape, that he'd placed across the gas cap cover before leaving for the States. Still there, good—he peeled it away. He checked that the index marks he'd made with clear nail polish on the hubcaps remained aligned, then inspected the ground for strange fluids or wire clippings. On the passenger side he repeated the procedure with the folded bill, moving on to do it around the hood, the whole time checking the ground.

Returning to his carry-on, he put away the telescoping mirror and withdrew a five-by-seven photograph of his engine compartment. Feeling first around the latch for trip wires, he lifted the hood and compared what was there with the photograph.

Strock said, "You are seriously creeping me out with all this."

"It's a funny country." Jude wiped his brow with his sleeve. "You can make funny enemies."

"Like who?"

"That matters?"

"What are you looking for? I mean, specifically."

"Anything strange." Jude leaned in to peer behind the engine block. "Sealed-up plumbing pipe or a rigged aerosol can. Smear of plastic explosive made to look like a patch job."

"You've actually found stuff like that?"

Jude didn't answer. He was staring at a spot tucked deep behind the engine, low on the firewall. He'd run through the protocol dozens if not hundreds of times, always finding nothing. It took a second to double-check, but sure enough, something was there.

Easing in closer, he saw a scrap of lined notepaper, about the size and shape of a finger, held fast with what looked like a wad of gum. There was nothing else attached, no wristwatch, no wires, so he guessed it wouldn't detonate or catch fire if he reached down for it.

Straining to get his fingers there, he pulled gently. The slip of paper gave way easily. The gum stayed put. Jude stood up straight beside the truck and brushed some grease off the paper with his thumb.

The note consisted of five words: *Hey, Jude—Don't Be Afraid*.

Thinking the handwriting might be Malvasio's—and Strock might recognize it even after ten years—Jude folded the paper over, put it in his pocket. "No big deal," he said.

"What is it?"

"Nothing. Little joke from one of my coworkers is all." True enough, Jude thought, possibly. He surveyed the parking lot, then looked past the rim of *almendra de rio* trees toward the crowded airport terminal, to see if anyone was watching.

"Some joke," Strock said. "How come you're not laughing?"

Jude leaned in to give the engine compartment one last good look. "You know how it is. Life with the guys."

"Yeah. I remember it well."

Jude slammed the hood down and pulled his keys from his pocket. His lower lip throbbed. Only then did he realize he'd been gnawing away at it like mad. He unlocked the passenger-side door, removed the spare, and threw it into the truck bed, then lifted their bags and tossed them in after the tire. "Let's get going," he said, climbing behind the wheel.

THEY HEADED OUT A LONG TREE-LINED AVENUE AWAY FROM THE airport. As Jude lodged into fourth, he glanced sidelong at Strock who stared out the window, gazing beyond a perimeter of eucalyptus trees at the U.S. Navy radar installation. Big C-130s and smaller P-3 Orions lined up along the airstrip, fueling for their patrols of the coast for drug boats and gun runners.

"They call it a forward footprint," Jude said. "For exporting force. This sad little country is turning into a very big deal. If we go into Colombia or Venezuela to make sure the oil keeps flowing or to back a coup or whatever, this'll be a staging ground—FOL, they call it. Forward Operating Location. You'll have more Americans down here than in Puerto Rico, which is pretty much what it's beginning to look like anyway."

It reminded Jude of Eileen's rant during the drive to her house that night. He missed her so bad it felt like an ache, and he intended to see her by day's end and patch things up if he had to crawl all the way to La Perla and beg.

Strock murmured something, his voice a lazy growl. Jude turned to ask for it again but Strock hunched sideways, leaning into the passenger-side window. His head was bathed in sweat and lolled heavily on his arm. The cane lay loose in his grip.

He was snoring.

18

THE NEXT THING STROCK KNEW, A PACK OF BAREFOOT AND SHIRTLESS boys were chasing the truck, running alongside, shouting "¡*Parqueo!* ¡*Barato! ¡Parqueo!*"

Rubbing the muck from his eyes, Strock checked his watch, saw more than an hour had passed since he'd last paid attention, then looked out the window into the face of one of the boys. The kid seemed eager to the point of rage—wild-eyed, slapping the side of the truck as he ran.

Strock turned for some explanation but Jude kept his eyes straight ahead, steering down a narrow lane of dense gray sand between lines of sagging vendor stalls. The place felt eerie, like a deserted carnival, especially with the pack of feral boys keeping pace. Strock was drenched in sweat and felt parched but thought better of suggesting they stop somewhere for a drink.

Jude turned sharply away from a cluster of wind-scarred restaurants and accelerated toward a vast, open thatch structure where a shirtless old man in a blue skipper's cap rose from a folding chair to guide them into a parking place. The old man, dark and bandy-legged with a scant, nappy beard, wore frayed sandals and bright blue swim trunks with yellow piping. When Jude pressed a bill into the old man's hand, the badgering youths finally stopped shouting, turned about, and headed back the way they'd come.

"End of the road." Jude turned off the motor and lodged home the parking brake. "We take a boat from here."

Strock shook his head to clear away the cobwebs. A channel of blue-green water glimmered nearby. In the distance, he heard the muffled drone of breaking surf.

"Where are we?"

"La Puntilla. That's the Estero de Jaltepeque straight ahead. Around the point you've got the Bocana Cordoncillo and the ocean."

Jude got out, unloaded Strock's bag from the pickup's bed, stored his own plus the spare tire in the cab, then locked up. The two of them followed the old man down to a long, narrow boat anchored in the shallows. The sun beat down as the old man stepped into the brackish water to drag the boat closer to shore.

The thing looked ancient—blistered paint, speckled with rust. Jude planted Strock's bag in the midsection, then held the gunnel as Strock, clutching Jude's shoulder for balance, climbed in and sat near the bow. Jude took up position behind him as the old man collected his anchor, coiled its line, dropped it in the stern, then shoved off with one hard push. Stepping aboard into the only space left for him, the old man sat down, cranked the little Yamaha outboard and, once the motor caught, grabbed the tiller and steered them out into deeper water.

The boat rode low, the weight of the three men sinking the gunnel to within inches of the water. The spray and a tepid breeze cooled their skin. They passed the channel leading out to the Bocana Cordoncillo, a rim of whitecaps forming where the incoming surf collided with the outgoing current of the estuary. The sky beyond seemed impossibly blue.

As they traveled deeper along the estuary, thick mangroves covered the shore, the roots tangling atop the calm green water while tiny swallows darted among the branches. Fishermen lingered in small inlets, tending crab traps and the plastic jugs they used for float markers. Pelicans drifted sleepily in the mangrove shade or took off with slow, loping thrusts of their wings. Here and there houses sat in ruins, overgrown by flowering vines.

After twenty minutes, the old man steered the boat toward a wooded sand spit. A trio of open rickety thatch structures occupied a clearing near the shore. Cutting the motor, the old man let his boat drift in beside a small dock lined with ancient tires crusted in sea salt and barnacles.

"From here," Jude said, gathering Strock's bag, "we walk."

The old man stayed behind as first Strock then Jude climbed onto the dock and headed up a set of log stairs. At the top, three dark Indian women in varying states of heftiness waited in the thatch shade with strained smiles, gathered around an ice chest smudged with char. Something stringy and small—rabbits, Strock guessed—roasted over a smoldering fire pit. Buckets teaming with live crabs rested nearby in the sand beside piles of mangos and coconuts. Jude gestured for Strock to keep walking as he said something to the women that sounded apologetic. They nodded their understanding but it was clear they would have preferred hearing something else.

Leaving the shelters behind, Jude and Strock trudged along a path of dirty sand lined with palms and thorn thickets. They passed a primitive wellhead topped with a bicycle wheel chained to a crank. Off in a clearing, two emaciated horses grazed in a patch of scrub.

Jude turned toward the ocean and Strock followed, digging into the sand with his cane. The wind blew stronger into their faces, its intensity matched by the rising sound of the surf, till finally they came within sight of the shoreline.

The deserted beach extended as far as Strock could see in both directions, the bright sand scruffed with sprawling plants and dotted with horse apples. Hermit crabs, tiny and faint as tufts of hair, vanished into pencil-thin dens. Sun-bleached driftwood lay scattered about and a three-foot sand cliff extending the length of the shoreline marked the tide break. It seemed odd, Strock thought. Such a getaway. No one around.

Jude pointed to the left, where beyond a border of indigo plants a tall cinder block enclosure stood. Razor wire coiled atop the walls. As they drew closer, Strock could hear the thumping chug of a generator coming from inside.

Jude led the way around to the leeward side, where a thick wood gate stood locked. He reached and pulled on a thin line of hemp rope connected to a bell, ringing twice.

"Who are we waiting for?" Strock asked.

Jude shrugged. "Your guess is as good as mine."

The gate opened. A dark-skinned Latina stood there, tall and hipless, her black hair tied into a ponytail with a white ribbon. She wore a simple blue dress, belted and modestly buttoned up the front all the way to the lace-rimmed collar. Smiling shyly, she waved them inside.

"*Buenas,*" Jude said, passing through the gate. He gestured for Strock to follow along. Strock obliged, feeling a twinge of arousal as the Latina closed the gate behind them.

PALM TREES SHADED THE WALLED YARD. FALLEN GREEN COCONUTS AND sun-bleached palm fronds littered the sand. The house, erected on slab, was modest in size and run-down, with cracked, badly patched wall plaster and dry-rotted wood around the windows. A pelican perched atop the ragged tile roof. Strock looked around, leaning on his cane. The generator was silent now. An almost eerie stillness lay just beneath the sound of the wind and surf.

He felt the Latina approach from behind and turned to greet her. She was slightly bucktoothed and wore no makeup. Dark freckles mottled her cheeks. Her blue tennis shoes matched her dress but had no laces.

Extending her hand, she said in a soft, birdlike voice, "*Mucho gusto, señor. Me llama Clara. Estoy su servienta.*"

"Clara." Strock took her hand and smiled. He had no idea what she'd said except for her name. "Call me Phil." When she seemed confused, he shortened the introduction to just his name, which she then repeated back to him, making it sound like "Feel." That'll do just fine, he thought. Call me Feel. Clara smiled and sauntered into the house. She walks like a girl, he thought, not a woman.

Jude nudged Strock's shoulder. "Let's get you stowed away."

Inside, the house was tidy but in much the same state of disrepair as outside. The refrigerator, run off a storage cell charged by the generator, was relatively new but looked like it had fallen off a truck. In contrast the iron stove, run on propane, looked primordial. How did they heft all this stuff out here, Strock wondered.

The kitchen opened onto a large dining room, bare except for a wood-plank table and roughly carved chairs. Sliding glass doors opened onto the sandy yard.

"This way," Jude said, tugging Strock's sleeve. "Your room's back here somewhere."

Strock followed Jude down a musty dark hallway to a small room at the end. Dust motes hovered in the light filtering in through a screened window. The furnishings included a narrow bed, a chest of drawers painted an almost psychotic shade of yellow, and a rickety desk of such blatant shabbiness it didn't even merit the lunatic paint job.

None of that caught Strock's attention, though, as much as the Colt AR-15, fitted with a Redfield three-to-nine power scope, perched on its bipod atop the desk. A crate filled with ammunition boxes sat on the floor against the wall, along with cleaning rags, a bore brush, and a tin of Hoppe's No. 9 solvent.

He stepped toward the weapon. "Somebody wants me to practice out here."

Jude hefted Strock's bag onto the bed. "The place is isolated enough, I suppose."

Strock looked out the window screen at the swaying palm trees. "The wind'll create havoc with shot placement. Blow me around like a boat. Hard to settle in, get a stable sight line." He noticed there was a spiral notebook in the crate with the ammunition, for logging his practice shots, he supposed. "But I guess none of that's your problem."

Jude looked puzzled and bored and ready to go. "It's just not my end of things."

Strock lifted the rifle, measuring its balance in his hands, smelling the sheen of oil, like invisible sweat, on its metalwork. "I trained on a weapon just like this. We stopped using it long-range ages ago. You got a .223 round, hard to bring a man down with a load that light. You've got to hit him square in the middle of his face or his ear hole or straight through his heart to do the job. Otherwise, he's hurt but he's still walking. You hit him in the skull, the round can just bounce off. I'm not joking. Seen it happen. That's why we switched to a retooled Remington 700—hogged-out stock, free-floating bull barrel, fires a big fat nasty 7.62 NATO round."

Outside, the pelican on the roof shrieked and flew off toward the beach, its shadow flickering across the sand. Jude said, "My guess is you'll just be there to scare off thieves. See a guy digging under the fence, you fire off a warning round. He doesn't respond, you wing him."

Strock set the rifle back down on the desk, then nudged the crate of ammunition with his foot. "Wing him? Oh, you mean *shoot to wound*. Sure. That always works. Nobody ever fucks that up and kills the guy by mistake."

Jude glanced at his watch. "I'll let you straighten all that out with the people you'll be working for."

"And they'll be coming around when?"

"Tomorrow morning as I understand it." Jude turned to go.

Strock caught him by the arm. "You'd leave me here with no more to go on than that?"

Jude dislodged Strock's hand. "Go outside. Look around. A thousand guys would trade places in a heartbeat. If anybody meant to screw you over, why would they leave you with a weapon and enough rounds to hold off half a division? Not to mention, ahem, they gave you a maid. I'll bet there's even beer in the fridge. Stop worrying. Everything's going to work out."

He said it like he meant it, then turned away. Strock hobbled behind, thinking what the kid said made sense. And yet, with Jude on his way out, Strock felt an odd streak of almost boyish lonesomeness. "I don't even know where I am. There's no phone."

Jude stopped at that. Over his shoulder, he said quietly, "Hold on." After a quick trip to speak with Clara in the dining room, he came back carrying her cell phone. "Correction. On one front anyway." He thumbed the dial pad. "There. I've logged in my number, in case something comes up, nobody shows, whatever. Okay?"

"Yeah," Strock said. "Sure. Thanks."

"Just ask Clara for the phone. *Teléfono.*"

"Okay."

"I don't answer, no big deal. I'm back on duty come tomorrow, and I don't pick up all the time. Leave me a voice mail. I'll answer when I can."

With that he went back to the dining room, returned the phone to Clara, then headed out. He crossed the sand toward the gate; Clara followed, to secure the lock behind him. Strock stood in the doorway to the house, leaning on his cane, watching Jude disappear. Kid McManus, they used to call him. Pop Gun's son.

Clara walked back to the house and, as she came close, offered the warmest smile, pretty despite her horsey teeth. Her eyes seemed sad, he thought. Maybe it's me.

"*¿Quiere su almuerzo ahora?*"

He shrugged, not knowing what she'd asked, then limped after her on his cane into the house. Again, he caught that same queer silence lingering beneath the roar of the wind and the breaking waves.

19

JUDE DROVE FROM LA PUNTILLA UNDER THE SAME BLISTERING MIDDAY sun, storming in a back-blast of dust past the pricey hotels and elegant *ranchos* along the Costa del Sol. He tapped his horn as he passed the teenage bread vendors on their *bicicletas de la carga,* the women balancing baskets of *tamales* atop their heads, the wandering dogs and cows and pigs rooting along the roadside for fallen mangos or cashew pods or even half-rotted cabbages, while armed men watched from behind iron gates. The jarring clash of luxury and want prompted an uneasy candor: He felt guilty but grateful to leave Strock behind. Just one last connection with Malvasio, report on things, then he'd put this curious little picaresque behind him for good.

He'd been lied to, sure. Used, maybe—and for what? He couldn't tell. That's just the way things get done sometimes, he told himself: No harm, no foul. God loves drunks, fools, and Americans. Here's hoping. But then, rounding a bend, he felt a surge of nausea build to the point he had to pull to the side of the road. He opened the door, leaned out over the billowing dirt of the roadbed, ready to hurl. Nothing came, just a trickle of bile up his throat, while from somewhere nearby a rooster shrieked. He felt ridiculous. Until that moment, he hadn't realized what a buildup of fear he'd been sitting on. It seemed odd, not to know a thing like that.

Glancing up, he saw a billboard for Schafik Handal, the FMLN candidate for president, looming over the road. The old guerrilla's beaming, bespectacled, white-bearded face was gone, obscured by a giant blotch of black paint. The country had held its elections on Sunday, while he'd been in Chicago, and the *efemelenistas* had lost big. More to the point, as the vandalized billboard made plain, the *areneros* were ugly winners.

It made him wonder about Eileen—out of concern for how she was taking the election, sure. He'd ask her about that, ask her about everything. But ever since he'd landed, despite all this business with Strock and Malvasio—or maybe because of that—she'd become the star of increasingly shameless daydreams. He felt like a ten-year-old with a crush on the babysitter, a state of puzzling arousal humming in his groin. And, bowing to the humility inspired by his sudden bout of dry heaves, he admitted to himself he felt unworthy of her.

What do you do with something like that, he wondered. Sit on it, like your fear?

✦

Malvasio sat waiting at the same beachfront restaurant in San Marcelino. This time there were other customers too, two men, one woman, sitting together: the men filthy from fieldwork and stormily drunk, one of them wearing a sweat-stained cowboy hat of yellow straw; the woman young, dark, and willowy, with doe-like eyes that belied the fact she was a prostitute.

Malvasio offered a *Hey buddy* smile. "Everything squared away?"

Jude sat down across the table, the artery in his neck throbbing. "I'd get somebody out there to follow up quick. Before somebody we both know goes batty."

"No worries. That's the plan."

"I gave him my cell number to call if he gets edgy and I'd prefer he didn't blow up my phone wondering what the hell's going on."

Malvasio cocked his head a little. "You guys do some male bonding on the way down?"

"What's that crack for?"

"Nothing. I just—"

"I felt for the guy. God knows he's a drunken pain in the ass, but he's out there alone, middle of nowhere."

"What about Clara?"

"She doesn't speak English. He doesn't speak Spanish."

"My point," Malvasio said, "is he's not alone." He reached across the table and gave Jude's arm a little buck-up shake. "And he'll get connected work-wise tomorrow, first thing. Relax. He'll be okay." His eyes warmed again. "He's somebody else's worry now. You did great. I'm grateful. Really."

Despite his own better instincts, Jude felt reassured by the attaboy. Malvasio had the gift. "You were right about one thing, incidentally."

"Just one?"

"He says he'll kill you if he sees you down here."

Malvasio looked out across the white sand, the rustling palms, the shimmering blue water. "I wish I knew what to say to that."

"He filled me in on the Winters story. The parts you left out." And more, Jude thought, holding on to that for now.

Malvasio turned back. "And which parts might those be?"

"Mainly, the part about planning the hit two months before Winters died. And leaving Strock with his knee torn up when he fell through a rotted stair trying to get into position."

Malvasio looked like something had crawled up his pant leg. "Come again?"

"I think you heard me."

"Jude—"

"That's not your recollection of what happened?"

"I haven't got a clue what you're talking about," Malvasio said. "Phil and your dad always told me they were working in your basement and there was an accident. Phil fell off a ladder, I think. A screwdriver or saw blade or something went through his knee. You're telling me that isn't his story now?"

Jude felt another lurch of nausea but he tamped it down, picturing how it might have happened—not Malvasio but his dad the one who wanted Winters dead, the hooker snitch too, planning it out with Strock, only to have it all go wrong. It made sense, actually, after a fashion. But then why blame Malvasio? *Because he's the lucky prick who got away clean.* Give yourself ten years to perfect a fable of blame every time you've got a drink in front of you, God only knows what you'll concoct.

"No," Jude said. "That's not the way he tells it."

"You ever talk to your dad about what happened?"

Assuming I'd believe my dad, Jude thought. "Never."

"So it's Phil's word against mine."

"Yeah. Seems so."

Malvasio rubbed his eyes and groaned. "The funny thing? It's not like I didn't know this might happen—I told you he puts every-thing on me, right?"

"You're saying he's lying. His version of what happened to his leg, Winters—"

"Jude, let me stop you, okay? I can't make this right. I can't go back and prove anything for you. I've already told you my side, he's told you his, there's no getting from one to the other. You just have to decide who to believe. Him or me. Maybe neither." Malvasio shook his head with a sad little laugh. "If you don't mind me chang-ing the subject, how'd you find him?"

"The kid you told me about," Jude said. "I tracked her through Vital Statistics, found the mother in East Chicago. She told me enough I could figure out the rest."

"You met her. The mother."

"She's a dancer. The exotic kind."

"Okay, that fits the picture. She got a name?"

Jude thought about that. "Listen, don't take this wrong. I don't mean anything. But given the bad blood—"

Malvasio raised his hand. "Jude, we're good. Fine. Don't tell me. I don't need to know. I was just curious, okay?"

"He's not crazy about the weapon you left for him, incidentally."

"Not my problem. Or yours. Besides, that's just him. Olympic-class whiner, that guy. Give him twenty-four hours, he'll be knock-ing caterpillars off coconuts at three hundred yards, trust me. Be doing the same if you left him a slingshot and a box of rocks."

"He says it's too windy to practice out there."

"So they'll find someplace else he can practice. Look, it's covered. Your worries are done. Let's wrap up—any problems along the way I should know about?"

Jude thought through what had happened the last few days—from tracking down Strock to finally dropping him off at the *ran-cho*—the whole time not knowing whether he was doing a good thing or a dumb thing, wondering what came next and would he get dragged into it somehow, getting his mind whipsawed by one tale after another with no way to tell what was true: Did any of that constitute a problem?

Malvasio said, "Don't do that."

Jude snapped to. "Do what?"

Malvasio pointed to his mouth. "That thing with your lip. The way you chew at it. It's a nervous tic. Gives you away."

Jude could feel the blood rush to his face. "Sure." On a sudden impulse he searched his shirt pocket for the slip of paper he'd removed from his pickup's firewall—unfolded it, set it on the table, turned it so Malvasio could read the hand-scrawled lettering: "This look familiar?"

Malvasio glanced down, read the message, then lifted his eyes again, his face imbued with an almost pitying impatience. "What are you going on about now?"

Jude felt his defiance melt away as easily as that. Telling himself to give it up, he fluttered his hand, like he was shooing away a bad idea. "Never mind. Stupid. Sorry." He gathered up the paper slip and stuffed it back in his pocket.

Across the room, the girl and her two johns were drinking hard; the talk was heating up. The one in the cowboy hat had his arm around the young woman and he leered at her, pinching her nipple through her halter, his fingers black. Jude guessed he'd been digging by hand through cold trash fires for scrap metal. And he'd found enough to cash in, pay for a party—which meant five bucks for the girl, two more for the beers.

Malvasio produced an envelope and slid it across the table. "This is for you."

Jude stared at it. "No need. Really."

"What I gave you before was for out-of-pocket costs. This is to say thanks."

"You're welcome. Thing's done. Hope it got done well and everybody ends up happy." Standing, Jude left the envelope where it was. "I'd best get back to what I do down here."

Malvasio looked up at him with an expression that said, *So that's what you think of me*. He nodded toward the envelope. "You're sure you won't take this? I don't want you feeling taken advantage of."

"It's not a problem."

"I didn't say it was a problem. I just want you to have it."

Across the room the grimy cowboy reared back his head and roared, laughing, reaching with his beer bottle to clink it against his friend's. A toast. May the best man win. Loser gets sloppy seconds.

"You want me to handle that?" Malvasio said.

Jude blinked. "Excuse me?"

"You want me to take care of it?"

"Take care of what?"

Malvasio took the envelope with the cash inside, stood up, and ambled over to the table where both men were pawing at the young woman now. He let the envelope drop onto the table.

"*¿Cuánto te pagan? Yo te pago más. Mucho más.*"

How much are they paying you? I'll pay you more. Much more.

The man in the cowboy hat cleared his throat and glared while the other one blinked. The young woman eyed the envelope. Malvasio gestured for her to stand up and go. It took a second but, smiling nervously, she turned sideways on the bench to get out. The cowboy stopped her. To Malvasio, he said, "*A la chingada, baboso, y—*"

Malvasio snatched the beer bottle from the cowboy's grip and slammed it so hard against his nose his face exploded in blood. His friend jumped back with a sick little shriek. That much Jude had half expected. It was the next move that stunned him—Malvasio picking a fork up off the table, gripping it like a knife, then plunging it into the cowboy's throat.

The man sat there, face bloody, white eyes gaping while a faint, bubbly hiss leaked out from his punctured windpipe.

Malvasio lifted the envelope, dotted with blood now, handed it to the girl, and told her to leave. She kicked off her sandals, the better to run, grabbed them from the floor, and vanished down the stairs. Malvasio turned away from the two men and walked slowly back to Jude.

He said, "I had to do that or he'd have come back sooner or later and taken it out on the girl. You understand that, right?"

The cowboy's drunk friend finally overcame his shock and inched to his companion's side. He reached tentatively for the fork but the cowboy shook his head in whimpering panic and swatted the hand away.

Malvasio said. "You should go. I'll wrap this up. Thanks again for all your help."

PART III

SINCE I MET
THE DEVIL

The true purpose of masks, as any actor will tell
you, is not concealment, but transformation.

—SALMAN RUSHDIE, *The Jaguar Smile*

20

WANT ME TO HANDLE THAT? JUDE TORE WEST IN HIS PICKUP FROM SAN Marcelino, trying to convince himself nothing he could have done would have mattered. By the time he'd caught on to what was happening, it was too late—but everything had that sense to it now. What other little reckonings were in store? It dawned on him that for someone whose job was protecting people, he'd done a piss-poor job looking after himself, and no doubt there was a moral to be had in that, but for now it just brought to mind the way his father died, with a whole new take on just how fitting it was: a miscalculation, a thoughtless slip. Then tangled up underwater. Trapped.

He told himself to calm down. Again, there was no way to tell who was lying and how much or whether it mattered—besides, that had nothing to do with this last bit of theater. That was just what it was, a bar fight, settled the old-fashioned way, except for Malvasio's novel use of flatware. He hadn't even seemed angry, though. The man you found so humbled, so convincing, in a snap there's a casual menace to him, the kind of thing you wondered about but told yourself no, he's different, more complex. Have you been paying attention to what's in front of your face all along, or just trying to talk yourself into what you wanted to believe?

Oh for fuck's sake, lighten up, he thought. Even if the worst imaginable were true—and you've got nothing but your fear to convince you it is—what could you do about it? Realistically, your options are pretty limited. The man's got friends down here, remember? The kind of friends who can make problems disappear, make people disappear maybe, no matter what a slow learner like you tries to do to make it all right. Forget about it. Like the man said, not your problem anymore. Chances are you can't find out more about him or his business without exposing your own role, and what does that solve? Don't blunder your way in deeper.

As he reached the bridge spanning the Río Jiboa, traffic suddenly slowed to a crawl. Up ahead, beyond the knot of cars and trucks and the grainy shimmer of heat they created, three PNC Nissans had pulled to the dusty roadside, plus a pair of military jeeps and a seven-ton truck, the kind called a Dragon Wagon. Something was going on beneath the bridge.

The river was almost dry, just a trickling stream of oily brown muck, one foot deep at best, threading down a chalky *quebrada* lined with tuff beds and cluttered with struggling almond trees. Beneath the punishing sun, PNC officers scoured the underbrush. Soldiers joined them, poking with their bayonets into snarly thickets of thorned *iscanal*. From the lip of the *quebrada,* a trio of women grape pickers from the nearby vineyards pointed, trying to help, while overhead a circle of buzzards—*zopes,* they were called—drifted in lazy flight.

Jude got waved forward through a choking cloud of exhaust by a pair of women officers trying to keep traffic moving. When he finally reached the far side of the low-walled concrete bridge, he passed a cluster of onlookers parked along the road. He recognized a face in the crowd—Waxman, the reporter—then spotted Aleris and Truco, the *marero,* and wondered if Eileen was with them. That's all it took. He eased to the berm with her husky voice spiriting up from memory, pulled to a stop about fifty yards farther on, then locked up the truck and hurried back toward the bridge.

People gathered along the road or stood on the hoods of their cars, craning to look while from somewhere a radio blared a thumping, incongruous *reggaeton*—like someone in the crowd might want to dance. A group of *campesinos* dressed in sweat-streaked work clothes crowded the back of a flatbed truck, clinging to the guardrails as they peered toward the riverbed. Farther on, a family looked dressed for the beach: the father—chubby, ruffled, bespectacled—

wore a T-shirt bearing the slogan BE ALL YOU USED TO BE. It wasn't the only English on display nearby. Emblazoned on the side of the Dragon Wagon, the local brigade's slogan read: HONOR, VALOR, LOYALTY. It doesn't take much imagination to see where things are headed, Jude thought, if even the military no longer bothers with Spanish.

Near the edge of the *quebrada*, Waxman argued with a soldier. Aleris stood beside him while Truco hung back, dressed in long sleeves despite the heat—to hide his banger tats, Jude supposed. He looked around for Eileen, but the only other person he recognized was Waxman's photographer, standing twenty feet down the dusty slope toward the riverbed, fending off two soldiers trying to grab his camera. He held it high, rattling away with a mollifying patois of smiling Spanglish, and Jude remembered his odd name suddenly: Abatangelo.

The soldier going at it with Waxman was a corporal, dark and knobby and fierce. He rested one hand on his hip, the other gesturing wildly in the air.

"*¡No! ¡No fotografías!*"

"*Soy un reportero.*" Waxman's accent belabored the words, robbing them of all conviction. "*Las fotografías están para—*"

"*¡Oíme, tripudo—no fotografías!*"

Taking the corporal's insult as a cue—he'd basically called Waxman *fatso*—Aleris waded in, peppering the corporal with machine-gun Spanish, half pleading, half badgering, as Jude ambled closer to Waxman and tapped his shoulder.

"What's going on?"

Waxman turned, shading his eyes with his plump freckled hand. "Well . . . hello."

Jude detected no conspicuous disdain in the greeting. An omen, he hoped. Maybe the bridge back to Eileen hadn't burned down completely. Nodding toward the corporal now being browbeaten by Aleris, he asked, "There some kind of problem?"

Waxman drifted a few steps till he stood behind Truco and

gestured for Jude to follow. "That remains to be seen, I suppose." He folded his arms across his chest, casting a sidelong glance toward Abatangelo as he added uneasily, "For the moment, I'm still hopeful."

He wants a favor, Jude thought, like I've got pull with the troops. "What's everybody looking for?"

Waxman nodded toward the riverbed. "A boy working in the vineyard saw a bunch of buzzards feeding on something in the underbrush this morning." He squinted upward at the eerie black *zopes* circling overhead in the ash white sky. "When the boy went down and shooed the birds away, a pair of eyes stared back at him."

"A body."

"Just a head." The reporter winced. "They're trying to see if there's anything else to find."

Jude scanned the length of the *quebrada*. Soldiers maundered about, seeming as keen on avoiding something as finding it. "Why not just let the *zopes* do the work? They did it once."

Waxman smiled wanly. "Then everyone would have to find another way to look busy."

Truco quivered like a fighter, rolling his shoulders. "The head, we saw it, got a snapshot. It had long black hair. Guy who bagged it lifted it up for his buddies to see." He licked his teeth and spat. "Long hair, I say that means a *puta* or *mariposón*. Fuckers can scream all they want about gang jobs but the *maras* don't go hunting for hookers and fags to wax. Leave that to Los Soldados de San Miguel."

It was the name of a recently active death squad, plying its trade in the east. Waxman raised his palm: *Keep the volume down.* "Let's not get ahead of ourselves."

Truco grimaced at the corporal. "Why you think *flaco* here's so jacked about pictures? They're in on it. They wanna grab all the evidence, make it go poof." He snapped his fingers. "Like that."

Jude turned back to Waxman. "I get the feeling you'd like me to help out somehow."

A schemey hope flashed in Waxman's eye. "Could you?"

"You seriously overestimate my clout here. No offense."

That fast, Waxman slumped. "You lack our political baggage. If you don't mind my saying so."

It didn't sound like an insult but it felt like one, and Jude had to make an effort to hold his tongue, thinking: Why should I mind? I'll just sneak these fellas the secret sign. We'll go off arm in arm, singing the *himno nacional*. "I may have baggage all my own, you know."

"My point is, I think they might see you a little less as an outsider."

"On the basis of what—honestly, who do you think I am?"

Before Waxman could answer, Truco muttered under his breath, "Couple old ladies, you two," and strode toward the edge of the *quebrada,* clapping his hands, trying for Abatangelo's attention. Sticking two fingers in his mouth, he let rip a quick knifing whistle, then called out, *"¡Oye, chele!"* Hey, whitey.

Truco gestured for the camera and Abatangelo, still fending off the two soldiers, lobbed it uphill. Truco lunged, genuflected, and cupped his hands, catching the camera before it hit the ground. Then he turned on his heels and ran.

The corporal who'd been arguing with Aleris shouted *"¡Pare!"* and took a dozen listless steps in pursuit, then just stood there and watched as Truco darted down the line of cars, skirting the crowd. He slid down the roadbed as it sloped toward a vast concrete slab dotted with sand piles and scattered with rebar and cinder blocks, then skated across the drifting sand, ducked behind a storage building, and raced toward a cluster of *champas* at the edge of a sparse wood.

Waxman collected Aleris by the arm. "I think we'd best be going."

Abatangelo broke free of the two dumbstruck soldiers who'd been hassling him and clambered toward the road. The soldiers scurried behind him, calling for others nearby who soon followed, including the lieutenant in charge, all of them struggling uphill from the dusty riverbed. The corporal circled back as well. Shortly Waxman, Aleris, and Abatangelo were surrounded. Jude stepped up to intervene, sensing that any sway he might actually have with the soldiers better be used now. He barely got the first word out before a shove landed in his chest that sent him tumbling toward the others.

The lieutenant—a bug-eyed man with a feral grimace and no hat—drew his pistol and raised it toward Waxman. Then, from beneath the bridge, one of his men shouted, "*¡Teniente!*"

The soldier who'd called out pointed to something hidden in a dense thorn thicket of *iscanal*. An almost comical look of horror crept across his face, then he turned, dropped to one knee in the chalky mud, and vomited into the shallow river.

Two other soldiers rushed toward him, pulling up when they came upon what he'd found. One just stared. The other put his hands to his head. On the far side of the *quebrada,* the three women from the vineyard lowered their hands. They didn't have to point anymore.

THE SOLDIERS LINED THE FOUR OF THEM UP ALONG THE ROAD IN THE choking heat, their legs spread wide and their hands held up above their heads, each of them forming a human *X*. The pain gradually built from a dull ache to a knifing throb, but whenever Jude lowered his arms, even for an instant, just to wipe the sweat from his eyes, a soldier came up and screamed insults laced with obscenities—*jodido* (fucker), *mamón* (cocksucker), *hijo de la verga* (son of a prick). It was the same for the others, Waxman earning *panzón* and *gorda cerote* (both variants, again, on "fatso"), Aleris *zorra* (slut) or *hembrita* (a barnyard term for anything female). Abatangelo largely escaped the abuse; he was better than everyone else at keeping his arms up.

Soon enough the name-calling stopped being scary, so the soldier tore off a switch from a eucalyptus in the roadside windbreak and used it to thrash the bare flesh of their arms: all of them, punishing the group as a whole for any slacking off from just one. Meanwhile, overhead, the *zopes* continued circling in the parched thermals, sensing something worth sticking around for even after the soldiers slopped the dead woman's dusty, butchered remains into a body bag.

It took two hours before the questioning began. Apparently, that was the province of the BESM—Brigada Especial de Seguridad Militar—specifically a captain named Dominguez who arrived by jeep from the capital. Odd, Jude thought, they could wait for him but not a morgue unit from the forensics lab.

Captain Dominguez reviewed everyone's passports, listened as the bug-eyed lieutenant reported his fevered understanding of who was who, what had happened. Dominguez said little except to interject curt, clipped questions now and again, pointing to this person or that. He returned to his jeep, made a long-winded call on his field radio, then came back and paced along the roadbed in front of them, studying faces. Finally, he said, "You can put your arms down."

A shudder shot through Jude's whole body. Waxman groaned and shook out his arms, and Aleris uttered a soft little gasp, wringing her hands and massaging the fingers, trying to get the blood back. All of them checked the welts on their arms too, except for Abatangelo, who just tucked his hands in his armpits, making no sound whatsoever.

Reading one of the passports, Captain Dominguez said, "Stay where you are for just a moment more, if you would, please." His English was too accomplished and free of accent, Jude thought, to be the result of just a few training forays to Fort Benning. More likely he'd matriculated up through the British or American academies in San Salvador, which meant a sound middle-class background or better. He was short but muscular with an easygoing grace, more like a cop than a soldier, which wasn't surprising since he was both.

He stepped up to Jude, held out his passport, and said, "You can go."

Jude knew better than to think this was luck. He'd been expecting questions—where had he come from, where was he headed—and had prepared the lies he'd need to avoid any mention of Malvasio. Given the fork episode at the restaurant, that troubled him far more than explaining why he'd stopped here. But somehow the captain already knew enough to single him out from the others. And who was it, exactly, that had put in the good word?

Jude took his passport and started for his truck, then checked himself. *I'll just sneak these fellas the secret sign.* The quip felt slimy now, and though relieved he'd not said it out loud, he still knew how this looked.

Captain Dominguez stood there reading the next passport. Finally, sensing Jude's continued presence, he glanced up. "I told you. You can go."

Jude checked the man's face and decided to trust him. "I was wondering if—"

"Please." The voice possessed a soldierly tact but the eyes turned to stone. "You'll only make this more difficult for everyone."

"I can vouch for these people."

"Can you?" The captain shifted his weight to inch his face a little closer to Jude's. "If that's the case—and it's not my understanding that it is—you'll do them no favors. Now, I'm not in the habit of repeating myself."

"What understanding? Who did you talk to?"

"I'm losing my patience, Mr. McManus."

The others wouldn't look at him but Jude knew none of their prospects would improve if he didn't do as he was told. He walked to his truck at a pace to satisfy the captain and climbed behind the wheel. Checking his passport, he found it intact, then turned the key in the ignition and released the emergency brake. As he drove away, he saw Captain Dominguez shaking his head as he stepped toward Waxman.

TRAFFIC REMAINED SLOW ALONG THE HIGHWAY PAST THE AIRPORT turnoff, then picked up speed as Jude turned onto the coastal highway toward the Costa del Bálsamo. When he came to El Dorado Mar he just kept driving, through the rough-hewn tunnels and around the cliff-side switchbacks till he passed the white stone church where he slowed for the turnoff into La Perla.

Barefoot children, slick with sweat, chased chickens around the central pen as adults looked on from makeshift chairs of lashed wood, fanning themselves. Stray dogs lazed in the chalky dust, and a teenage girl led a swaybacked goat down a narrow lane between crumbling houses crowned with barbed wire. Jude dodged the larger stones in the sandy road, following the parallel ruts toward the beach. He needed to see Eileen now more than ever, tell her what had happened, explain it his way before anyone else could poison it. Like you didn't have enough to apologize for already, he thought.

He found her house empty, locked up. He pounded on the door regardless, peered in through the barred windows, then went around back and put his shoulder to the wood door till the old, rusted lock hasp gave way.

Her belongings were gone, the blouses, scarves, skirts, handwoven mats. Everything. The place smelled stale from being closed up and felt hot as an oven.

As he made one last look around, he spotted a crumpled sheet of notepad paper tossed into a corner. Picking it up, spreading it out flat, he discovered a handwritten poem:

Walls with broken glass on top
protect the caudillo's garden.
You don't belong in there.
But handsome bruiser who guards the place?
The mug who looks at you

like you're his favorite problem?
You took a chance, invited
him over to your place and
he came—you know—then vanished like a punk
to crawl back to his paymasters,
stifling the little ditty in his heart,
the tune he sang for you when
you were alone together.
The one that goes: I didn't want this
I didn't want
I didn't—
But here I am.

21

JUDE CLIMBED BACK IN HIS TRUCK AND FLED LA PERLA, TURNING EAST on the Carretera del Litoral. The prospect of twenty straight days on the job suddenly felt like a perverse stroke of luck, and not a bad way to fend off the epithets ticking through his brain: *Mug. Punk. Bruiser.* Quite a kick down the stair, he thought, from *You're the best-looking guy I've ever done the deed with.*

He told himself he'd see this current assignment through, make sure Axel finished up his work in one piece, but after that some time off was in order. He needed to screw his head back on straight and he'd always wanted to travel the subcontinent—Rio de Janeiro, Montevideo, Buenos Aires, the Punta del Este—maybe he'd even take the train south through Patagonia to Tierra del Fuego, the end of the world. It might help put recent events and their sad little in-dignities in perspective. Then he'd circle back here because, yes, he loved the place. Who knew, maybe he'd extend the sabbatical for a while, sign on with an NGO—Habitat for Humanity, Engineers Without Borders—they could use a good carpenter, roofer, driver, anything. He was rethinking the whole protection racket, and that ambivalence seemed at the heart of a whole stew of misgivings. The macho pretensions had worn thin. I'm good with my hands, he thought, always have been. I take pride in what I build. Not that construction wouldn't have the same old tedium to it or wouldn't bring with it moral conundrums all its own; it just seemed a better fit with his gifts, his wants. He knew it might make him sound like Miss America to the guys he worked with, let alone Malvasio and Strock, but he wanted to help people, wanted his life to matter. Wanted the voices in his head to be happy for a change. He wondered what might be different if he'd seen that more clearly or admitted it sooner—opened up, told Eileen about it. Maybe nothing. Maybe everything.

When he arrived finally at El Dorado Mar, the doldrums had given way to an offshore breeze. Even with its charge of sunbaked heat the wind felt good on his skin as he unloaded his bags from the truck, and it seemed like forever since anything much had felt good.

Once inside Horizon House, though, he found three men waiting. Two were FBI agents, men he'd met briefly before, the third he didn't recognize. It seemed clear now why his roadside interlude with Captain Dominguez had been so brief. The locals had deferred to these three.

The lead agent was a man named Ed McGuire—olive-skinned and black-haired, with the kind of fluency in Spanish the bureau wasn't known for. Jude had made his acquaintance during a liaison visit to the embassy by the Trenton crew, and he'd puzzled over the ill fit of the man's name, until he'd learned Ed was short for Eduardo. He came from L.A., had a task force background battling *sureño* street gangs, and was uptight, unhelpful, arrogant, and dull as a sock—but scary smart, too, something Jude made a point to remember at that moment.

The other agent was Jimmy Sanborn—pinched blue eyes, a

flaming red crew cut, and eyebrows so wispily fair they all but disappeared, making him look a little like a burn victim. The story on him was he'd been a bank robbery specialist of some renown, stationed in Saint Louis, till a poisonous divorce had him begging for transfer to a place as far from his ex as possible.

McGuire and Sanborn had been sent to El Salvador through the LEGAT in Panama City to liaise with the PNC regarding the recent terrorist threats and to haggle for intel on gang matters. Jude could halfway understand why they might want to talk to him, given Truco's performance along the Río Jiboa. The last man, though, was troubling.

Normally, when the agents traveled outside the embassy, they were plagued by the Regional Security Officer or the Chief of Mission or their State Department pixies, to be sure the host country remained unembarrassed by the bureau's work. But Jude knew those folks, and this man wasn't one of them. He had the brushed, well-tanned cut Jude associated with the military, which seemed like overkill but so had the army's presence at the Río Jiboa. The Peace Accords had tried to end such arrangements, but the Salvadoran armed forces had begun nosing in on routine police work again, doing so at SOUTHCOM's urging, in the name of combating terror. Then there was the Juventud Sana program, through which the Pentagon, rather than the Justice Department, was training PNC officers now. Maybe that's the connection, Jude thought, eyeing the man a little more mindfully.

He wore a gray cotton shirt and black linen slacks with a crease straight as a plumb line, despite the heat. It was his face, though, that jumped out at you: angular, hard-bitten, pockmarked, and unavailing, framed with impeccable short-cut hair. His eyes were heavy-lidded, small, and gray.

The three men sat in the living room area with Axel, near the balcony with its view of the sparkling beach in the distance. Everyone else—taciturn Pahlavi and froggish Dillahunt plus the EP crew—sat eating supper in awkward silence at the opposite end of the common area, beyond earshot. Jude could smell the food—*gallo en chicha,* a chicken stew made with corn liquor—as he set his bags down and said to McGuire, "I'm guessing you're here to see me."

McGuire rose from his chair, and his shirt peeled away from the leather with a sound like tape being stripped from a dispenser. "We can talk outside, if you like."

Axel got up too, leading with a smile that seemed both valiant and false. "They say it's just routine." Then, lowering his voice: "Something about a woman found beheaded under a bridge."

Jude gestured for them both to sit back down. "No need to go anywhere. Here's good."

He pulled up a chair and sat facing McGuire, with Axel on one side, Mr. Gray Eyes and Sanborn on the other. Shortly, Fitz got up from the table and crossed the large open room to join them, wiping his lips with a napkin. "Mind if I . . . ?" There was no point protesting: He was the advance man, it was his job to know all. And the fact the agents seemed open to a group chat boded well, Jude supposed. Even so, his pulse throbbed. He told himself: Get ready.

McGuire started it off. "A Captain Dominguez from the BESM contacted us at the embassy. He mentioned you'd been detained."

"Detained and released," Jude said.

"Fair enough, detained and released. In any event—"

"Look, let me tell you what happened. How's that?" Jude glanced around, face-to-face, more for stage business than to register anyone's permission. "Just be shorter that way. I was driving over the Río Jiboa bridge—"

"Which direction?" McGuire asked.

"Excuse me?"

"Where were you coming from?"

Jude worked up an innocent smile. "What difference does it make?"

The smile went unreturned. McGuire said, "You landed this morning in Comalapa and went through Immigration with a man named Phil Strock. He used to be a cop in Chicago, with your father. Went down with your father, as a matter of fact."

"And a guy named Bill Malvasio." Sanborn's contribution.

In the corner of his eye, Jude spotted a shimmering cloud of blue-green dragonflies hovering in a ball of sunlight near the balcony railing. It distracted him long enough for Axel to step in, saying with a shake of his head, "Excuse me. I'm a little—"

"Same here," Fitz said, less pleasantly.

McGuire just waited—like he already knew everything, oldest cop trick in the world.

Jude took a deep breath, inhaling someone's sour cologne. "Yeah. I flew down with Phil Strock. He was a friend of my dad's. What's the question?"

McGuire studied him. "What's he down here for?"

"Vacation. That's what he told me, anyway."

"Alone?"

"Anything wrong with that?"

"Not wrong." McGuire looked like he'd just remembered a so-so joke. "Just odd."

"Spend some time with Phil. You get way beyond odd real quick."

Sanborn puckered up his face. He'd been pulling his freckled ear as he listened. "He just happens to be on the same plane as you, coming down here for vacation?"

"I didn't say that. We came together. I hooked up with him back home because my mother asked me to." The lie rolled out naturally and Jude felt glad for that. He'd practiced for this mentally on the flight down, figuring the questions might come up sooner or later. If anyone from the bureau bothered to follow up with his mother, she'd just slam down the phone. "Mom heard from Phil over the holidays, said he didn't sound so good, asked me to check in on him. I did, we had a beer, talked shop. I told him how much I like it down here and he got interested. Said he'd like to see for himself."

"Just like that." Sanborn tented his shirt. Out came another jolt of rank cologne.

"He's not leaving a whole lot behind, trust me. Look—"

"You drive him someplace from the airport?" McGuire again.

"Yeah. I took him to the Costa del Sol."

"Why there?"

"He read about it in a brochure, I guess."

"Where'd he get the brochure?"

"Oh, come on."

McGuire smiled, giving it up. "Where'd you drop him?"

"All the way at the end, La Puntilla, this *pupusería* overlooking the estuary. He said he wanted some local fare then he'd walk around, see if he could book a room in a boarder house."

"He didn't have reservations anywhere?"

"I get the feeling Phil's pretty much a spur-of-the-moment kinda guy."

"He gave Immigration your name and number for contact information."

They're thorough, Jude thought. And quick. He shrugged. "I'm the only person he knows down here."

"Except Bill Malvasio."

Okay, Jude thought. Here we go. "Bill Malvasio's down here— you know that for a fact?"

"No." McGuire wiped at a shimmer of sweat pooling in the hollow of his temple. "But you do."

Jude caught his reaction too late, which was unfortunate because McGuire was bluffing. The tip-off was the "No."

"I haven't seen Bill Malvasio in ten years, at least. That was back in Chicago."

McGuire leaned in a little bit more. "You sure about that?"

"Oh, yeah." Jude's heart thumped. "Real sure."

Sanborn said, "I wonder if Strock would back you up."

"Oh, get serious. What, you think I dropped Strock off with Malvasio? Listen to me—Phil made it real clear, if he saw Malvasio down here or anywhere else, he'd kill him."

Axel blanched at that, then traded glances with Fitz.

Sanborn said, "Some vacation. A little surf, a little sun, kill Bill."

"Regardless," Jude said, "it's got nothing to do with me."

"Strock brought Malvasio up," McGuire said. "That's interesting. What else did he say?"

"He told me my dad saved his life once, he's grateful."

"Here's an idea," Sanborn said. "Let's drive over to La Puntilla. Maybe this Strock guy's checked in somewhere and we can sit down with a beer and straighten all this out."

"What's to straighten out?"

"If you don't mind . . ." Axel sat forward in his chair and stuck out his hand, as though venturing into a verbal cross fire. "I have to interject here that I was under the impression this was entirely routine. It's grown adversarial for reasons which escape me since this all seems like a lot of fret and fume—over what? A man's vacation. Or something that happened ages ago." He turned to Jude. "Am I getting that right?"

Jude nodded. "Ten years."

Axel turned to McGuire. "You told me this had to do with a woman found dead—today—along the Río Jiboa."

In the corner of his eye, Jude caught Mr. Gray Eyes staring. Sensing a little more diversion might be wise, he said, "You know, I'm sorry, maybe you said your name, but I'm having trouble remembering it right now."

The man said nothing. McGuire spoke for him. "This is Al Lazarek. He works at the embassy." Like it was one of life's misfortunes. "Back to Malvasio—"

"Works at the embassy," Jude said. "What, he's the astrologer?"

"He works for ODIC. How—"

"So you're the elusive Alan Lazarek." Axel swung toward the man. "I was beginning to think you were a myth. Weren't you and I supposed to connect at some point?"

"He's not here to answer questions," Sanborn said, trying to keep things on track.

"From appearances," Axel sniffed, "he's not here to do much of anything."

Jude felt, finally, enough smoke was in the air. "Look. Let's get this over with. I have no idea where Malvasio is. As for Strock, go to La Puntilla, track him down, be my guest. But don't be surprised if he's hard to find, because I get the sense he wants to get lost for a while."

Sanborn wasn't having it. "Explain that."

"He's crippled and out of work, lives in a hellhole and has a little girl he adores but can't see because the mother won't let him. Maybe there's more, I don't know—he didn't share, I didn't probe, but one glance tells you a vacation's long overdue. Anything else about him or Malvasio are secrets to me, and I hope they stay that way. I've done my good deed, I'm back on duty tomorrow, and my business is here." Jude looked from face to face, checking in. "As for this other thing, the dead woman, I was on my way back from dropping Strock off when I saw Bert Waxman near the Río Jiboa bridge. I know him, Waxman, we've chatted now and again, nothing deep, and though I don't get along with the Guatemalan woman he hangs around with—"

"What about his photographer?" Sanborn was tugging at his ear again. "The ex-con."

"More importantly," McGuire said, "what about Truco Valdez?" From his shirt pocket he withdrew a sheet of paper folded into squares. He shook it open and handed it to Jude. "That face look familiar?"

It was an article under Waxman's byline, printed off the Internet, titled, *Double Bind: Salvadoran Gang Members Learn Leaving the Life Links Them to Terrorists*. A head shot of Truco led off the piece, with Abatangelo getting the photo attribution.

"I doubt I've said five words to either guy," Jude said. "Him or the photographer, I mean." He went to hand the article back.

Fitz said, "I'd like to see that," and took it from Jude's hand.

"But you recognize him," McGuire said to Jude.

"Sure."

"He was the man who ran away with the camera at the Río Jiboa."

"I think so. Yeah. The only thing I know about him is that he left the life behind. Or so I was told."

McGuire steepled his hands. "We hear his group, La Tregua, is just a front. The *mareros* join so they can tell the judges they're dropping the flag, try to beat the two-to-five they're looking at under La Mano Dura. But they're banged up bad as ever."

Jude vaguely remembered hearing something along those lines, but saw little point in sharing that with McGuire. "News to me."

"You sure? What does Waxman say about it?"

"Ask him. Only person I've spoken with about this Truco guy is an anthropologist who meets up with that crowd from time to time. Her name's Eileen Browning. We didn't say much but, yeah, we talked." Emphasis past tense, Jude thought. Because, you know, I'm a punk.

McGuire said, "How, exactly, did the discussion turn to Truco Valdez?"

"Night before I left, ten days ago, Truco and another *marero* named Jaime something-or-other—"

"Jaime Lacayo," Fitz said. "He's mentioned here too." His voice sounded vaguely relieved as he handed the article back. He refused to look at Jude, though. McGuire folded the paper up and put it back in his pocket.

"Those two," Jude said, "Truco and Jaime, they were down at the beach with Waxman, his photographer, the Guatemalan woman, and this anthropologist I mentioned, Eileen. The religious guy, Jaime, was all Bible this and Jesus that but Truco wasn't buying. I seem to remember Truco bitching about how his group—what was the name again?"

"La Tregua," McGuire said. It meant *truce*.

"About how the U.S. had designated La Tregua a terrorist front or some such, like that article says. They can't get money sent from the States to help with outreach down here."

"Outreach." Sanborn chuckled acidly. "That's poignant. I've got some vic pics on my laptop in the car, you wanna see some fucking outreach. What is it about these clowns and cutting off heads?"

"You think Truco Valdez had something to do with the woman they found under the bridge?"

"Why else run off with the camera?"

"Because he thought the soldiers were going to make off with it."

"It's evidence. Why shouldn't they take it?"

Don't get sucked into this, Jude thought. "Look, whatever, my point is I barely spoke to the guy, okay? And if Eileen knows him any better, you'll have to ask her about it." He waited, hoping someone might fill in the gap, mention where Eileen had gone to. Everybody just sat there, though, waiting him out. "Anyway, back to the Río Jiboa thing, I saw Waxman and the others by the road, the soldiers, the PNC. I stopped because I was curious."

McGuire mindlessly fussed with his wedding band, a nervous tic. "Where's Truco Valdez now?"

"You tell me. My two cents? Getting some pictures developed."

Finally, Lazarek said something: "You think this is funny?" His voice was flat but his neck muscles corded. "Terrorist gangs are a cancer down here. And these phony outreach groups, it's all a game. Like everybody's back in the school yard, as long as they're touching home base they can't get tagged. One gets a little sick of it, to be honest. Meanwhile money sails down here from the States, most of it dirty, some of it collected from dumb clucks who think these thugs are a charity. It buys guns, drugs, influence—"

Axel broke in: "And that, if I may, relates how, exactly, to your brief with ODIC?"

Lazarek shot him a look. "Business people say the key thing they consider before setting up shop down here is how stable the government is. And crime, especially gang crime, is destabilizing. You think I'm wrong, check out what's going on in Nicaragua, Honduras,

Brazil. And the punks are getting help. Venezuela's just ordered three hundred thousand AK-47s from Russia—for an army of sixty-two thousand men."

Axel waved that off. "Don't mistake this with support for Chávez, but only the whole world knows he thinks we're going to invade."

"Because he's psychotic. Three guesses where those guns end up. And if that's not enough to get your attention, we've actionable intelligence that al Qaeda cells are linking up with the *salvatruchos* to sneak operatives across the border into the States."

"I thought Interpol debunked that," Axel said.

"Interpol doesn't know its ass from a handbag. The point is we've spent a long time and millions of dollars and spilled blood getting this country where it is today. We're not going to see that undone by the *mareros* or any of their ilk, including the political hacks who kiss up to them."

He meant the FMLN but only Jude was listening: Axel's eyes had glazed over. McGuire shrank into his own world. Even Sanborn looked far away, despite the fact Lazarek had parroted his line. It was well known the bureau and the intelligence community despised each other, even when they shared goals, or especially then. And Lazarek could claim he worked with ODIC all night—he was a spook.

Jude turned back to McGuire. "I've got no clue where Truco Valdez ran off to. It happened real quick, the camera thing. I'd just walked up to see what was going on. Again, I was curious." He scratched his arm. "Which reminds me—any idea who the murdered woman was?"

It seemed like a cue. McGuire and Sanborn traded glances, then rose to their feet. "What we're told," McGuire said, "is she was a prostitute from Usulután, got reported missing a few days ago."

He was too smart to lie so badly. *What we're told?* Then an explanation that came out like the world's most contrived anticlimax. Meanwhile both he and Sanborn avoided Lazarek's stare like it gave them hives. Jude wondered at all that but not to the point he intended to say anything. It looked like they were ready to go. Please, he thought, do.

Apparently, though, Fitz caught something off as well. "Who told you this? About the woman, I mean."

Lazarek finally got up from his chair. "I'd say we're done here." He strode past McGuire and Sanborn toward the door. McGuire said, "Thanks for your time," then headed out too. Sanborn trailed after him, leaving behind a lingering whiff of his vinegary cologne.

Once the door closed behind them, Axel's eyes whipsawed between Fitz and Jude. "What did I just miss?"

22

DILLAHUNT, PAHLAVI, AND THE OTHER EPs WERE WRAPPING UP THEIR dinners as Jude, Axel, and Fitz finally sat down to theirs, Jolanda appearing promptly with her tureen of *gallo en chicha* to ladle out portions. Despite the almost hallucinatory aroma steaming up from the broth of corn brew, an uneasy silence lingered over the table, remaining even as the others peeled away to pursue their evenings. Axel tried once or twice to enliven the table with a little diversionary chat between spoonfuls, but Jude could muster little more than one-word responses and compulsory nods, at one point staring into his bowl with an eerie sense of comradery with his meal—he felt like he'd barely fended off something that thought he was food. Meanwhile, across the table, Fitz brooded, lost in thought.

In between his mindless assents to Axel's chatter, Jude tried to piece together the most likely sequence of events: his getting identified with Waxman and the others at the Río Jiboa; a call to the embassy, routed to McGuire, the on-site American whose brief was gangs; discussion of possible links between Jude and Truco Valdez; a little background, including a call to the Delegado de Inmigración; discovery of Jude's entry this morning with Strock; a little more background; discovery of the Laugh Master connection. Bingo. Something to pry Jude open—a bluff, basically—a wedge to get him to say all he knew about the *mareros* in his life. Which, of course, was next to nothing. And that meant if they'd known anything more about his contacts with Malvasio, up to and including today, the scene at the restaurant in San Marcelino, they would have brought it up. Why hold it back? Why hold back anything on that front—Malvasio's life here the past ten years, the people he was in with, the things he did for them? If there was anything damning in all that, they'd hardly keep it to themselves—they would have used it to impress him with their knowledge, embarrass him in front of Axel and Fitz, shame him into talking. But none of that happened. They had nothing more to say about Malvasio than I did about Truco, he thought, and that's why they bagged it up so quickly at the end. He told himself to relax. About everything.

Finally, Jolanda came to collect dishes. Getting up from the table, Fitz said, "I'd like both of you to join me in my room for a moment, if you would."

Fitz's bedroom doubled as his office and epitomized order—his desktop a shrine, his bed a tomb. Even the ceiling fan hummed with unnerving perfection. Closing the door, he turned to Jude. "The thing McGuire brought up about your father—what was all that about?"

Jude had hoped they were done with this. "It's ancient history, Fitz."

"There's nothing in your personnel file about it."

"Why should there be? The man's dead. Has been for ten years."

Fitz tucked his hands in his armpits—to hide their shaking, Jude supposed.

"He was a crooked cop?"

"Fitz, whoa. This is wrong."

"That's a material omission. Plus this new thing with his old pals, accomplices, cellies for all I know. Not to mention these people your girlfriend bangs around with—"

"Excuse me—bangs?"

"Girlfriend?" Axel's first contribution. He seemed oddly pleased.

"I haven't seen her, Fitz, since the night you gave me crap about it. I've been gone, right? Just got back, right? What's this about?"

Fitz looked off, thinking. Behind him, the screen saver on his laptop showed a pixilated sunrise morphing into a fetus dissolving into the Milky Way. "You've made some interesting acquaintances."

"Well, Fitz, your company, it's riveting, no argument there. But variety, the spice of life—you following me here?"

"You think this is all some kind of joke, it'll all blow over. But I've gotta call Jim."

He meant Jim Leonhard, the man who'd first recruited Jude at Los Rinconcitos in the Zona Rosa. He supervised the region now.

"Look, Fitz, the gas pressure on this is kinda needling into the red for no good reason, don't you think?"

Axel reached out and touched Fitz's arm. "I have to agree with Jude on this, Michael. Your reaction seems a little out of proportion for such small beer. He hasn't done anything to jeopardize me, that's for sure, and that's the only consideration I can see meaning much of anything."

"It's not about that."

"Yes, I realize." Axel's blue eyes warmed. "That's the troubling part. Whatever it's 'about' seems oddly personal, if I may be so blunt, and I think you should stop for a moment and consider that." He let go of Fitz's arm. "Beyond which, I've just spent ten days with Jude's replacement and God save me from another stretch of time outside an alligator farm in such company."

It was astonishing, the transformation—like that, Fitz was groveling. "Look, I realize Bauserman's got some rough edges—"

Axel turned to Jude. "Do you know what this imbecile who replaced you did? We have, in Jolanda, quite possibly the best cook

I've ever known outside my Swedish grandmother. Then this moron shows up with a ten-pound bag of grits. He tells her he wants a bowl for breakfast every day, plus three eggs over easy—'runny as cum,' he says. I wish I was making that up. Of course, Jolanda indulged the idiot, and you should have seen her, mixing that slop. She said it looked like something she'd feed her parrot." Axel turned back to Fitz. "The man doesn't know the difference between an honest-to-God thought and raw mental sewage. Nor does he know when—or perhaps even how—to shut up. He ought to be running a Ferris wheel. So he can die a happy man, peering up girls' skirts."

Fitz was backpedaling mentally, looking for something to say but apparently finding only empty space where the words should have been.

"I have been looking forward to Jude's return," Axel continued, "because he's conscientious and smart. I feel safe with him and, when we get the opportunity to drop our guard at day's end, he's a pleasure to visit with. And, since I'd say my opinion on this matter should carry some weight, I'm going to ask that you let go of whatever it is that's got you feeling so shirty and we'll all get back to our day-to-day routines. Jude, welcome back. Michael, I appreciate your hearing me out." Axel reached out for the shoulders of both younger men and gave them a fatherly squeeze, then a glint of mischief twinkled in his eye. He smiled like the best part had finally come. "Now, Jude, let's hear a little more about this anthropologist of yours."

Jude blushed before he could catch himself.

"I mean," Axel prompted, "I'm assuming from the way you looked when you talked about her that you're somewhat fond of her?"

Fitz cut in. "Maybe you guys can double-date. How swell."

The scorn in Fitz's voice caught Jude off guard, then something occurred to him, a sudden insight long overdue—about Fitz, his work in the Kuwaiti minefields. All that carnage, not just humans but animals, too—dogs, camels, sheep, ripped into pieces alongside the Iraqi war dead, rotting black under the desert sun. The flies, the stench, the sweaty tedium—then a coworker blown to screaming meat before your eyes. All that lying in wait whenever you touched someone. And Fitz resented it, resented the world's indifference and his pitiless, disgusting thoughts, resented the women he'd never love and the men who would love them instead.

Beyond that, though, Jude was lost. "I'm not following."

"No, of course you're not," Axel said, avoiding Fitz's gaze and apparently immune to his derision. "There's been no time to tell you. It happened while you were away." He looked suddenly years younger. "I've met someone."

STROCK HAD DISCOVERED THERE WAS, INDEED, BEER IN THE FRIDGE. A mere six-pack, though—he'd rationed himself. With sundown, he popped open his third. It was a brand called Bahía, bright and yeasty with a gassy head. One must make do, he thought, hobbling into the dining room.

A soft light lingered along the dingy walls, shadows swelling in the corners. Clara sat in one of the rough wood chairs, wearing a distant smile. Shoes on the floor, hands in her lap—she looked like a daydreaming nun.

Turning her glance toward Strock in the doorway, she tucked a strand of hair behind her ear. "*Hola, Señor Feel.*"

She'd made him two meals so far, a lunch of thick pancake-like tortillas filled with cheese that she called *pupusas,* served with warm salsa and a kind of pickled slaw, and a dinner of grilled shrimp with peppers and fresh-squeezed lime, followed by slices of a tart pink-meated fruit she called *guanabana*. A man could get used to this, he thought, except the isolation was taking a toll. He was used to solitude—how often had he holed up alone in his apartment, days at a time, ignoring Dixie's knock?—but this was different. So far from anything familiar to anchor him, no one to talk to beyond the clum-siest Spanglish, no TV to fake companionship, only three more beers. If somebody didn't show up first thing the next morning, he'd get on the horn to Jude just to milk him for conversation.

He ventured outside to flex his knee. It throbbed a little but the milky heat had limbered it up some, good news on that front at least. Overhead, the blue of the sky had mellowed with dusk. The wind rustled through the palm fronds, the sun-salt tang of the ocean riding the heat, and the surf thundered gently beyond the wall, modulating strong and soft in endless random surges. It made him think of Florida. Like anybody who'd endured a Chicago winter, he'd often dreamed of retiring near a beach.

Suddenly, he felt Clara at his side. In that soft, birdlike voice of hers, she said, *"Camino contigo."*

What's it going to take for her to realize I haven't a clue what she's saying, Strock wondered, but she gestured for him to follow her toward the gate. We're walking somewhere, he realized. Well, fine. Something to do.

They headed toward the windswept beach and turned east, walking with the surf to their right. Crimson swirls of feathery cloud lingered above the glassy ocean. Clara kept a modest gait, pausing so Strock could catch up every now and then, their progress slow, the sand deep and soft. She walked with her arms folded, her chin high, the wind fanning her black hair in every direction at once. She looked less homely in the fading light.

Suddenly, it dawned on him that this was a trap. She was leading him out of the house, away from where he had a weapon. She'd step away suddenly, the men would appear from beyond the trees.

He stopped, to see if she stopped with him or just kept walking. That would tell him, he thought, just as she paused and turned back. Her eyes in the blustery twilight seemed so guileless and free of menace he felt ashamed—and yet he'd suffered morbid fantasies all day. It was hard, alone in a strange place, not to feel the paranoia worming away. I'm sorry, he thought, smiling apologetically. She smiled back. They resumed walking.

Finally, about a hundred yards along, she stopped and faced a break in the line of palms. In the dimness, Strock saw within a clearing the ruins of a large, plain house—the roof gone now, walls crumbling, windows shattered. Clara stared at it for several seconds, gripping her hair in a fist, then began to speak. Her words came out in a soft plaintive drone and she gestured along with her story, so Strock could try to follow. From what he could tell, the house had been full of people once, children perhaps, a lot of activity, coming and going, good and bad—opposites, of some kind, or turmoil. No. A storm—Strock remembered Jude mentioning Hurricane Mitch, pointing out the destruction as they'd boated deeper into the mangroves. The winds tore the big house to shreds, Clara seemed to be saying, miraculously leaving the smaller house down the beach untouched. Many of the children had died. That, at least, was what Strock made of the pantomime. He realized she could just as readily be telling him that one night a horde of banshees had howled down from the sky to ransack the house and drive out the merry band of circus midgets who'd taken shelter there. He liked that version, actually.

Clara turned away from the house, finally, with a shy look of heartbreak, and silently headed back the way they'd come. Strock took one last look at the ruins, gripped his cane, and followed behind.

By the time they were back inside, he was wringing wet from the exertion. Strange, he thought, how even sunset and the ocean wind didn't cool things much. He thumped back to his room, gripped by a sudden need to lie down. His thoughts squalled, he felt dizzy and weak and closed his eyes.

When he opened them again, he saw Clara's silhouette in the doorway. At last, he thought, here comes that good thing. She was holding a bowl, though, and from clear across the room he could smell the rough tang of wood alcohol. She padded forward and knelt beside his bed. First soaking a cloth in the spiked water, then wringing it out, she began a sponge bath—gently mopping his brow, wiping his face and neck and throat, his arms and hands, his feet. Her touch was intimate but not erotic and she avoided his glance, removing any hint of seduction—on top of which the smell of the alcohol gave the procedure a distinctly medicinal taint. More peculiar than that, though, was his own lack of arousal. The heat, maybe, or his spinning head. He considered testing it, removing his shirt to see where that might lead. When he reached for the first button, though, she rose, whispered something that sounded prim, and turned to go, leaving the bowl and cloth behind so he could finish by himself.

23

MALVASIO STOOD IN A DIRT-FLOORED HUT ON THE EDGE OF THE mangrove swamp, watching a *bruja* stir her decoction of *espino ruco* and *tolu balsa* in a tin pot over a wood fire. The grimy cowboy with his broken nose and the fork in his throat sat on a stool, awaiting her care.

The *bruja* wore a T-shirt and jeans and a Red Sox cap over short black hair that looked like she cut it with a pocketknife, her skin the color of tree bark and her face gnarled up and sunken from age and long-lost teeth. Her limbs were as thin and knobby as kindling. She claimed to be from Izalco—to Salvadoran witches what Paris is to chefs—but Malvasio suspected that was just marketing. Waving one skeletal hand dreamily in the air, she stirred her repulsive goop with the other and murmured a chant in a language Malvasio presumed to be a dialect of Nahuatl. Her eyes rolled back in her head at times, a great trick. She was laying it on.

People called her La Ciguanaba, which meant "river woman" and referred to a folklore creature similar to Medusa—a woman who seems beautiful from a distance, washing her hair by the side of a stream, until you venture too close, at which point she lifts her head and exposes a face so unspeakably hideous it unhinges your mind. Malvasio simply called her *señora* and she seemed okay with that.

As for the cowboy, the fork in his throat was held fast with a swath of cellophane Malvasio had applied at the restaurant in San Marcelino. By some bizarre chance he'd missed the carotid artery— otherwise the guy would be dead already—and the cellophane wrap had stopped the external bleeding and had helped seal the cowboy's trachea so he could breathe, which he did through his mouth, his nose being flat as a sponge. The internal bleeding, though, remained unchecked and there was no telling what the damage was there— not without getting the guy to a proper clinic, which wasn't going to happen.

The cowboy coughed a lot, not just from the smoke of the *bruja*'s fire and the woody, putrid stench of her folksy medicinal stew but from the blood bubbling in his throat and trickling down his wind-pipe into his lungs. His eyes still flared with panic but he was woozy, fighting unconsciousness, so his terror had a helpless, soulful quality and it almost made Malvasio pity him.

The cowboy's sidekick hunched in the doorway, clutching a bot-tle of La Tenzuda and murmuring prayers and incantations and as-surances that it would all be fine, all of it: *"Todo, chero, todo."* He had fifty dollars in his pocket, his payoff from Malvasio, with promise of another fifty on the back end. He could afford to be nice.

The levels we sink to, Malvasio thought, meaning not just the sidekick but himself.

When he replayed the scene at the restaurant in his head, he could pinpoint the spot when he should have said: *Whoa, horsey.* But something about Ray's kid, the backwash of feeling that sludged up from nowhere and the righteous Tom Sawyer indignation the kid gave off like a smell, it just galled him. You think you know your-self, you've got your weaknesses cataloged, you're in charge of your own mind—but then something sneaks under the skin and you're watching yourself like it's somebody else and by the time you get a grip, the thing is done. The guy's stabbed—by you—with a fork. Because you wanted to say: *I'll tell you a real story now about your old man, you snotty little prick, about the time he slammed his nightstick into his whore girlfriend's throat because she mocked his meat, called him Sergeant McMannish.* That was the subtext, as they say, but you kept that to yourself and resorted to a little show-and-tell instead. And the next thing you know, you're wrapping the guy's neck in cellophane and telling the cook and the waiters to stay cool, pretend nothing happened, then you're paying off the cowboy's pal to keep him quiet and so he'll help you get the guy out of there and into the van, and then you're on the edge of a swamp full of pelicans and four-eyed fish, standing in the foul, airless hut of some goofball Indian witch and you're thinking: This is why your old man handed you a hundred bucks when you graduated from high school, saying, *I'm tired of your mouth. Tired of your stealing from your mother and me. Pack up and get out.*

It wasn't like he didn't have enough to worry about already. The woman found dead beneath the Río Jiboa bridge, for example. She was the *campesina* who'd been crowing to anyone who'd listen about how the wells south of San Bartolo Oriente had gone bad. The authorities didn't know that as yet, and if all went well, they never would, but Malvasio had confirmed it in a flurry of cell phone calls while waiting for Jude at the restaurant in San Marcelino. The *veteranos* he'd hired to deal with the woman had lied about where and how they'd disposed of the body. In a drunken, lazy bit of improvisation, they'd driven not all the way to the western hinterlands but had stopped midway at the Río Jiboa bridge. There, using an old bayonet, they'd cut off the woman's head, tossed it over in one direction, and heaved her naked body another.

Why did they lie? The same reasons anybody lies, he thought: To cover their sloppy, indifferent hides. To mock me, show me up, maintain a little ass-backward dignity. For the sheer hell of it. Someday they'd pay for their insolence, of course, but that wasn't topping his list of concerns right this minute.

The fact the body'd been found was a problem. Hector had to line up a ringer to misidentify it now, claim it belonged to a street-walker from Usulután who'd gone missing last week (and who in truth had returned home to Nicaragua, where she'd stay if she was smart). A plan to have the dead woman's remains cremated as soon as possible had to be put in place, and Ovidio would track the investigation inside the PNC, let the colonel know if anything went screwy. It wasn't effort anyone had expected, and the resentment ran high. The job was Malvasio's and he was expected to do it well, without this need for cleanup on the back end. So okay, he thought, I'll take the heat for that. But given where things stood, it would still, more likely than not, work out just dandy. Only a matter of time before the whole thing blew over, right? The way killings do here.

But there was another complication. It wasn't just the PNC at the scene. The military had shown up at the bridge for some reason, even taking the lead in the hunt for the woman's remains. Malvasio had no idea as yet what to make of that. He tried to tell himself it was no big thing, the army barged into everything now, whether they were welcome or not. It could be dealt with, let the colonel earn his cut. But he still had a bad feeling. Wherever the army showed up, the Americans tended to follow. And it was the Americans he had to worry about.

THE *BRUJA* STOPPED HER MURMURINGS AND REACHED UP TO THE cowboy's throat, picking at the cellophane so she could unravel it. The cowboy's eyes swelled from terror but she cooed to him in soothing, toothless whispers. Malvasio hated to think what her breath smelled like.

The cowboy sat still while she finally peeled away the first layer of cellophane, tugging hard now and then, her arm circling his head as the stuff unraveled. Once she had it all stripped away, she balled it up and tossed it on the fire. The filmy strand, laced with blood, flamed blue and yellow and hissed as it burned.

She spooned a little of her pulpy concoction onto a square of cloth, puckered her lips, and blew to cool it off, then reached up and without warning grabbed the fork and yanked it from the cowboy's throat. Quickly, she squeezed the rank poultice against the wound and counted in a whisper to three, then nine, then thirteen—magical numbers. The cowboy's eyes ballooned and he made to scream, but only a hissing, gargley rasp came out, followed by coughing sobs. Malvasio supposed the man finally realized he was going to die and there were no prayers or magic tricks or witchy goo that would change that.

Malvasio made for the door of the hut and gestured for the cowboy's sidekick to follow.

Outside, the air was just as thick and hot but it felt like a godsend to be out of the smoke. His clothes felt tacky against his skin, soaked through with sweat.

The clearing outside the *bruja*'s hut was lit by a kerosene lamp hung from a pole. In its hazy, flickering light the sidekick threw back another mouthful of La Tenzuda, his face a mask of shadows. Staring up at the night sky briefly, then closing his eyes, he wailed, as though the words were lyrics to a tuneless song, *"Lo siento, chero. Lo siento."*

I'm sorry, my friend. I'm sorry.

He lowered his head and put his face in his hands and wept miserably and dishonestly, and Malvasio decided right then not to wait. He'd planned to pay the guy the other fifty bucks first and let him at least count it—it seemed right, letting him feel happy—but there'd be no better chance than this, so he reached inside his shirt, pulled the .380 from under his belt, placed it in the hollow where spine meets skull, and fired. The bullet snapped the man's spinal cord and he dropped like an empty coat.

Malvasio returned to the hut, where the *bruja* was drinking from a warm bottle of beer, already aware from the sound of the shot that her party was over. The cowboy had stopped weeping. He just stared, like he'd see them all again in hell, as Malvasio pressed the pistol barrel to the bridge of his shapeless nose and pulled the trigger. The cowboy's head lurched back in a thin cloud of blood and he crumpled off the stool, flailing, twitching. Malvasio fired an insurance round into the base of the skull, same spot as for the first guy, then put the gun away and turned to the *bruja,* saying he needed her help.

HE'D DONE THE OLD WOMAN A FAVOR ONCE, SCARING OFF ONE OF THE young, snotty doctors from the rural *clínica popular* who'd wanted to shut her down. None of his kind came out here anymore. The old woman's assistance with the cowboy had been payback for that service. She didn't bat an eye when the price ticked up a bit. As for the violence, Malvasio assumed that, like a lot of *indígenas,* she interpreted the cruelty of life as God's way of reminding you He existed.

They rowed out into the estuary in an aluminum *cayuca,* the body of the cowboy huddled between them under a tarp. It would take two trips to get rid of the bodies; the tiny boat would get swamped if they tried to carry both at once.

Malvasio let the *bruja* guide them in the darkness into a narrow inlet carving a path through the mangrove forest. About fifty yards in she stopped rowing and gestured for Malvasio to hold up as well. She was smoking a Marlboro and her ash glowed red as she inhaled, burnishing her shrunken face. The *cayuca* thudded against the slick tangled roots and she turned around, drew the tarp off the cowboy's body, and clambered out of the boat.

She perched on the tree root and held the gunnel with her feet, to keep the boat from tipping over as Malvasio reached under the cowboy's body, hefted him up, and dropped him into the black water. The cowboy sank with a *ploosh* then bobbed back up again and half floated beside the *cayuca,* air pockets ballooning his shirt. Malvasio shoved the drifting body away with his oar as the *bruja* clambered back into the boat. They paddled it backward into the estuary, then retraced their way to the old woman's hut.

The procedure got repeated with the sidekick but he got dumped in a different part of the swamp. Sooner or later the bodies, in whatever stage of decay by then, would get found by fishermen but the fishermen were Indians. They knew better than to get involved with the law, even with the best of intentions.

Back again at the *bruja*'s hut, Malvasio counted out the hundred dollars he'd promised to the sidekick, having retrieved the first fifty from the dead man's clothes. One thing he'd learned in this place, the desperately poor were no different from the miserly rich in one way at least—only money got trusted. The old woman rolled up hers and stuck it in her pocket, then lit up another Marlboro and said in Spanish, not Nahuatl, *"El camarón que se duerme, se lo lleva corriente."* It was a local saying, meant to chide the lazy: The shrimp that sleeps gets carried away by the current. She dropped her chin and cackled, the sound clenched and wheezy, a toothless smoker's hack, reminding Malvasio he was dealing with the woman they called La Ciguanaba. He looked away.

24

JUDE TRUDGED DOWN THE WINDING PATH OF SAND FROM HORIZON House to the beach, the hint of an unseasonal storm carrying a humid, metallic scent inland. The cloud front was shallow and narrow, only the Costa del Bálsamo would get hit, if the storm landed at all. To the east, toward the Costa del Sol and the Estero de Jaltepeque beyond, the sky remained clear.

He considered phoning the beach house just to check in, ask the *servienta*, Clara, how Strock was holding up—maybe speak to the Candyman himself. It might be a good idea to get our stories straight, he thought. Almost instantly he talked himself out of it. He remained convinced that McGuire and Sanborn's interest in Malvasio was nothing but a ploy, which meant Strock was unlikely to face scrutiny himself. Besides, there was no way they'd find him, not out where he was. And by tomorrow he'd get picked up by whomever and mosey along to the coffee plantation to begin work—assuming, of course, Malvasio hadn't lied about that. Which brought up the real reason Jude didn't call: He wanted nothing to do with either man anymore, wanted the whole sorry episode behind him. If down the road Strock wound up in a bind, got slammed into a chair and told to talk and then handed up Jude's name on whatever pretext, Jude would deny it all and trust his credibility would win out. Strock just tagged along, after I found him on his knees outside a strip club in East Chicago. I'd tracked him down to check in on him as a favor to my mother. Ask her if you don't believe me, assuming she'll give you the time of day.

In the meantime he wanted to get off alone, swim a little, think. He seemed to be the only one at Horizon House, especially after dark, willing to forgo the pool and brave the rocky beach, the notorious undertow, the occasional slithery critter—not that he was complaining. Tonight in particular he wanted solitude.

As he broke into the clearing he found dark-skinned Erika closing up her *comedor* for the night. Using a damp towel, she wiped a sheen of sweat from her face, then lifted the braided rope of her hair and did her neck. Her ten-year-old daughter sat on a rock feeding leftover rice to a famished pup, while a lone customer lingered inside the thatched *glorieta,* lit up like a prisoner by the single bare bulb.

It was Waxman.

Jude felt his pulse quicken, and he wondered where the others might be. The thought Eileen might be with them sent a little shock of longing through him, followed instantly by regret, then finally shame, as he tried to figure out what Waxman was doing there. The *efemelenista* professor, he supposed, the one who had a house here at El Dorado Mar, he must have made some calls, contacted some friends with clout, and asked them to step in, make noise. Maybe they just paid somebody off. Regardless, there Waxman sat, impossible to avoid.

The reporter had bathed and changed, his russet hair darkly wet as he hunched over a Pilsener that seemed more an object of contemplation than last call. Jude walked up quietly and took a seat. Lifting his glance to see who it was, Waxman froze.

Jude said, "I was afraid you . . ." That was as far as he could get.

Waxman glanced away. In a tone that managed to be both snide and forgiving, he said, "It's all right. Captain Dominguez conducted himself with exemplary decorum."

"He let me go because he knew I was going to be questioned here. A little while ago, the FBI and some guy from ODIC."

That piqued Waxman's curiosity. "They questioned you here?"

"We keep the embassy informed about where our people are at. It's never hard to find us. Did they come see you?"

Waxman smiled abstractedly and finger-combed his hair. Shadows played across his face as the wind blew the bare bulb overhead. "Let's just say I'm not as fastidious about keeping the embassy informed of my whereabouts. Besides, I've nothing to tell them I haven't already told the locals, and only an idiot answers the same questions twice."

Jude could almost hear the doubts crawling around inside the reporter's head. About me, he thought. "They wanted to know where Truco was. I told them I had no clue. They have a serious hard-on for that guy."

"Yes, I'm aware of that. Truco Valdez, secret terrorist. Secret even to himself." Waxman thumbed a grain of sand from the lip of his beer bottle. "They scream about the evils of gangs, then make it impossible for anyone to leave. You have to give the old boys credit—they are the most ingenious psychotics on the block."

"They were interested in your photographer, too. Abatangelo."

"If they have any questions for Dan, they'd better hurry. He's on his way to the airport this minute. Has a pair of soldiers for company, to make sure he doesn't tarry. Same with Aleris. They're letting me stay, for now, a friend at *El Diario de Hoy* intervened. Never plays well, kicking journalists out of the country." With that, Waxman finally took a sip of his beer.

"They wondered what I knew about him. Abatangelo. Which is nothing. I told them that. They didn't ask me about Aleris."

Waxman perched his chin atop the bottle and blinked his eyes, bringing to mind a sunning lizard.

Jude said, "Why do they have to leave?"

"Their kind are unwelcome here." Waxman shook off his pose. "Like the contingent of Lutherans the government held at the airport last week and accused of coming down to influence the elections." He grinned mordantly then took another, lustier swig. "Paranoia strikes deep. Into your life it will creep."

"The FBI agents, they said they'd been told the woman whose body was found along the Río Jiboa was a prostitute from Usulután. Somebody reported her missing a few days ago."

Waxman uttered a sad, breathy little laugh. "Interesting."

"That's not true?"

"I didn't say it was untrue. I said it was interesting."

Jude waited for Waxman to elaborate but he didn't. It seemed time for the question he'd been itching to ask all along. "I went to Eileen's place in La Perla. She's packed up and gone. Any idea where she went?"

Waxman faced Jude fully then, regarding him like he was hopelessly thick-headed. "You might wish to consider the general mood here. The election results have caused considerable bad feeling."

"And that's got what to do with where Eileen is?"

Waxman's smile suggested he knew something he wasn't ready to share. "Jude, you seem like a reasonably decent guy. And Axel, the man you're working for, is the kind of American I'd like to see more of down here, all things considered, though I'm not sure the people who hired him feel the same way. I mean, ODIC's involved, what does that tell you?"

It had been a long, wretched day. Jude was losing track of where all this was going. "I don't know. You tell me."

"ODIC steps in when the social or environmental costs of a project make it unpalatable to the World Bank or U.S. Ex-Im—and God knows they've hardly been squeamish when it comes to screwing the third world. That's changing, some say. We'll see. I'm not holding my breath. But ODIC remains in a class by itself. It provides the back channel the government wants in the event something really, truly, conspicuously stinks. The suits can claim the World Bank's guidelines are being followed, it isn't involved and neither is U.S. Ex-Im, which will appease most of the know-nothings and go-alongs who work that beat. Then Mister Whiskers'll slip the money through ODIC and life goes on. Axel stands out for that reason. It doesn't fit, his being mixed up with Estrella."

Jude realized finally that Waxman might be fishing. That seemed to present an opportunity—a little give-and-take, with Eileen's whereabouts up for trade. "Axel had some words for the guy from ODIC who showed up. Tonight, I mean. His name was Lazarek."

"Al Lazarek," Waxman said.

"You know him?"

Waxman shrugged. "His connections with the world of international finance strike me as, how shall I put this, a bit improvisational."

"He looked like a spook."

"Imagine that."

"Meaning?"

"Just the usual rumors: He worked black ops for the crazies in the basement during the Reagan years, he's with Joint Special Operations Command." Waxman shrugged. "Could be rubbish. Those kinds of things are almost impossible to fact-check."

"What would a guy like that be doing working for ODIC?"

Waxman chuckled. "Surely, Jude, you've heard of economic hit men and the military-industrial circle jerk. They're among our favorite folktales." He downed the last of his beer.

That kills tit-for-tat, Jude thought. Time for flattery. "I appreciate what you said about Axel. I feel lucky to work for him."

Waxman lifted his eyes to the wind-racked palms, withdrawing behind an indulgent smile. "Yes, Jude, but really. If Estrella or its American investors or ODIC weary of Axel's contrarian instincts, they'll cut him loose and hire someone who knows how to toe the company line. That isn't true of you. You'll protect the next man the same as the last. Or am I missing something?"

Jude remembered Eileen saying much the same thing. It stung a little more, hearing it rewarmed through Waxman. He wondered if they'd talked about it. "I'm still not getting—"

"Eileen doesn't want to see you, Jude. She doesn't want you to know where she is."

Jude recalled the crumpled sheet of paper, the poem he'd found on the floor of her house. "And you know this how?"

"She told me."

Jude decided to bluff. "I don't believe that."

A slight twitch quirked Waxman's eye. "Well, that's neither surprising nor terribly relevant."

The overhead light went out. Erika called out apologetically, *"Lo siento, señores. Buenas noches."* As their eyes adjusted to the cloud-patched moonlight, they watched the long-skirted *indígena* gather her daughter's hand and lead her beneath the swaying palms, up the sand path toward the highway, where they'd walk along the roadbed toward their village. The little dog trailed behind.

Jude said, "I want you to give Eileen my number. Tell her I'd like to talk to her." He opened his cell for the sake of its light, hoping Waxman had brought something to write with. But the reporter made no move for his pockets.

"This ardor of yours, Jude. It's touching. Really."

Jude had to control an impulse to shove the pompous fat-ass off his seat. "You've got no reason to talk to me like that."

"I don't mean to insult you, Jude. I'm just commenting. It's so typical, this attitude you have. I suffer from it myself. Why is it so hard for us—Americans I mean, American men in particular—why is it so hard for us to conceive that we might not be wanted?"

25

JUDE CLIMBED BACK UP THE HILL TO HORIZON HOUSE THINKING IT was classic—boy meets girl he has no business wanting and learns the hard way: Reach for the moon, you fall off the roof. He turned from the road and was halfway to the front door when someone whispered his name. He pulled up short—only then noticing the solitary figure lingering among the shadows of the short, broad-leafed *marañón* trees beside the porch.

"Don't go in just yet. I'd like to talk with you alone for a moment."

Axel stepped out into the moonlight. His face, deeply shadowed, seemed masklike, an effect intensified by the fixation in his eyes. And yet his shoulders sagged, he seemed weary. He reached for Jude's arm.

"I was beginning to wonder if you'd come back at all tonight." His smile was listless but warm; he turned toward the road. "Let's just head up the hill a ways. It's a pleasant night. A walk might feel good before we turn in."

It was a hopelessly transparent lie, but Jude left it alone. It hadn't been said for his sake, but in case anyone inside, sitting in the dark just beyond the window screens, might be listening.

The two men returned to the road in silence, then walked together uphill. Axel set a restive pace, glancing behind or to either side every few steps. Houses sat dark in lush ravines off the road, nestled into gardens thick with orchids, flowering *tulla, chichipince* vines.

They rounded a bend at the crest of the hill and Axel gestured for Jude to stop. As though looking for some way to begin, he said, "Interesting, all the intrigue about your father. It sounds, if you'll excuse my saying so, like he must have been a grandly imperfect man."

It didn't sound catty or insulting, Jude thought, just inquisitive. "My father was a lot of things, none of them much worth talking about."

"I'm willing to accept that, particularly since it has nothing to do with your work for me. And that, by the way, is what I brought you up here to discuss."

A sudden, stormy wind whipped the tree cover. Axel waited for the rustling to subside.

"You've always told me to let you know of anything I become aware of that might affect my safety. Or your ability to protect me. Well, in keeping with that spirit I think I have a few things to share with you." His eyes darted down the road behind them, checking one last time to see if they'd been followed. "I've kept all this to myself so far. That Bauserman fellow, your replacement these past ten days—I wouldn't tell him my shoe size unless someone got me drunk first. But even Fitz has been odd of late. You saw a little of that. I don't know, perhaps I'm overreacting, but the only person I feel comfortable discussing this with is you."

Axel was not a man of many moods, which made this one, with its odd mix of wounded loneliness and fear, all the more exceptional.

"I've been putting on the rakish façade for Fitz and the others whenever I discuss this woman I've met. Consuela, is her name. Consuela Rojas—daughter of an outcast colonel, a socialist, how's that for drama?" He looked up into the sky at a flock of shimmering moonlit clouds. "I'm not sure exactly what I've gotten myself into."

I've met someone, Jude thought, recalling Axel's first mention of her. He'd said it like he was bowled over and proud of it. Jude hadn't realized what a nifty liar the man could be.

"You know how I feel about my work down here," Axel said. "For all the faults of the people who run things in this country—and those faults are insidious—I still believe it's possible to get this economy kick-started with some wise investment and good, solid development. I'm not one to wring my hands overly much about how rough life can be or how corrupt its machinations are. When in doubt, build—with the caveat, yes, build wisely. The Salvadorans are nothing if not resilient and hardworking. Give them opportunities, they'll deliver. The key is crafting the opportunities. That doesn't come from mere good intentions. As for corruption, think of it as a cost of doing business and forge ahead. That's how I've always seen it, at any rate."

With his foot, Axel poked at a green coconut that had fallen to the ground, nudging it to the roadside.

"That said, I've been receiving e-mails the past few months from Consuela. That's how we met, I guess you'd say. She started writing when she learned I'd been retained to look into the Estrella plant expansion. She was never entirely frank, afraid her messages might fall into the wrong hands. She wouldn't say who, exactly, scared her. But I gathered soon enough from what she did say that she had a story to tell.

"She's incensed by Estrella for a variety of reasons, not merely because of the water issues. She also thinks there's some kind of shell game going on, to protect Torkland Overby from charges that they're helping exploit children down here."

Jude had heard before from Axel that Torkland Overby, the American conglomerate retaining him to review Estrella's water usage, had reason to be skittish about public relations disasters. Slave labor charges linked to a *maquila* that Torkland partially controlled, operating in the capital's free trade zone, had depressed the corporation's stock nearly 16 percent over three quarters the year before. Then, for good measure, the factory shut down and the local owners vanished, stranding both workers and creditors to the tune of ten million dollars. News of that fiasco had barely died down before hints of a water problem in San Bartolo Oriente hit the Internet—by which time Torkland had already supplied not just working capital for the soft drink plant's expansion but new assembly line conveyors, filler machines, mixing tanks and cap sealers, even a fleet of trucks. ODIC could insure the capital transfers but not stock value. If Estrella had any more skeletons in the closet, Torkland might have to fend off a shareholder revolt, especially from its institutional investors.

"Consuela says she has proof there are eight-year-olds working some of the cane fields that supply Estrella with its sugar. Say what you will about the harpies of feel-goodism, she has pictures of kids with these awful wounds from the machetes they use to cut the cane. She gave up getting Estrella to care long ago, so she's moved on to Torkland, but they've given her nothing but double-talk. Everyone's bound by their contracts, they say, and 'by contract' Estrella doesn't purchase directly from suppliers who use anyone younger than fourteen in the fields. I mean, that's bad enough, I suppose, but it could just mean Estrella slips in a local factor or some other kind of middleman so Torkland can claim ignorance about kids younger than that. Consuela was hoping I'd step up and say something, denounce the pussyfooting. I told her it wasn't my area of expertise and I didn't have enough hard evidence to say much of anything, regardless. But she pressed the issue so relentlessly I decided to meet her, at least.

"That was last week, while you were away. We got together for supper. It became obvious immediately that with Bauserman present she wouldn't speak freely. I mean, it's hard to describe how ghastly he was. He just sat there, eyeing her. It was beneath sexual. Like he'd already had his way with her just thinking about it. I told him to show some manners but he just ignored me. That's when I invited her up to my room."

Axel wandered over to the roadside. A *morro* tree lay just inside a low stone wall surrounding the nearest garden. He reached for a cluster of the tiny leaves, rubbed them together between his fingers and thumb, then smelled the nutty fragrance on his skin.

"I'm not saying it was a brilliant move. And I'm sure it had something to do with showing up Bauserman. I'm not proud of that. But there we were, Consuela and I, in my room, alone together." He smiled winsomely. "Interesting turn of phrase. Alone. Together. You're still quite young, Jude, I'm not sure I can make this intelligible to you. But I'm sixty-two. My wife divorced me when I was fifty—she was forty-five—because she feared the rest of her life would be as sexless as it had been for twenty years." His blue eyes rose to meet Jude's. They seemed ashamed. "I realize that's overly personal, but I need you to understand. I've spent my life on the job, the kind of projects people crow about—many in the wrong place, most at the wrong time, and nearly all for the benefit of the wrong people. And whenever I felt dismayed by that, I just told myself that was life. 'I mistook disenchantment for the truth,' I think is how it's said. And for ten years after my wife left I just went on working—like it was all that mattered. Life was an exercise in dealing with one's bitterness and the rest was inane, self-involved rubbish. Then one day I woke up from a bad sleep and felt a terror like none I've ever known. I saw everything decaying before my eyes and thought if I put my feet to the floor, my skin would come away contaminated with rot. Sounds silly when I say it out loud. Believe me, it was quite real. So real that for three days I didn't leave the bed.

"I didn't overcome it or figure it out. I just decided to pretend it hadn't happened. As you can imagine, that didn't work. The dread was still there, always. In the background." He waved vaguely toward the windblown palms, as though they were examples, the things we ignore. "And gradually I came to realize the terror had nothing to do with disease, it was because my wife had genuinely loved me and seen me for who I am, then left in disgust. Long-suffering woman, she was. In any event, I've reached that point in life when death seems to be getting nearer, faster. This pitiless blank slate coming at me, and what do I have to show for it? A revolted ex-wife, no children, and a life of dubious work—including this odious business with Estrella, for which I was hired only because three other hydrologists Torkland would have preferred were unavailable.

"Then suddenly this woman is with me in my room. She's lovely, but more than that she's simply, ineffably feminine—all that amplified by her intensity, this ferocious commitment to these children. That's when she told me what was truly bothering her about Estrella. Not *what* so much, actually, as who. But I wasn't listening, not yet. I was smelling her perfume and trying not to stare at her breasts the way Bauserman had. And either I sensed a return interest on her part or I invented it. In any event, I heard her out as best I could, paid just enough attention to be able to say honestly I'd do what I could, and then she sat there, not getting up, looking at me. She wanted something more. Something stronger. And I took that to mean what I wanted it to mean."

Axel's eyes clouded over. A dove cooed somewhere in a nearby garden.

"Looking back on it now, I realize she must have felt trapped. Maybe she wanted to trap me in return. Regardless, she stayed. Till morning. And I ignored everything except the way she made me feel young and worth something and unafraid for at least a little while."

He looked straight into Jude's eyes as though he might find forgiveness there. But all Jude could think of was that line of Waxman's: *Why is it so hard to believe we're not wanted?* Axel had gone one better: *How hard we pretend we're wanted regardless.*

"This woman's going to extort you."

Axel recoiled a little. "I hadn't considered it along those lines, to be honest." He reached up absently to scratch behind his ear. An odd gesture, it made him look old. "I mean, what I figured might happen is she'd use our liaison as leverage, to get me to press her concerns."

"Use it how?"

"Guilt, I suppose."

"You mean, what, nag?"

Axel lifted his chin in defiance, but the rest of him sagged. "Basically. Yes."

"And if that didn't work, expose you."

"Of what—having a libido at sixty-two? Welcome to Viagra. Besides, I'm a divorcé. Where's the scandal?"

"Axel, the woman came to you for a sympathetic ear, not a revitalized dick. And she'll get first shot at setting the scene as to what happened in your room."

A sudden shadow darted along the moonlit wall behind Axel. Jude turned toward it just as the *gorrobo,* a small brown lizard, vanished up a low-hanging tree branch.

Axel let out a brooding sigh. "I've been foolish, I suppose."

"There's nothing here that can't be handled. We keep her away from you."

"That's not possible."

That caught Jude off guard. "Why not?"

"I'm quite fond of her." The words came out with sapped strength, as though Axel were their victim. Then he added, even more abashed, "I'm in love with her, actually."

Jude felt like he was talking to three different people. "You're making this too hard."

"I'm going to ask that you try to understand."

"You realize what this exposes you to?"

Axel scoffed, "Now you're sounding paranoid."

"I get paid to be paranoid. Why drag me up here if there's nothing—"

"Look, I've put all this in its worst light. Let's get things back on track." Axel closed his eyes to regain his focus, his hands scrubbing together worriedly—another aging, enfeebling gesture. "I told you, Consuela's issues with Estrella go beyond what it's doing, to who's involved. Does the name Wenceslao Sola mean anything to you?"

Jude could put the name to a face but little more. "He's on the Estrella board."

"Hasn't a whiff of business sense, let alone experience, but he's connected by family to some influential people. I'm not sure there's a scam going on, exactly, but it's damn odd how miserly the well-to-do down here can be when it comes to investing in anything local. The money sails offshore to banks in Miami, the Caymans, Luxembourg, wherever. Nobody's going to risk anything of his own to see this place improved. So development capital comes through loans— the World Bank or IMF or export-import banks like U.S. Ex-Im or export credit agencies like ODIC—and as often as not gets skimmed or paid out to cronies in kickback schemes, some quite clever, or just stolen outright. That's what Consuela suspects is going on here. The bottling plant's expansion is just an elaborate reward to Sola and his cronies for their continuing support of U.S. plans down here. That's why ODIC's involved. To ensure that Torkland Overby isn't on the hook for plowing money and equipment into a white elephant being used principally for payoffs."

"And again," Jude said, "she knows this how?"

"She doesn't know," Axel said wearily. "She suspects."

"Because?"

"Because of this Sola character!" Axel threw up his hands. "She was married to a cousin of his. A disaster of a marriage, apparently, but it gave her an inside glimpse at the clan. Wenceslao is the family scapegrace, spends money like a whore on holiday, is rumored to have a thing for little girls, and is generally just one of those louche, pampered little deviants who couldn't make his own way in life, let alone earn an honest buck, if his soul hung in the balance."

"Axel, I don't mean to sound harsh, but that's the way the sewer runs down here."

"During the war, Sola joined a group called Los Patrióticos, a kind of bourgeois brotherhood cum weekend death squad—I know, I know, death squads, the great bogeyman of Latin America. But hear me out, all right? He also has ties to Judge Regalado, the owner of the sugar operation upstream from the bottling plant. He's practically an institution when it comes to venality." Axel scratched his head and sighed. "I'm sorry this is so complicated. I'm doing my best to crib it, believe me. Consuela, for all her virtues, can be a tad scrambled in her tale telling, and her delivery is, shall we say, a bit on the breathless side."

Jude said, "Axel?"

"Yes, yes. I'm coming to the denouement. Despite all the disavowals Estrella tries to make, it's unthinkable it doesn't get at least some of its sugar from Judge Regalado's plantations, given not just their proximity but the links between families, his and Sola's. And it's one of the worst-kept secrets in El Salvador, apparently, that the judge has no compunction about children working in his fields. Christ, he almost insists on it—builds character, helps support families, all that rot." He let out a long, shuddering sigh, looking spent. "There. That's what I was trying to get out."

A cluster of *golondrinas* suddenly scattered in frantic wing bursts from among the swaying branches overhead. Another *gorrobo,* or maybe the same one, scurried down the stone wall and burrowed in the sand.

Jude locked his hands behind his neck. "Well, that's quite a yarn."

"Yes. And I've only told you half."

"You're joking."

"My mention of death squads wasn't for the sake of drama. Whenever Sola visits the bottling plant in San Bartolo Oriente, he stops for lunch at a restaurant owned by a man named Hector Torres. Consuela may have little kind to say about Sola, but he's a mere pest compared to Torres. Consuela's terrified of him."

Jude considered that for a moment, taking full account of the gravity in Axel's eyes and voice. Then he said, "Sola, he has lunch. At this guy's restaurant." He didn't mean to spoil the party, but really. "That's it?"

"Torres has long played the role of pivot man for the death squads operating in the eastern departments. Not just during the war but after. He's the godfather of Los Soldados de San Miguel, and you've heard of them, I'm sure. They're particularly fond of snatching uncooperative prostitutes, gutting or beheading them, leaving the bodies on the steps of local churches, to flaunt their impunity. He's made all the right friends and people fear him. Consuela hears he runs a protection racket now, muscling theft rings, kidnap rings, drug dealers—prostitutes, naturally—even street vendors. He's ruthless, has a little army of *veteranos* and *mareros* he uses for henchlings. People pay."

Of course they do, Jude thought. He recalled what Strock had said. *We taxed them, sure.* And suddenly Torres the respectable gangster got conflated with the Candyman and Malvasio, the Laugh Masters. Jude's father. Overhead, the *golondrinas* resettled in the palm branches.

"Axel, correct me if I'm wrong, but none of this involves you unless—"

"The day before you got back from the States—and shortly after the last time Wenceslao Sola paid his respects to Hector Torres—a woman named Marta Valdez disappeared from a tiny village outside San Bartolo Oriente. She'd complained to people—in particular, to Consuela, who works with a few citizen committees in the area—about the *pozos,* the wells, below her village. The wells, they've become brackish with mineral deposits because the water table's dropped so low, partially because of the bottling plant—or so everyone suspects, including me, but I've still not been able to confirm it satisfactorily. Regardless, Consuela went up to the village when this woman, Marta, didn't appear for a follow-up interview. No one there would so much as talk to her. Except, as she was leaving, a boy came up. His name is Oscar. He's all of eight years old.

"He says he heard a car drive up the hill and park outside Marta's house. Four men were in the car. Two went inside the house and stayed for a while. When they came back out, they were carrying what looked like a body wrapped in a blanket. Then they drove down the hill again. No one's seen Marta since."

A light came on in the window of a nearby house, then almost instantly went out again. Jude gestured for Axel to start walking with him downhill. Once they'd moved on a ways, Jude said, "This boy, he's told all this to your friend Consuela. Anybody else?"

"He's too terrified to tell the authorities. I don't know, I can't help wondering if this prostitute-to-be-named-later from Usulután, who's now been found beheaded—"

"And you didn't mention any of this to McGuire why?"

"Once I heard the way they were going at you, I didn't trust them. You didn't either, obviously. And then this Lazarek character. ODIC doesn't have an ongoing presence at the embassy. People come and go, and beyond the pencil pushers it's always a bit of a game, figuring out which consultants are spies and vice versa. But Lazarek was a different story altogether—a name people whispered. I was looking forward to meeting him face-to-face, actually, just to see if he really existed. Well, now I have. All that crap about stable government and gangs. Spare me. If the gangs were pro-ARENA, we'd pay for their weddings."

"But if ODIC is Lazarek's cover—"

"That could mean they're not turning a blind eye just to Sola and the other trough-feeders on the Estrella board, but to this crooked judge and Torres and whoever killed this woman." Axel sighed at the strangeness of it all. "As for the FBI, I haven't a clue why they're involved."

"My guess is they're not." Jude wouldn't be sending McGuire or Sanborn any valentines, but their contempt for Lazarek now seemed reassuring.

"One last thing," Axel said. "Excuse me if this seems intrusive, but what might your father or this man you flew back with or the other one they were harping about—"

"Malvasio."

"What have they to do with any of this?"

"Nothing." Jude tried for nonchalance. "Cop tricks. Trying to put me off guard." Nothing had changed his mind about that. Yet. And if anything, Malvasio now seemed less a menace than a seer: *For all you know, the people involved in your hydrologist's project could be the worst of the worst down here.* "Back to Lazarek for a minute—any chance he or somebody else at ODIC would know about your thing with—"

"Consuela? Possibly." Axel cringed. "Thing, please. God. But Bauserman knows, yes. Fitz knows. I've no idea whom they may have told in turn."

"And the fact she knows that this Sola character, the judge, Torres are all connected?"

"I've shared that with no one but you."

26

Malvasio reached the San Bartolo Oriente city limits just before midnight—hours late, delayed by his detour into the mangrove swamp. He was driving the van with its telltale dark-tinted glass, pistol in his lap, doors locked, his eyes always trained not at the cobbled tunnel-like street twisting before him in his headlights but at the mercurial shadows melting into the doorways to either side.

By day you'd see the streets jammed with women shopping at the *mercado central,* boys making bread deliveries on their basketed bikes, and schoolgirls in blue pleated skirts and white blouses walking arm in arm, while horn-honking traffic squeezed through the crowds beneath the blistering sun. But the night belonged to the *mareros.* The city was too poor for after-hour police patrols. People shuttered their homes come nightfall and waited for dawn.

He slowed at the cathedral plaza, dodging stray dogs rooting through trash. On the plaster wall of the cathedral itself, a recent inscription in loopy spray paint read: *Por mi madre nací y por mi barrio muero.* By my mother I was born and for my brothers I will die. It was punctuated with the customary *MS 13* in Gothic lettering, marking the area for Mara Salvatrucha, and surrounded by a bilingual roll call: Poison, Travieso, Snorky, Choca . . .

Malvasio turned uphill again, another narrow, snaking road. Near the top, a smaller church named El Niño de Atoche stood in a grove of *amate* trees with their ghostly white bark. Malvasio spotted the tip of Sleeper's cigarette glowing on the vestibule steps. On seeing the van, the boy flipped his butt into the street, the red ash arcing like a rocket through the darkness.

Sleeper was bare-chested, his long-sleeved shirt knotted around his waist, the better to show off his ink. His chest was adorned with prayer hands and rosary beads, a *pachuco* cross. On his back, two long-haired women in clown face appeared, one happy, one sad—the traditional Smile Now, Cry Later. Variations on MS and the number thirteen sleeved up and down his arms, while the back of each hand bore the inscription "C/S" for *Con safos*: untouchable.

Climbing into the van's passenger seat, Sleeper said, "The fuck you been, Duende?"

His English came softly inflected with an incongruous drawl, the result of six years spent in rural Virginia. He'd landed there at age twelve with his mother, who'd fled Soyapongo and her abusive drunk of a husband to seek a better future for herself and her son in the Shenandoah Valley, a growing haven for Salvadoran émigrés. Things didn't turn out as she'd hoped. Armando, as she knew him, was a bored and restless sort, lousy at school, prone to fights, and he fell in with a Salvatrucho *clica*. He got banged in at fourteen and, in accordance with the irony of gang handles, was rechristened Sleeper because he was constantly wired. By age eighteen he was honing his flair with a blade by logging sixty-hour weeks at a poultry processing plant carving up chickens, then working on his entrepreneurial skills by driving down to the Carolinas each weekend to score meth for sale back in the valley. He and his pals were outhustling the biker outfits who'd once dominated the local trade, and

crank was taking the rural backwaters by storm. Not that the Salvatruchos were the only ones testing the darker edges of American
ambition: Some of their biggest buyers were the hayseed managers
at the poultry plant, who offered free rails to anyone willing to work
a second shift. Then, six months ago, a multi-agency sweep came
down: The homegrown managers lawyered up and pointed the finger at their immigrant suppliers, who got rounded up by the DEA,
deported by the ICE. Shortly thereafter, Malvasio came upon
Sleeper trying to hustle up a connection at a bar here in San Bartolo
Oriente, and saw possibilities.

As for "Duende," it was the name Malvasio used with his
hirelings. It referred locally to a kind of spirit, not unlike a faerie or
leprechaun, who could be charming or devious or even malevolent
depending on his mood. Behind his back, he'd learned, they sometimes called him Dundo instead: Stupid. Such were the indignities
suffered by middle-management everywhere.

In defense of his tardiness, Malvasio said, "A situation came up."

"Yeah, well, a situation almost came up here. I was ready to book
my ass on down the road."

Malvasio didn't respond. He was looking past Sleeper at the thin,
dark, rawboned youth emerging from the shadows of the church
steps.

"Who's Buster?"

Sleeper did a little sheepish dance with one hand while the other
stuffed his Marlboros into the back pocket of his sagging jeans.
"Thought a posse of two with your particular business in mind just
wouldn't cut it, know what I'm saying?"

The youth lingered on the sidewalk. He was somewhere between thirteen and sixteen, with dull, fathomless eyes. He wore a
Raiders jersey and baggy Dickies, both counterfeit no doubt, a black
bandana wrapped tight around his head, a machete tucked into his
belt.

"He old enough to have a name?"

"Chucho."

Malvasio nodded. It came from *chuco chucho,* Nahuatl for "dirty dog."

"Open the door. Tell him to get in."

Sleeper reached behind his seat and undid the lock on the van's sliding door, gesturing for Chucho to climb aboard. Before sitting down, the boy turned the machete so the blade rested upward and wouldn't damage the seat vinyl. The perfect passenger, Malvasio thought.

"Put your shirt on," he told Sleeper, putting the van in gear again and pulling away from the curb. "Just give people one more thing to ID you by."

Sleeper unknotted the sleeves around his waist and pulled his shirt on. Buttoning the cuffs, he said, "You don't look so hot, Duende. Like you could use a rail, get you through this thing." He reached into his front pant pocket and removed a short straw and a bindle of crank wrapped in tinfoil. Methamphetamine had made its way down here, along with Ecstasy. They were the latest drugs of choice, pushed by the Mexican cartels, sometimes used as payment if the *mareros* helped move product—which Sleeper, given his pedigree, was more than happy to do. "Chucho and me could use a bump our own selves."

He laid out a line for Malvasio in his palm. Malvasio braked, slipped the tranny in neutral, and leaned over, then took the straw and horned the line of yellowish chalky powder off Sleeper's skin. It flooded his nostril with an odor like gun metal wrapped in dirty sock and soured the phlegm trickling down the back of his throat. As the first little kick quivered through his neck muscles, he thought: forty-five years old, look at you. Sleeper tapped two dots of powder into his palm, took the straw from Malvasio, and passed it to Chucho, holding out his hand. The boy leaned forward and hoovered his bump, fussed with his nostrils. Sleeper knocked back his own recharge as Malvasio put the van in gear again and headed downhill.

"I thought about you today, Duende, know that?" Sleeper grinned like he knew a fabulous secret. "Heard on the news about this cat in Afghanistan—you know the one I'm talking about? This guy pretending to be some kind of freelance special forces hotshot. Says he was a Green Beret down here in the eighties, no lie. The local angle. Any event, he's over there now, hoping to cash in on the twenty-five-fucking-million-dollar bounty on Osama bin Laden's head. He's taking guys prisoner, says the U.S. government knows all about him, they love what he's doing, on and on and on like this till he gets arrested by the *afghanilistas* for torturing guys in this house he's, like, renting? Got 'em tied to the toilet or hanging upside down from the ceiling and shit. And the guys he's capturing, he says they're al Qaeda and Taliban, but the cops or whoever look into it, and his prisoners, they're just, you know, guys. Meanwhile, the real special forces, State Department, who-the-fuck-ever—they can't scrape this guy off their shoes fast enough, man. They say he's crackers, totally messed up and shit, so—"

Malvasio cut him short. Crank talk. "And why, exactly, did this remind you of me?"

Sleeper's eyes narrowed to slivers. The grin lingered. "He's like you, man. Doing *el mero mero*'s bidding. But if you're ever caught—you hear what I'm saying? They'll back off you like a fucking leper. Call you nuts. Do it so fast, make your head spin. Then they'll let you hang."

THEY DROVE SLOWLY WITHOUT HEADLIGHTS DOWN A SIDE STREET lined with dark market stalls two blocks from the cathedral, the beginning of the *barrio bajo*. Sleeper leaned forward in his seat, peering through the windshield at the dark doorways of the decrepit shops and shabby walk-ups lining the sidewalk. Behind him, Chucho hunched forward, one hand on the handle of the sliding door, the other on his machete, ready to bolt into the street when Sleeper gave the word.

They were searching for a small-time dealer named Ziro who understood imperfectly the proprieties of hustling in San Bartolo Oriente. Anyone with a dose of smarts knew that Hector Torres, *el mero mero,* got paid for such privileges. His reputation as the godfather of the local death squads instilled the required level of fear, but he was also a businessman, and he'd come around to the perfectly reasonable position that it made better sense to extort the *mareros* than to slaughter them. The point was maintaining a certain level of order, not eliminating vice, especially when there was money to be made. And so the *mareros* were permitted their minor scams—hand-to-hand drug sales, stickups, muscling street vendors and small businesses—but they kicked back to Hector for protection, which kept the mayhem reasonably in check. Those who didn't play along suffered—that was where Malvasio came in.

The work reminded him of his Chicago days, not in the good sense but in the gone-to-hell sense. Not that he regretted what he and Ray and Phil had done, jackrolling fools—they'd deserved worse, and he'd pocketed a tidy bonus from the Gangster Disciples for harassing the competition. It was the grim sense of déjà vu that weighed on him, as though he were trapped in a bad dream—pulling the same tricks as ten years ago but for shabbier reasons in an even drearier place, and having to soil his hands with hopeless little deviants like this Ziro creature who'd not only skipped on his taxes three collections running but was bragging about it now. Finding him, getting his account in balance, teaching him some manners—that was the new bit of business Hector had brought up the night before in the bar at El Arriero, when all Malvasio had wanted was sleep.

If Ziro didn't listen to reason, it would be up to Los Soldados de San Miguel to take it from there. Malvasio would try to get that through to him: This little visit from me is the good news. Don't be *dundo.*

The air smelled of rotting garbage and urine, a carryover from the street markets in the baking sun earlier that day. Here and there, faces emerged from the shadows—scowling boys, fat tattooed men with lacquered hair wearing shapeless *guayaberas,* the occasional prostitute squeezed into a spandex top and miniskirt. Then just as quickly the faces pulled back into the swallowing darkness again.

Malvasio said, "You're sure he's out tonight?"

"You never hand up your spot, Duende. Never."

They crossed a steep narrow alleyway cluttered with lumber, leading back toward the main plaza. Sleeper held out his hand, signaling Malvasio to stop.

Rolling down the passenger-side window, Sleeper pursed his lips and let go with a soft lilting whistle. At the same time, with his hand hidden, he gestured for Chucho to get ready. Almost imperceptibly, a figure edged back farther into the shadows.

Sleeper whispered to Chucho: *"¡Ahorita!"*

The kid slid open the van's side door and darted into the alley. Ziro, running for his life, scattered two-by-fours behind him, but Chucho hurtled past or fought through them, possessed. Malvasio gunned the motor and, a hundred feet ahead, turned sharp, racing down a brick-paved side street, then turning back again at the next corner just as Chucho flushed Ziro from the mouth of the alley. The two boys raced downhill half a block toward the cathedral square, then Chucho tripped Ziro up and tackled him. Malvasio sped to the spot, braked hard. He and Sleeper jumped out to join in as Chucho pulled the machete from his belt with a spinning flourish and pressed the blade to the other boy's throat.

Faces stared from black doorways. Ziro—scrawny and small, boxers high, pants low, no shirt or shoes—lay on his back in the street, chest heaving, his breath a soft, wheezy shriek from the sheer force of the air pumping in and out of his lungs. Sleeper strolled up grandly, leaned down, put his hands on his knees and cocked his head, peering into Ziro's bloated eyes.

"Hola, chero. Tienes el culo a dos manos ¿verdad?" Hey, buddy. Scared shitless, am I right?

He and Malvasio each took an arm and hefted Ziro to his feet as

Chucho kept the machete blade pressed to the boy's neck. They trundled him into the van, forcing him to lie on the floor where Sleeper tied his hands behind his back with hemp cord and stuffed a filthy rag deep into his mouth. As quick as that, they were on their way, out of town.

They drove to a deserted spot along the dry riverbed of the Río Conacastal, where the proceedings would be shielded from view by a copse of spindly fernlike *carago* trees. The three of them dragged Ziro out and stripped off his pants, then pulled his pockets inside out, collecting his bottles—the boy was dealing crack mixed with crumbled Alka-Seltzer, drywall for the cluckheads—and the measly fifty dollars he had on him, a fraction of his nut. Then, as he knelt in the brittle, black *carago* pods, Sleeper went to work, whipping him with a car antenna he liked to use, finishing up with a few good blows to the head, the gut, the kidneys, using a fish billy he'd brought along as well. Chucho, a mere spectator now, sat to the side on a rock, bored, twirling the handle of his machete between his hands. One of Ziro's eyes had swollen closed and a deep gash along his brow oozed blood down his face. He hung his head, choking back tears.

Malvasio gave the signal and Sleeper pulled the rag from Ziro's mouth. The boy gasped and spat out the noxious taste and caught his breath, then looked straight up into Malvasio's eyes. He said, "I know a boy you want. He see. He see the woman get take."

The kid had the gall to bargain. "What woman?"

"*¿Qué mujer?*" Sleeper translating, just to be sure.

Ziro licked his lips. The dried blood clotting there glistened. "*La mujer del pozo.*"

The woman from the well.

The *caserío* sat among low hills, the five tiny houses made of *bahareque,* a mix of cane stalks and wood sticks glued together with mud. As the van pulled up, climbing the last of the rutted path from the nearest road, Malvasio spotted a small figure darting into the forest. Sleeper saw it too. He and Chucho jumped from the van and gave chase, thrashing through the underbrush beneath the dark tree cover.

Ziro, barely able to sit upright or even see much given the damage to his eye, remained behind with Malvasio, still bound but not gagged. Minutes passed. Sleeper and Chucho reappeared finally, alone, drenched in sweat, cursing and swatting at buzzing mosquitoes as they trudged back to the van.

Malvasio drew his pistol, got out of the van and gestured for Sleeper and Chucho to take the back of the hut, he'd take the front. Once he knew the other two were in position, Malvasio stuck his head through the beadwork hanging in the doorway.

A candle burned in a wood holder and quivering shadows stretched across the dirt-floored room. An *indígena* woman sat on a *pepeishte,* a woven mat for sleeping. She wore only a light cotton *falda* and had a homely, square, girlish face belied by her eyes, which seemed to belong to a much older woman. She cradled an infant in her arms. There was nothing else in the tiny house except a log to sit on, a *guacal* filled with corn, and a *metate* grinding stone.

Malvasio called the others inside, then asked the woman where her boy had run. She tried to pretend she didn't understand, but then Chucho tapped her alongside the head a few times with the broad side of his machete. When she still wouldn't answer, he went to grab the child.

The woman spoke then, in a rush of Spanish tinged with Nahuatl: "My son didn't see what he thinks he saw. It was all a mistake. I will tell anyone who asks that he admitted to me he was lying. He never saw the woman who was taken away, the woman who complained about the water going bad in the well." She looked at Malvasio with heartsick eyes, then crossed herself, kissing her infant's head as she clutched its body tight against her own.

Malvasio returned to San Bartolo Oriente, climbed the hill past the cathedral square, and parked in the shadow of the *amate* trees outside El Niño de Atoche. He'd dropped Ziro off a mile from the *bahareque* village to make him walk—one last exercise in the tutorial—so only Sleeper and Chucho needed out. He paid them for the night's services, and Chucho left promptly, gladly. Sleeper lingered.

"I don't know, Duende."

He looked at the infant, swaddled in its cotton *manta,* lying on the backseat. They'd told the woman her baby would be returned if her other child, the boy who'd fled, said nothing about what he thought he saw. That meant the abduction was open-ended, but that seemed the least of the mother's concerns. She'd begged and sobbed and promised while Chucho ripped the infant from her arms and Malvasio dictated terms.

Malvasio gestured for Sleeper to take off. "Let me worry about it."

Sleeper shook his head, muttering, "*Muy fregado.*" Fucked up. Reaching into his pocket, he took out the tinfoil bindle with the last of his crank inside and tossed it onto the dash. "You gonna need that more than me." He got out, slammed the door, and, not looking back, melted into the church shadows with Chucho.

Malvasio turned in his seat, reached back for the child, and managed to lift it onto his lap without waking it. It'd bawled like a banshee when they'd taken it from its mother—the mother's howling hadn't helped—but once the van had started up, the little squirt had dropped into a dead sleep. Not so much as a chirp since. He wondered if it was retarded, or already had mother issues. Christ, maybe it's sick, he thought, laying his hands against its brow. He felt no conspicuous fever but he knew nothing about children or their afflictions. He needed to find a place where the kid would be safe for a few weeks, maybe longer.

The obvious choice? Take it to the judge's *finca,* let the women on the house staff fuss over it. But he could imagine the judge, the colonel, or Hector deciding the child was too big a risk, or too needless a bother, to keep around that long. Bodies moved quickly in their business. The baby would be sold or given away, or they'd find some other way to make it disappear.

Just then the infant stirred and Malvasio adjusted the *manta* around its body. Its face was broad and dark and gnarled up in wrinkly flesh with a porcine nose and bubbly pink lips. Thin tufts of black hair smeared its skull, and its skin smelled oddly like grass. Stretching, it reached out a chubby arm, flexed its fingers, then settled back into sleep, its black-lashed eyes never opening.

Malvasio thought of Anabella, the girl who'd shared his bed, as he racked his brain. He came away with nothing but senseless ideas until, after the fifth time it occurred to him, he stopped discarding one particularly reckless option and considered it more mindfully.

27

STROCK AWOKE WITH HIS SKIN SHEATHED IN SWEAT BUT HIS MOUTH bone-dry. He'd slept like a stowaway, mind crawling with shadows that loomed and receded in time to the monotonous ocean, the taste of salt water pickling his throat. He sat up in the lumpy bed, rubbed his gluey eyes, and stifled a yawn. Finding his cane, he rose, tottering a second, then hobbled to the door of the tiny, airless room and headed down the narrow hall, craving something cold to drink.

As he entered the kitchen, he heard voices murmuring somewhere nearby. He hadn't expected that, figuring he was alone here with Clara the maid, housekeeper, slave, whatever. He'd been thinking he could stand another alcohol bath. Senseless not to take full advantage of the perks. The sliding doors leading outside from the dining room were open and he headed that direction.

On the concrete patio, under the shifting patchwork of shade and sun beneath the windblown palms, he found Clara in her blue and white uniform sitting with a man, the two of them facing each other in the rough-hewn chairs. The man's back was turned and he cradled a swaddled child. Clara cooed and stroked the infant's face with her fingertips—rapturous, glowing, impossibly happy. Strock felt a bewildering surge of nausea tinged with rage. He realized why when the man turned suddenly, glancing over his shoulder.

Strock lurched as fast as he could on his cane back through the kitchen and down the hall to his room. He slammed a magazine into the AR-15 and primed a round into the chamber. When he turned, Malvasio stood there in the doorway, still holding the infant. The years had worn him down, his face washed out, even those dagger eyes a little spent now—and the rug rat, what was that about?— but there was no mistake. Strock shouldered the rifle and sighted the barrel on the bridge of Malvasio's nose.

"Put the kid down."

Malvasio said, "Like this close, Phil, you'd miss." Then: "Sure. Hold on." He turned to hand the child to Clara who'd scrambled up behind him in the hallway. Malvasio stroked the infant's head and murmured something to Clara in Spanish, then gestured for her to take the child away. Strock sighted on Malvasio's ear, the easiest pathway into his brain at this angle, and told himself, Don't wait. Pull the trigger. Now.

"What are you telling her?"

"Phil, relax. Okay?"

"Tell me what you said."

"She's not calling anybody, Phil, if that's what you're thinking. There's no one to call. Just me." He leaned into the doorway, like he hadn't slept and it was all he could do to stand upright. He seemed wired, though, a bit of a twitch here and there. "Ray's kid mentioned you felt like this."

"He's in on this, I'll kill him too. Kill you both."

"And accomplish what?"

"You left me for dead, shitbird. I lay there damn near eight hours before Ray showed up. Tendon and nerves in my knee cut to crap. Never has healed right."

"I didn't know you were hurt that bad."

"How bad did it need to be, asshole?"

"Ten years ago, Phil. If it'll do any good, I'm sorry."

Strock nudged the barrel to one side and pulled the trigger. The report was deafening in the confined space and plaster shattered on the wall. Malvasio dropped to his knees and covered his head with his hands as, from the kitchen, Clara screamed. The ringing in Strock's ears muffled the sound as the tang of cordite filled the air, scalding away the smells of mold and brine. Malvasio, brushing plaster dust from his neck and hair, shouted back, "*¡Está okay, quédate allá!*"

Strock said, "You're sorry?" His voice sounded muddy inside his own head.

Malvasio glanced up. The baby was wailing in the kitchen now, distant but gradually more clear, Clara sobbing as she tried to comfort it. "You want to kill me, Phil, fine. But not here. Not like this."

"Here's perfect. You, your kid, your third world squeeze."

"Jesus, Phil, no, you've—"

"How many times we see that, Bill? Break down the door and find the little kids in their rooms, baby in the crib, wife in the bed— always the bed, remember that? Daddy last to go, can't live with himself now. Happened a lot around the holidays. Easter's coming up. I'm sure it happens down here."

"Phil, you've got it wrong. They've got nothing to do with me. With this. And you're not that kind."

Strock cackled at that. "What kind would that be, Bill? Kind who backed you up every time some saggy-pants turf toad needed his money roll lifted?"

"And you blame me."

Strock fired a second round, closer than the last. A ricochet of plaster caught Malvasio's cheek and drew a thread of blood. Clara screamed again and Malvasio called back—they jabbered in clipped, fevered Spanish, Strock reveling at the fear in Malvasio's voice, regretting it in Clara's. And the baby, its bawling, he was having trouble with that.

Malvasio turned back to Strock. "Let them leave, Phil."

"You got the say here? I don't think so."

Malvasio, already on his knees, seemed to shrink a little more. "This thing between you and me, they shouldn't have to pay. That's crazy."

Strock gestured with the rifle barrel. "Move."

"Promise me, Phil."

"I said *move*."

Malvasio got to his feet, shedding coarse white dust. The floor was hazed with it now. The baby's shrieks remained unabated and Strock still felt haunted by that.

"I won't hurt them," he said. "I promise."

"Thank you." Malvasio inched back till he butted up against the wall. "One last thing. I brought you down here to help me look after Ray's kid. Jude. Don't blame him for any of this. I put him up to it, sure, told him not to mention me and he went along, but I sold him some bullshit about having work for you, wanting to do you a good turn. The truth? I did it for him. He's in over his head down here. The guy he's protecting, he's made some enemies and this is the wrong place to make enemies. They're going to do what they want to this guy, and if Jude gets in the cross fire, tough. And that's Jude's job, right? Take the bullet meant for the guy he's hired to protect."

Strock's finger eased on the trigger. The rifle's stock separated from his cheek. "And you know this how?"

"People I work for down here, they're staging the hit."

It was the first thing Malvasio said that Strock believed.

"I've been mixed up in a lot of things the past ten years, it's how

I get by. What did you think, I came out of it clean? None of us did."

Strock's finger tightened around the trigger again. "What happened to you, what happened to me—you think they're the same?"

"Phil, all right, I get it. But did you hear what I just said? Ray's kid is gonna get taken out. You want to just sit by and let that happen?"

PART IV

THE ONE LOST SHEEP

One rarely rushes into a single error. Rushing into
the first, one always does too much. So one usually
perpetrates another, and now does too little.

—Friedrich Nietzsche, *Twilight of the Idols*

28

NOTHING HAPPENED OVERNIGHT TO IMPROVE FITZ'S HUMOR. As HE provided his Monday morning advance report to the EP crew, he could barely bring himself to meet Jude's eyes, as though the unannounced visit from the FBI, Jude's failure to mention his father's past, and the dubious company he'd kept of late were a scandal. The fact that nothing had come of this wickedness seemed to matter little. He'd let everybody down, created a needless bother, an irritant. He'd overtaxed Fitz's mind.

And so, as Fitz recounted his litany of reported atrocities that had occurred throughout the country the past seventy-two hours, noting their locations on a wall map, followed by a recitation of known post-election demonstrations planned for the coming days—"Have alternate routes in mind ahead of time," Fitz warned, "don't leave it up to the drivers"—Jude decided Axel was right, Fitz was best kept in the dark for now about the disreputable entanglements among the men connected to the Estrella project. He'll only compound the problem with a load of blame, Jude thought, or denounce us for slandering the client's in-country partners. And the men presented no immediate danger, as long as Axel remained discreet in his liaison with Señora Rojas and kept any untoward findings about the water plant's expansion to himself. It seemed wise he withhold his final determination on the aquifer drawdown until he left the country. Till then, Jude surmised, as long as they kept their eyes and ears open and smiles at the ready, ruffling as few feathers as possible, they were safe. It might get tricky if Consuela demanded more of Axel than he could reasonably provide, but Jude figured they'd just have to burn that bridge when they came to it.

He nearly leapt from his seat, eager to escape, when the briefing session wrapped up. Back in his room, he collected his weapons: a .22 he carried in an ankle rig, and a Sig Sauer 9mm, small for its caliber and thus easy to conceal beneath the ballooning contours of his *guayabera*. Strike fear with fashion, he thought, regarding himself in the mirror. He looked more like a barber than a bodyguard.

Jude had never fired his weapon on the job, didn't know a man outside a war zone who had. It was a commonplace in the trade: If you have time to draw your piece, you have time to shield and remove the client. Your responsibility is not to win gun battles but elude them. Even so, the pistols were more than props. Jude practiced often, different times of day, at least once every two weeks from a moving car. More prosaically, in his valise he carried his maps and daily log, his roll call of contacts, a list of hotels and restaurants deemed safe. The only visible clues of his profession would be his build, his vigilance, and the close proximity of his principal.

The drivers arrived at eight. Carlos, Axel's chauffeur, had washed and waxed the black Mercedes and it glimmered in the morning sun. The car wasn't armored—the client wouldn't pay for that, which was pound foolish since the immense sedan, insanely *caudillo,* presented a conspicuous target for kidnappers, but all Jude's protests in that regard had fallen on deaf ears.

Carlos stood beside the thing like a proud uncle. He was stocky but solid, gray flecking his mustache and temples, with strangely delicate hands, more suitable to a schoolteacher than a former paratrooper. He greeted them in a raspy voice with clipped businesslike English: "We're off for the capital, no?"

They set out on the coastal road for La Libertad. In accordance with Axel's wishes, Carlos had a Haydn symphony, the "Trauer," playing softly; it provided a stately if incongruous sound track for the curving tree-lined Carretera del Litoral. Upscale *ranchos* sprawling behind high walls and guarded gates stood within calling distance from wretched *tugurios* and smoldering trash fires along the highway, while every hundred yards or so a glimpse to the south revealed the sunny palm-crowned beach.

Children walked along the roadbed on their way to school, some of the girls in blue uniforms, white socks sagging down their calves in the heat, books teetering atop their heads in imitation of the women carrying water jugs called *canteros* to and from their villages.

At La Libertad, Carlos turned north toward the central plateau, and soon they were passing sugarcane fields sprawling for miles to either side of the road, some stubbled from the harvest, others thick with green ratoons, a few bordered with small groves of banana trees.

A tractor chugged smokily along the berm, a wizened old man naked from the waist up bouncing in the iron seat. A few shabby houses of mud and thatch hid in the shade of sprawling *ceiba* trees. A mother and daughter, both barefoot, lifted their damp laundry from a stone *pila* and hung it out to dry on the rusted wire fence along the curving highway.

Carlos hit the brake.

Beyond the turn, the PNC had set up a roadblock—three officers in dark blue drill and high-laced boots were stopping traffic between the airport and the capital. In the backseat, Axel glanced up from the geological chart blanketing his lap. "Is there some kind of trouble?"

A battered pickup loaded with *campesinos* had been pulled over, and the workers shambled in a line along the roadside ditch, staring at the ground as their driver negotiated with one of the officers. An old *obrero* fanned himself with a straw hat as he waited on his perch atop an oxcart piled high with woven corn husks called *tusas*. Carlos slowed the Mercedes but the cop directing traffic waved them on after barely a glance.

As the Mercedes gained speed again, Axel said, "I've heard the officers get a percentage on the tickets they write. Is that really true?"

Carlos smiled in the rearview mirror. "So one's told."

Axel returned to his chart. "Screwy system, you ask me."

"It keeps people in line."

"Poor people, you mean. I notice they didn't even think of pulling us over."

Carlos was spared further defense of his stance by the sudden trilling of Jude's cell phone. It was Fitz. "You've got a change of plans," he said coolly, forsaking a greeting. "I just got word of a protest march blocking the Alameda Juan Pablo II from the soccer stadium to the Centro de Gobierno. I've relocated Axel's meeting with Rubén Manrique at ANDA. Head for the other side of town, the Hotel Elena José, it's in the Zona Rosa. They've got a nice little restaurant and bar there. I think you guys can make do." With that, he hung up.

As they neared the capital, the landscape changed to rolling hills. A roadcut of *tierra blanca* rose like a monument of chalk a hundred feet above the highway. Beyond it, a new development of small, stark concrete houses defiled beneath the brutal sun. A billboard outside the project read: *"Las Casas: Tipo Americano."* American-style houses. They were human storage sheds really, selling for twenty thousand a pop. No surprise, most stood empty.

Carlos switched off Haydn and turned on the radio to get news of the demonstration. The protest Fitz had reported was an anti-CAFTA march sponsored by the unions and swelled by church groups, even a contingent of farmers from Iowa. They were protesting ARENA's unexpected introduction of the agreement to the assembly for ratification at three in the morning, when only its supporters knew it was coming up for a vote.

The demonstration was being met by counter-protests from the right. ARENA was staging a march to celebrate its presidential victory, show support for the troops in Iraq, and rally solidarity in the face of the recent threats from al Qaeda. Already clashes had broken out between the opposing factions, and other protests were flaring up downtown in the Plaza Barrios between the Metropolitan Cathedral and the National Palace, even in the Santa Elena neighborhood outside the U.S. embassy. A couple dozen people had been injured. Two cars had been set afire.

Carlos kept the radio on as San Salvador came into view. Even without the political tensions, Jude always experienced an odd frisson, half expectation, half disappointment, whenever he saw the hazy, uninspiring skyline against the hills. Even as third world capitals went, it was lackluster, a sprawling, decaying stepsister to East Los Angeles, unworthy of its people—its monuments neglected, its churches sad, its museums wanting, and its nightlife tame or hidden while its commerce metastasized without any sense of prosperity, despite the perpetually crowded streets.

They arrived well before noon at the Hotel Elena José in the tony Colonia San Benito, near the incongruously located Monumento de la Revolución; there they waited on the patio over coffee, then lingered over lunch until half past two. A well-heeled crowd came and went for the midday meal, indifferent to the disorder across town. The next table over, a portly woman lingered, draped in pearls and clutching a Chihuahua that bared its fangs with a wheezy snarl when Axel leaned over to pet it.

No one from ANDA appeared or even sent word. Jude called Fitz but he said he'd tried and failed to get through to the agency since he'd rescheduled their meeting. "Just sit tight. God only knows what's happening over there."

Finally, as Jude was about to propose they head for the hotel, a secretary appeared, arriving by cab. She was pretty but flustered, wearing stylish eyeglasses and Italian heels, her hair in a prim bun. She made no apologies for the delay, not even to blame the demonstrations. Rather, she explained that Señor Manrique and a half dozen others had been placed under house arrest that morning on charges of embezzling three million dollars from the water agency.

Axel sat dumbstruck. After a moment he gathered his wits and managed to ask who he could contact to schedule a follow-up appointment. The secretary pleaded ignorance, said she had no further news, then fled.

Axel stared after her, watching as she climbed back into her taxi and rode off. When he turned back to the table, he said, "I feel like I've finally run off and joined the circus."

THE DRIFTWOOD LITTERING THE BEACH HAD BEEN SCRUBBED CLEAN by the sea and blanched by the sun till it resembled bone. A lone pelican soared low across the whitecaps, plunging suddenly, disappearing between waves, its wings splashing furiously till it rose again, a silver mackerel convulsing in its beak. On the shore, tiny sandpipers called *chillos* hopped and skittered across the wet sand, dodging the surf as they fed on the even tinier hermit crabs scuttering about.

Malvasio watched the tableau, nature feeding on itself, from just outside the wall of the *rancho*. He sipped from a mug of Clara's coffee, and that, with the knife-tip of Sleeper's crank he'd stirred into it like sugar, had him crackling and ready and would keep him that way, he hoped, through the day.

Not that ragged edges didn't remain, no small thanks to being shot at. Overall, though, he had few complaints. The headiness of having stared down the barrel and survived helped focus his mind. He'd managed not just to get Strock on board but to instill a sense of mission. We gotta rescue Pop Gun's son. Malvasio smiled. Never sell short the average drunk's obsession with heroics. And yet, who knew—maybe they would, in the end, turn out to be the heroes in this, at least to themselves.

He'd yet to settle on a clear-cut plan, just its elements. He'd always known he'd have to improvise once things started moving—too much remained in flux—but he hadn't expected it to start so soon or take such a wild turn. He still felt a little in shock. He'd heard it in his voice when he'd called Ovidio earlier to tell him he wouldn't be needed now to collect Strock. "I've got it under control." Things had strangely, mystically worked out.

Odd, he thought, how sometimes chance, in its random blindness, can put things together better than any plan, no matter how long and hard you think it through. There was something for the bumper stickers, he thought. Not: *Let Go. Let God*. Rather: *Give Chance a Chance*.

Down the beach he saw the outline of the old safe house, destroyed by Hurricane Mitch. During the war, the colonel's intelligence unit brought suspected insurgents or their sympathizers there—students, reporters, aid workers—interrogated them, tortured them, murdered them, then dropped their naked remains into the ever convenient sea. The Final Campaign of the Cold War, they called it. The time before that, in the thirties, they kept it simple: La Matanza. The Massacre. Anybody's guess, Malvasio thought, what they'll call it next time.

After the war, the colonel continued using the place as a safe house, for his and the judge's underground railroad of orphans and runaways. Twenty of them died when the hurricane hit, crushed by the roof and other debris, more bodies to dispose of. Clara had been working at the safe house then, looking after the children passing through; she'd lived here at the *rancho,* which had been transformed into servants' quarters. She'd survived because of that—strange how the one had collapsed, the other remaining intact, but every disaster left behind stories of that sort. Random chance, again. Clara remained in the colonel's employ—a steady, dependable, even cheerful worker, smart enough to keep her mouth shut, too desperate for work to beg off. She was a gift, Malvasio thought. Right now he had no clue what he'd do without her.

He poured the dregs of his coffee into the sand, then rang the bell at the gate. Shortly Clara answered, cradling the little girl—that point, the child's sex, was now settled. Malvasio hadn't been curious or perverse enough to poke around, but Clara had bathed the tyke straight off and: bingo. As she slept in Clara's arms, her tiny brown face puckered into fleshy creases.

Strock sat at the dining room table, finishing a lunch of soup and tortillas washed down with cold beer. Malvasio had arranged with the women of the *pueblito* on the estuary that there be a six-pack on hand every day. More than that, Strock could get sloppy. Less, he might get the shakes.

The AR-15 sat atop the table like a killer's centerpiece, several boxes of ammunition stacked beside it. Spotting Malvasio, Strock downed the last of his beer and rose, gathered his cane, and hefted the rifle over his shoulder. Malvasio collected ammunition boxes, stowing them in his rucksack. Neither man spoke. They'd had the morning to discuss particulars.

They headed out and hiked away from the beach, wind at their backs, following the path beneath the palms and shaggy eucalyptus trees through the thorny scrub brush toward the estuary. The thick-bodied women of the *pueblito* were serving rabbits and crab to a table of workmen with machetes who'd been gathering thatch. Everyone pretended not to notice as the two Americans, one of them armed, walked past.

Malvasio had anchored his *lancha* in the sandy mud at the bottom of the log steps. Strock plopped down in the bow, sitting backward so he could face Malvasio. With Strock watching his every move, Malvasio pushed off, cranked the outboard, then steered toward a branch of the estuary leading deep into the mangrove swamp.

In time, Malvasio called out above the growl of the outboard, "Mind if I play tour guide? This place is pretty interesting, if you know what's what."

Strock worked up a grin, adjusting the AR-15 across his lap. "Suit yourself." He thought back to earlier, aiming for Malvasio's skull, then firing, pulling off-target at the last instant. Doing it a second time, a third time. It had felt far more delicious than killing him could have. Once he was dead, that was it. What was there to look forward to? To have that chance again, here, now, but to forbear once more—yeah, that was the word exactly. Delicious. And listen to him, how humble he is, how palsy. Strock felt like luck's new buddy. He felt like God.

The way Malvasio had told it, saving Jude would require some precision shooting, and none of the snipers to be found down here could be trusted—they'd turn their allegiance to the men in charge. Malvasio realized he was in a bind and had to come up with a plan of his own. He depended on these men for his safekeeping—they'd turn on him in a heartbeat if he voiced any objections. He had to follow through, make the thing look okay. But it couldn't succeed. And all that depended on the Candyman, which Strock found appealing. He could see Laugh Master Bill getting cornered like this and needing an old pal he'd screwed to bail him out. It had a certain moral symmetry to it. And yet Bill hadn't begged. If he had, Strock would have grown suspicious. He just laid it out, let Strock think it through, ask his questions and decide. And the longer Strock had the weapon in his hands, the more certain he became.

He put these musings aside as Malvasio began pointing and naming. In a dark tangle of mangrove roots, a pale blue *garza* stood sentry, resembling a flamingo with its slender body and long curved neck, but smaller, delicate. Schools of sardine-size *cuatro ojos*, four-eyed fish, darted to and fro—two eyes below water, trained for food, the other two pointed skyward, looking for predators—and the flickering mass of bodies created silvery green trails in the shallows. An eagle—stark white head and body, pitch black wings—perched high above the impenetrable mangroves in a stately *conacaste* tree.

Malvasio steered the *lancha* into a narrow inlet on a thickly forested sand spit. Wild parakeets darted branch to branch in the thick foliage overhead. The deep, humid shade smelled of moss and rot. Fifty yards in, he cut the outboard, drifted the last few feet, then tied up to a mangrove root.

"This is the spot," he told Strock.

They scrambled out and headed for a clearing just beyond a rim of trees. Once they broke through the tree line, Strock slipped the rifle off his shoulder.

"What the hell . . . ?"

The clearing was maybe sixty-by-forty yards, obviously man-made, but to what end? As though reading Strock's mind, Malvasio said, "Used to be a soccer field here. A group of *zacateros* from La

Herradura on the other end of the estuary built it, cleared away the trees, put up goals, painted boundary lines. But after Hurricane Mitch and the earthquakes the thing just got forgotten. The swamp's already reclaimed most of it." He pointed to the mangrove roots sprouting everywhere in the loosening sand. "And the goalposts got pilfered for lumber or firewood."

Sixty yards created a shorter zero point than Strock would have liked. The Redfield scope was three to nine, so he cranked the power down to four to get some background in his field of vision. Malvasio had shooting range targets, a human silhouette circled with white rings, that he tacked up to a tree. He didn't mention where he got the targets and Strock chose not to ask.

That wasn't all Malvasio had brought along. From his rucksack he withdrew a Larand sound suppressor and handed it to Strock, saying, "An ounce of precaution. So we don't make what we're doing out here any more obvious than it needs to be."

Strock took the device from him, studied it briefly. He'd used one before, target work, never in a SWAT situation. It wasn't the kind of thing cops needed normally. A combat sniper, maybe. Or an assassin. It was made of copper mesh discs, perhaps two hundred, packed tight inside the black steel cylinder, decent enough though hardly state of the art. He screwed the silencer onto the end of the rifle barrel, saying, "I've heard some guys say you're more accurate with one of these on your piece than you are without."

Malvasio said, "You think that's true?"

Strock shrugged, eyeing the target sixty yards away. "I guess we'll find out."

He spent the next hour acquainting himself with the weapon. They were deep enough within the swamp that the wind wasn't a factor, so he didn't have to dope the scope. He did have to fuss with eye relief, though, until he could sight through cleanly the instant he had the stock shouldered, the target jumping to life in the crosshairs. The trigger pad felt natural, the action was a standard two-and-a-half pounds, smooth and clean—he could hold a dime on the barrel on dry fires. The rounds were light—fifty-five-grain boattails—tapered to minimize wind drag. Recoil was negligible. By midafternoon he was shooting half-inch groups of five, sitting, standing, prone. His chops were rusty, not lost; it all came back like an old habit—a little like sex, actually, a rhythm you never have to learn and never really forget. Just need practice. The pain in his knee flared up every now and then, but he could focus through it if he just relaxed. His cold shots—first rounds fired before the barrel heated up—were high right a quarter inch. Normal. As for whether he was more or less accurate with the silencer, it seemed a moot point—Strock had a pretty good idea the thing was staying on regardless.

He logged his shot placements and the atmospheric variables in his notepad, already bored.

Given he was using the silencer, the parakeets in the branches overhead seldom scattered when he fired, and when they did, they settled down again quickly. The humid air was thick with their chirps and trills. Hitting one square would prove an interesting challenge, he thought.

Following his glance, Malvasio said, "You want to shoot birds, go for the big black jobs. They're called *zanates*. They raid other birds' nests and eat their eggs, which is why you see them damn near everywhere."

"Yeah, but they're bigger and slower. I wasn't thinking of it in terms of pest control."

"Whatever. I'm just saying—killing them would be God's work."

"Then let God do it." He handed the gun out to Malvasio. "You want to take a few swings at the bat?"

Malvasio considered it, looked at his watch, then said, "We've got a while. Sure." He took the gun and lay down on the sand and settled in, not rushing as he fired off his first group of five. Watching him, Strock spotted several errors in technique right off.

"You tend to look up after every shot, know that? Stay married to the weapon. Keep your eye trained through the scope."

"I tried that. Things go in and out. Sometimes I can see, other times it's all black."

"That's because I've adjusted it to my eye relief, not yours. We can fix that easy. After that it's just practice."

A devilish glint rose in Malvasio's eye. "What'll I need you for, then?"

"To hit something that moves." Strock took the rifle from him and ejected the magazine for reload. "Or that's more than sixty yards away."

29

IN THE CAPITAL, MEN AXEL HAD ARRANGED TO MEET DURING THE week found themselves unexpectedly engaged. Follow-up meetings would have to be scheduled at an always unspecified later date. Various excuses were made, each less credible than the one before, though it seemed apparent the embezzlement scandal was at least partially to blame. Few officials, it soon became clear, welcomed the prospect of outsiders asking questions in the charged climate the criminal inquiry created, no matter how far afield those questions might be. Even men unaffiliated with ANDA seemed hopelessly elusive, not that gathering information hadn't been a challenge before. An alphabet soup of twenty-five disconnected but stubbornly territorial and ultimately toothless agencies oversaw water issues around the country, ANDA being the dominant player but other outfits possessing critical data of their own, data they guarded jealously: You had hydrologists at ASPAGUA, social workers with FIS, environmentalists from SALUD, engineers on behalf of EYCO, businessmen representing CEDES, and so on. They coordinated poorly even during the best of times, and arranging meetings typically resembled herding cats. Getting even four men together at a single time and place bordered on the miraculous, and Axel had wasted the better part of numerous visits during the past year trying to correlate data obtained from competing authorities. Now, just as he was trying to finalize his analysis, the flow of information virtually stopped.

Compounding the problem was the strange tendency of agency lackeys to abscond with government files when they left their jobs, doing so with the hope of launching second careers as consultants. The rumors of ANDA's imminent privatization only accelerated that trend—and no one was ever punished for the thefts—meaning Axel all too often had to chase down these freelancers and pay a fee for the privilege of reviewing documents that should have been public record. Now, with the embezzlement scandal a daily headline, these characters apparently decided it was unwise to push their luck, and most refused to so much as return calls.

But not even that was the worst of it. Charts and data Axel knew to be on hand not just at ANDA but at other entities in the capital—materials he'd reviewed cursorily only weeks before, and needed for his final follow-up—now could not be found or were delivered to him ridiculously piecemeal. Streamflow records for the Río Conacastal—data already frustratingly spotty due to destruction of river gauges during the twelve-year civil war—were suddenly missing or in suspicious disarray. The only recharge and groundwater yield analyses now available for the alluvial plain bordering the river had puzzling gaps, most notably the drought of 2002. Geological maps of the fractured basalt formations running through the area, suggestive of large-yield aquifers, were maddeningly incomplete. It made the task of confirming his prior analyses all but impossible.

Meanwhile, traveling about the city became more problematic as the protests in the streets escalated. Archbishop Saenz, a member of Opus Dei, the right-wing Catholic brotherhood, addressed a crowd of *areneros* in the cathedral plaza, exhorting them to stand firm against terrorists and to support the heroic troops in Iraq. Unfortunately for the archbishop, a jury in Fresno, California, had just awarded a multimillion-dollar verdict against Álvaro Saravia, a former air force colonel responsible for hiring the gunman who'd martyred the much-loved Archbishop Romero in 1980. When *efemelenistas* at the rally waved placards accusing Archbishop Saenz of complicity with his predecessor's assassins, the predictable melee broke out. Dozens were injured, one woman blinded. Revenge assaults flared up throughout the city.

Intent on keeping order around the cathedral, the police cracked down on street vendors in the nearby Mercado Central. The vendors responded by throwing rocks, but the PNC claimed shots were fired too. The police answered with bullets of their own, then tear gas, killing one man and sending two dozen others to intensive care.

As though that weren't bad enough, a riot broke out in La Esperanza, the hellish overcrowded penitentiary in Mariona near the capital. Homemade grenades exploded in fireballs along one wing of the prison, creating a stampede as inmates fled for their lives to escape the fires and blinding smoke. Battles in the yard broke out almost instantly between members of Mara Salvatrucha and Mara Dieciocho. They went at each other with homemade pipe guns called *chimbas* as well as shanks fashioned from broken chapel benches and steel bed frames. Thirty-one inmates were dead, some scalped, some burned to scorched meat in the fires. Dozens of others were wounded. Rumors of retaliatory atrocities were already circulating as prison guards fought to reassert control of the prison.

Word of the riot scarcely leaked out before a patrol car was bombed in Ilopango. Police patrols in Zacatecoluca and Sonsonate took fire. Gang-on-gang violence erupted in the capital and smaller cities in the countryside, compounded by a sudden surge in gunpoint robberies and carjackings. Curfews were enforced nationwide.

The Mercedes seemed too easy a target in that environment; Jude imposed a house arrest of his own, restricting Axel to his room at the Hotel Camino Real unless travel outside was absolutely necessary. Not that it mattered. Only two of the dozen contacts Axel had arranged to meet that week followed through, joining him for lunch at the hotel. They responded to all his inquiries with vague assurances that the information he needed would be available once all the disruptions died down—the civil unrest, the embezzlement inquiry. "But that could take ages," Axel protested, to which his luncheon companions could only shrug.

Then, late in the week, an American was killed. A Teamster of Salvadoran descent named Gilberto Soto had come back to visit family and meet with cargo drivers in Acajutla to discuss unionizing. While having dinner at his mother's house in a working-class barrio in Usulután, he stepped outside to take a call on his cell phone. Alerted by an accomplice on bicycle, three men walked up and opened fire, then ran off.

The union called it a death squad hit, but the port authorities and truck companies were parroting uncredited accounts that the crime was drug related. Some, given the recent mayhem in the wake of the riots at La Esperanza, blamed the gangs. Back in the States, the Teamsters were burning up phone lines, pressuring everyone from trade representatives to congressmen to the ambassador, demanding a credible inquiry from the PNC. But the police said only that the investigation was in progress. They had, as yet, no suspects.

As Jude passed this news along, Axel gazed from his balcony down the Boulevard de los Héroes, his hands folded, fingertips tapping against his chin. "They're not going to beef up your protection detail," Jude said, "since this killing looks like an isolated incident. That means we just have to take even greater precautions than we have already until things settle down. That may happen overnight or it could take a week. Maybe longer."

Axel seemed distracted, his gaze unfocused. "Consuela called this morning," he said finally. "She's coming here tomorrow, to the hotel, to stay with me." Almost imperceptibly, he blushed, despite the sobriety in his voice. "I trust she'll be safe. All things being relative, I realize."

THURSDAY EVENING, WORKING BY CANDLELIGHT, STROCK LASHED TWO pieces of driftwood into a cross and dressed it in a spare shirt and trousers, stuffed the clothes with palm fronds, cinched the cuffs with twine, then fashioned a head from an empty coconut, drawing in googly eyes and a knucklehead smile with burnt cork.

He showed his creation to Clara who sat hunched on the floor of her room beside the mattress, watching the little girl sleep. Clara, glancing up, indulged Strock with a shy, puzzled smile, and it warmed him. He'd grown increasingly, protectively fond of the woman the past few days—her kindness, her gentleness, her uncomplaining decency. Those things defined her in a way he'd once thought only a woman's looks could.

Not so long ago his worldview could have been summed up in the old joke: *Why do women have vaginas? So men will talk to them.* Now he would have liked nothing more than to just talk, reach through the language barrier and let Clara know how much he admired the way she cherished that child, carrying her everywhere, cooing to her, caressing her. Watching her sleep, for chrissake. He hoped, once this business with Malvasio and Ray's kid was done, to live up to that example. He ached to see his own little girl, make things right by her and her mother, drop the anger and self-pity and step up. He wanted Chelsea and Peg to know they could rely on him. If he could manage just that, he'd feel like a millionaire.

And yet he couldn't keep the pretty picture in focus for long. He was down here to keep Jude from getting killed, but that just meant other men would have to die. That was the plan as it stood so far. And he couldn't tell which was worse—the fact he knew that was wrong or that he didn't care. He had a talent. Didn't the nuns always say it's a sin to bury your talents?

When Malvasio arrived the next morning for their daily trip into the mangrove swamp, Strock collected the rifle, his cane, and a coil of rope he'd found in a closet. Then he handed Malvasio the scarecrow, saying, "Meet Sparky. Another day of just shooting at targets, I'll go batshit. Let's have some fun."

Out at the abandoned soccer field, they hung Sparky from a mangrove limb and Strock told Malvasio to let him swing. The scope's optics gathered illumination from the shafts of sunlight spearing down through the tree cover as Strock tracked the swaying target. Before long he was drilling the head and chest consistently. To make it harder, Malvasio went one better, twisted the rope tight, stepped behind the tree, then swung Sparky out like a tetherball. Strock fired five rounds and connected only once. To himself, he whispered, "Yee-haw," then called out to Malvasio: "Okay, collect the ornery fucker and let's do it again. Round two, the Sparky Challenge."

Strock slaughtered three different lengths of rope and made a hash of the shirt and trousers before finally managing to reliably nail a head shot. By noon he'd nicked the coconut into a garish little sculpture, at which point boredom settled in again. He traded places with Malvasio and let him shoot for a while, just letting Sparky swing back and forth, which was challenging enough. Strock was a natural, but he'd been on a gun range often enough to know that with a good scope, a good weapon, a little composure, and enough practice, anybody could hit just about anything. Not to say Malvasio was merely average. He'd become a good, steady shot over the week, a little slow on the trigger but deadly accurate, even when they placed the target farther away, a hundred yards, one fifty, threading their shots through the mangrove forest. Malvasio compensated for his lack of native skill by being patient, not chasing the target. As Strock watched him wait out Sparky, drill the dummy square five times running, an idea came.

While Malvasio was collecting his spent casings and reloading the rifle's magazine, Strock broke off a branch from a *ceiba* tree, cut Sparky down, and lashed the thick branch to the dummy's vertical axis, more than doubling the upward length of the pole. Malvasio, noticing finally, called out from the far end of the field, "What the hell are you up to now?"

"You can hold him up in the air this way." Strock demonstrated, limping forward, hoisting Sparky overhead like a bullet-riddled effigy. Finally, once he reached normal talking distance, he let the thing drop. "We used to do this on the target range, use a wig head on a broomstick—or two, make like it was a guy with a hostage."

Malvasio, sensing he'd be the first one on walkabout duty, said, "Yeah, but I'd guess the man holding the broom was down in the spotter's trench."

"When did you turn into such a pussy? Hell, if I was gonna kill you out here, I'd have done it Monday."

"That's comforting." Malvasio gathered up his rucksack. "We gotta cut things short today, anyway. Got some people to meet out east. After that, hopefully, I'll have a better idea where things go from here."

THREE HOURS LATER, MALVASIO SHOULDERED THROUGH THE CROWD at the street market in San Bartolo Oriente, then turned up a cramped, meandering alley. The buildings on either side provided welcome shade but scant relief from the heat. On a balcony above a beauty parlor, a chunky prostitute in red spandex with a helmet of canary yellow hair vamped for him, fanning herself with a postcard, smiling through a yawn. Fatima, Malvasio thought, recognizing her. A good taxpayer. She was, if he remembered right, sixteen.

Continuing on, he swam through a heady stench of dog piss, rotting trash, frying grease, and spilled beer, passing a man in a filthy apron hawking slices from a massive block of cheese, waving flies away with the blade of his cleaver. At a shoe shine stand, an old *campesino* watched stoically from his chair as, for some inscrutable reason, his sneakers got lathered with shoe black. Finally, Malvasio spotted Sleeper and Chucho perched on wood stools at a *comedor,* chowing down. Tiny *fuís* hopped about, pecking at crumbs beneath the tables.

Sleeper, dabbing fingers on a napkin, said, "*Quiubo,* Duende," through a mouthful of fried plantain. Despite the sweaty heat the kid wore his long-sleeved shirt buttoned at the collar and cuffs, a wise strategy given the recent police sweeps. Beside him, Chucho hunched over his steaming paper plate as he shoveled cheesy pork rind into his mouth. Unlike Sleeper, the kid was shirtless, his shiny dark skin immaculate. The ones coming up got it: Skip the ink.

Malvasio took a slip of paper from his pocket while *batucada,* a Brazilian drum music based on samba, tripped along rhythmically from a nearby sound system, lending an air of Carneval.

"So," he said, "the vampires brave the light of day."

Sleeper did a little shoulder shirk as his eyes darted side to side, scanning the crowded, twisting alleyway in both directions. "Man's gotta eat."

Malvasio laid the slip of paper on the table. "I'm assuming if you'd heard anything yet about what we talked about, you'd have told me." He'd instructed Sleeper to spread word town to town—he wanted to know if anyone had brought in a roll of film to be developed concerning the beheaded woman found along the Río Jiboa. Sleeper had sent out *chamacos* he could trust, from here to the capital, making it known. Word would be rewarded. Silence wouldn't.

Sleeper licked his teeth. "I told you. Truco Valdez ain't a dope. He gets that developed, it'll be in San Salvador, and there's damn near no way to track that."

"Speaking of Mr. Valdez. You know his organization, La Tregua."

"Yeah, I know." Sleeper spat. "Punks give up the flag? Fuck 'em."

Malvasio turned the slip of paper so Sleeper could read it. It contained an address. "You're going to pretend you want to join."

Sleeper's eyes hardened. "No way."

"Excuse me?"

"You can't. This is wrong. This is . . . This is evil, man, you can't do this."

"I said 'pretend.'"

"I'll get the mark on me, understand? They'll say I'm tricked up."

In the background, Chucho licked his fingers, paying a bit more attention now. Nervy little bastard, Malvasio thought. It was a talent.

"Your friend here can vouch for you. Besides, the group has a rep as a front. *Mareros* try to make it look like they're boning out when they're really not. Run with that."

"You don't get it."

"No, I get it." Malvasio turned to leave. "I just don't care."

"I do this," Sleeper said to his back, "you're gonna do like you promised, right? Get me to the laser clinic." He meant one of the newer tattoo removal salons, run by the Catholic church with funding assistance from, of all places, the U.S. embassy. It would spare him having them burned off.

"Your own mother won't recognize you," Malvasio assured him, speaking over his shoulder, then walked away. It was time, finally, for him to suffer a little kiss-up-kick-down of his own. At the hands of *el mero mero*.

30

HECTOR TORRES WAITED IN A PRIVATE ROOM AT EL ARRIERO WITH
the colonel and the judge and Wenceslao Sola. The occasion for the
gathering was the completion of a new chapel for the local orphanage, which the judge had generously financed. Fresh from the chris-
tening ceremony—at which, Malvasio imagined, the nuns had
prostrated themselves in gratitude—the four men dined on grilled
goat, basted with mango and lime, served with rice, chunks of yucca
fried to a golden brown, and glasses of ice-cold beer.

Glancing up as Malvasio entered, Hector said, "I was beginning
to wonder if you'd withered up in the heat, like a spider." The others smiled darkly or ignored the remark, and Malvasio figured that
was as good as it was going to get. Meanwhile, Hector gestured for
him to take a chair against the wall and wait.

Malvasio had received a serious dressing down earlier in the
week for the screwup with his *veteranos*—and he had every intention of passing the abuse along tenfold when the time was right—
but for now, it was his understanding a second flogging wasn't in
store. He was there to provide a progress report that would make
everybody happy, to show a suitable level of contrite resolve, and
then he'd grovel his way out the door. The last two wouldn't be a
problem, he thought. It was an act he'd mastered long ago. As for
making anyone happy, though, a glance around the table convinced
him that would take some doing. These were men who equated
happiness with perfection—in particular, perfection from others.

Sitting next to Hector, Judge Regalado seemed almost ethereal—
a thin, waxy man with a sharp nose, cold pale eyes, and wisps of
white hair curling out from a narrow head that tapered to a point at

the chin. He could pass for a Spaniard, and it took an effort, some-times, to remember that a man of such Gothic delicacy could be so roundly feared.

The source of that fear, of course, was in many ways the man across the table from him: Colonel Vides. He was as dark as Hector but taller and better-looking, despite a beak of a nose and a tiny, pinched mouth. He carried himself with the clipped grace of a man who had commanded other men and earned their respect. But his eyes, if studied carefully, revealed something else—a base and strangely volatile pride. He was, after all, a country boy at heart, raised above his station by his military career, and his newfound status as a civilian among influential men seemed to encourage a certain venal bravura, tinged with an almost operatic mean streak. Even so, Malvasio had to concede the colonel a grudging respect. He was the only one, other than Hector, with the remotest clue how to actually accomplish anything.

Lastly, Wenceslao Sola hunkered over his plate, pudgy, self-conscious, ill-tempered, seldom glancing up as he chewed his food. He inspired neither fear nor love as far as Malvasio could tell, except from the ratty terrier of garbled breed that sat at his feet, waiting for scraps.

While Malvasio waited, the colonel inquired after one of the judge's grandchildren, a girl named Rosa. Apparently, she was thirteen but looked seven, and for the past year she'd suffered terrible pain in her joints. After ruling out lupus, her doctors sent her to an endocrinologist in Miami who uncovered a rare thyroid disorder. Rosa was now on a regimen of pills and nightly injections of human growth hormone, plus monthly shots to suppress puberty—bone growth stops, the judge explained, when a girl has her first period. Meanwhile, her hair had begun falling out, and the family had pulled her from school to spare her the ridicule. Though the pain was better, the medications had side effects: She was sluggish and dull-witted, with no interest in things she'd once loved, even her pets; she'd grown fat and slept sixteen hours a day. Everyone murmured their sympathies and invoked the help of God and family, then Hector at last turned to Malvasio.

"So, you have news," he said. It was a command, not an invitation.

Malvasio nodded. "I'll know the whereabouts of Truco Valdez in a day or two. Latest, beginning of next week." A godawful promise, practically a lie.

The colonel screwed up his withered mouth; his lips all but vanished. "He's had a week already with the pictures." He tilted his head back when he talked, as though to look down on you. His voice was reedy. "Long enough to pass them along to whomever he pleases."

"There are only so many places between here and the capital where he can get film developed," Malvasio said. "I've put out word. If anything like those pictures shows up, I'll know."

The judge, holding aloft a morsel of goat impaled on his fork, said: "But soon enough? I believe that is Narciso's point."

"I can't control that."

The judge shook his head in disgust, then inserted the sliver of meat into his mouth, eyes rolling back behind fluttering lashes as he chewed.

Hector sat forward, hands clenched over his plate. "It is what it is. We don't even know if there's anything in those pictures to bother over." Malvasio, though gratified by the show of backhanded support, knew it was motivated by self-interest. Hector was, after all, the one ultimately responsible for these recent mistakes, such was the chain of command. "What about this boy, the one who says he saw the woman abducted?"

"He hasn't been found yet, but I received some good news right before I came here. We're close." Another lie. Malvasio had yet to tell anyone about the boy's baby sister, now in Clara's care at the *rancho*. He was keeping that to himself for now, among other things. He still held out hope the mother would choose her innocent little girl over her rash, mouthy son. No news till good news, he thought. That's my motto.

"You're not very good at finding people," the colonel remarked.

"It's not a big country." This was Sola, his first contribution, made between mouthfuls. He tried to look menacing, then slipped a bit of gristle from his mouth to the dog.

"With seven million people in it," Malvasio said. "And it was my understanding I wasn't the only one looking." He glanced the colonel's direction, wondering: What, your guys took the week off? He knew better than to say it out loud. "Regardless, the boy knows, he opens his mouth, his mother suffers. Plus, the rigged ID worked out, the dead woman and her runaway head got cremated. She is who you say she is, and nobody's the wiser."

Everyone glanced up, stunned by his impertinence. How dare he hide behind what everyone else had been obliged to do to bail him out. Hector, sensing a need to move things along, said, "For now, you're right. Let's hope it stays that way." He shooed a fly from his plate. "What about this other thing, regarding the hydrologist?"

"That's all in place. But given the killing of the American, the Teamster—"

"We had no part in that," Hector said. A smile: "Not to say we don't know who did."

"Or that we object," the judge added, carving another portion of goat.

"No one's heard?" It was the colonel. Everyone turned. "There's been a break in the case. It should be on the news later." He puckered up a smile. "I won't spoil the surprise."

"My point," Malvasio said, trying to get things back on track so he could wrap up and leave, "is that it's not like some tramp from the hills you can claim is a hooker and get believed. You've got a dead American. Perks people up. Following suit on the hydrologist right now—"

"It is, perhaps, a moot point." This was Sola again, asserting himself—an odd move for him, among these men at least. He glanced around the table, wiggling his knife and fork, then focused on Malvasio. "As I was saying before you arrived—the Teamster, good result, bad timing, granted. But we caught some luck earlier in the week with the ANDA fiasco. Ironic, actually. I had a friend in the administration contact the acting head of that department, tell him to slow things down to a crawl. I couldn't do that with Manrique in the picture. He couldn't be bribed because he was stealing." He laughed, tipping his chin down to keep from spitting food. The little mutt tensed at his feet, waiting. "Word has gone out to a number of others too. Let this Odelberg beg all he wants, he won't get the information he needs. Better no answer than an answer that fucks us—at least till Strickland, from Torkland Overby, visits next week. He'll ask for a report on this Odelberg's findings—it's been almost a year, after all. If nothing's final, the hydrologist bags up and goes home. I have that on good authority from Lazarek, our friend at ODIC. The company will say his work was inconclusive. That suits everyone's purpose for now, and life goes on. Simple." He looked from face to face, wearing a bent little smile, then resumed the attack on his plate.

Malvasio had to restrain himself from reaching across the table and strangling him. *I have to arrange to kill a man for you, an American, pin it on the* mareros; *I have to find a way to avoid taking out my dead best friend's son in the bargain; then, just for a kicker, I have to stand there while an old sidekick, who not so long ago vowed to see me dead, takes a few potshots at pointblank range— you couldn't come up with this before?* But of course that was crazy thinking. *Who needs to plan ahead when nothing costs you?*

"So I can stand down," he said, "from getting my guys into place."

All of them glanced up as one, like before, their eyes even more disapproving than earlier—his initiative was impudent, reckless— but once again only Hector spoke. "No, continue with that for now. One never knows."

Sola saw this as an opening to say something else. He spoke to Malvasio without looking at him. "Incidentally, I got a call from someone who works with the hydrologist's bodyguard. He apparently found out the *puta socialista* that the old goat is screwing was married to one of my cousins. He wanted to know if I thought there was anything he should know about her, anything that might raise concerns—I mean, beyond the fact she's disgracing herself and her children. Revenge against me or my interests, that sort of thing. I told him nothing specific, just that we considered her a little crazy, moody, unrealistic. I didn't want him getting any ideas he should take some kind of action that might complicate what you've been planning."

"I appreciate that," Malvasio said. It took everything he had to give the man credit for so much as a viable impulse, but he knew his place. Then, feigning upbeat: "This keeps up, I won't have anything to do."

"I wouldn't worry about that just yet," Hector said, sitting back as a waiter cleared his plate. "And following up on what Wenceslao said earlier, about making the hydrologist's work difficult—confusion is good, more is better." He smiled wickedly, leaning forward on his elbows, licking his teeth. His odd good humor seemed to echo around the table; shrewd grins appeared all around. He said, "Have you ever worked with animals?"

THE CATTLE GRAZED IN A PASTURE RIMMED WITH PARCHED *tiguilote* trees on a rise above the Río Conacastal. To the north, beyond a misty haze, the volcano known as Chaparrastique loomed darkly over the scorched plain.

The herd consisted of several hundred scrawny piebald shorthorns with goatish ears and primitive brand markings. They belonged to a cattleman named Humilde Lopez who with his sons tended them on land owned by Judge Regalado.

Malvasio parked his van and stared down for a moment at the river lazing muddily at its dry season low. The water was largely untreated runoff from the judge's sugar processing plant, an undrinkable brew of plant matter and sludge. For all he knew, it was poisonous to the cows.

Have you ever worked with animals?

Even with the sun dipping toward the horizon, the open air felt like a furnace. Lopez and one of his sons were shoeing a horse in the lengthening shade of a lone *ceiba* tree in the center of the pasture. Malvasio got out of his van and called out his greeting as he approached. The father handed the hammer to his son, and Malvasio, as he came closer, noticed that the young man lacked two fingers on his right hand. Malvasio gestured for the older man to follow him, a little ways toward the dusty riverbed, so they could talk alone.

"I just left the judge and Señor Torres," Malvasio told him. "I was asked to tell you that they want you to move your herd from this pasture to the one across the river this weekend."

Humilde listened as though receiving penance for someone else's sins. He was a dark, reserved, bony man. A milky cataract hazed one eye. "There is hardly any water here, except for the river, which is no good. There is none over there."

"I'm sorry."

"The judge said he would send water trucks so I could fill the cisterns for the cows to drink. None have come in over two weeks. And the wells. Believe me, I do not want to complain"—something in his voice suggested he was thinking, *Everyone knows about the woman who complained*—"but the wells are going bad. They need to be redrilled." Gesturing with his hand for emphasis, he added, "Deeper."

"I can pass that along," Malvasio said. "I'm just supposed to let you know you're to move the herd. And the judge wants you to follow the *quebrada* to where the line of shrubs heads off uphill. Cross over there, pick up the shrub line again on the far side, and follow it through those fields to the lower pasture."

The cattleman seemed puzzled. The shrubs were believed to follow the path of an underground stream. "But the American has his instruments there. He dug wells."

"It's my understanding none of that matters anymore. In fact, everyone will be much obliged if you and your herd make short work of all that."

Humilde Lopez realized finally what he was being told to do. "There is still the problem with water."

You're talking to the wrong man, Malvasio thought. Not that there's a right man. He reached into his pocket and withdrew his cash. "I'm to pay you for your trouble."

HECTOR HAD SAID TO CONTINUE WITH THE OTHER PLAN AS WELL, AND so Malvasio headed back into San Bartolo Oriente to where the hydrologist's woman lived. The development was called, somewhat extravagantly, Villas de Miramonte and was located on the outskirts of town behind a high graffiti-tagged wall.

Shortly after the hydrologist's interest in Consuela Rojas became known, Malvasio learned where she lived and discussed with Hector and the colonel the best way to proceed. Though she was known to Sola and his relatives, it seemed best to avoid further involvement of the family. It turned out that one of the bartenders at El Arriero had an uncle whose mechanic knew someone who knew someone else, the daisy chain of acquaintance ending finally with a retired bank teller with the appropriate inclinations who rented a house across the street and three doors down from the Rojas woman in Villas de Miramonte.

The old man, whose name was Osorio, had been one of the government's *orejas* during the war, informing on bank customers who deposited suspicious amounts of cash or whose transactions hinted at allegiances with the popular front. He was a wizened, shambling, cheerful man who wore white socks and glistening shoes and crooked bifocals.

Malvasio had introduced himself to Osorio last week. He'd dropped the appropriate names and mentioned that the object of his interest was one of Osorio's neighbors. The old man cagily guessed which one right off, saying he'd had his doubts about the Rojas woman for some time. Her father had been a *socialista:* not a Marxist exactly but close enough, especially for a military man. And the woman herself was a divorcée, which meant she'd fallen away from the church. Visitors appeared at her house whom Osorio recognized from their faces alone as the complaining kind, the sort who use pity for the poor as an excuse to shun work and mock God.

Malvasio had asked that Osorio provide his house as an occasional surveillance post, with the possibility that some of Malvasio's assistants, posing as workmen, might also appear, conducting their observations from a van parked just outside. Osorio had responded that he was only too glad to help.

"Criminals run free like dogs these days," he'd said. "They should be dealt with like dogs."

NIGHT HAD FALLEN BY THE TIME MALVASIO DROVE UP TO THE TALL iron gate at the entrance to Villas de Miramonte and provided Osorio's name to the two men manning the guard station. They wore no uniforms and carried no weapons, though an ancient M1 stood ready in the wood shack where they sat playing cards by lamplight, listening to the radio.

Inside the gate, a hundred homes stood packed one against the other along several long culs-de-sac. The houses were the standard cinder block structures, a little better than average in craftsmanship but still limited to propane in their kitchens plus no hot water. Despite those drawbacks the average price ran eighty to a hundred thousand dollars. It was something of a miracle anyone but the rich could afford property. If she hadn't had a decent lawyer and a wealthy ex-husband, Consuela Rojas wouldn't have been able to afford her home either.

Given it was after dark, people hid inside their homes, content to be barricaded with their families. Malvasio parked in front of Osorio's house, but rather than heading to his door, he made his way across the street to the home of Consuela Rojas, carrying a cloth kit bag.

The woman was gone, Osorio had reported, having traveled to

the capital to be with her American *marinovio*. The house stood empty and dark.

Using the shadows for concealment, Malvasio removed his rake gun and torsion pick from his bag. The lock had a five-pin tumbler but it was old and loose and he worked all five pins up to their shear lines without much bother. The lock cleared within ninety seconds. He pushed the door open, took out his flashlight, and stepped inside.

The decor, though immaculate, almost out-humbled the neighborhood. The woman had once lived with her wealthy doctor husband in a colonial era mansion in San Miguel. She'd had a personal chef, *servientas*. Now this.

A rough cedar table, covered with a simple linen tablecloth, consumed the small dining room. The living room had a couch, one chair, a lamp, and a simple cabinet containing memorabilia and photographs. From the pictures he learned she had two children, boy and girl, both in their twenties now, off studying somewhere. An elfin mother with saintly eyes. And the socialist colonel father, a handsome man, wearing a suit, not his uniform. No evidence of Dr. Ex.

There were two bedrooms upstairs, both barely big enough to hold a bed and a dresser. He searched cabinets and closets and drawers for anything the hydrologist might have left behind, something that indicated what he was thinking, planning, but found nothing beyond the tidy little things of a woman with flawed luck. He even searched her lingerie, taking in the flowery scent of her perfume, fingering the lace. The underthings were surprisingly chic. He went to the closet and saw that she'd kept some of her clothes from her marriage, too, relics of her former station.

But now she's met an American, he thought. Her hay's made. Barring any unforeseen calamities.

Malvasio had considered bugging the house, an RF transmitter for each room, planted inside a light socket, but Jude was smart enough to sweep the house and the radio frequencies would be impossible to miss. It would be great to know what they all were saying here, thinking themselves safe, but not at the cost of having them bag up and go elsewhere. The front of the house was a perfect kill zone, better than anything he'd expected when he'd first decided to enlist Strock in the plan. No point getting greedy.

He looked out the rear bedroom window to confirm that the set-up outside resembled Osorio's. If anything, it was even more confined. The houses on either side and to the rear shared a high cinder block wall draped with thorny *veranera*.

He came away from the window, thinking all in all the house would be hard to escape but easy to defend. It would be important to lure people outside, he thought, if it came to that.

31

CONSUELA LEANED FORWARD OVER THE DINNER TABLE, HER FACE marbled with shadow from the guttering candlelight, her pearls chiming against her plate. "They killed an American."

"And arrests were made," Carlos shot back, "within twenty-four hours."

"Arrests are hardly a problem—unless, of course, you want the real killers."

"Go ahead and mock. People trust the police."

"The suspects were taken away in hoods, tortured. One was raped."

The four of them—Carlos, Consuela, Axel, and Jude—were seated in the corner of a small, tony restaurant in the Paseo General Escalón, not far from the hotel. The neighborhood had held secret torture chambers for the counterinsurgency during the war, now it featured embassies. In the background, dated American music burbled gently—Peggy Lee, Nancy Wilson, Vic Damone.

"You sound like the *efemelenistas,*" Carlos said. "It's obscene the way they're making this political. Death squads—what a load of crap. It was a family affair. End of story."

"If it's a family affair," Consuela responded, "how do you explain the break-in at the Center for Labor Rights? Why won't the PNC disclose their sources?"

"If it's a political hit, explain the hatred between this guy and his wife's family. Explain the life insurance."

"The life insurance named the children as beneficiaries, not the wife. They were divorced, she has nothing to gain. No one in the family believes her mother hired the killers."

News of arrests in the killing of the American Teamster had broken just before dinner, generating controversy instantly. The suspects were the dead man's mother-in-law and two *mareros.* The mother-in-law, paraded before television cameras, wept openly and begged for help, claiming she was innocent and had no idea who her two so-called accomplices were.

Carlos said, "The family's lying for her. They're all ashamed."

"It's a cover-up. Everybody says so—the Teamsters, the unions here, even the Human Rights Ombudsman."

"How would they know?"

"It's obvious!"

Carlos grimaced and shook his head. "You only see the bad."

"I see what's staring me in the face. Meanwhile, how convenient, they find two gang members to share the blame."

"The *mareros* are terrorists."

"Everyone's a terrorist! The gangs, the priests, teachers, unions. Same as it was during the war. Ask the men who had the American killed."

"He was killed by his family!"

Axel, a look on his face like a ref who's lost control of his fight, finally saw the wisdom of breaking in. "Anyone like to join me in an Armagnac?"

One table over, a trio of Americans from a pharmacy chain

dined with their Salvadoran associates. They'd been glancing this direction now and again as voices swelled. In a little reverse eavesdropping of his own, Jude had overheard some curious observations: *The drugstore has become the female convenience store. . . . You have to nail down the corner of Main and Main. . . .* It was astonishing, Jude thought, how bland their voices were and how much they looked alike—same oxford shirts, same pleated slacks, same mama's-boy hair.

Elsewhere, a Salvadoran businessman, elegant and bald, dined with his two bodyguards. Jude had watched them throughout the meal just as he'd watched everyone who came or went—not many, slow Friday, the week's upheaval to blame. He'd even scrutinized the servers marching to and from the kitchen, to make sure no new faces suddenly appeared. They looked like clerks here. All was staid. All was calm.

The waiter appeared, and the table ordered coffee. Hoping to lighten the mood, Axel also requested a ginger flan; then, remembering his mention of Armagnac, he asked the waiter to bring along a snifter of that too, adding to no one in particular as he handed back his dessert menu, "What the hell, since I brought it up."

As it turned out, only he showed any interest in either indulgence, listlessly picking at the one, halfheartedly sipping the other, while everyone else lingered over their coffee. Carlos fumed with stoic pride. Consuela smiled valiantly, wringing her napkin in her lap. Then, at last, *la cuenta*. Jude paid, as was his custom—it was his job to leave Axel with as little to manage vis-à-vis strangers as possible—while Carlos went out to bring up the car.

Mortified, Consuela dropped her cheek into her palm and sighed. She was an attractive *morena* with soft dark eyes and wavy shoulder-length hair, and she wore a simple but elegant sleeveless black dress, set off by her pearls. Jude could see how Axel had fallen so hard, so fast. And any concerns he'd had about her wanting to extort, manipulate, or otherwise influence Axel had melted away almost instantly— she seemed honorable, guileless, and unabashedly enamored.

"That was wrong of me," she said. "I should have kept quiet. I'm sorry."

Axel reached across the table. "Don't be silly."

"It reflects badly on you, Axel." She pronounced his name "ox ale."

"Carlos is an adult. We all are." He squeezed her hand. "Disagreements aren't fatal."

THEY TOOK THE ALAMEDA ROOSEVELT PAST THE PLAZA DE LAS Américas, Axel sitting in back with his arm around Consuela, the two of them discreet but tender. Outside, street vendors waited at every corner, hawking papayas, bananas, dolls, thread, even the two-liter cans of olive oil that the relief agencies, for whatever reason, doled out to people who had no use for it. Carlos, in an excess of caution, kept the car moving without a single stop all the way to the hotel.

Fire trees thick with their distinctive, fleshy red blossoms lined the drive to the lobby entrance. Uniformed guards bearing shotguns strolled the parking area.

As Carlos pulled up to the entrance, Jude told Axel and Consuela, "Give me a moment," then got out. Carlos immediately relocked the doors as Jude checked the area. Three taxis waited at the cab stand. The doorman chatted over smokes with the parking valet. Seeing nothing amiss, Jude signaled for Carlos to unlock the doors, then helped Consuela out, followed by Axel, and accompanied them both inside past massive urns brimming with flowering *izote*. Carlos waited, the Mercedes idling, in case a sudden getaway became necessary.

Jude led the way across the lobby to the elevators and up to the second floor. He tried never to book a room higher than that, in case a fire or other emergency dictated jumping from the balcony.

He entered Axel's room first and ensured that it and the balcony were clear, then checked the bedside kit—two smoke masks, a panic alarm linked to Jude's cell phone, and a fire bag containing a flashlight and directions out of the building—then let the couple in to resume their evening together. Once they were safe and locked tight, Jude went to his own room, called down to Carlos on his cell, thanked him—deciding not to mention his disagreement with Consuela over dinner—and told him they'd call in the morning when the car was needed.

JUDE STRIPPED TO HIS SHORTS AND SAT WITH HIS LAPTOP ON THE BED, reviewing his security brief for the next day and checking e-mail for updates from Fitz. *House Party 2,* in English with Spanish subtitles, played quietly on TV in the background, amusing if only for the hip-hop translations: "motherfucker" became *puta madre,* "bro" morphed into *chero*. According to Fitz, the PNC had reasserted control not just throughout the capital but in the smaller cities too. The unrest had settled down, the highways were safe. This wasn't, and wouldn't become, Haiti. The trip east to San Bartolo Oriente on Sunday was cleared.

Come midnight Jude put his laptop aside, turned off the TV, and settled back on his pillow, staring at the shadows flickering across the ceiling. He couldn't sleep. He pictured Axel and Consuela naked in bed, even imagined once or twice a giddy little moan from beyond the door that connected the two rooms.

From his briefcase he removed the poem Eileen had written, reading it for the thousandth time—*handsome bruiser . . . vanished like a punk*—stung by her mockery all over again but telling himself he'd roused some feeling in her. Wounded her. That meant something, right?

He went out to the balcony and, scratching his hindquarters, gazed out across the city, vast and sprawling—a million lights, none of them beckoning to him. He nudged that miserable little despair aside with thoughts of how Strock might be faring. He'd felt back-handedly grateful for the week's tumult, the anger in the streets, the violence, the minute-by-minute need to stay focused on Axel's safety. It had proved a welcome distraction from that other bit of business. And yet, on a handful of occasions, he'd snuck a call to the cell numbers he had for Malvasio and Clara, only to reach dead air or, finally, recordings that the numbers were no longer in service. He told himself that there was nothing so strange about that, an excess of caution on Malvasio's end. Predictable, really. Maybe he'd found out about the FBI's visit and was playing it safe. But that was just so much whistling past the graveyard. What have you been part of, he wondered. What kind of luck will it take to never find out?

32

"GET YOUR CLOTHES," MALVASIO SAID, "WHATEVER ELSE YOU HAVE. It's moving day."

Strock glanced up from the table where he sat in morning diagonals of shadow and light, a dripping hunk of *pan dulce* suspended over his coffee. "Moving where?"

"Time to get you into place."

Strock smiled, set the pastry down, and licked his fingers. "And I was just getting into the swing of things here."

From the tone of the quip, Malvasio wondered what had developed between the Candyman and Clara the past few nights. It wasn't sexual, that seemed obvious—and odd, given Strock's appetite on that end—but there was something. "Vacation's over. Sorry."

Strock mugged a pout then got up, grabbed his cane, and thumped toward the hallway back to his room. As Malvasio went to the stove to pour himself coffee, Clara passed behind him with the baby, hurrying outside. She did everything in her power to avoid eye contact, and he was struck again by the sense that something was going on between her and Strock. Then it dawned on him—it wasn't about Strock at all. It was the girl.

Malvasio knew Clara's story: a war orphan from San Francisco Gotera, brought to the judge's plantation at ten with a noxious dose of clap—bad enough to make her sterile—sent to the nuns in Santiago de María, kept at the orphanage till she was fifteen, then farmed out as a *servienta* and ultimately enlisted into the operation. She'd been kept in the dark about its uglier aspects but she wasn't stupid. Children are commodities, they change hands. She knew that better than anyone. But she'd given the little girl a name—Constancia—and it tumbled from her lips nonstop as she carried the little one everywhere, doting on her, singing to her. Now, though, with Strock leaving, Clara's little game of house was ending. Malvasio guessed she knew that. He had to come up with something to tell her.

He'd yet to think through the how or when of the baby's return to her real mother. Maybe once Jude's hydrologist was out of the picture. Maybe never. So what was the harm in standing pat just a little longer?

He went outside and crouched before Clara who sat in a sandy patch of palm shade, bouncing the infant gently in her lap. The brine from the ocean, ripe with heat, thickened the air, the surf a rumbling hush beyond the high wall. Malvasio smiled, tugged on one of the little girl's heels, then told Clara he had nowhere to send them just yet and needed her to stay here, with Constancia, until something developed. She and the baby would be all alone. Would she mind that?

Clara looked puzzled, unsure she'd understood. Then she shook her head—no, she wouldn't mind. The tiniest of smiles appeared, as though she'd gotten away with something.

They reached San Bartolo Oriente just before noon, turning onto an overgrown dirt road near the edge of town and following it through shabby woods to a deserted construction yard. As they pulled up, Sleeper's pal Chucho jumped from the shade of a ragged-barked *amate* tree to undo the padlock, pull back the wire gate, and let them in. He looked ill, with rheumy, bloodshot eyes and a fidgety case of the sniffles—all of which earned him a mad dog stare from Strock.

The yard was half an acre in size, with windblown trash stuck to the fence around the perimeter. Any usable vehicles, tools, or lumber had long ago been carted off by thieves. All that remained were drifting piles of sand and gravel, a Dynapac roller with a burnt-up engine, and the rusted carcass of a dump truck stripped of its motor, tires, and seats.

At one end of the yard stood a high wood-frame garage, built to hold four trucks. On top of the garage, the old owners had erected a set of offices from two-by-four framing and plywood sheets, and on top of that two rooms sat by themselves, sharing a common wall and roofed with tar paper. Sleeper, wearing a bandana but no shirt, called down from one of the topmost rooms.

"Got you fixed, Duende. Hustle on up, check it out."

Wood-plank stairs led from the garage to the first floor of offices, the cedar rotting away in places. Malvasio could see from the look on Strock's face that the arrangement brought back infuriating memories. Strock didn't say anything, though, and Malvasio took that as a good sign.

From atop the garage, a wood ladder led the rest of the way. Malvasio steadied it as Strock struggled up. Chucho scrambled up after, taking Strock's bag. Malvasio brought up the rear, carrying the rifle and cane.

The two rooms were small, connected by an open doorway. The windows, if there'd ever been any, had been stripped away with the doors, and that helped with the heat. Later in the afternoon the shade from the *amate* and a pair of even taller *ceiba* trees would help cool things down some more. The plywood walls bore water stains and a taint of mildew soured the air.

Sleeper had cut away a jagged hole in the outer wall, just this side of which lay a thin mattress. Must've been a clown act getting that thing up the ladder, Malvasio thought, especially with Mr. Jittery Sniffles involved. Candles and matches lay atop a makeshift table made from an upturned crate. A bucket sat in the corner of the other room—the toilet.

"Welcome to your sniper hide," Malvasio said.

Strock looked bereft. "Bit of a switch from where I've been."

"You'll only be up here through Wednesday. Friday at the latest. Good news is, there are things going on that may render this whole exercise pointless. If that's the case, we'll bag up quietly and go our merry way. But if that falls through, I want to be ready."

Taking that as a cue, Strock flipped down the bipod legs on the AR-15 and lifted its scope caps front and back, then eased down into a prone position on the mattress, sighting the weapon through the hole in the wall. Malvasio knelt behind him, peering down the line of the rifle barrel beyond the feathery green crest of several *mariscargo* trees. A couple hundred yards away lay the wall surrounding Villas de Miramonte, and beyond that the cul-de-sac down which the hydrologist's woman lived. It was that sight line, from here to Consuela's door, that had crystallized the plan in Malvasio's mind. No need to rent a room across from the man's hotel, be seen, leave a paper trail. Sooner or later he'd come by to visit his lady friend. With patience, it would all fall together.

"I'll go down tomorrow," he told Strock, "point out the target house. Nobody's around this weekend. Meanwhile, make yourself as comfortable as you can. I'll send Sleeper or Chucho back with some water and food, soap and towels. They'll check in every morning and night."

"I'm gonna want a bag of kitty litter," Strock said.

Malvasio took a second to process that. "Do I need to hear this?"

Strock slapped his left elbow with his right hand. "Prop it under my arm, brace my shot."

Malvasio checked to make sure Sleeper caught that. The kid

looked like he was ready to bust. "Duende, that other thing you had me working on. I got news."

Malvasio assumed he meant Truco Valdez. "Tell me at the bottom." He added a head nod to suggest he and his buddy start down now. "I'll be right there."

Strock waited till Sleeper and Chucho were on the ground, then said, "Where'd you find the two grease spots?"

"Around. More just like them everywhere you look."

"The tall one, guy who speaks English?"

"Sleeper."

"Looks like the Crocodile Man, all those tats. But he's normal compared to this sidekick."

"Chucho."

"Kid acts like he eats Sterno."

"Lot of crank and chemicals down here. He's not always that bad."

"Keep him away from me. Can you do that?"

Now he's dictating, Malvasio thought. "Sure. I'll try. Him and Sleeper are like Cisco and Pancho lately, but I'll try."

"I don't mean to second-guess your judgment. I'm just saying, given the way things might have to go down—"

"No problem. Consider it done. You'll only have to deal with Sleeper."

Strock nodded absently, then yawned. "Appreciate it."

"Just so you know—you'll be seeing more of him than me the next few days."

"Oh, this just gets better."

"I'll try to stop by at least once a day, but I've got a lot on my plate. So Sleeper's gonna be your main source of face time. He can get pretty buzzed himself and he's chatty when he is. Just so you know."

Strock turned back to his weapon, closed one eye, and sighted through the scope again. "Let's hope that's the worst of my problems."

When he reached the ground, Malvasio gestured for Sleeper to join him by the van. He counted out money for groceries. "Buy the stuff we talked about, plus the kitty litter if you can find it. And water, make sure he's got plenty. It's gonna get hot up there." He handed the cash over. "Another thing—let's think about keeping your pal away from my pal the next few days."

Sleeper counted the bills, then stuffed them in his pocket. "What's his hang-up?"

"It's a cultural thing. You said you had something to tell me?"

"Yeah. Me and Chucho, we went to one of those meetings, La Tregua? On the button, man, like you said, bunch of *putas chavos* just want their tats removed."

"Fascinating. But Truco."

"He's around."

Malvasio waited. In the background, Chucho squatted in the shade, gripping his head. "That's it—he's around?"

"What do you want? I press too hard, I get made, then what?"

"You're going back."

"Tonight, yeah—What's *with* you, man? Lighten the fuck up."

"Tonight, what?"

"Me and Chucho, we got a bead on a guy who's in touch. Think so. We'll chat him up, tail him if we have to. By tomorrow—day after, tops—I'll have your guy."

"There," Malvasio said, grateful the prediction he'd given Hector wouldn't need revision. "Better." He opened the van door and climbed behind the wheel.

Sleeper stepped away into the sun, glancing up at the sniper hide. "That's an evil piece your buddy's got. Chucho and me gonna get the same?"

"That what you want?" Malvasio already had identical weapons put aside, minus silencers and scopes. Part of the plan. "Let me see what I can work out."

Sleeper liked that. *"Qué chivo."* Awesome.

"Put your shirt on."

Sleeper, clowning, mimicked *boo-hoo.* "Poor Duende. So much on his mind." He undid the knot in his sleeves. "Give us a lift to town?"

"No. I just thought of something I forgot to tell my guy. I need to go back up."

"We can wait."

"It's gonna be a while."

Malvasio waited for Sleeper and Chucho to sulk away, then retrieved from the back of the van a cell phone with an earpiece and a box of sabot rounds.

The cell phone was so he could communicate with Strock during the shooting if it came to that. He'd try to limit use before then so no one could trap the signal.

The sabot rounds were boattail bullets sheathed in a thin plastic shell that split and fell away after firing. The barrel's striations wouldn't appear on the round itself, just the plastic, which normally landed no more than ten yards away from the shooter's position, easy to pick up afterward. If Strock hit anyone, there'd be no way to trace the bullet to his weapon—or, given ballistics down here, no way to prove for sure it hadn't come from someone else's.

Like Sleeper's. Or Chucho's.

And so it goes, he thought, drawing no pleasure from how well things were falling into place. In fact, the more the plan crystallized, the more his mind turned ashen. He couldn't shake a forbidding sense of waste. God help me, he thought. Help me and Phil and Ray's unlucky kid.

33

OVER A LATE, LEISURELY BRUNCH ON THE INTERCONTINENTAL'S
sun-washed restaurant patio, Axel clutched Consuela's hand in the
shade of their tasseled umbrella and gamely tried to broaden the
conversation to invite Jude in.

"I miss waking up to the parakeets," he said with a sigh. "What
do we get instead? *Chicharras*. Criminy, what a racket."

He was referring to a variety of cicada that bred noisily and laid
its eggs during March each year, then died off, like something from
an insect opera. Their eerie trilling echoed down through the hillside canyons above the city and resembled wind through high-
tension wires.

"I guess I tuned it out," Jude said, unable to take it further. He'd
risen early, checked his e-mails, and confirmed arrangements for
the coming trip east to San Bartolo Oriente. Then he'd cleaned his
weapons, checked the spring tensions on his magazines, practiced
speed reloading and presentation—grip, clear, clasp, sight—from
both his belt and his ankle holsters. Next he'd dry-fired two-shot
hammers and split hammers at imaginary targets around the room,
then worked up a good dense sweat with calisthenics, after which
he'd taken his longest cold shower in memory as he waited out the
lovers dallying in bed next door. *Andante amoroso,* was how Axel put
it. They still had that sated afterglow.

"I'm beginning to think that everything I love about this country
is getting overrun by bugs, blackbirds, and buzzards. Well, not quite
everything." Axel smiled at Consuela, who indulged him, rolling
her eyes. "Imagine the wildlife you'd still have here, though, if they

hadn't clear-cut ninety percent of the forests for the sake of planta-tions."

Or the locals didn't need to eat everything they could lay their hands on just to survive, Jude thought. Then something caught his eye. Turning, he stared across the patio of sandstone pavers to the French doors leading into the restaurant. There, framed by two large urns overflowing with *mano de leon,* stood Eileen—dressed comfortably, seductively in a white camisole, denim skirt, and san-dals. The sun reflected off her glasses, causing her lenses to flare. She clutched a manila envelope to her chest.

Sensing Jude's bewilderment and following his gaze, Axel said, "What in God's name is it?"

Before Jude could respond, Eileen started walking toward them, negotiating a path among the other tables, tapping people on the shoulder and murmuring, *"Con permiso,"* with a smile. If she'd been a jumpy, sweaty stranger—or brandishing a gun—he'd have known exactly what to do. As it was, he just sat there, watching her ap-proach, his meal churning in his stomach and a vein thumping in his neck like a plucked string.

Reaching the table, she bent a little at the waist, so her face could be seen beneath the umbrella's tassels. "Hello, Jude."

That voice, he thought. Axel and Consuela shot mindful glances back and forth. Eileen spared him further agony by extending her hand to Axel.

"I don't believe our paths have crossed. Eileen Browning. I'm an anthropologist who's been working down here for a year or so."

Axel brightened. "Delighted. Axel Odelberg. This is Consuela Rojas."

"I know. Actually, it's Señora Rojas I've come to see."

Consuela blanched quizzically. Axel said, "You know each other?"

Jude, mastering his shock finally, looked about for a chair. "Let's find you a seat."

"Actually, I was going to ask if there was someplace private we could talk. Señora Rojas, I've been working with a reporter named

Bert Waxman the past week, ever since his former assistant was told to leave the country. I have some pictures here I would like to show you."

ON THE BRIEF RIDE UP IN THE ELEVATOR, EILEEN LEANED TOWARD Jude and whispered, "You look well." It stunned him, all things considered. *Punk. Bruiser.* And her eyes conveyed a fond warmth, reminding him how much he'd missed her. Now here she was, like a conjurer's trick, but before he could process all that into an appropriate response, the doors slid open. Everyone filed into the hall.

He felt awkward making them wait outside Axel's room while he cleared it, as though Eileen might have lured them into a trap, but as he'd heard more than once, one can't sacrifice the client's safety on the altar of good manners. He'd explain later; for now, he ventured in himself and asked everyone to wait just beyond the open door.

Housekeeping had already tidied up, but the room felt close and hot, the maid having switched off the air-conditioning since no one was in the room. Jude opened the sliding glass door to let in a breeze, knowing Axel's preference for fresh air, and checked the balcony for anything out of the ordinary. He cast one quick glance down, onto the hotel grounds, then out toward the Boulevard de los Héroes and the gentle, smoggy hills of the European Zone, before returning inside.

The room was typical of the local hotels, spacious but bland as a box, and yet the drab decor had the advantage of making it easy to search. A pool of sweat formed in the small of his back as he went about things quickly to compensate for a little more thoroughness than usual, in case somebody who'd known of Eileen's coming, or who had followed her here, had somehow managed to sneak in while they were all downstairs. He checked the closet and behind the curtains and wall hangings, then inside every drawer, under the cabinets, the bed. He unscrewed the mouthpiece and earpiece on the phone, checking for transmitters, then did the same with the most accessible wall sockets, using a small screwdriver on his key chain to undo the faceplates. He even lifted the toilet lid to see if anything lay in the reservoir—a microphone, or a bomb sealed in plastic—but found only a pair of dead mosquitoes and a dissolving puck of chlorine. Last, he tried the TV remote to make sure all that happened was a program came on.

Satisfied the room was clean, he invited everyone inside with: "Sorry to make everyone wait."

Axel directed them all to a circular table near the patio door, where the curtains rustled in the parched wind. He took the chair next to Consuela's, then inched it closer till their arms touched. Sensing his protectiveness, Eileen addressed her words to him.

"Jude may have told you about the woman whose body was found along the Río Jiboa about a week ago." She waited, received an acknowledging nod, then: "A photographer took some pictures at the scene. In particular, he was able to get a shot of the woman's head when one of the soldiers lifted it up for his . . . for the other soldiers to see."

The blood drained from Consuela's face. A whisper: "My God . . ."

Eileen turned toward her. "Another man named Truco Valdez was able to get away with the camera. He had the pictures developed here in San Salvador. You met with a woman named Marta Valdez who complained about the wells near her village below San Bartolo Oriente. I have the pictures here. I'd like to know if you'd be willing to look at them."

Squirming in his chair, Axel mustered the beginnings of a protest, but Consuela stopped him. "Of course," she said.

Eileen undid the envelope's clasp and removed several prints, sorted them, then handed one across the table, saying, "This will be hard."

Consuela took the picture, studied it, then put her hand to her mouth. The hand began to tremble and her eyes hollowed out. Axel reached his arms around her and unwittingly knocked the picture to the floor. Even looking at it upside down, Jude nearly got sick. It was one of those grainy, hideous images that could make a photographer famous: the soldier jubilant, arm held high, with a fistful of matted black hair—the dusty, marble-eyed face with its crooked, gaping mouth; the sawed flesh of the neck; the clinging mass of flies.

Eileen said, "It's her, isn't it?"

Consuela nodded.

"There's no mistake?"

"No. No."

"Because right now, officially, Marta is simply missing. The PNC claims someone came forward, identified the body as that of a runaway prostitute."

"Yes, I've heard that. We all have. But I recognize her."

Eileen leaned closer. "There's a boy who saw the men who abducted her."

Consuela nodded, collecting herself. "Oscar."

"Yes. He said he'd spoken to you. About Marta. It's why I came here today. I tried you at your home, but—"

Axel broke in. "What is it exactly that you want?"

"Please, Axel," Consuela said.

"Oscar's in hiding," Eileen said. "The people who have him are already being watched, though. They think. No one knows for sure. But it would probably be wise to move him. They've asked for our help, me and Wax—Bert, I mean, Mr. Waxman."

"Bring him to me," Consuela said, her revulsion already quickening into anger. "That's what you're asking, yes?"

"It's too dangerous. Bringing him all the way here, I mean. Sooner or later we'll have to, I suppose. There are lawyers here in the capital, the Human Rights Ombudsman—"

"Bring him to my house then. Until it's safe to move him. I'll go back today. With you."

"Consuela," Axel said. "Think for a moment."

"It's not just him now," Eileen said. "It's his mother as well."

"Very well." Consuela seemed impatient, conflicted—her sense of obligation, her outrage, Axel's concern. "I don't—"

"Men came to their home recently," Eileen continued, "looking for Oscar. He isn't sure whether they were the same men that killed Marta, but they took his little sister, an infant. They told his mother the baby would be safe as long as Oscar tells no one what he saw—which, of course, means nothing. The woman's half-mad with fear."

Jude leaned down finally and lifted the picture off the floor. He set it back on the table, facedown, as Axel said, "I'll be staying at the Hotel Gavidia tomorrow night. Why not bring the boy and his mother to me?"

Jude cut in. "Axel, wait."

"I don't think," Eileen said, "bringing Oscar and his mother to a hotel would be wise. Too many people could see them."

"They'll be safer in the company of an American."

"Axel," Jude said, "you know that's not true."

"I'd have to agree with that," Eileen said. "If we didn't have reason before not to trust the authorities, we do now. The way they're handling Gilberto Soto's killing—"

"Let's put it this way then," Axel said. "An American without the baggage. I don't mean any offense, but let's put it plainly. Mr. Soto belonged to a union people think of, rightly or wrongly, as an arm of the Mob, and the killing occurred here. To most Americans, that's a man they don't much care about killed in a place they've never heard of. I'm not trying to slander the man, I'm just saying . . ." He fluttered his hand suggestively. "I'm a little different. Perhaps. I could be their uncle. That could mean political heat back home if anything happens to me, and even the creatures who run things here don't want to alienate the boys in Washington."

"Actually, it's more the reverse," Eileen said. "El Salvador is the only Latin American country with troops still in Iraq. Now they're sending private security contractors too. It's the boys in Washington, as you put it, who want everything smoothed over here."

"Even so, can we agree it would be something of a statistical oddity, two Americans killed here, one right after the other? Even during the war, it was very rare. I know that much local history."

Jude rose from the table. "I don't think whoever's behind all this will be swayed much by the math. Would anyone mind if Axel and I spoke alone for a moment?" Without waiting for a response, he gestured for Axel to come with him to the adjoining room.

Axel didn't move. "Anything I have to discuss on this issue, Jude, I'll discuss with Consuela present."

"I think—"

"I know, Jude. Please." Axel's eyes hardened with a sad, protective defiance. Jude felt oddly helpless against it.

"I'll go," Eileen said, getting up from her chair. "I don't mind waiting alone."

JUDE UNLOCKED THE DOOR CONNECTING AXEL'S ROOM WITH HIS AND showed Eileen through. Suddenly modest, he ducked a quick glance around to make sure housekeeping had hit here as well. All was neat, tucked away, but stifling. "Go ahead and open things up," he said, "or switch on the air conditioner if you like." He turned to leave, but Eileen snagged his arm.

"Could I talk to you alone? Just a second."

Jude stepped all the way into the room and closed the door. Despite himself, his pulse was jumping. "We really do need a breeze in here," he said, needing the distraction every bit as much as the air. He went to the sliding glass door, opened it, drew the curtains. Turning back to the room, he found Eileen sitting on the bed, her ankles crossed. She ran a finger along the lace rim of her camisole, the fabric sticking to her skin. A sheen of sweat glistened on her face and throat. Her glasses slid down her nose, and he found himself wishing she'd take them off.

"I realize this is awkward," she said, fanning herself with her hand. "But the boy, Oscar, he specifically mentioned Consuela and—"

"It's okay. I understand."

She nodded self-consciously, then pulled back her hair. "Good. Thank you. I just mean it's difficult, clumsy, given what happened between us."

She made it sound so final, he thought. "I'm not sure I could tell you, one way or the other, what happened between us." It came out needlessly flip.

Her eyes flared. "What I mean is, Jude, the situation here, it's bigger than a sport fuck, okay?"

"Excuse me?"

"Don't act like—"

"Wait. Hold on." He could feel heat rising to his face, his neck. "My sole concern right now is keeping that man in there out of harm's way."

"He's not the only one in a bit of a jam here, big guy."

"I'm sorry about the woman, the boy, his little sister, all of it. But—"

"How American. They ought to start putting that on the dollar bill, don't you think? 'We're sorry. But.'"

"Oh, great, drag that in."

"Now don't get snide."

"You want snide?" Before he could catch himself, he went to his briefcase and fished around for her poem. Stop this, he thought, but the thing had a momentum all its own. Finding the worn sheet of notepad paper, he unfolded it and held it out for her to take. "You forgot this at your house in La Perla."

Staring at the limp sheet of yellow bond, laced with her script, she pushed her glasses up her nose. "Good God. Listen, Jude—"

"Let's get this straight. What *happened* between us, as you put it, has nothing to do with how I go about my job."

Cooly, she met his eyes. "Convince me."

"If Axel decides to go ahead, it's his choice. I'm going to argue against it—out of concern for keeping him in one piece, and nothing else—but it's his call."

"I'll make you a bet. The minute I saw the two of them together,

I had this much figured out—he sticks with her. Even if you refuse to protect him."

"Refuse—that's what you think of me?" He wagged the poem at her. "That and this?"

She finally took it from him. Scanning her words, she smiled ruefully. "This isn't the only note I left behind—you know that, right?" She looked off, as though bringing a memory to bear, then pulled a few damp strands of hair off her neck as she tilted her head and began to sing in that raspy voice of hers: "Hey, Jude. Don't be afraid."

It took a second for him to place it.

"That's right. The little note stuck with gum under the hood of your truck?" A half shrug, and she bit her lip. "A day or two after that night you came out to my place, one of the women in La Perla, Alma's her name, needed somebody to drive her to Comalapa. Her brother was coming back from the States. Everyone there's been great to me, of course I said yes.

"As I was parking at he airport I noticed your truck. I don't know, something just came over me. I got this idea. I told Alma to go on ahead, I'd wait in the car. I needed to tell you something, speak my mind, and yet I didn't want to come across like some mad bitch stalker, either. So it just came to me, that line from the song, and it seemed perfect somehow. A little anonymous observation from out of the blue. Because yeah, I think you're afraid, Jude. We all are, I realize, and I don't just mean you're afraid of me, or what you feel for me, though I think that's true. I feel like I know you—not just that you're afraid, but the good things about you, too. The fact that you're kind, for example. You understand the people here. You want to do the right thing. I see all that and more, but you're scared to death you're going to screw it up somehow. You've got two modes: kinda okay and complete disaster. Happy? Forget about it, too much to lose. Better hold back, wait the thing out. Because sooner or later it's bound to head south." She closed her eyes and let out a long, burdened sigh. "That's sad, Jude. I don't mean it's weird, and God knows it's not uncommon. I don't think it's set in stone though, either, or I wouldn't be sitting here talking about it."

He felt stunned by what she was saying, but oddly relieved as well. Wasn't this what he'd really wanted, especially from her? To be seen for who he was: good, bad, indifferent. She was right, he'd spent much of his life waiting things out, watching from a slight remove. Did that mean he was scared? He'd always thought of it simply as a way to fend off his joyless mother's relentless disapproval, a way to bury the embarrassment of never quite living up to his jaded dad's expectations, a way to keep his impatient needs and pointless wants in check. He couldn't pinpoint exactly when it had happened, but the strategy had become as effortless as breathing. Nothing insidious in that, he realized, it was human nature: The truest person you met had a practiced air. Character is habit, after all. And everybody falls for his own act in the end. Eileen, as far as he could tell, used a disarming mix of tomboy smarts, feminine charm, and an oddly brassy lack of guile to face the world. It made her terribly convincing. But he wanted more than anything to be convinced, so he was a poor judge.

"Given what a rust bucket that truck is, I figured sooner rather than later you'd be sticking your head under the hood. Well, hey. Now you know the whole story." She shrugged dramatically. "I was hurt. And when I'm hurt I get royally pissed and I don't always make a lot of sense. That's me."

He wanted to say something, tell her what he was thinking, that she was right, about everything, but the words he wanted, as always, got lost in a muzzy incoherence. Only then did he notice he was chewing his lip.

Finally, he managed, "That's . . . interesting."

Subtly but unmistakably, the light in her eyes dimmed. "Okay. I get it. Look, I've got brothers so I know the routine. Quicker's easier, easier's better." She tore the poem into shreds. "Stupid to make too much of this anyway, given what that woman in the next room has to decide."

"I told you I was leaving the next day. The trip back home, it was . . . a job. I just—"

"Sure." She crushed the shreds of paper in her hands. "It feels obscene, talking about this now."

JUDE CLOSED THE DOOR BEHIND HIM AGAIN AS HE RETURNED TO THE other room. Axel, looking lost, sat with his arm locked around Consuela's shoulder, clumsy, stiff. Her eyes were desolate. The manila envelope had been rifled, the pictures gone through. They'd looked at them all. Beyond them on the balcony, set against the empty sky, a *pujillo* perched on the iron railing and fluttered its blue-black wings.

Axel turned to Jude, unhinged his arm from around Consuela's shoulder, and said, "Join me out in the corridor, will you?" He murmured something brief to Consuela, she nodded blankly in return, then he led Jude out.

The hallway was decorated with the same powderpuff beige as the rooms, and to Jude the lifeless fleshy color seemed to speak of the futility of desire, the mockery of death. It whispered: *You're afraid. You're obscene.* Axel, meanwhile, merely crossed his arms and stared off blankly, taking a moment to frame his thought. Down the way, a hefty man in a terry-cloth robe, an unlit cigar in his teeth, helped himself to extra towels from the maid's cart.

"I'm reminded," Axel said, once the stranger disappeared, "of something you told me once, something to the effect that I assume the threat level—I believe that's the phrase—of the person I'm with. Well, it occurs to me that works both ways. The person I'm with assumes my safety level, if you will. That sounds tautological, I realize, but the point is she's not safer because of me. She's safer because of you."

It wasn't a compliment. "I'm not sure where you're heading with this."

"There's another thing you once said, Jude, that keeps running through my mind. Something about how my security is not intended to be my enslavement."

"That's not how I put it." The axiom was: Don't constrain the principal to the point he becomes a victim of protection instead of a victim of attack. "And the point is, I shouldn't limit your normal day-to-day life."

"Well, *my* point is there's a moral dimension to that as well as a physical one. I'm not going to let the fact that I owe someone else for my protection prevent me from doing what I think is right. And I'm not leaving Consuela to fend for herself."

"Axel, I wouldn't ask that."

"There's a lot of blather these days about personal responsibility, more times than not from people who can't blame someone else fast enough when things go wrong. Well, I'm the one responsible here. I have what they want."

"You've lost me. Who's 'they'?"

"The men who've done this. One way or another it all gets back to that damn bottling plant. The water. I sign off on the usage rates, everything moves forward."

"But you can't sign off. You've been saying that for a while now."

"I said nearly everything I've seen indicates the drawdown on the aquifer is most likely unsustainable, but the thing's a goddamn puzzle." He ran his hands through his hair absently, eyes hazed. "From a distance, sure, the geology suggests you've got high-yield aquifers throughout the region. The bedrock's composed of younger volcanics that are highly porous, with excellent recharge, and the groundwater flow rate reaches four hundred thousand gallons per minute in places. That's more than enough to support industrial wells. But up close, you find out the story's different. The further downstream along the river you get—the closer to the bottling plant, that is—the more rhyolite and basalt you find, volcanic slag, with minimal fracture zones. That means it's a poor source for groundwater. The only aquifers you've got there are shallow, and given the pollution levels—the DDT's three times the lethal limit for fish, never mind the fecal chloriform bacteria and other waste—that means any wells you drill around there could prove worthless. But even further upriver you've got the same problem: Drill too shallow, you get contamination. Drill too deep, you risk mineral intrusion. The records for well abandonment in the area tell you that much—I mean, the ones you can get your hands on.

"Then, to the south, you've got the Laguna de San Juan and the river running from it to the Río Grande de San Miguel. It's fed by a thermal spring that's so heavily mineralized the water's useless. Any wells you drill too far out in that direction risk hydrothermal intrusion, which is what I suspect happened to the domestic wells this woman, Marta Valdez, complained about. The drawdown from the existing well field probably caused those shallower, southerly wells to go bad, though I can't prove that.

"On top of that, the aquifers are largely composed of uncompacted pyroclastics, a sort of volcanic gravel. The good news is, that means excellent hydraulic conductivity: The aquifer can transmit considerable water. But that's also the bad news. High hydraulic conductivity means poor retention. Why do you think the river runs dry when the rains stop? Plus, with the deforestation from the cane fields, you've got a serious runoff problem. That means insufficient ground saturation and poor recharge levels. Add to that the serious drawdown caused by the cane field irrigation and the sugar processing plant, you've got more than enough to suggest that expanding that bottling plant is foolish. Hell, the plant as it is may not be viable for long.

"But none of that means squat without the numbers. From June to October you've got tropical rains, which as you know are exceedingly generous here. Who knows, maybe it turns out recharge and retention are higher than you'd think, and everything squares. But that's where things go completely haywire. The company's records become funny right around the time of the 2002 drought.

The weekly static water level and pumping records look fudged, to be honest. They're too consistent to be genuine, nature's not like that. My guess? Somebody's trying to hide the drop in head across the well field, not that anybody at Estrella's going to tell me that— the process manager out there's a born genius at agreeable stalling. I've had to stand right there with him like we were on a date whenever he ran well tests—at least, if I wanted to trust the numbers. And what I got for available drawdown for each of the wells doesn't jibe with what the company claims it's been getting the past two years, which everybody dismisses as a one-year anomaly, of course. That's why I needed the government's data, to cross-check. I thought I'd begun to get a handle on that, even with the crazy, confusing, contradictory information I found. Every trip I made down here, I spent most of my time trying to pull all that together. But I needed one last shot at those documents to finalize my conclusions. You know what happened this past week— suddenly, nobody's home, and the data I got was slaw. With so many gaps in the record, even if I ventured an educated guess at what's happening out there, I can't be confident anyone else could confirm my findings, no matter how hard they tried. I could end up looking like a fool."

The same heavyset stranger they'd seen earlier re-emerged from his room, dressed now in a garish floral shirt and tan slacks, his un-lit cigar still firmly wedged between his teeth. Watching him lumber away toward the elevators, Jude waited until the man was well out of earshot before turning back to Axel. "So what you're saying is, you can't say anything."

"I'm saying I can't reliably conclude the drawdown's unsustainable. But if that's true, why not take it a step further? Make everybody happy. I'll say the evidence as it now exists doesn't rule out that recharge levels will keep the aquifer viable for the foreseeable future."

From some of the men Jude had protected, such a comment would have seemed all too typical—facts are marketable. You want the truth? Make an offer. But he'd never heard such things from Axel. "Why would you do that?"

Axel uncrossed his arms and reached for the doorknob, ready to go back in. "It gives us something to offer in exchange for getting that little girl back to her mother."

34

WHILE AXEL HELPED CONSUELA PACK, JUDE RETURNED TO HIS ROOM. Eileen waited on the sunlit balcony, gazing out at the sprawling capital's bustle and haze. Coming up behind her, he felt a momentary impulse to wrap her in his arms.

"Consuela wants to drive back with you to San Bartolo Oriente right away, if that's all right."

She turned her head at his voice, the sun bearing down on her face and arms, which were milky with sweat, the perfume on her skin fragrant from the heat. "That's fine," she said quietly.

His mind rattled through an inventory of untimely, inappropriate things to say—not that he would've had the wherewithal to put them into words even if they were timely or appropriate. He settled on, "I wish I could travel with you, to make sure you get there safe. But—"

"I understand." She shook off her reflective mood and offered a gallant smile. Mimicking the prettiest girl in the wagon train, she drawled: "Your work is here, sheriff."

It felt good, he thought, joking. "You'll be careful?"

"I'll do my best." Her eyes betrayed a dozen emotions. "Cross my heart."

Feeling a need to prolong the encounter, if only for a moment, he said, "I'm going to give you my cell number. I want you to put it on speed dial, in case anything happens. Your phone has a GPS, they can pinpoint where you're at if—"

She reached up with her fingers to touch his lips, silence him. "I know." Peeking over her glasses, she smiled. The warmth in her eyes helped disguise her fear. "And another thing I know? You wouldn't have kept that damn poem if I didn't mean something to you."

ONCE CONSUELA AND EILEEN LEFT FOR SAN BARTOLO ORIENTE, Jude and Axel put their heads together to devise a strategy for arguing their change of plans to Fitz. Figuring simple was best, they kept the story lean: Consuela had invited Axel to stay at her home in San Bartolo Oriente rather than the hotel, and that was the kind of request a gentleman obliges—read between the lines, et cetera. They refined it a little, adding detail, shoring up the weak spots, then dialed the phone. Axel, it was decided, would take the lead. Harder to deny the man in love. Fitz, predictably, dug in his heels.

"There's no time to work up a proper risk assessment, a thousand things I can't predict."

"In a neighborhood," Axel sighed, "enclosed by a high wall with guards at the gate."

"Do you have their names?"

"We'll get them. Or perhaps the local police—"

"Don't know dick. Sit around all day waiting for trouble to come to them."

"Michael," Axel said, dredging up Fitz's given name, "really, I'm tired of flogging this."

"Just a reminder, you're the principal, Axel, not the client. I have to call back to Torkland to get this okayed. If they say no—"

"Then I'll hire Jude myself, either through Trenton or, if that's not acceptable to you or whomever, on an individual basis. I'm quite serious. And on that note, I'll hand you over."

He passed the receiver, looking just a little smug at his improvised ultimatum—now it was Jude's turn to keep the ruse alive. Fitz launched on in the same vein, adding that he'd done some extra background on Señora Rojas. "I made a call. There's some serious bad blood in the Sola family, meaning she could have an ax to grind. I didn't get the sense she was dangerous, just a flake, but—"

"If she's not a danger," Jude said, "why are we discussing it?" Secretly, he felt glad Fitz had uncovered nothing more recent than the divorce—Consuela's work on the local citizen committees, for instance, her contacts with Marta Valdez.

"All I'm saying is, I think it's unwise, Axel spending so much time alone with that woman."

Jude could only wonder at the lewd scenarios tripping through Fitz's mind. "Honestly, I haven't seen anything much to worry over. She's a nice lady. They're sweethearts. That's it."

"She could be filling his head with God knows what."

"So? We're here to protect Axel, not his ideas. Or his results, if that's what you're worried about. He's a professional. And an adult."

Fitz wouldn't let it go, and when Jude could take no more, he broke in and recited a list of extra weapons and equipment he wanted for his own peace of mind, figuring they'd mollify Fitz's paranoia in the bargain. He ended with, "I think at that point we can say we've taken all necessary precautions and then some, don't you?"

He understood the cost of this deceit. If the truth leaked out—as it almost certainly would if things went badly—the industry would shun him like bad luck. You can't trust his word, they'd say, let alone his judgment. No one would care that Axel had made up his mind and intended to proceed with or without protection, which meant Jude's commitment to stand by him showed real spine. And yet, he reminded himself, he'd been planning a change after all this was done, mixed with a little travel: Rio, Buenos Aires, Patagonia. The end of the earth.

Suddenly, Fitz threw in a trick pitch. "By the way, while we're on the subject of extra background, I followed up with McGuire about the two guys he was asking you about—those friends of your father's? He admitted he had nothing that wasn't ten years old on the guy you flew back with, Strock. But the other guy, Malvasio—if you told me you'd had anything to do with him, I'd have you committed. Or arrested."

Jude went cold—He's doing background on me? "What's this about, Fitz?"

"About two years ago the FBI sent a fugie unit down here to find the guy because of something he pulled in California. They couldn't track him down, though. Nobody knows where he is, McGuire confirmed that. He would've brought all this up the day he paid his visit but he hadn't had time to catch up on all the details. Then, when you said you hadn't seen the guy in ten years, he just decided it was all a dead end and moved on."

But you waved him back, Jude thought. "So why are we talking about it?"

"This Malvasio character, he's slipped onto the back burner down here with al Qaeda and the *maras* to worry about, but I get the feeling the Feds would be thrilled if he turned up. McGuire didn't get callbacks in time to bring this up when he was here, but an agent in California finally got in touch. Malvasio torched a whole neighborhood in this town north of San Francisco. About twenty people died, damage in the major millions. The weird thing? He confessed. Malvasio. After a fashion—called a cop by satellite phone, nobody knows from where, admitted the whole thing, just to get even with the guy who'd hired him because he only paid half the fee. The guy was some political honcho who couldn't get the city council to move off the dime on eminent do-main, so he just had Malvasio burn the place down. Emptied nine thousand gallons of gas from a tanker into the sewers, the fumes backed up into the houses. Boom. Nobody's seen him since. But I get the sense he's got a whole lot more hanging over his head back home. That's where he does his dirty work—uses different aliases, then hides down here."

Jude felt the walls of the room quivering from the heat. But it wasn't the walls. Or the heat. "How do you know that?"

"Know what?"

"That he hides down here. How do you know that if nobody can find him?"

"Just a hunch, a theory. Whatever."

"And this other stuff he's supposedly part of, back in the States, how do you know that?"

"After McGuire told me about the thing in California, I made a few calls. Most came up dead ends, and the few guys who did get back to me had nothing solid, rumors chasing rumors. Still, when I called McGuire back to follow up, he got very cagey and quiet. That's when I figured I was on to something."

But there's been no follow-up with me, Jude thought. They're not interested in me. He felt craven and small, being worried about that, and yet it sprang to mind unbidden. "So why are we talking about this, Fitz? The guy's a menace, okay, but that doesn't change the fact I haven't seen him in ten years."

"I'm just trying to give you some good advice. This would be an excellent time to play things straight."

"I'm doing that. It's called my job."

"Your job is keeping Axel safe, not agreeing to whatever he wants."

"Christ, Fitz, the man wants to stay with his lover. This is hardly the first time the issue's come up. And, yeah, I'll keep him safe—no matter who pays the freight. Everybody can work out the money on the back end. But if you're going to pull the plug, let me know so I can arrange for a driver and everything else I'll need."

After he hung up, Jude went out to his balcony to think. The sun had dipped toward the horizon. Soon the late-day heat would turn bearable, given the city's altitude, but that was little solace. So, he thought, Malvasio hadn't kept his nose clean the past ten years—Christ, his little game of pin the fork on the cowboy tipped you off to that much. Working for a prominent family? He has connections here, no doubt, but his employers are up north, it turns out. And apparently, for whatever bit of work he's up to now, he needs a sniper. Strock. And I was just the rube to serve as go-between. Malvasio couldn't risk tapping Strock himself. No, he needed a patsy. Me. The son of the man who saved the guy's life—how could he refuse? And leaving a rifle for him at the *rancho*—it was genius, really. Making everybody feel safe, Strock all alone out there.

And yet none of that made sense. He couldn't picture Strock falling back in with Malvasio, given the hate he still carried around. So maybe it was true, he thought, somebody down here really did want Strock's services. For what? A little guard duty on the ol' plantation seemed unlikely, given the kind of services Malvasio provided now. Strock was here to kill somebody. And as soon as that idea formed clearly, Jude felt his insides coil up.

He couldn't tell his guilt from his fear—my God. Axel. Then: No, get a grip. Strock wouldn't do it, not when he owes his life to the old man. *What if they threaten him. Better yet, what if they threaten his little girl?* They don't know where to find her. *You led them to her, idiot.*

Jude rushed back inside, checked that Axel was packing in his room, then dialed down and asked the hotel operator to connect him to a number in the Chicago area that he recovered from his briefcase: the investigator's report on where to find Peggy Check. A variety of clicks and hums and then a sheen of white noise, followed by the blurred ring of her phone: once, twice, three times. Four. The machine picked up. No, he thought, listening to that drawling familiar Appalachian twang: "Hey, it's me. You know what to do—"

The message broke off. A voice came on. "Hello?" A child.

"Is this Chelsea?"

A long pause. "Yeah?"

"Is your mom home?"

Another pause, punctuated with a sigh. "She's sleeping." Jude checked his watch. Four o'clock. Chicago was in the same time zone. An afternoon nap. Maybe Peg was working again.

"Could you get her up, please? Tell her it's real important."

He heard the receiver drop, then the girl keened for her mother as she thumped away from the phone. Jude hadn't even considered what he'd actually say, and was only halfway to something he thought might work when a new voice came on the line, murmuring groggily: "Real important? It damn well better be."

"Peg? This is Jude. The guy you met last week, I was looking for Phil?"

A bleary, ragged moan, followed by a bottomless yawn: "Where the hell are you?"

"I'm down here. El Salvador."

Another drawn-out silence. Finally, she said, "So what's up? Anything wrong?"

"No. No. It's just Phil asked me to check in, find out how you were. Nagged me half to death, actually. You know what a pill he can be."

"How'd he find out you know how to reach me? You said you wouldn't tell."

"I didn't." It was the truth, buried inside lies. "He just assumed."

Her voice turned cold: "He doesn't know where I am, does he?"

"I promised you I wouldn't do that. I'm good for my word. Just trying to be a nice guy, play the go-between."

"There's no 'between' to talk about, not with me and Phil."

"I get that. He just wants to know you're okay."

"Little late for that. Besides, why shouldn't I be?"

Jude wiped the sweat from his face with his hand. "Well, the thing at the club. He knows you got tapped around."

"You told him that?"

"No, he just figured, given the trouble he caused and the kind of people we're talking about, it was more likely than not you got roughed up."

"Ah jeez, you kno-o-o-ow . . ." She drew the word out like taffy. "Look—my business ain't his business, not anymore. It's over."

Let's hope so, Jude thought. "Okay. But for my piece of mind, not his, anything suspicious going on? Anybody following you around?"

"Like who?"

"I dunno, the guys from the club. Maybe somebody working for them. Hassling you, whatever."

"You serious? That sounds like work, and we're talking Vince's guys here. They called me into the office, slapped me around, called me names, told me to get the fuck out of Dodge. That's enough strain for a month, those losers. Anyway, old story, boring boring. I've got a new job now—"

"That's great," Jude said. And it was, on more levels than she knew.

"Yeah, and I'm on tonight, so I could use a little shut-eye, okay?"

"No problem." His body relaxed. Only then did he realize how hard he'd been gripping the phone. "You're okay then. That's all I wanted to know."

"Good as ever, which could be better, but hey."

"Same all around, I suppose."

"Listen, just so I'm real damn clear—there's no more need for Phil or you or anyone else to know diddly about me or my girl, okay? I get you were just checking in, but I want you to listen to me now. I don't hate Phil. I don't spend my days putting everything that's gone sour with my life on him, okay? I was young and stupid and full of pity and I've learned my lesson. Only good thing to come out of that whole sorry episode is Chelsea, and I'm gonna do right by her. I know I seem like a heartless bitch keeping Phil away from his own little girl, but I want her to grow up a little before she has to deal with him any more than she already has. If at all. Not the kind of lesson I want her to learn. Man who throws his own damn life away and blames it all on bad luck? No. She don't need that. I don't want her thinking who he is and what he's let happen to himself is normal."

This from a stripper, Jude thought. And yet he wondered what his life might have been like if his own mother had seen things like this, had the sense, the foresight, whatever, to recognize his father for who he was and act on it, rather than seal herself away in bitterness and blame, call it a marriage. But then again, no one else saw his father clearly either, not till it was too late. "I hear what you're saying," he told her.

"I mean, you seem like a reasonably okay guy, but I really, really, really don't wanna hear from you again."

"Understood."

"Okay then. Well, take care of yourself." She seemed to be hanging up, then: "By the way, what was so damn important about this call?"

"Honestly?" Jude had to mentally backtrack, fast. "I just, you know, wanted Phil off my case. I was sick of being pestered."

She chuckled acidly. "Get in line."

She hung up, and Jude sat there a few more seconds, bobbing the damp receiver in his hand. He felt light-headed. All right then, he thought, setting the phone down in its cradle. She's okay. Nobody's come around, threatened her, followed her that she knows of. And if anybody was planning to twist Strock around, that's the leverage they'd have, and it would've happened by now. It doesn't make it all better, he realized. It just means Axel's most likely not the target. But somebody is. You may never know who—or even when or where it happens—but there's a dead man on your conscience. Maybe it's already done. Call McGuire, he thought. Call him, tell him, explain it any way you need to but make the call—and say what? I'm sorry? What information have you got that would save anybody? The name of the cop, Ovidio Morales. But if Malvasio lied about so much else, would he really tell the truth about that? And if he had, no doubt Morales had been contacted before when the fugitive units passed through. A dead end. I've got the name of a restaurant in San Marcelino, the location of a *rancho* on the beach near the Estero de Jaltepeque that's most likely long deserted, a junk cell phone number that's already worthless. I've got nothing.

He reminded himself he couldn't get distracted by all this, he had enough to occupy his mind. Axel trusted no one else. He needed somebody keeping an eye out now more than ever, even if Strock and Malvasio weren't the issue. And maybe it wasn't Chelsea Check, but a little girl's life was still at risk. You fail at all that, he thought, on top of everything else, what you're feeling right now will seem like peace of mind.

35

As it turned out, Fitz didn't pull the plug—shortly after sunset, Carlos arrived with the Mercedes, bringing the hardware Jude had requested. Sensing that something had changed, the former paratrooper packed a little hardware of his own—an old G3 salvaged from his war duty, plus a Beretta 9mm. He stored the big rifle, loaded, in the trunk; the pistol he slipped under his seat. He made no secret of his indignation, pulling Jude aside to whisper, "You're letting him make a fool of himself. That woman's nothing but trouble."

Jude shook himself free. "Let me guess—you told Fitz the same thing."

"I was asked a question." Carlos blanched, he looked caught. "I answered honestly."

"I don't have a problem with that," Jude said. "Just make sure you do the same with me."

He kept especially alert as they traveled by twilight out the Alameda Juan Pablo II, past the stadium and the Iglesia San Francisco and the old bus terminal with its little circle of junk-food huts like McServipronto's, the area notoriously poor and ripe with gang activity. His mind boiled with imagined threats, the possibilities seemingly endless now. There was so much he hadn't seen with Malvasio—what was he missing now? He had to keep reminding himself that even if a new threat source existed (and he had no proof it did), the means of likely attack were still ones he'd been trained for. He gestured for Axel to sit low in the backseat, then kept an eye trained for trail cars, or vehicles poised at cross streets, waiting to veer out suddenly and cause a collision. He paid a little more mind than usual to the roof lines as well, checking for irregularities in the shadows—silhouettes, men with weapons. He relaxed a little once they reached the city limits—though roadblocks and carjackings, he knew, could happen anywhere, and the last five minutes' safety never guaranteed the next. They continued east out the two-lane Pan-American Highway past the shabby, crowded suburbs and the Lago de Ilopango.

In time, they left the central plateau's moderate climate behind for the dense heat of the lowlands. The increasingly long stretches between towns—flanked by vast cane fields, massive volcanoes looming in the distance—seemed eerily desolate in the cloudless moonlight. Random stabs at chat got strangled quickly by the tense mood, so they switched on the Haydn and said nothing, mile after mile. Finally, just before midnight, they pulled up to the gate at Villas de Miramonte.

Consuela had let the night guard know they'd be coming, and the old man rose from his rickety chair outside the tiny clapboard shack to wave the Mercedes in with the *novela policiaca* he'd been reading, giving them not so much as a second glance. How diligent, Jude thought, wondering how many strangers, on any given day, just talked their way inside.

Consuela lived on a cul-de-sac named Senda Numero 6, down which the plain two-story row houses lined up chockablock, one nudged tight against the other, to the end. No places for someone to lurk, waiting. Finally, Jude thought, some good news.

While Axel telephoned Consuela from his cell to inform her they'd arrived, Carlos pulled to the end of the street, then circled back so the passenger-side door opened directly toward her house. Jude told Axel to wait, then got out. Carlos, as always, locked the doors behind him.

Jude checked the street in both directions, seeing no one, not even a face at a curtain, though given the darkness someone could have been staring straight at him from a window and he might not have known. The night was still and hot. In the far distance, a glimmer of light came and went too quickly to pinpoint. It didn't reappear.

He stepped to Consuela's door and knocked softly. She greeted him wearing a white cotton dress and a tight smile, explaining straightaway in a hushed voice that Oscar and his mother were upstairs. Eileen had dropped them off earlier. They'd left the house where they'd been staying without incident, and she'd felt confident they hadn't been followed. Needing to get back to where she was staying, though, she'd headed off about an hour ago, saying she'd call Jude's cell phone if she sensed any trouble.

"Was anyone in the neighborhood watching when the boy and his mother arrived?"

"No," Consuela said. "And I checked, just to be sure. It was dark, everything was quiet."

Jude tucked all that away. "Let's keep the boy and his mother out of sight until Carlos leaves, all right?" Consuela nodded with an expression of calm complicity, and he found himself liking her more by the minute. The time would come when Carlos needed to be filled in, he figured, but that time wasn't now. Then he explained he wanted to do a quick look around before having Axel come in. "There might be something I see," he said, "that you wouldn't notice."

The entire first floor was the size of a two-car garage. The picture window looked out on the street from the dining room, with small side panels to crank open for a breath of air. The connecting walls along each side of the house were solid front to back. He smelled no propane leaks in the kitchen and the electrical hookups looked safe. A sliding screen door opened onto a tiny backyard with patchy Saint Augustine grass, but more to the point, the high walls with their thorny vines would be hard for anyone to get over.

Upstairs, the door to the rear bedroom was closed. A flickering light shone through the crack at the floor. He rapped gently. "*¿Perdón?*"

Bare feet padded against the floor within. The door opened a little, revealing a shirtless boy with eyes that seemed both dull and furious. Oscar, Jude thought. Beyond him, his mother sat on the bed in a threadbare *falda,* knees tucked to her chin, so lost within herself Jude wondered if she'd even heard him knock. Several candles lit the room, and the raw scent of tallow lingered in the close air.

The boy was tiny and thin, his boniness exaggerating the stoop of his posture and the hard angles of his face—thus the pop of his haunting eyes. And just as the boy was too small for his age, the mother seemed far too young to look so old—the same gaunt thinness, a face creased into a mask. She stared at nothing unless the boy moved, then her eyes flashed with terror.

Jude went to the window, pulled the filmy curtain aside, and looked out at the night. Across the back wall, perhaps as close as twenty yards away, in the house the next street over, another curtained rear window faced the one he was looking through. The same was true for every house up and down the block. A gunman, if patient and positioned correctly, could hit anyone standing where he was, and though he still couldn't convince himself Strock was his problem, it didn't mean somebody else couldn't fill that role. Don't confuse reasonable preparation with imagining things, he told himself. It's doubtful anyone knows you're here. Eileen said she hadn't been followed; keep the boy and his mother out of sight, they should be safe. As for Axel, the danger wouldn't be here, anyway, not yet—it would come once they began negotiating for the little girl. After that, sure, it would pay to take every precaution, here and everywhere.

Jude let the curtain fall back into place and turned to go. The woman was staring at him now, her eyes narrowed as though she were trying to place him. Jude apologized for intruding, slid past the boy, and left, closing the door behind.

He checked the front bedroom as well, staring out the window at the silent neighborhood for a moment, then went back downstairs and out the door, studying the street in both directions one last time. Satisfied it was safe, he gestured for Carlos to lift the locks. Opening the rear passenger door, he said, "Axel, you go on. Carlos and I will bring things in."

They unloaded Jude's and Axel's luggage, plus the weapons and hardware brought along for the house. Consuela was upstairs, keeping Oscar and his mother out of sight. Carlos had made it clear he intended to stay in town at the Hotel Gavidia, and grew more sullen as he worked, barely disguising his disdain, to the point Jude had to hide his relief once the man finally got back behind the wheel and drove off. It might be wise to find another driver, Jude thought. Or a car of our own.

He mounted a perimeter sensor in the backyard so anyone coming over the walls would set off the alarm, then did a quick sweep with a radio frequency detector, waving it across the electric outlets like a stud finder, searching for transmitters, finding none. He told Axel and Consuela they could head off to bed then, suggesting they stand clear of the windows just to be on the safe side, and giving Axel a second Sig Sauer that Carlos had brought, as well as two protective vests. Axel held his up like he was being asked to wear a dress.

"You do realize it's terribly hot. And you're not going to tell me we should wear these to bed, I hope."

"I'd be happy," Jude said, "if you wore them just about everywhere else. Not the shower, obviously, but—"

"Is there really any indication I'm in danger at this point?"

Jude nodded upward toward the rear bedroom. "Indication enough."

"But that's my point," Axel said. "They're the ones in danger.

When they see we have these"—he shook his vest—"and they don't, what do we say?"

"I'll tell them to stay away from the windows," Jude said helplessly. "And not to go outside."

Axel sighed with an air of uneasy forbearance, then slipped the vest on and gestured for Consuela to do the same. Once they were upstairs, Jude checked his pistols, chambering a round in each, then loaded nine-shot into the Remington 870 he'd asked for. He hoped to God none of the weapons would be necessary. Tucking the shotgun and his own vest under the couch in the living room where he'd be sleeping, he glanced up and noticed only then that Oscar sat crouched at the top of the stair, staring at the guns with that same numb ferocity in his eye.

JUDE SLEPT LIGHTLY, ROUSTING HIMSELF EVERY HOUR TO CHECK THE doors, look things over, inside and out, listening for flaws in the silence. The night passed uneventfully, though, and he felt himself calming down.

He rose for good at six when the bells of a local church tower pealed, reminding him it was Palm Sunday. Consuela came downstairs and made a pot of thin scalding coffee that he and Axel shared until Carlos appeared for their trip out to the Río Conacastal.

Another gratefully uneventful drive ensued, and an hour later, the three of them—Axel, Jude, and Carlos—pulled up to a parched field along the trickling river. Almost as soon as he got out, Axel noticed something wrong. Jude, sensing his agitation, kept close. As they drew closer to the series of test wells Axel had ordered drilled along a jointing line of shrubbery, they saw that they'd been all but ruined by an errant herd of cattle that remained grazing only a hundred yards away.

Axel had ordered that the wells be drilled after surveying aerial photos of the region, hoping the ragged green line descending from the foothills traced a significant water-bearing fracture the bottling plant could tap into. Analyzing the rock formations, he'd guessed that a valley once lay here. At some point basalt flows from volcanic activity had covered the valley over, and then been overlaid by fine-grained sediments deposited later, then basalt again from subsequent eruptions, and so on. A hydraulic transition between basalt layers could prove fruitful. Maybe there were several.

They'd drilled on both sides of the river, to determine what if any percentage of the underground streamflow was siphoning off there, both during the rains and during the dry season. Axel had performed both step tests and seventy-two-hour pump tests over the past ten months, logging drawdown and recharge readouts back to the previous May, then loading the numbers into a modeling program on his laptop and watching the simulator replicate visually the movement of water through the aquifer before, during, and after the tests. The good news: There was a decent supply of water. Bad news: not decent enough to sustain industrial usage or even irrigation—about two hundred gallons a minute at peak flow during the rains, a fraction of that now. It was enough, perhaps, for domestic wells, if anybody bothered to drill them. Axel had hoped to make several more dry-season readings, with the faint promise that retention was better than he'd expected, but now all he saw was wreckage.

Jude spotted, at the far end of the field, two men on horseback collecting stragglers amid lazy clouds of dust. Gesturing that direction, he said, "We should ask them what happened."

Axel gazed down one of his wells, its casing torn away, its borehole choked with debris—not just dirt but brush, dung, scrap metal, garbage. The monitor had been shattered, its pieces strewn about the ground. He knelt to pick up the ruined flow gauge from the dirt. "You know what they'll say. The cows did it. The evil, stupid cows."

"We can at least try."

Axel dropped the gauge and dusted his hands on his pant legs. "Don't get me wrong, I intend to speak to them." He headed off across the hoof-marked dirt toward the two riders. "Because I know who owns the land around here. I know who had this done."

Jude gestured for Carlos to stay with the car, then hurried to catch up with Axel. He snagged the older man's arm. "I said let's ask what happened, not start something we can't finish."

Axel shook off his grip. "You know what this means, right? Just as I'm trying to phony up what these mobsters want to hear, they've made it all but impossible for me to say anything at all and still come across as credible. It would be comical if a little girl's life weren't involved."

The two horsemen watched from their mounts as Axel strode toward them, Jude following behind. The younger of the two was in his twenties, wearing a grimy bandana around his neck, a sweat-blackened ball cap flattening his black curls. As Jude got closer, he saw the young man's hand lacked its ring finger and pinkie. The other rider was older, perhaps the father, a dark and leathery *vaquero* wearing no hat despite the punishing sun, staring at the approaching Americans with wooden eyes.

In Spanish, Axel asked, "What happened here?"

The younger one deferred to his elder, who said, "We lost control of the herd, moving from pasture to pasture yesterday. We had permission to use the road along the river. Then some fool, wanting to get through, took out a gun and fired it in the air. There were only four of us, we couldn't manage them all." He waited for a moment, as though to see how that sat, then added, "I am sorry for the damage to your wells."

"What's your name?"

The young one shot a disapproving look, but the older man said, "Humilde Lopez. I will pay you for what the cows ruined."

Axel turned to Jude, saying in English, "Oh, they'll pay. Doesn't that just make everything swell."

Jude, returning to Spanish, asked the father, "Who gave you permission to use the road?"

He might as well have asked the circumference of the moon. Neither man spoke. The horses swished their tails, and beyond them a cow let out a moaning bleat.

"You said you had permission."

"We always take the road," the father said finally.

Axel barked, "Which one of your cows stuck rubbish down my wells?"

Father and son glanced at each other, feigning incomprehension, despite Axel's use of Spanish.

"Your cattle didn't do this damage. Men did. You did. Who put you up to it?"

The son flicked his reins and turned his horse about. The father reached into his shirt pocket, took out a greasy pencil stub and a small notepad, and began to write. "I told you I would pay," he said, then tore off the page and handed it out for Jude to take.

Jude stepped forward for the slip of paper. Humilde Lopez had written his name and a phone number in blocky script. The man turned his own horse about then and followed his son.

"How Gary Cooper." Axel watched their horses move lazily away, swaying their hindquarters and trailing dust. "I wonder how strong and silent they'd feel if they realized what they've actually done."

Jude folded the slip of paper over and stuck it in his pocket. "Axel, how smart are you?"

The engineer blinked in the dusty sunlight. "I beg your pardon?"

"All the problems gathering data, that made things difficult. But the fact they've gone so far as to ruin your wells, that makes things impossible—that's what you're thinking, right?"

"If I make any projections about the possible yield along this fracture, yes, they'll know I'm bluffing."

"Who are you to judge that?"

Axel swatted away a fly with one hand, wiping at the grime on his neck with the other. "If I didn't know better, I'd think you were trying to insult me."

"If they understood everything they needed to about water, Axel, why hire you?" Jude took one final look at Humilde Lopez and his disfigured son as they slowly gathered their scattered herd. "You know things they don't. Now, down the road, sure, you're right. If Torkland Overby's investors hire experts to review your work, you'll get found out. But that's way, way down the road. There's time to prepare for that. For now, don't underestimate how much people want to hear what they want to hear. Even if they know you're lying."

I speak from ample personal experience, Jude thought of adding.

36

THE CALL CAME IN WHILE MALVASIO SAT PERCHED ON A WOOD FOLDING chair at a tented café in San Bartolo Oriente's *mercado central,* sipping guava nectar over ice. Across the street in the cathedral plaza, the faithful poured out of church and milled among the parishioners sculpting devil piñatas from papier-mâché for the upcoming celebrations of Semana Santa: Holy Week. Malvasio took out his cell, checked the number, saw it was Sleeper, and flipped open the phone.

"I got good news and I got bad news, Duende." Sleeper's voice was lilting, cautious. "Bad news is, Truco Valdez ain't where we thought he was. You're gonna have to drive a ways."

Malvasio shot up straight in his chair. "You found him?"

"Damn. Beat me to the good news."

"What did you do?"

"Nothing you wouldn't." In the background, a voice broke in. Sleeper said, "Hold on." The sound grew muffled, a hand pressed over the mouthpiece, as the background voice said something else, longer, more elaborate. Sleeper laughed. Back on the line, he said, "Chucho wants me to tell you don't worry, no animals were harmed in the making of this movie."

———

Smoke rose from the lip of Volcán Usulután as Malvasio turned south off the Coastal Highway. The road all but petered out in a shabby little town of dirt streets, crumbling stucco, and rampant weeds, with gang graffiti everywhere. Suddenly, on the south side of town, the pavement returned and Malvasio headed on to Puerto El Triunfo.

The tiny fishing village sat on the Bahía de Jiquilisco, which the government was pimping as the future site of tourist hotels, golf courses, a convention center—if they could just convince well-off emigrants living in the States to part with some money. The village houses were modest but well kept, the brick streets lined with shady *maquilishuat* trees. Malvasio drove all the way to the water and parked outside the *terminal turística,* a two-story open-air market built by Canadians. The vast blue bay spread west and south along heavily forested shores where out-of-work fishermen illegally scavenged for firewood. A sailor with an M16 slung from his shoulder lazily patrolled the dock, nudging a stray pig out of his way with his boot. Streams feeding the bay shimmered with pollution while tiny one-clawed crabs struggled in the tarry foul-smelling mud.

Malvasio searched the food stalls in the *terminal turística* till he found Sleeper in the farthest corner, drinking a cold *champán,* a sort of fruity cream soda. He was wearing long sleeves again, the shirt crisply pressed and buttoned to the neck.

"Gonna find you a pill," Sleeper said, slipping off his stool, "take care of this bad case of late you got." He gestured for Malvasio to tag along, then walked with his distinctive forward lean out to a battered brown Datsun. "Show you the way."

Malvasio tailed Sleeper to an isolated road outside town, rimmed with bare fields, where a small clapboard church faced a funeral parlor that resembled a bunker, with a stamped-tin door and windows fortified with wrought iron grating, as though someone might come to rob the dead. Beyond it lay a rustic cemetery lined with tottering sun-bleached headstones. Malvasio pulled up behind the Datsun and parked, then followed Sleeper along an overgrown path past the church to a remote, isolated house of concrete block surrounded by a high, sagging tin fence.

"Is it just me," Malvasio said, "or don't you find it odd—an empty church on Palm Sunday?"

"There was a *desfile* this morning," Sleeper replied. "Everybody in this church headed over to some other church back in town. They had a guy dressed like Jesus on a donkey and people wore robes and shit, everybody waving palms. It was freaky, specially with the party we were throwing inside here."

He gestured Malvasio through a scrap wood gate in the listing fence. Inside, Chucho sat on the stoop, reading a comic titled *Violencia en la Jungla,* the front door open behind him. *"Buenas, señor,"* he said, getting up to let Malvasio by.

A third man waited just beyond the door, introduced by Sleeper as Magui. He rose from his perch on a tiny wood stool and just kept going, six-foot-four at least and three hundred pounds easy, most of it muscle, none of it hair. Well, eyebrows. He could have worked in the circus, the ink on his skin—face, neck, throat, arms, chest, back. He glowered till Malvasio shook his hand, at which point he broke into a sunny, job-hunting smile.

Meanwhile, the uptick in heat indoors was instantaneous, the stench of an abattoir. Something very bad had happened here. It took passage through only one room to find it.

A heavily tattooed but otherwise clean-cut Latino lay bound with duct tape on the floor, half his face burned away. Dead. To his right, another Latino sat bound to a chair, duct tape again. Naked, like his pal, burned too but alive. Truco, Malvasio guessed. Hoped.

Malvasio realized now why Sleeper wore a crisp clean shirt—to remove the taint, because he'd worn something else to work in. Malvasio wondered where it was, the laundry bag. Meanwhile: "Who's the stiff?"

"His name's Jaime Lacayo," Sleeper said. "Bible-thumping boned-out motherfucker."

The room was a shambles; they'd searched everywhere for the film. Among the debris lay Christ and his cross, prayer cards, a rosary, votive candles. A bible lay facedown on the floor. Malvasio stooped to pick it up. A passage from the Book of Ezekiel was marked with a paperclip: *They shall loathe themselves because of their evil deeds.*

"You said they had a procession today," Malvasio said, dropping the book back where he'd found it. "I'm guessing this Jaime is the kind of guy they'll miss?" Everybody looked at everybody else: a riddle. "My point is, somebody may come nosing around, wondering where he's at." He turned to Truco. "But maybe I should be asking you about all that."

The bound man drifted in and out of a twitching stupor and his skin was crawling with flies. He'd been worked on, his face almost black from burns and bruising, cuts on both cheeks, and his arms were deeply scored from a razor or knife, the wounds gluey with blood. The skin was clean, though, and from the smell Malvasio guessed they'd used *chicha,* corn liquor, to wipe him down, knowing it would burn.

Malvasio waved the flies away and picked at the edge of the tape gagging Truco's mouth, then ripped it away in one rough pull. Someone had forced a rag into his mouth too, and Malvasio pulled that out next. It stank of piss. He grimaced and wiped his hand on his pant leg as Truco gasped for breath, eyes rolling in their sockets.

Malvasio asked Sleeper, "What's he told you so far?"

"Not much." Sleeper cocked his head to the side and spat. *"Puta jodido."*

Malvasio turned back to Truco and bowed down, till their faces all but touched. "I'm going to get you to a hospital," he whispered. "You have my word. It should never have gone this far." He touched Truco's face, his fingers cool against the scalded skin. "All we want is the film. You know what I mean. I'm going to help you. I promise. Now, please, help me."

Truco looked down at the body of his companion. Flies were gathering there as well, dotting the gray skin.

"Your friend doesn't need help now. You do. I can help you. Look at him. You don't have to end up like that."

Truco shuddered and Malvasio thought for a moment he was ready to talk, but instead he merely reared back his head and let out a gasping howl. Blood gathered on his tongue and he spat, spraying more on himself than Malvasio.

Sleeper, standing nearby, shrank back. *"¡Hijueputa pendejo!"*

Stepping to the side, Malvasio gripped Truco by the hair. "I'll try it this way, then. By the time thirty seconds is up, you will either tell me what I want to know," he shoved Truco's head down, "or you will be as dead as he is. Look at it. There's nothing noble about it, nothing heavenly about it, no kind old man at the top of the big white stair telling you to come on home. Just that. Meat. A dead fucking fool." He shook Truco's head back and forth hard. " I can help you or kill you. Talk."

Truco coughed, spattering a foam of saliva threaded with blood across his lap. Struggling hard against Malvasio's grip, he managed to lift and turn his head till their eyes met. Drool lathered his chin, then a grimacing smile creased his lips as he worked himself up to hiss, "He was my friend." He laughed miserably, closing his eyes. *"Adios, chingados."* So long, fuckers.

Malvasio let go of Truco's hair. The dampness left on his hand felt slimy so he wiped it on his pant leg. To Sleeper, he said, "Wrap this up." Then he leaned down, whispered into Truco's ear, "I don't loathe myself," and walked out.

Two hours later, Malvasio was back in San Bartolo Oriente, eyes lifted toward the blanching sky as Strock stood on the roof of the garage, dressed in nothing but his shorts, shiny with sweat and leaning on his cane. He looked tanner, more fit, healthier than when he'd first arrived. Not that he'll thank me, Malvasio thought.

Strock shouted, "Where the fuck your little helpers run to? Been on my own up here all goddamn day."

Malvasio shaded his eyes. "They were doing a favor, out of town, for me."

"Then you owe *me* a favor, Buckwheat."

Malvasio lifted the bag of *tamalitos* and beer he'd bought on the trip back. "I'm way ahead of you."

He climbed up the tricky wood stairs to the roof. When he got there, Strock grabbed the bag, looked inside. "Smells good. Looks greasy. Let's eat."

"Help yourself. I'll go down, spot the house for you so you can set your zero point."

"I wouldn't." Strock unwrapped the oily napkin folded around one of the *tamalitos*. "They're already there."

"Who?"

"Jude. The guy he protects."

"The hydrologist?"

"Him."

Malvasio turned, looked out past the wire fence and beyond the scraggly treetops toward Villas de Miramonte as Strock stuffed half the *tamalito* into his mouth. Heat shimmered off the cul-de-sac's blacktop till the air seemed to vibrate. "They weren't due till later. A lot later."

"Showed up about midnight. Mercedes dropped them off then left."

"Dropped them off?"

"Yeah. They spent the night. Given the way they unpacked, I'd say they're staying a couple days at least."

Malvasio thought that through. It seemed an unwarranted stroke of luck and he didn't want to make too much of it until he was sure it was true. Then he remembered the scene inside the house in Puerto El Triunfo, the chaos, the gagging smell of blood and *chicha*. No, he thought, don't trust your luck just yet.

"The car came back again this morning," Strock said. "Jude and his guy got in, drove off, then reappeared a little while ago. Would've told you all that already, but you said stay off the cell."

"Smart." Malvasio took out a handkerchief, wiped his neck.

"For a minute last night," Strock said, "I thought Jude made me, or made the sniper hide. He stood there, staring this direction." He lifted what was left of the *tamalito* and nibbled at the gooey edge. A slimy thread of cheese leaked out. "But then he turned away. I watched them unload the car, but it was too dark to see much. Think he brought along a shotgun, though."

Malvasio stopped wiping his neck. "Oh, fuck me."

"Yeah. Maybe he got wind of your gig, because he seems ready for some whoop-ass."

Malvasio tried to think how that might have happened. The only weak link was Strock. "Wait. If it was dark, how did you see that, the shotgun I mean?"

"Caught him through the scope in the doorway." Strock stuffed the rest of the *tamalito* into his mouth and wiped his fingers on the paper bag as he chewed. "The light in the door gave me my zero point. Two hundred thirty yards, in case you're curious."

Malvasio stuffed his handkerchief back into his pocket. "That's a chunk of real estate."

"It's nothing. Got a straight lane, hardly any wind. We were hitting targets at two hundred in the mangroves, needling shots through the trees. This is a duck shoot." Strock rummaged in the bag for another *tamalito*. "They've got visitors now, by the way."

This wasn't getting better. "Who?"

"How the fuck should I know? Man and a woman."

"Describe them for me."

"Americans, I think. Guy's chunky, reddish hair, glasses." He started his second *tamalito,* unwrapping the napkin daintily, then digging in. "Girl's tall, nice looking. Not great, but nice."

Malvasio turned back toward Villas de Miramonte. From the

description, the man sounded like the reporter everyone was moaning about. He couldn't place the woman. "I almost put a bug in there. Now I wish I had."

"Jude woulda made that. He's not that dumb."

"That's why I didn't do it."

Strock twisted open one of the beers and drank, his Adam's apple bobbing as he chugged it back. Malvasio settled against the ladder, using a rung for a seat. The sun was dipping beneath the tree line. The leaves of the *ceiba, amate,* and *mariscargo* trees hung limp in the heat.

Fed, Strock looked transformed, content. He leaned on his cane. "Checked in on Clara out at the beach since yesterday?"

Malvasio found the question odd. "No. Should I?"

"You tell me. I was just curious how her and little Constancia were doing."

Inwardly, Malvasio cringed at the name, thinking it was bad luck. And it hinted again at something deeper between Strock and Clara. "What exactly went on between you two?"

That quick, Strock's humor turned. "That some kind of crack?"

"Not at all. It just seemed like you two connected somehow."

"I liked her," Strock said. "She had a way with that little girl. That a problem?"

"No, Phil. Look, let's drop it. I didn't mean anything."

Strock reached out with the cane and rapped the tip against the side of the ladder. "Don't presume you know what's going through my head."

Oh for fuck's sake, Malvasio thought. "I won't, Phil. I'm sorry. Can we change the subject?"

Strock looked off for a moment, leaning on his cane again as he mulled something over. The whiteness of the sky beyond him looked infinite, empty. "I'm assuming the plan's still the same."

Malvasio wasn't sure he liked where this was headed any better. "More or less. How do you mean?"

"You want me to pick off your own guys. When they pop out of their van, I take them down before they can so much as cross the street."

A *zanate* cawed from somewhere in the nearby branches. "Something like that."

"It's risky."

"I know. I'm not thrilled with it either, but I'm not the evil genius I used to be."

Strock grinned. "I doubt that."

"What do you mean?"

"I've got a pretty good idea, the first way you figured this? I'd be the guy to take out the hydrologist. And Jude, well now. He kinda comes out looking like a sucker, don't he?"

Malvasio wanted no part of this. "Phil—"

"I mean, all in all, it's the perfect scheme. Jude never has to step in front of a bullet. He never sees it coming. Boom, his guy's down. Your crew rushes up but they're just for show, they shoot high, whatever, make it look good. Happens real fast, their weapons match mine, no one's the wiser. And the sabot rounds? Impossible to prove where the kill shot comes from. Your guys are safe because Jude's not going to fire back, it's not his job, he'll be focusing on his guy, who won't be getting up." Strock looked proud, the puzzle solved. "Tell me I'm wrong."

"That's not—"

"I won't go for it."

Malvasio took out his handkerchief again, this time wiping his throat. "Yeah. I know."

"Don't get me wrong. You wanna waste Sleepy and Dumbo—"

"Sleeper and Chucho."

"—I'll whistle while I work. But I draw the line there."

"Fine," Malvasio said. "If it comes to that. I wouldn't ask otherwise."

Strock laughed. "Yeah. Sure."

"Look, Phil, think what you want but a lot of this is academic at this point, okay? Like I said, the people I work for have done everything in their power to make it so this doesn't have to happen. The company honcho flies in tomorrow, he's due to meet with the hydrologist sometime early this week, and we've squirreled his work so bad he can't say anything to hurt anybody. That makes my guys happy, no harm no foul, life goes on."

"But if he kicks up a fuss?"

"If he launches into stuff he's got no business talking about, yeah, absolutely, we may get the good-to-go." That was the wild card, Malvasio thought. The woman.

Strock lifted his cane and planted the tip against Malvasio's chest. "I won't kill him."

Malvasio chose to let the cane tip sit. "Even if it saves Ray's kid's life?"

"There's another way."

"It's not foolproof."

"We gotta make it foolproof. If it comes to that."

"Okay. I'm with you." Get this fucking thing off my chest, Malvasio thought. "Good."

Strock worked up a satisfied smile, then pulled the cane away. "The guys who hired you, what'll they say when your little troop of cat turds doesn't come home?"

"I don't know. Not sure I care."

"They'll just slip you the envelope, give you a shrug and a wink. Better luck next time."

"What can they say? Trust me, the PNC's not gonna waste time on a ballistics trace for a gunfight where all the bad guys go down."

"Even if the shots come out of nowhere?"

"What difference will it make?"

"Ray's kid'll figure it out. He kinda knows I'm down here."

"So what? His guy's alive, the shooters are dead—you really think he's gonna open that can of worms? He brought you down here. He's screwed, he brings that up."

"What about your end? Your target's still standing."

"Think about how it'll look. He survives, then bad-mouths my people, who are gonna be the ones who crow loudest about the shooters. Trust me, my guys are gonna stomp and fume, demand a crackdown—and that old bird's gonna crap in their faces? Let him. He'll sound like a whiny flake, which is as good as shutting him up. I'm thinking, he reads between the lines, realizes what a lucky schmuck he is, and goes home, never to be heard from again."

Strock frowned and shook his head. "Sounds like wishful thinking."

"Yeah? What doesn't."

A scant breeze rustled the nearby branches. Strock lifted the beer bottle to his lips again, drained it, then tossed the empty onto a growing mess on the sandy ground, scattering a cluster of *zanates* picking through the trash. "Just so you know. Something goes wrong, Jude takes a bullet or I get the feeling the whole thing's sliding sideways and I don't like where I sit, I'm gonna make the call: 9-1-1 works the same here as back home. I know. I tried it."

Malvasio suffered a sudden flood of wrath so intense he could feel it pricking his skin. "I hear you, Phil."

37

"I'M NOT FRUSTRATED," WAXMAN SAID. "I'M CONFUSED."

They sat around the dining room table drinking thin, tepid coffee—the reporter, Axel, Jude, Eileen—each of them sagging. The heat of late afternoon turned liquid against the blank white walls. Consuela was upstairs, consoling Oscar's inconsolable mother.

"The last time we met," Axel said, "I was very off-the-cuff in my speculations and probably spoke out of school." He looked spent, eyes glazed, shoulders rolled forward. He tugged at his shirt and fluttered the fabric to cool his skin. "There are a great many variables and complex calculations that go into analyzing water table variation."

"On the other hand," Waxman said, "it could be as simple as this: The bottling plant is depleting the aquifer."

"I don't know that for a fact."

"A woman died, trying to get people to notice."

Axel glanced over his shoulder. Oscar sat perched on the stairs, chin pressed into the fold of his arm, gazing with an otherworldly calm at the strange adults below, yammering in their meaningless language. "I realize that," Axel said, turning back again. "And it's a terrible turn of events. But many of the wells the villagers use are dug by hand and very shallow, five to ten meters, and they routinely go dry by the middle of April every year."

"The ones downstream from the bottling plant have been drawing up muck since January."

"Mr. Waxman, it's easy to assume the worst about these things. But trust me, analyzing water involves a little more than parading around with a dowsing rod. Aquifers are inaccessible. The only way you can venture a guess how vast they might be, or how exhausted, is through tracking very specific data." He ticked them off on his fingers: "Transmissivity, hydraulic conductivity, porosity, specific capacity, specific yield, specific retention. You have to track head loss versus change of gradient across the well field, then cross-check it against regional water level trends, precipitation, evapotranspiration. Then you have to load all that data into a computer modeling program, and I'm sure I won't shock you by confiding that computer models can be inaccurate. And on top of all that, you have to microscopically analyze the rock samples obtained when you drill your test wells. You have to measure the total dissolved solids in any water you draw, to check for organic and inorganic contaminants. And all those factors have to be logged over lengthy periods."

"You're saying you haven't had enough time to draw a sound conclusion."

"I've not completed my work yet. Normally, a full climate cycle should be enough to make reasonable evaluations."

"But not enough to make a simple, honest statement about whether the bottling plant's water usage is negatively impacting the domestic wells nearby."

Axel slumped back in his chair. "Mr. Waxman, pardon me if what I'm about to say begins to sound a little like a game of snow-the-reporter—"

"In contrast to everything else you've been saying?"

"—but I'd like to at least briefly sketch a few things it appears you imperfectly understand. Now, as it has been explained to me—"

"Marta Valdez said the water in the well near her village started going bad when the bottling plant was built a few years back, and it's steadily been getting worse. First there's poor draw from the pump, then what water does come up tastes wretched. Like most people down here, poor people in particular, she tried to get along as best she could and not make waves. This year it got so bad she decided she couldn't keep quiet any longer. She meant to be heard. Her courage cost her. But that's a lesson everybody understands down here: You interfere, look what happens."

Axel blanched. He'd heard all this from Consuela, of course. And Waxman probably guessed that.

"If you'll just permit me—"

"You think it's all just a coincidence, the bottling plant's draw-down and the wells going bad."

"I'm saying assumptions aren't facts. The problems you're describing can be caused by a great many things. First, all over the country, alluvial aquifers outside the coastal areas are often only thirty meters deep, and shallow aquifers disproportionately suffer from high contamination, especially ones close to populated areas. Second, the villagers here aren't terribly sophisticated when it comes to understanding how underground water moves, and many times you find they've built latrines too close to the wells. It's a surprisingly common problem, and the major reason why so much drinking water is contaminated. Third, a great many smaller wells are poorly constructed and badly maintained. Most last less than five years. They go bad for any number of reasons. Fourth, the well for this village is not terribly far from the alluvial plain for the river leading from the Laguna de San Juan, which feeds off a geothermal spring and is notoriously brackish. The well's drawdown may have been enough to cause hydrothermal intrusion, which would lend a very foul mineral taste to the water, rendering it undrinkable."

Waxman shook his head. "That's nonsense and you know it. The well's too shallow, the drawdown's nothing. But if you throw in the cone of depression created by an industrial well field, like the bottling plant's, sure, I could see that happening." Waxman tip-and-tailed his pen against the tabletop and a coldness settled in his eyes, as though he meant to say: *Snow the reporter? Go ahead. Try.*

"But you could still get heavy sediment or mineral intrusion," Axel countered, "if whoever drilled the well inadvertently struck a perched aquifer. That's a reservoir suspended above the water table—"

"I know what a perched aquifer is."

"Then you know they're often limited in capacity and tap out quickly."

Waxman reached up beneath his sweat-streaked glasses to pinch the bridge of his nose. "You realize that you're speaking almost entirely in hypotheticals."

"Granted, most of what I'm saying is speculative. By necessity."

"But what you intend to tell Estrella or your client, Torkland Overby, that won't be speculative, will it?"

"I've not been authorized to discuss that with you."

Almost desperately, Waxman leaned forward, saying quietly, "This really is beneath you."

"Suppose we leave considerations of that sort—"

"If you really—"

"Even if the plant were, in fact, causing significant exhaustion of the aquifer, it wouldn't mean the end of the world."

"Not for you."

Axel bristled, his blue eyes flared. "Look. First of all, you've got SOUTHCOM and USAID and God knows how many NGOs stumbling all over each other trying to help with this issue. The Salvadoran government has a plan to drill wells throughout the country, with one hand pump well for every five families."

"A plan. How noble. What's the funding? And what difference will it make if the aquifer's depleted?"

"Second, as you know, water trucks visit these villages—"

"They're unreliable at best, and the farther from San Miguel you get, the less reliable they are."

"Well, that can hardly be blamed on Estrella, can it?"

Waxman snorted. "Not until the national water system's privatized, and they take over for the region."

"Well, let's stick to the present, shall we?"

"Sure. In the present the wells are going bad."

"I've personally drilled test wells along a water-bearing fracture not far from here, and I found a significant amount of untapped groundwater there."

For the first time, Waxman seemed taken aback. "Enough to make up for the bottling plant?"

"Certainly enough to provide the locals with a healthy supply of fresh water."

Waxman studied Axel's face. "Estrella would be that magnanimous?"

"I think Torkland would be willing to make that a condition of the capital outlay."

"And if Estrella takes the money, then doesn't perform?"

Axel waved dismissively. "Let the lawyers slug that one out. Meanwhile, another way to mitigate any drawdown problem would be to install a recirculation system in the sugar processing plant located upstream."

"You're joking. Judge Regalado owns that plant."

"I'm aware of this."

"Why would a man like that go to the trouble, let alone incur the expense, of installing a recirculation system—what's in it for him?"

"Pressure might be applied from ANDA or some of the other national water agencies."

Waxman barked out a grim little laugh. "Excuse me. I could've sworn I saw a pig fly by."

"It's not so inconceivable."

"They have no enforcement capability. Not that the judge would obey them if they did."

"It's also not inconceivable, as I suggested earlier, that Torkland might consider having Estrella divert some of the capital for the bottling plant's expansion—"

"Into the judge's pocket? I'm sure. But it won't build a recirculation system unless somebody puts a gun to his head. And maybe not then."

Axel grimaced wearily. "How am I supposed to respond to statements like that?"

Waxman made a disgusted little huff, shifting in his chair, then wiped the sweat from his face and dried his hand on his shirt. "Fine. Let's get back to square one, a simple yes or no—can you come to a conclusion or not about the bottling plant's impact on the aquifer?"

"As I stated earlier, I'm not at liberty to divulge specifics."

"If it's the truth, what's the problem?"

"It's proprietary. But Bob Strickland from Torkland Overby arrives this week, and we'll review matters. That's high on the list, believe me. I will say this, however: The plant has deep-bore, high-yield wells that were properly engineered. The well field's being competently maintained. The wells continue to be productive."

"That sounds like damning with faint praise to me. Beyond which, it's not an answer."

"At the risk of repeating myself—"

"Have you discussed this with your friends at ODIC?"

"They are hardly my friends."

"You've met with Al Lazarek."

"Not by choice. And I would hardly be shocked to learn his role with ODIC is merely cosmetic."

"You think he's with the intelligence community."

"It would not surprise me. Be that as it may, it has nothing to do with the water table along the Río Conacastal."

Eileen touched Waxman's arm lightly, preparing to step in. "I may be wrong, Axel, but I get the sense something has changed since I told you about Oscar's sister being abducted."

There, Jude thought. The little dark heart of the matter. When Eileen had shown up with Waxman, she'd looked helpless, as though to say she'd had no choice, he was coming here one way or another and she might as well tag along. Secretly, Jude had felt glad to see her, but then Axel had pulled him aside to whisper, "What can your friend be thinking, bringing a reporter here?" Jude hadn't missed the reproach lurking in *your friend*. Now she was asking questions herself and getting straight to the point—maybe a rebuke was in order.

Axel, meanwhile, hid behind a blank stare. "I'm sure I don't know what you mean."

"We all want to do anything we can to help this family," she said, lowering her voice as though Oscar might somehow crack the language barrier and understand. "But if you think not telling the truth about the bottling plant might somehow—"

Axel waved her off. "Listen. My job here—"

"You can't trust these people. God only knows what else they might do, who else might suffer."

Axel, never one to be lectured to, looked off, his face knotted up like a fist. A tin clock atop the dish cabinet chimed the half hour. Finally, he came back and leaned forward, lacing his fingers together on the table. "Can I tell you a story? An old story, admittedly, but one that's apropos, I think."

Eileen sank back against her chair, eyes blighted. "Of course."

"It goes back to when I was studying geology at Purdue." Axel dropped his gaze to contemplate his coffee dregs. "I attended a

Lutheran church near campus. The pastor was quite old-school, but the younger ministers who came through there for their studies were decidedly au courant. Two in particular, Bill Dickey and Frank Fairchild. I had a number of discussions—arguments, I guess—with both men about the war, about race relations, about everything. It was a strange time, the sixties, with people like myself being every bit as naïve in a phony, hardheaded way as others were in their flakiness. But there's one discussion in particular that has always stuck in my mind.

"I was visiting Reverend Bill, we were teamed together for some sort of fund-raiser for the church. Can't even remember what now. But Reverend Frank came in, clearly in a state. He took Bill aside as though I weren't even in the room and told him what the trouble was. I just sat there, fiddling about my business, but listening in, too.

"It turned out there was a boy at a local high school who'd gone down to the steps of city hall and in a fit of high drama burned his draft card. He was young enough to think this was heroic—women would weep, boys would cheer. This is West Lafayette, mind you, the heart of the corn belt. He got arrested on the spot, tossed in jail, and told he should prepare himself for ten years in prison."

Axel unlaced his fingers and began turning his cup slowly in its saucer.

"The young man didn't call his parents from jail. Or a lawyer, or someone from the War Resisters League. He called Reverend Frank—and was scared to death. Like a lot of high school kids in town, he'd come down to the church coffeehouse to hang out, smoke cigarettes, talk Kafka and Camus, that whole scene. That's where he'd met Reverend Frank and, like a lot of young people, was smitten. If there is such a thing as Lutheran magic, that man had it. Not a handsome fellow—shortish, pockmarked face, kinky brown hair—but very genuine, very sharp, very committed. This boy, I wish I could remember his name, he asked Reverend Frank to come to his defense, say something in the papers or from the pulpit, let them know he wasn't the craven pinko deviant they were making him out to be.

"The problem was, Reverend Frank was already on probation with the church hierarchy. His sermons were meant to comfort the afflicted and afflict the comfortable. Not surprisingly, they'd drawn complaints, nasty ones from important people. He'd been warned in no uncertain terms that one more little scandal and he was gone. That meant no more pursuit of his master's in sociology. It could well mean giving up the cloth.

"He poured all this out to Reverend Bill and said he knew he could do more good for more people if he gained his degree, stayed within the church. It wasn't just the safe choice, it was the practical choice—the compassionate choice when you balanced the benefit for the many against just one. But, he said, every time he thought about telling this young man that he'd have to seek help elsewhere, he thought about the parable of the one lost sheep. And he could not bring himself to abandon this scared, asinine boy, even if it meant giving up so much else."

Axel left off fiddling with his coffee cup and folded his hands again.

"It left quite an impression on me, like I said. I'd never seen anyone grapple with his conscience openly like that—haven't seen much of it since, to be honest. It was the first time I'd seen the Gospel treated as something concrete, something to live by, not the shopworn taradiddle you normally get from the pulpit on Sundays." He looked out the dining room window, past the gauzy curtains at the fading daylight. The street beyond was empty. "You can pray, you can examine your conscience, search every book you please, holy or not. But none of that provides guidance the way you want. What would be the point of faith if it did? You choose. If you err, as you inevitably will, hope for forgiveness." He turned back finally, meeting Eileen's eyes with artless conviction. "Well, I've made my choice. I hope it's the right one. If not, please forgive me."

No one spoke for a moment, and Jude found Axel's words resonating in a way he couldn't quite place. Gradually, though, it came to him: *If we fuck up, as we invariably do, we try to make good for the people we've screwed, which is the best we can offer*. He felt a sudden moral uneasiness, a sense that men like Axel and Malvasio, the honorable and the conniving, might in fact somehow be indistinguishable. How many ways, he wondered, does a man remain a stranger to himself? The thought devolved into a wormy little terror—that from this point forward every step he took would be not just blind but tragic. *Cry your eyes out, sucker.* Then the sound of a door opening and closing upstairs rescued him, luring him back to the here and now.

Shortly, Consuela appeared, gently stroking Oscar's head as she passed him on the stair. The boy seemed oblivious to her touch. She dropped into the chair beside Axel, fanning herself with her hand.

"I do not believe," she said, "that young woman will survive this." She glanced at Jude. "She told me something I hadn't realized before. The men who came and took her little girl—one of them, the leader, was an American."

The import didn't hit Jude all at once. Then his insides clenched. "Did she describe him?"

"Yes. She said he was tall, like you—which was why she stared last night when you came into her room. But he was older. Darker. And his eyes, his voice—this is odd, but she said they made her think of Chupacabra. He's a monster, a scary story the country people tell, a kind of vampire who roams the hills, sucking blood from goats."

Jude's mind raced. Nothing came. He just sat there staring at the blank white wall while, beneath the scrabble of unspoken words, an undertow of guilt thickened into rage.

Axel said quietly, "Jude?"

"I was thinking," Jude managed finally, "of people at the embassy or anyone else who might fit that description."

Waxman said, "This man's linked to the embassy? My God—"

Axel waved the notion away. "Let's not be idiots."

Jude nodded. "I didn't mean—"

"Are you all right?" It was Eileen, staring across the table at him. "You look a little, well, *friquiado.*" Freaked out.

"I'm fine." Jude shook his head. "I'm just fading a little. Spotty sleep the last few nights."

"Which should serve as our cue." Axel rose from his chair.

"I'd like to talk to the boy's mother," Waxman said. He looked bitter and spent. The story was slipping away. "Would she be willing to do that?"

"She is terrified," Consuela said. "A reporter, these people, the danger to her child—"

"But you'll ask?" Waxman made another rat-a-tat with his pen. "Please."

Consuela trudged back upstairs, an empty exercise. Everyone knew that, even in the unlikely instance Oscar's mother felt inclined, Consuela would talk her out of it. Around the table, amid the smells of cold coffee and bodies ripened with sweat, no one spoke. *These people,* Jude thought. People like Bill Malvasio. Like me. You stupid, needy, gullible fool.

Soon enough, Consuela returned, shaking her head. "I'm sorry."

Axel, still standing, gestured ungraciously to the door. His manners had frayed—the heat, the questions.

Waxman didn't move: "What if this girl ends up dead? What if she already is? What will you have gained?"

The blood drained from Axel's face, aging him ten years in an instant. "I really do think we're finished here."

Jude showed Waxman and Eileen out, feeling light-headed and numb. Evening was falling, scarcely a breeze, the air smelling of metal and foul water and dust. An old couple walked a small, quivering dog down the shadeless street. Waxman plodded to his car but Eileen lingered, telling Jude, "I know you two are up to something, and if it's what I think it is, you're insane."

"That's interesting, coming from you. Remind me—who brought Oscar and his mother here?"

"Does Axel really think he can bargain with these people?"

Don't let her drag you into this, he thought. "Your imagination's getting the better of you."

"That little homily about Reverend Frank?" The sun caught her hair as she shook her head. "I don't think so."

"He just wants to do the right thing, and he's having a hard time figuring out what that might be." He wanted to add: *Now let it go.*

Her eyes scoured his. "What about you?"

"Me?"

"Say what you want, I can tell something's wrong."

Secretly, he enjoyed the scrutiny, though he felt pretty sure that wasn't wise. He glanced away. "I told you, I'm just tired."

"I'm checking in on you tomorrow."

He mustered a smile. "If you come, don't bring Wax along, okay? You didn't score any points there."

She looked stung. "He wouldn't do anything to hurt anyone. That's the last thing he wants."

Like want has anything to do with it, Jude thought, but all he said was, "Be careful."

BACK INSIDE, MUSIC WAFTED FAINTLY FROM A SECONDHAND BOOM box in the living room—Kiri Te Kanawa, the "Four Last Songs" of Richard Strauss. Consuela had grown up at the Salvadoran embassy in Bonn, her father the socialist colonel exiled to Germany for his support of the leftist coup in 1960. The Strauss played sadly, fatefully in the background as Axel sat at the dining room table again, mindlessly smoothing the coarse linen tablecloth.

Sensing someone there, he glanced up at Jude. "Well, that was an experience." His eyes floated in their sockets; he looked baffled and dour. "Think I'll make an early night of it." But he just sat there, staring at nothing, till Consuela finished washing the cups and saucers, turned off the music, and led him upstairs.

Alone finally, Jude dragged a chair from the dining room table, propped it in the front doorway, and sat there, staring blankly out at the staid, shabby neighborhood in its sweltering Sunday calm. His stomach roiled and the same numb dizziness as before returned—

only now he realized it came from a kind of inner free fall, as though all his psychic moorings had come undone. It wasn't just that he felt duped and used—what particularly galled him was that same phrase circling back to haunt him, *The people involved in your hydrologist's project could be the worst of the worst down here.* Malvasio had known all along who Axel was working for; he was working for them himself, just to different ends. And worst of the worst, as it turned out, hardly came close.

Too bad knowing all that doesn't solve anything, he thought. You got thrown a curve by what Fitz told you, that stuff about the fire in California, the work up north, but you can't pretend anymore, hope you left this problem behind somehow. It's right here. You can't see it just yet, but it's here, has been all along. Not just Strock working for whomever, but Malvasio, who faked you out of your jock from that very first phone call, worse than he did the old man. Down the road somewhere you can take the time to flog yourself properly for being such a perfect mark, but right now you better smarten up and do it fast. You won't have the luxury of figuring out the plan ahead of time—who knows if the two are in it together, if they buried the hatchet somehow, what it took to make that happen? None of that matters. God only knows what's in play—you've just got to stay on the ball, prepare for anything and everything, because something's going down. It's been in the works all along.

Gradually, as he sat there staring out into the hot dusty night, he began to sense why it was that he'd not seen any of this clearly until now. What was it Eileen had said: *You've got two modes, kinda okay and complete disaster.* She was right, of course, and not just in the way she'd intended. That wasn't just how he dealt with the outside world—it was how he faced himself. From the very beginning, those first get-togethers with Malvasio, collecting Strock—Christ, even his bungled night with Eileen—every time he'd sensed something wrong, he'd gone from being savagely critical to blindly stoic, nothing in between. And invariably he'd resolved his doubts, cured his paralysis, by telling himself to forget about it: Keep your head down, soldier on. It was why he'd never seen what was coming. Given his training, he had an intuitive sense of how to predict trouble, avoid danger, at least when it came to protecting someone else. But he had no reasonable critical faculty when it came to his own actions—he either eviscerated himself or numbly kept on moving. Moving toward disaster, as it turned out—and not just for himself now.

As much as he could see where this behavior came from—the logical result of his upbringing, he supposed—he also realized it was pointless to dwell on that. Mom and Pop won't be taking the fall if you screw this up, he realized. He'd set himself up for a real test, the defining moment of his life, maybe. Bummer for Axel and Oscar's little sister—and God only knew who else—if he fucked it up.

He caught himself: There you go again, he thought, cutting yourself off at the knees. Come on, do something—not just anything this time, the right thing, the smart thing, the necessary thing.

He got up, closed the door, and climbed the stairs. Rapping on the bedroom door, he called out, "Axel?"

The door edged open. Consuela peeked out, dressed in a cotton *falda,* her hair held back from her face by a broad white band and her skin smeared with cold cream.

"I need to see him alone a minute."

Consuela glanced over her shoulder. Axel sat on the bed, already stripped to his boxers. Nodding, he rose wearily and stepped barefoot into the hall. Closing the door behind him, he crossed his arms, covering the down of white hair on his chest. His voice was soft but strained: "I had an idea you'd be coming up."

"Tell her to stay away from the window."

Axel started, "Jude, what—"

Jude reached past him, opened the door, went in, and switched off the bedside lamp. "Stay away from the windows," he told them both.

Axel, still standing in the doorway, said, "You've told us that already."

"Then do it."

"Jude—"

"If you have candles, use them. The shadows on the curtains won't show so clear. And put your vests on. I've told you that, too, haven't I?"

Consuela stared, alarmed at his tone. Finally, she reached down to pick up the vest from the floor beside the bed and strapped it on. Jude collected the second vest and handed it to Axel, then pushed past him and hurried down to the living room, where he gathered his own from beneath the couch. Hurdling back upstairs, he knocked on the back bedroom door and went in.

The boy sat on the floor beneath the window, folded up like a knife, clicking his teeth. The curtains hung motionless above him as he gazed at his mother, curled up on the bed. Her eyes were savage, a rosary in her fist. Jude repeated the same directive—lights off, use candles, stay clear of the windows—then he crossed the room, knelt down before the boy, and told him to lift his arms. As he attached the Velcro straps in place, he told the boy not to take the vest off, no matter how hot it became.

Back in the hall, Axel waited, looking ashen. Above the rim of his vest a wisp of white hair tickled the hollow of his throat. "My God, what is it? I saw something in your face, earlier, at the table. Something's wrong, obviously. I should have asked but you seemed—"

"Come downstairs. Please."

They settled in across from each other at the dining room table. Jude had no idea how to frame the thing, so he just launched in— from his father's days in the Eighteenth District to Malvasio's recent contact, Jude's trip to Chicago to bring Strock back, everything learned since. As the words rushed out, he flashed on what he'd always told Axel, the importance of hiding nothing—for his own good. The irony of the role reversal felt shaming, especially since all this candor came far too late, but for once he refused to let that stop him.

"I have no idea," he said, "beyond his taking Oscar's sister away, what Malvasio has to do with Estrella. As for Strock, he's a wild card at this stage. But I think we should assume the worst, prepare for it."

Axel sat there, a look on his face as though his brain had begun to tick. He said, "Give me a moment, please," then glanced down at the tablecloth. Shortly he reached out, as he had before, and absently smoothed the fabric until he caught himself and drew back his hand. Glancing up with a sort of pitying dismay, he said quietly, "I'd wondered, ever since McGuire first brought up your father, what the whole story was. It must have been pretty rough, going through all that. And excuse the dime-store psychology, but I'd venture a guess that the roughness of it most likely explains why you got involved with these men again. To show you're better than they are." The dismay and pity melted, only to be replaced a moment later by something colder, more demanding. "It's not the noblest motive, you realize. And certainly not the smartest. But I suppose you've figured that out."

It occurred to Jude it might be best if he stepped aside. "I'll understand," he said, "if you call Fitz, get someone to replace me."

Axel recoiled. "Who—Bauserman? Please."

"I'm sure they can find someone capable."

Axel waved off the idea. "I don't believe merely capable will fill the bill at this stage, do you? Certainly not after the song and dance we handed Fitz. And another lie to cover the last will hardly make anyone safer."

Jude felt as though a pile of ashes had formed in the pit of his stomach. He nodded. "I suppose you're right. Still—"

"No, Jude. I'm afraid we're in this a little deep, my friend." Axel glanced over his shoulder toward the upstairs bedrooms. "And I don't mean just you and me."

38

BEFORE TURNING IN, JUDE SAT WITH CONSUELA ON THE LIVING ROOM couch and had her map out the houses in the neighborhood and name and describe everyone she could, down this block and on the next street behind. There were both *areneros* and *efemelenistas,* even a few die-hard Christian Democrats, but by and large the neighbors were simple working people, a baker, two mechanics, a widow hairdresser, several teachers, a pair of evangelical missionaries from Chile, a music professor (there were whispers he was a *mariquita,* a ladybug: "Homosexual," she explained), a retired bank teller who was also a bit of a gossip. None enjoyed the social station needed to rub shoulders with the likes of Judge Regalado or Wenceslao Sola, Consuela said, nor could she imagine any of them being thoughtless enough to dare any involvement with a man like Hector Torres.

"But one never knows," she said helplessly. "After the war, you learned things about people you'd never suspected. Never. And I've only lived in this neighborhood a few months."

She asked if Jude was going to speak with anyone, and he said no, that wouldn't be wise. It would just pique their curiosity about Consuela and whoever was staying at her house. He just wanted to know who was who as best he could, plot out the most likely sources of trouble. He thanked her for her help, then wished her goodnight.

Jude stayed up awhile longer, opening the front door and standing there sideways, to form a harder target, studying the houses he thought, given what Consuela had told him, were most likely to harbor unfriendly folks—the gossipy old teller, the *arenero* mechanic, the professor with a secret. The entire neighborhood was dark and still, not so much as a stray dog slinking about, and after five minutes he returned inside, heading for the back door now. Standing at the edge of the garden, he repeated the routine, peering up and over the high wall, listening for movement. The heady fragrance of the *veranera* blossoms hung thickly in the close heat, and from one of the nearby houses the fleshy gargle of deep-throated snoring rumbled softly into the night from an open window. He listened for another minute, trying to guess the weight and girth of the snorer, then came away from the back door and settled in on the couch.

He hardly slept. His mind was a zoo and the blood sang in his veins from the adrenaline, his thoughts riddled with doubt and guilt. Whenever he did, at last, drift off, he entered flickering dreams thick with voices. Then, just before daybreak, he opened his eyes and felt startled to confront a middling sense of clarity. No scathing inner voices. No countering robotic vigilance. It'll have to do, he told himself as he switched on the lamp. He dragged the Remington out from under the couch and filled its magazine with nine-shot, then loaded extra clips for his .22 and the second Sig Sauer. He wanted to make sure, in his absence, Axel was prepared for anything.

He dressed and then, for the next hour, sat at the back screen door to the tiny garden, watching the glow of daylight swell like mist inside the high vine-covered walls as he thought through what he'd say, plotted out what he'd do, preparing for every twist he could think of, every wrong turn. He felt strangely clearheaded and calm. Meanwhile, upstairs, the others gradually rose and shuffled or thumped groggily back and forth, their bedrooms, the bath. Then, about eight o'clock, someone knocked at the front door.

Jude collected his pistol, released the safety, and went to the dining room where, keeping the gun out of sight, he edged back the curtain to see who was outside. Dressed in a sleeveless embroidered cotton shift, Eileen stood there alone in the soft morning light, clutching a grease-stained bag.

"Tamales for breakfast," she said. "That down-home tropical treat."

Jude holstered the pistol and draped it with his shirt, then went around to open the door. He pulled her inside, then looked up and down the street to see who might be watching.

"My God," she whispered, "what's wrong?"

Jude closed the door. They were standing very close in the hallway, face-to-face. "We're just being extra cautious from here on out," he said. It sounded coy.

She searched his eyes, then leaned in and delivered a swift dry peck on his cheek. "Well, I'm not the enemy, okay?"

They warmed the tamales in the oven until the late risers tottered downstairs, everyone but Axel wearing a vest—he'd given his to Oscar's mother. Jude met Axel's eye to suggest they discuss this, but the older man just fiddled him off as though to say he'd made up his mind—he intended to be a gentleman and that was that. And if you die, Jude wanted to say, what becomes of getting that little girl back? But he knew Axel would just turn the argument around, point out that Jude's safety was just as crucial but his vest now protected Oscar. Meanwhile, Eileen shot Jude a curious glance of her own at the sight of the vests, and he responded merely, "Like I said, we're being extra careful."

They sat down to eat. Oscar's mother merely picked at her food, her dark eyes seeming to sink farther into her skull each time Jude glanced her direction. For once, though, the boy dove in, stripping away the steamy corn husks, devouring the soft hot cornmeal with its cheesy filling and licking his fingers afterward. Consuela made a pot of her anemic coffee and Jude threw back three cups before it dawned on him that Eileen's presence solved a problem.

He asked her to join him in the garden. Along the way, he dragged the shotgun from under the couch.

Inside the high-walled enclosure, dragonflies skittered back and forth between sun and shade. Jude said, "I have to go somewhere. I need someone who can use a weapon to stay behind, look after everybody. Axel has a pistol of his own and he can handle it okay, but I was wondering—" He held out the shotgun. "I don't know why, but I've got a feeling you know how to use this."

Her eyes bulged, moving from him to the gun, back to him again. "No, no, wait." She cocked her hip. "Back up."

"Please. Do this for me, I promise, I'll fill you in on what's been going on the past two weeks or so."

"Like that's a gift?" Then her eyes narrowed. "You've been lying."

"There's a lot to tell."

"But you've been lying."

"I haven't been entirely candid, no. But I haven't lied."

She looked away, rocking foot to foot, testy in that way of hers, then turned back and eyed the shotgun again. Taking it from him, she measured its balance in her hands, then brought the stock to her shoulder and aimed down the barrel. In her white dress and glasses, she looked like Annie Oakley's improbable sister. He remembered that first night together, the two of them swaying naked in her hammock. It seemed a million years ago.

"My dad had a Remington pump," she said, lowering the weapon from her shoulder.

"So you know how to handle it."

She sighed morosely, as though it were a curse. "Don't ask me to hit a duck."

He took the shotgun back, set it aside, then handed her the .22. "I'm going to take my Sig with me just in case, but I won't be needing this." Her hands were almost too big for the thing and she fumbled with the safety and magazine release. "Just a heads-up," he said, "Oscar's had his eyes on these. I wouldn't leave them out of your sight."

"You really think all this is necessary?"

"I've got this theory. Well, superstition actually. The more you plan for something, the less likely it is to happen. But don't open the door for anybody, I don't care who it is. I mean that. I'll explain later."

"I want to know where you're going."

"Let me borrow your car, I'll answer all your questions when I get back. I promise."

He got Axel and Eileen to trade places, and now it was Axel's turn in the small sunlit garden. Jude said, "It's time to do this."

Shading his eyes, Axel furrowed his brow and pursed his lips. "I'll go get ready."

"No. You stay here. I'll handle it."

"I'm more than willing—"

"I know that. It isn't the point. I had a lot of time last night to think it through. What have we got to trade for that little girl? You. What's in your head, anyway. Be stupid to lose it in the first face-to-face, wouldn't you say?"

Axel blanched. "You're taking too much of this on your own shoulders."

"No," Jude said. "I'm not."

The gravel parking lot for El Arriero was bordered with towering, shaggy *conacaste* trees and packed with dusty cars. It was Holy Week and the shrinking Salvadoran middle class was on holiday. A limp white banner strung above the restaurant's brick archway announced:

¡SEMANA SANTA! ¡ESPECIAL! ¡LANGOSTA!

Jude lingered in Eileen's VW wagon, looking things over. Two guards manned the entrance, bulging out of their uniforms, sporting wraparounds and armed with MP5s. He tucked his Sig Sauer into the glove box, realizing he'd never get past the door with it anyway. And if Hector Torres meant to do anything truly serious, he wouldn't do it here. He'd send somebody along afterward, cut Jude off on the street and hustle him out of the car, drag him off to somewhere remote, where it wouldn't interfere with lunch.

He locked up and headed across the gravel lot beneath the wilted trees. In the shadow of the brick archway, the two guards patted him down, more like they were hoping for cigarettes than searching for a weapon, then they waved him on—that quick, he bored them.

Inside it was hot and deafening—a hundred wood mallets slamming against tabletops, the tang of steamy brine. The open central courtyard and a large dining room beyond were both jammed, the locals having turned out in force—men in swim trunks and T-shirts, boys in tank tops and ball caps, women in culottes with their hair pinned up, ponytailed girls in halters—everyone bedecked in sloppy white bibs. Those not hammering away or sucking meat from splintered red claws fanned themselves with their menus or threw back tumblers of cold beer or soda—Estrella, Jude noticed, wonder of wonders.

Amazingly, despite the noise, the lobster feed came with entertainment. At the far end of the courtyard, a guitarist sat perched on a tall wood stool, slumping toward a gooseneck microphone, struggling to be heard—a throwback to a lost trend, Jude thought, long hair and wire glasses, denim shirt and jeans. Glancing up, the musician spotted Jude—an American!—and hastily abandoned the *bachata* ballad he'd been torturing, fiddled with his keyboard drum machine, slowed the beat to a mushy *Boom-bapbap-Boom-bap* and started in at the top with "Yesterday," butchering the English so farcically Jude couldn't tell if he was being welcomed or mocked.

Love was up and he's ashamed to pay.

The shapely *morena* hostess at her podium smiled coquettishly, revealing a gold tooth, and asked if Jude was dining alone. He smiled back and told her in Spanish he'd come to see Señor Torres. "I'm a friend of Bill Malvasio."

Like that, her face clouded over. The gold tooth vanished.

"Please." Jude said. "Let Señor Torres know. It's very important."

The hostess fussed with some papers, excused herself, then stepped primly in her flowing slacks and backless sandals along the edges of the thronged courtyard, disappearing behind a thick wood door. The pounding racket continued. Jude could feel his irritation ticking upward, and the singer wasn't helping. After a second listless verse, crooned above the din, he bailed on "Yesterday" and switched to "Black Magic Woman."

Got a black plastic woman . . .

Finally, the hostess stuck her head out and waved for Jude. He followed the same path she had, skirting the crowd, garnering stares from various tables. As he approached, she stood aside in the doorway, eyes down. Once Jude passed, she fled, unable to vanish fast enough.

Put a smell on me, baby.

Jude closed the door and it clicked shut. A grainy haze filtered in from a dirty skylight, revealing a small, strong, gnomic man with a singularly ugly head counting money from a register drawer as he sat beneath a slowly turning fan. He wore a lot of gold, a pair of cheaters, and a bracelet of rubber bands, his arms matted with thick black hair.

Jude stepped forward. "Señor Torres."

The man did not glance up. "Adriana said you wished to speak to me."

"Yes. I'm a friend, I guess you'd say, of Bill Malvasio."

Torres licked his thumb. "I don't know who that is."

The sound of a glass shattering came from beyond a side door leading to the bar. Torres looked up.

"Strange. Bill told me he worked in your security detail."

"I know the men who work for me." Torres returned to his counting. "I know them each by name. Most, I know their wives and children. The name you gave is not familiar."

"Perhaps I misunderstood him. It may be Wenceslao Sola he works for."

Torres stopped, lifted the reading glasses off his nose, and set them down on his ledger. He had quick dark eyes, a man with a temper. Jude realized, then, this wouldn't take long.

"You want something, Mr.—"

"McManus. I work for Axel Odelberg."

Torres considered that, then let go with a plaintive sigh. "Mr. McManus, I have two hundred lobsters on ice. Ever smell two hundred lobsters go bad? I need to sell them. To do that I need to make change." He held up the bills remaining in his hand. "And for that I need to count this out, so I beg you—"

"Some pictures have shown up."

Torres froze, almost despite himself. Then, recovering: "I don't understand."

"A woman's body—her body and her head—got found under the bridge over the Río Jiboa. The PNC claims she was a prostitute, but her name's Marta Valdez. That's been confirmed through a photograph taken at the scene. She complained about salt in the wells south of town."

Torres still said nothing, but his gaze hardened.

"A boy saw the men who abducted her. Later, Bill Malvasio came around but the boy escaped. Malvasio took the boy's infant sister hostage instead, telling the mother if her son told what he saw, the little girl would be killed."

For the first time, Torres showed a genuine reaction. Nothing much, a deepening groove in his brow, an idle twitch at the edge of his mouth. Surprise, perhaps. Jude didn't know what to make of that. Regardless, Torres regrouped quickly.

"Let me say this again. I do not know who or what you are talking about or why you came here—"

"Axel wanted me to let Señor Sola know that despite all the effort that's been made to make it impossible for him to do his job—ruining his wells, sabotaging data—he's actually ready to provide a full analysis. A favorable one, in fact. Depending."

Another twitch—Torres recognized the cue but refused to jump in. He sat, waiting.

"Axel will do that, sign off on the aquifer's drawdown and recharge levels. What he asks for in exchange is the safe return of this little girl." Jude reached for a pen resting beside the ledger at Torres's elbow. "I'll leave you my number."

"Enough." Torres ripped the pen from Jude's hand and slammed it back down on the table. "I don't mean to be rude, Mr. McManus, but get out. I have food and drinks to sell. That is who I am. That is what I do. I cannot help you."

Just then a woman burst in from the bar in a panic of muttered curses. She wore heels, pedal pushers, a scandalous blouse, her hair a lacquered swarm of black curls. She carried a fan of bills tucked between her fingers—a cocktail waitress—threw her hands up in despair, and was about to let loose with a full-blown cry when, seeing Jude, she caught herself. That fast, she buried her indignation and nodded a silent, apologetic hello. Approaching Torres, she leaned down and whispered feverishly, almost tearfully into his ear. He patted her arm as he listened, then twisted his head around, whispered something back. She smiled, took his face in her hands, and kissed his hair. "*Gracias, gracias, amorcito.*" Turning to Jude, she whispered, "*Lo siento, señor,*" then minced in her high heels back to the bar.

That's how easy it ought to be, Jude thought, to beg for a little girl's life. The folly of the whole business hit home then. He felt ridiculous, the butt of a cosmic joke: The devil feeds the multitude. The devil comforts Mary Magdalene. The devil suffers the little children.

Torres turned back. "If there's nothing more—"

"Just this," Jude said, determined to see it through. "The pictures, the ID of Marta Valdez, even the child labor on Judge Regalado's cane plantations—we know he's the source for the bottling plant's sugar—nothing will be said. That silence plus a favorable report on the water issues. All we ask in return is for the mother to get her little girl back."

A fleeting shadow crossed Torres's face, as though he were tallying the cost of dropping the pretense. Dealing. Encouraged by that, Jude added, "It's a generous concession. All things considered."

Torres said, "Please. I'm trying to be polite. Don't make me call my men."

Jude pictured that, pictured as well making short work of Torres in the meantime. To what end, though? "Fine," he said. "But I think Señor Sola will be disappointed if he learns I tried to get this information to him, through you, and you refused to pass it on." Jude reached down again, took the pen, and, fending off Torres's hand this time, jotted his cell number in the margin of the ledger. "In case Bill's misplaced my information." He dropped the pen and turned to go, glad at least he'd gotten through the thing without gnawing a hole in his lip.

As he reached the door, Torres said from behind, "I foresee a day, Mr. McManus, when you realize how badly you have misjudged me."

MALVASIO HAD TRAVELED ALL THE WAY OUT TO THE *RANCHO* THE NIGHT before. He should have stayed in town, but he'd figured the numbing monotony of the surf and the ocean breeze would help with sleep. The last few days of crank excess had taken a jittery, mind-hissing toll, but he'd crashed into a dead black stupor and dozed till noon, then gone out to the beach for a drop-dead run, miles and miles of empty beach. He was sitting in the garden now, eyes closed, back against the trunk of a shading palm, sucking wind and drenched in toxic sweat. His legs and lungs were on fire. Behind his eyelids, neural flashes shimmered. The pain felt cleansing. Not bad for middle age, he thought, then his cell phone trilled. Checking the display, he saw it was Hector. Save me a lobster, he thought, flipping it open. "Go ahead."

"What's this about an abducted girl?"

Looking in through the glass doors, Malvasio saw Constancia clasping her little hands tight around Clara's thumbs as the two of them marched around the dining room table—Clara bent over like a puppeteer, the little girl bow-legged, pudgy feet slapping pavers, happy as a peach.

"Excuse me?"

"I've just been visited by the hydrologist's bodyguard, the one you told me about, the son of your old friend? He used your name with the hostess, said he knew you worked for me. Said you told him so, actually."

"That's a lie." Then: "He showed up at the restaurant?"

"Those pictures you've been looking for? Don't bother. He has them. And, like I said, he claims you kidnapped a girl."

Malvasio looked in through the glass doors again. With Clara still guiding her, little Constancia wobbled on her feet, about to peal with glee. Jumping up, he moved as far away from the door as he could. If she makes a noise, he thought, say it's a parrot.

"I don't know what you're talking about," he said. It seemed absurd now, one of those thoughtless little blunders that turns out to be a cancer. Why hadn't he told Hector about the girl? He couldn't say exactly. He'd been improvising when he'd taken her, improvising when he'd brought her here, and the problem with improvisation, of course, is predicting how it will end. He'd trusted his instincts, though, and they'd said keep quiet, just as they told him now it was out of the question, if not insane, to own up. Hector Torres wasn't a man to indulge mistakes, let alone confessions. "What girl?"

Static on the line echoed the wind scouring the beach. "The little sister of this boy you've been looking for. The mother says you took the girl as a hostage, to keep the boy from talking."

"No. That's . . . It's nuts, frankly."

"Why would she claim such a thing?"

"Hector, how would I know? She had a kid, a baby, yeah, I saw it when I was there. If the kid's gone now, I'd bet she hid it, made up the story of a kidnap to keep it safe. Now she's trapped in her own lie. Other than that, you tell me."

Hector dragged out the next silence even longer. "The hydrologist is willing to write off the water usage if the little girl is returned. And nothing said about what the boy saw, the woman who was killed. The old fool gives us what we want and goes away."

Well, let's crack out the good stuff, Malvasio thought. "What are you saying?"

"If you have any access to this child, she could be very valuable to us."

No, Malvasio thought. I turn around, admit I lied, the girl's here, it's just a matter of time. May as well put the gun to my head myself.

"You want me to try and find her?"

The next, final silence was the longest yet. Then: "Strickland, the man from Torkland Overby, he arrives tonight. He's due to meet with this hydrologist tomorrow, and there's no telling what the old fool knows or doesn't know, what he'll do or say if he doesn't get what he wants. God only knows who he's spoken to already. I've already discussed all this with Wenceslao, by the way. No surprise, he's furious. We were so close, now this. Judge Regalado, the colonel, I've spoken to them as well. This young man, the bodyguard, he's been very foolish. And whoever helped him cook up this scheme must have been mad. What were they thinking? It's like dealing with children. . . ." His voice trailed off. Malvasio considered prompting him but thought better of it. Finally, a growling sigh, then: "You know what's expected. I realize it will not be pleasant, since we're talking about the son of a friend."

Malvasio caught something coy in Hector's tone. "You name the need, I do the deed. That's how it works. I know it, you know it."

"Unless, of course, you hear something about where you can find that child easily."

Malvasio looked back toward the house. Clara and the little girl stood in the doorway, looking up into the palm trees as a pelican fluttered back to its nest.

"I'll get things together."

Squinting through the Redfield scope, the crosshair optic gleaming in the bright sunlight, Strock watched Jude putter back up the cul-de-sac in the VW station wagon he'd left in two hours earlier. Quite a step down from the Mercedes he'd styled around in yesterday, Strock thought. The car belonged to the lanky woman in the glasses, she'd shown up again this morning. Jude's girl, maybe, except she'd stayed behind while he'd gone off, all on his lonesome. Strange, him doing that, given it was his job to protect the old man, go where he goes, stay where he stays. But now the kid was back and everyone would tell him the place had been deader than dead while he'd been gone.

Strock pulled his eye away from the scope and rested his chin on his arm. A sense of malaise swept through him, a mood he'd been suffering more and more the past two days. And yet who wouldn't get morose, he thought, cooped up in a room this size, lying stock-still hours on end like a turkey in the oven.

Deciding it was time to stretch, he hitched his way down the ladder till he stood on the roof of the garage, the sun high and hot. He found a corner of shade and set himself down there. A parrot fluttered its huge green wings in the feathery branches of a nearby *ceiba* tree and, in time, turned its eyes toward Strock. Shortly they were staring each other down. He found it calming, gazing into the small obsidian eyes, and as he sank deeper into the meditative mood, something he'd been thinking about quite a bit lately drifted slowly to the surface of his mind.

He began to talk quietly aloud: "Ray, I don't know if you can hear me, don't know if you even exist in any meaningful way. Hell, you could be this fucking bird for all I know, or I could just be sitting here, talking to myself. But if I'm lucky—and I realize I've got no right to think I am—but if I'm lucky you can hear me, because I've got something to ask. I'm going to save your boy's life. I realize that makes us even, you having saved mine way back when, but I'm going to ask you for just a little more. I've no idea how this thing is gonna play out. Dumb, I realize, trusting Bill all over again, and I could tick off the reasons for that but mostly I couldn't leave your boy to fend for himself, not with these jackals in the picture. I've got a little plan in mind, might work, might not, we'll have to see. But I realize I may not come out the back end alive. So here's my request—look after my little girl. Chelsea's her name. I'm fond of her—God, why is it so hard to say I love somebody? I love her. There. I love my little girl, and she's got more of her mom than me in her so watch over her, if you can. And, while I'm asking, look after Clara and little Constancia, too, if possible. I'm not sure why, but I just can't stop thinking about those two. They deserve a better break than I've a feeling they're gonna get."

He wiped away a thread of sweat quivering down his brow. The parrot ruffled its wings again and glanced away.

"That's enough to ask for, I suppose. I don't mean to be greedy. Just do what you can if you're up there, and thanks, partner. Over and out, amen, whatever."

39

THE PHONE DIDN'T RING TILL SUNSET, AND A MERE GLANCE AT THE incoming number crushed Jude's hopes: He'd been waiting for a call from Malvasio, Torres, Sola, anyone. But it was Fitz, telling him that Bob Strickland, Torkland Overby's chairman, would be landing at Comalapa as scheduled that night, staying over at a hotel on the Costa del Sol, then heading on to San Bartolo Oriente in the morning. He intended to meet with Axel first, a working lunch at the Hotel Gavidia to review his findings, then indulge the Estrella board with some face time. "I'll e-mail the security plan in a bit," Fitz said, sounding overwhelmed, as always. "Anything happening on your end?"

Jude squelched a laugh. It did, given events, sound a little like the setup to a punch line. "Weather's been a beast," he said truthfully. Then: "Too hot for trouble."

"Good. Glad to hear it." Fitz pulled back from the receiver to clear his throat. "Look, maybe I did go over the top about all this, your staying there, the woman's house. Looks like it's all worked out."

Give me one more day, Jude thought, I'll second that. And yet he felt oddly moved by the apology. Something had happened; Fitz seemed untypically subdued. "Nothing wrong with playing devil's advocate, I suppose."

"Like sex in the movies—good for you, good for me."

Poor sad, lonely Fitz, Jude thought. "Well said." He signed off, taking heart from his enhanced knack for lying, then went upstairs to pass on the news.

Consuela sat on the bed, propped on pillows, ankles crossed, listening to the radio while Axel tapped away on his laptop, sitting in a chair and using the foot of the bed for a desk. The contented couple, Jude thought. With the curtains closed, the air was hot and stale except for a hint of perfume.

"That was Fitz on the phone," Jude told Axel. "You're set for tomorrow with Strickland." He might as well have said they had a funeral to attend.

"We'll hear something by then," Axel said, trying to buck everyone up, himself included.

Jude rested his back against the wall, feeling the pitted surface of the cinder block through his T-shirt. "If not, they win anyway. You said so yourself—you don't have the data to prove the aquifer depletion."

"That's not precisely what I said." Axel returned his glance to his laptop screen. In its glow his facial features hollowed out, his eyes shimmered eerily. "Besides, funny things can happen with data."

"Funny as in . . . ?"

"Extrapolations, projections, best guesses." Axel tapped away at the keys. "If I could do it to fudge up an analysis to get that little girl back, I can do it to mock up something like the truth."

For what, Jude wondered—revenge? It never buys back what you lost. "Your reputation's on the line, Axel. With nothing to show for it now. Or am I missing something?"

Axel stopped typing. His hands, poised in midair, looked unearthly. "Let's just say I'm rethinking my reputation." His eyes turned to Jude's, bringing with them the saddest of smiles. "Don't worry, I'll save my full presentation till I'm out of the country, as I promised. I won't make your job any harder than it already is."

DOWNSTAIRS, EILEEN WAITED IN THE DINING ROOM WITH TWO GLASSES of ice water, squeezing lemon into each, then stirring in sugar. Water, sugar—for Jude they conjured the bottling plant, the judge's plantation. Even the littlest things struck him as symbolic now. Perhaps it was the candles. They filled the room with a museum of shadows.

"Beating yourself up?" she asked.

She was uncannily wise to him. "Only on the inside." He pulled up a chair and sat down. "It's how I pat myself on the back."

She passed him his glass, went back to stirring hers, glancing up now and then. Finally: "Just because you're doing the right thing doesn't mean it's your fault when it doesn't work out."

Pithy, Jude thought, let's sell T-shirts. He couldn't help himself—comfort felt insulting, and that tapped into a reservoir of bile. "If you decide to run for Queen of the Obvious, let me know."

Eileen shrank back in her chair. "Touché. Sorry."

"No. That was out of bounds." His nerves were shot. So little sleep. "I'm sorry."

"Okay. We're both sorry."

Like sex in the movies, Jude thought.

"I said it before." She shrugged and sighed. "I get stupid when I'm scared. Whistle a happy tune, that's me." She took a sip of her drink, hiding behind her glass. "Mind if I spend the night here? That is . . . I don't mean—" She winced.

"It's okay. I understand." It felt impossible, this thing between them. Impossible and necessary, like everything else of late. "It may not be safe."

"Who outside your company knows that Axel's here?"

"That's just it, I don't know."

"And not even your company knows Oscar's here. So why would anybody be safer somewhere else?"

Jude smiled helplessly and tipped his glass, a salute. "There you go."

"You trusted me with the shotgun before. Be good to have some-one here who can use it."

If you tell her no, he thought, she'll just fight harder. Admit it, she's staying. He wiped his nose, tickled by tallow smoke. "Sure. Good. Make yourself at home. I can sleep on the floor."

"No. I will. I just need a sheet."

Jude pictured it, the two of them lying there, a few feet apart, awake, pretending not to be.

Eileen cut short his reverie. "That poem I wrote, you were never supposed to see that, you know."

"You told Waxman you didn't want to see me."

She blanched. "I overreacted. I'm sorry."

There she was again. Little Sister Sorry. He could relate. "No need."

"I'm not so good at the boy-girl thing."

"Me neither."

She laughed. "There. A trait in common. Something to build on." She rattled the ice in her glass. Her shadow quavered on the wall behind her. "What are you going to do after all this is over?"

"I beg your pardon?"

"Once Axel's gone, what will you do?"

Once again, she'd nailed where his head was at. "I'm not sure I'm cut out for this work." He drained his glass. The lemonade tasted even runnier at the bottom, plenty of sugar, though. It made him thirsty all over again. "I want to travel for a while. Then I think maybe I'll head back home, get a contractor's license."

That one hit with a thud. "No. Stay here. You like it here, you told me. And it's obvious, the way you treat people." She rapped her finger against the table, to get him to look at her. Candles flickered with the tapping. "You're thoughtful. It's one of the things that attracted me to you. People here need homes and schools and clinics. More than back home. You know that."

"Parts of Chicago don't look a whole lot better than here, trust me."

"You know what I mean. Sure, you'll make more money in the States, but then what? Buy a house, fill it with a lot of stuff."

Jude stretched and yawned helplessly, like a cat, then nodded. "Land of the free, home of the brave and lots of stuff."

"Absolutely, yeah. And little by little the stuff buries you."

"Said like the daughter of a marine."

"No joke. God knows I've got a lot to say about America and the military and the unholy marriage thereof, but I learned some damn good lessons from my old man. I hate him but I dig him, he drives me nuts but underneath all the macho bullshit is a guy who just didn't fit in. Why? Because he wanted a life that didn't feel bought and paid for. I admire that."

Jude pinged his glass dully with his fingernail. "Me too."

"I know." She leaned toward him across the table. Candlelight glimmered in her eyeglass lenses. "That night at my place, I tried and tried to get you to talk about your family, but you were so damn cagey I almost smacked you. Lunkhead." She worked up a smile that could have, another time, melted his heart. "Your dad. There's something there. I can feel it. I don't know, I just do. Tell me. Now. Please."

Jude recoiled at the suggestion. Then, just as suddenly, he surrendered to blind impulse and launched in. Like a first-timer at a Twelve Step meeting: *Hi, I'm Jude and I'm the son of a bent cop.* To her inestimable credit, she listened patiently. Given her knack for seeing right through him, he wondered how much she'd intuited already, though he decided against using that as an excuse to leave things out. She recoiled ever so slightly when he got to the recent bit about Malvasio and Strock—who could blame her?—but he saw little merit in a half-scrubbed conscience. He played tabletop bongo for comic punctuation at the end, then waited for her to get up and walk out.

She didn't. But she sat there in silence for what felt like forever, thinking through, he supposed, what it meant to feel for a guy who'd unwittingly been in league with men who'd abducted a little girl—and done God only knew what else.

Finally, she screwed up her resolve and managed to say, "Did I tell you I heard from my brother in Iraq?" Her voice faltered, and somehow Jude got the sense she wasn't changing the subject exactly. "He shot a kid. By mistake. He didn't go into full-blown detail so I only know part of the story, but they were on the northwest side of Fallujah, this neighborhood called Jolan. It's ancient, with all these twisting streets, a nightmare. He said they had good intel on a stash house—but they always have good intel, you notice? Except when some Hajj phones in that a cop's house is full of guns or *plastique*. They like doing that, letting the marines kill cops. Anyway, Mike—that's my brother—he and his squad busted in, screaming for everybody to hit the ground. This kid, this boy, you've got all this smoke from the flash-bangs and he just—" Eileen put her hand to her mouth, a finger twitching against her cheek. She sat like that for a moment. Then: "You hesitate, you die. Or your buddy dies. Okay. I get that. But what about next time? My brother says he won't let it happen but I know him, he's a good guy and I know he's going to think next time. And that's the jinx."

"I'm sorry," Jude murmured. There it was again, that mucky little placeholder.

She downed the last of her weak lemonade. "You're right, Jude. You've got to get out of this work. It's a living death. For you. Guys like my brother. You make mistakes like everybody else, but unlike everybody else you can't forgive yourselves. Build things. Here. Things people really need. You'd be brilliant at it."

MALVASIO WAS TAKING A BEATING AT BLACKJACK, WAITING FOR HIS call from Sleeper. The casino, about the size of your average Burger King, was attached to the Tropico Hotel and reeked, appropriately, like an ashtray. But it was air-conditioned, so why complain?

About three dozen slots lined the walls beneath tilted mirrors, positioned to help spot slug droppers. There were six card tables: four for blackjack, two for poker. All six were manned by a single dealer, business was that slow. He wore a threadbare tux and a chipmunk smile and his obsequiousness only made his cheating more insufferable. The cage cashier had something French about him, which was to say he looked like he'd done time for forgery, and the cocktail waitress wore a short black skirt so tight her tree-trunk thighs whispered *kiss kiss kiss* through her pantyhose when she passed by.

Malvasio was a wee bit drunk.

He was cursing his second sixteen in a row when his cell started throbbing in his pocket. About time, he thought, cashing out. He left a tip commensurate with being played for a sucker and that, at last, wiped the goofy smile off the dealer's face.

Outside, Malvasio headed north in the dark to the caged walkway over the four-lane Avenida Eisenhower, coming down again at the entrance to the Cementerio General.

The gate in the large white archway stood open, but he slipped a coin to the beggar pretending to guard it. The central path was lined with *almendra de rio* trees and Malvasio followed it straight back, past memorial statuary and mausoleums of varying hideousness or ostentation, bigger than houses you found here, some dating back to the eighteenth century, fashioned from marble and granite and enclosed within black iron fences. Others were scruffed with moss or soiled with guano, and more than one had a sapling jutting from a loose crack in the stonework, a little flag of grief's neglect. Stray dogs roamed here and there, scavenging among the bouquets left behind during the day and anything else that resembled food.

A giant *ceiba* tree marked the center of the cemetery—it was sacred to the Mayans—and beneath its dark, sprawling branches he spotted the red glow of a cigarette. He whistled three pitches, low-high-middle, and received in return the same three notes reversed. Sleeper emerged from the dark shade of the tree into the moonlight.

"We're over here," he told Malvasio, gesturing to a spot farther back among the graves as he dropped his cigarette onto the gravel and crushed it with his shoe.

They walked together in silence through a maze of white headstones to a mausoleum the size of a small garage and built in the form of a Gothic cathedral, complete with vaulted ceilings and bat-winged gargoyles crouched atop flying buttresses. Of course, Malvasio thought, seeing the thing, where else would the *chamacos* hang? Ghoulishness aside, it was quite possibly the most lovingly crafted structure he'd seen in the whole country.

Chucho waited there with Magui, the same huge *marero* who'd been at the house in Puerto El Triunfo, plus a fourth hood Malvasio didn't recognize who was pitching stones at one of the starving dogs. Sleeper introduced him as Toto, and since no one laughed, Malvasio assumed it wasn't a joke.

Malvasio pulled his money roll from his pocket and counted out a thousand dollars, two hundred fifty per man, half the full amount for the job, the rest due once the thing was done. But Malvasio didn't expect to render that. He was doling out cash to dead men. Even so, money well spent.

"Go home," he told them as they counted their pay. "Get some sleep. We meet at five AM, sharp. No hangovers, no druggy nods, or you hand back what I just paid you and get left behind. And don't get any slick ideas—you don't want me coming to look for you, hunting down my money. We'll circle up at the usual spot. You don't know where it is, ask Sleeper."

WHEN HE GOT BACK TO THE VAN IN THE CASINO PARKING LOT, HE SAT behind the wheel for a while, trying to think it all through. The drink had him morose, hazy, indignant. That's it, he thought, blame the booze. He took his cell from his pocket and thumbed in the number he needed to call.

A groggy voice answered. "Yeah?"

"Get some sleep tonight, Phil. We're on for tomorrow morning."

"I *was* sleeping. Fucking heat." Strock moaned throatily and sighed. The pause lingered. "Remember what I told you."

Malvasio bristled but kept his head. "I do. And that's the way it'll go down. I wish it hadn't come this far but . . . Never mind. Not your problem. Let's not talk about it on the cell."

"Sound a little gassed there, Buckwheat."

Malvasio rubbed his eyes till they felt raw. "Maybe."

"I've wondered about that. Seen you zoomed, figured you'd drink to even out. Not the best lifestyle. I speak, sadly, from experience."

Malvasio didn't intend to sit through this, not from Strock. "Just wanted to give you a heads-up."

"You okay with this?"

Malvasio barked out a miserable little laugh. "Okay? No. It's fucked up. But if I don't take the wheel, it'll just be worse."

"For Ray's kid."

"Him, yeah. And me. Some things I just don't mean to live with, you know?"

Strock didn't respond for a moment. Then: "I asked before. I handle your boys—how's this gonna sit with your people?"

"Here's the thing, Phil. Know what? I don't care. I'm done. After this, I'm done. You reach a point, you know?"

The sound of static surged then waned on the line. Malvasio thought he'd lost the signal. Then Strock came back. "Where you gonna go?"

Malvasio looked out the van's window. The casino cocktail waitress was on her break, sitting on the hood of her car, buffing her nails in the moonlit heat. She'd stripped off her kissy pantyhose, which now lay tangled beside her shoes on the ground. "Don't worry about me, Phil. I'm a ghost. I roam at will."

STROCK HUNG UP THE PHONE AND WENT BACK TO WHAT HE'D BEEN doing—sharpening the tip of a jagged piece of wood he'd ripped from one of the rotting stair planks leading up to the roof of the garage. It had taken him a while to find a suitable candidate, small enough to hold and thrust, solid enough to puncture flesh. The AR-15 would be good for long range, but if things got dicey up close, he'd need something else. And that was the problem, thinking ahead to how things might go wrong up close.

He'd torn off strips of cloth from a T-shirt, wrapping it tight around the hilt to fashion a handle, but the trick was the sharpening. He'd resorted to using an ordinary rock for a grinding stone and it was thankless work, hour after hour of rasping the edges, honing the tip, working by candlelight now. He tested it against the skin of his inner arm. It'd be useless at slashing, but if he went for the gut, drove it hard and deep and high beneath the ribs to catch a lung, he might buy the time he'd need to finish the guy off with the rifle. Or his bare hands.

It had seemed poetic, using pieces of a rotted stair plank to fashion a weapon. That night he'd ruined his knee, back in Chicago, waiting for Malvasio, expecting to die and perfecting his hate—it had all come back in the gaudy Technicolor of self-pity and he found himself cursing the meager, circular madness of things. Here he was again, reliving the same nightmare, except he wouldn't let that happen. He was going through with the plan because he'd seen a crucial change in Malvasio, a wounded, stymied, bitchy terror that made Strock feel a little like he was looking into a mirror, not just his old friend's eyes. And there, really, was the sad little secret driving the machine. They'd been friends. For all the misery that had come of it, Strock still looked back at those years in Chicago as the best of his life. Did he really think that now, on his own, he could hope for better? Like Bill himself said, neither of them got out unscathed. And so he'd agreed to do this thing, reassured by the bond that had quickened between them again and flattered that he was necessary, after ten years of meaning nothing to anyone, not even his own little girl. Amazing, he thought, when we decide to whore ourselves, how piddling a sum can seal the bargain.

That didn't mean he intended to be a fool. He set 9-1-1 for speed dial and hid the shiv where he could reach it easily, just beneath the lip of the mattress. And if it's your old friend you end up having to kill, he thought, don't blame yourself or even him. Blame the meandering turns of fate that bring you back around, time and time again, to the same ridiculous decision: Choose who you are.

He looked out toward the dark *ceiba* tree, where the big green parrot had perched that afternoon. Strock chuckled at the memory, his moment of churchy weirdness, talking out loud to Ray like that. And then the bird had flown off soon afterward, never to return. Carrying my prayer to heaven, he thought. Or sick of the sound of my begging.

JUDE AND EILEEN DECIDED TO SLEEP IN SHIFTS, SHARING THE COUCH, two hours apiece, one of them staying awake to keep watch. Once, while he was dozing, Jude cracked his eye open to discover, through the filmy blur, Eileen staring at him. She was sitting nearby in a chair, hugging her knees, her dress tucked just so, revealing nothing immodest. The shotgun lay across her lap.

"Go back to sleep," she told him.

He readjusted himself on the couch, obediently closing his eyes. "Anything to report?"

"No. Nothing. Quiet as a Quaker with naught to confess, as my grandmother used to say." She let a moment's silence pass, as though to demonstrate, then let go with a flubbing sigh. "I do like looking at you, though."

40

A SEAM OF WHITISH HAZE RIMMED THE HORIZON AS MALVASIO pulled up to the little church, El Niño de Atoche, above the center of town. The four *mareros* waited beneath the spectral *amate* trees—Sleeper, Chucho, Magui, and Toto—all of them blistered from crank, but Malvasio had expected that. Despite his admonition, he'd figured they'd spend the night horning rails, pumping each other up with feverish talk or sitting off by themselves, blasting around inside their own skulls, rehearsing the killing ahead.

They scrambled into the van, Sleeper up front, the others hunched in back. No one spoke. Malvasio drove them to the isolated strip of country road sheltered by giant *conacastes* where another van sat waiting, this one white with black lettering across the side:

PINTOR CONTRATISTA—PAINTERING
JOAQUÍN MOJICA
289-9674

Señor Mojica would report the van stolen this morning, but not before it could be put to use. Malvasio had seen to that. Everyone climbed out, and Sleeper strolled to the white van with a hammer and smashed the driver-side window to perfect the ruse. Working by flashlight, he swept away the shatters then pried at the ignition cap with a screwdriver while Malvasio introduced the others to their weapons, conducting his tutorial in the spray of his headlights, to make sure no one missed anything.

He showed them how to load the AR-15 magazines—they held twenty rounds but he told them to stop at nineteen, otherwise they tended to jam—showed them the safeties, and disabused them of the notion that the selector switches, suggesting triple-shot burst and fully automatic firing options, were functional. "But these will shoot as fast as you can pull the trigger," he said, and let them all try their hand through a magazine to practice not just their aim but load and reload. Birds scattered from the tree branches with the gunfire. Sleeper, after hot-wiring the painter's van and transferring to it the odds and ends they'd need—kerosene, rags, a sledge—came and joined the lesson in time for the last of the shooting. By now morning had seeped its whitish blue into the sky and everybody seemed happy, weapons in hand, the burnt, sulfurous tang of cordite in the air. They got three spare magazines per man and loaded them there, then picked up the spent cartridges in the dirt. Finally, the four *mareros* donned the white coveralls Malvasio had brought along and climbed into the idling painter's van. Malvasio took out his cell phone, recalled from memory the number he needed, and thumbed it in while Sleeper turned the van around, came abreast, and stopped. Only he rode up front; the others sat hidden in back.

"The old man know we're coming?" He meant Osorio, Consuela's neighbor.

"I'm taking care of that now," Malvasio said, putting the cell to his ear. "Don't go in before seven. That's almost too early as it is. But don't wait longer than that, either."

Osorio picked up before the second full ring. Old folks, they sleep like they're afraid they won't wake up, Malvasio thought, watching as the other vehicle, trailing dust, disappeared. He explained things to the old *oreja,* told him the van he'd said might be needed for surveillance was on the way. He was sorry he hadn't been able to provide better forewarning but events had taken a sudden turn. Osorio hacked, sniffed, then said he'd be ready.

"Of course, this is all very sensitive," Malvasio said. "I'm sure I don't need to tell you that. No one can know."

"I did my part during the war," Osorio snapped. Malvasio could picture him, wispy hair a mess, blinking without his bifocals, sitting straight as a flagpole in his underwear. "I'm not some little dog, yip yip yip."

MALVASIO STOPPED AT A *PANADERÍA* ON HIS WAY BACK THROUGH TOWN to buy coffee and *pan dulce,* then drove out to the old construction yard, letting himself in at the gate and pulling into the parking area beneath the sniper hide. From the glove compartment he first removed his Beretta 92, screwing on the silencer, tucking the weapon into his pants and covering the butt with his shirt, then he pulled out a pair of vinyl gloves and stuffed them into his back pocket. Finally, he collected the bag with breakfast inside and climbed up to join the Candyman.

"Hope you slept better than I did," Strock said, his eyes rheumy and bloodshot. "I just kept thinking about all the ways this can go wrong."

"Don't talk like that, it's a cinch. Listen." Malvasio handed a coffee to Strock and a chunk of *pan dulce,* wrapped in wax paper. "Come seven o'clock they drive in. It's a painter's van. There's four guys, they'll be inside, one at the wheel, the others in back—zero in on the van's back door. They're gonna wait till the car shows up and Jude brings his guy out. Once everybody's inside the car, the van moves to cut off the street and the three in the back tumble out. Plan is they take out the driver first then fire away at the car till Jude and his guy are dead too." Malvasio peeled off the lid to his own coffee and sipped. "That's how it's supposed to happen, anyway. You take down the three spilling out the back as soon as you see them. All that's left is the driver. Thing's done before it even starts."

"They're gonna shoot the car—it's not armored?"

"You've got Humvees and APCs tooling around without armor in Iraq—think anybody's gonna pay the freight to plate up a Mercedes down here?"

Strock shook his head, tore off a chunk of *pan dulce,* and dunked it in his coffee. "The world is illusion."

"To live is to suffer. Pass the pie."

"What's the backup plan? If I don't get all four guys in time, what then?"

"There is no backup plan. You're it, buddy."

Strock grimaced, chewing, chasing his swallow with a sip of coffee. He thought for a moment, then said, "Not to sound like a broken record, but have you checked in at all with Clara and the little girl?"

Malvasio thought better of remarking on Strock's odd obsession, remembering the tiff from the day before. "As a matter of fact, I did. Kid was hopping around like a monkey, Clara tickled to beat Jesus. We should all be so happy."

"I dreamed about them last night," Strock said.

My God, Malvasio thought. He checked his watch, five till seven. "I thought you said you had trouble sleeping."

"I did. It wasn't a fun night. Except this one dream, which was, I dunno, very vivid." Strock rubbed at his flaming eyes. "Not that I can make sense of it. You know dreams. We were at the little house on the beach except it wasn't that house, it was different, bigger. Not the one the hurricane ripped to shreds, either, but kinda like that, I suppose. Houses mean something in dreams, I heard that somewhere. Constancia was bigger, too, almost a teenager. She was like a little Clara, same face and body, different hair. Sorta blondish, like my girl. Anyway, they showed me a part of the house where the roof was gone, and we looked up at the sky and the clouds were amazing, so close you could touch them. Then Clara said—she spoke English, that's another weird thing—she said the fish would be plentiful now. Something about the weather, I dunno, and then it was night and there was this moonlit river like a Hallmark card and another house and I can't remember anything else. Except the way it felt. You said they were happy? My dream, it felt that way too." He shrugged. "Bitch of a night, but I woke up happy."

Malvasio resisted the impulse to glance at his watch again. "Anybody who says they can make sense of dreams is lying."

"Yeah. But like I said, it was almost more a feeling than a dream." Strock licked his fingers and turned to look out through the hole in the wall toward Villas de Miramonte. "Ah, Christ. Already?"

Malvasio crouched to look over Strock's shoulder and saw the white van moving slowly up the cul-de-sac. It pulled in front of Osorio's and parked.

Strock lay down, fit the weapon to his shoulder, and peered through the scope. The bag of kitty litter rested under his left arm like a pillow and it rustled as he settled in. "Not to quibble with your plan, but it'd be easier to take out the driver first, given how he's parked. That way there's no cutoff, the car gets away. I deal with the other three as they appear."

Malvasio leaned closer, hovering over Strock's back. "Yeah, but if the van doesn't move into position, there's no guarantee the other three come out." He reached for the pistol in his waistband. When he had the weapon clear, he placed the silencer flush with the base of Strock's skull and fired twice.

Strock's head and shoulders slumped forward, his body went limp. As quick as that, Malvasio thought. Thing's done before it even starts.

He shoved the gun back in his pants, pulled the gloves from his pocket, and tugged them on. Only got yourself to blame, Phil. Said it was your way or no way, you'd call it in if you didn't like the smell of things. Well, I don't like it any better than you, but who says we had a choice? If it means anything, of all the ways I saw this going down, I wanted this one least.

The day before, as he'd racked his brain trying to figure out how to do this, he'd realized that the gremlin in the machine was the timing of it. To make it all work, he would've had to devise a way for the little girl to show up as though he hadn't known where she was all along. If he'd had a week or even a few days to mock up a search, pretend he'd hunted high and low—then bingo, looky here—he could've wrapped this up beautifully for all concerned. Well, Clara would've suffered. She'd bonded with the kid to the point it was almost eerie, but he could've found her an orphan. Hell, the judge's *finca* was crawling with them. But such thoughts were fantasy. Time. There just hadn't been time. In a moment of desperation, he'd considered simply ripping the kid from Clara's arms, coming here to Villas de Miramonte, and dropping her like a foundling near the security gate. But he'd remembered that undertone in Hector's voice, the suspicion lurking in the silences. The girl shows up that quick, he'd thought, no matter how or why, he'll see through the ruse. No such thing as parting friends, not in that crowd. Not with what I know.

If time was the gremlin, though, Jude was its sidekick, him and the old man, Axel Stumblefog. All they had to do was admit the obvious, give up, go away. But no, they had to blunder into what they didn't understand to accomplish the impossible. Like the upright Americans they were.

And that was the sum of it, he thought. Nothing else to say. You tried, they jinxed it, and there was no time to make it right.

He dragged Strock's body away from the weapon and tucked it into the corner. Both rounds had exited through the mouth and blood drained out. The eyelids had slid down to half-mast and Malvasio closed them the rest of the way. Sleep now, he thought. Or head off to wherever it is restless, bitter drunk souls go. Back to Indiana, for all I know. Send me a postcard.

Using a T-shirt of Strock's for a rag, he wiped away the blood on the rifle, making sure in particular the scope and trigger were clean. He searched Strock's things, looking for surprises, found none. The cell phone's outgoing calls were limited to his test of 9-1-1 two days earlier, the hopeless ass. The incoming numbers included Malvasio's, and though he'd be ditching that particular phone soon, there was no point being sloppy.

Strock's wallet contained a picture of the little girl, Chelsea. She was three maybe, but no telling how old the picture was. Strawcolored hair, milky skin, the kind of smile kids figure out early, playing the grown-ups. I'll send her some money, he thought, and tucked the picture back where he'd found it.

He flipped the mattress to avoid lying in blood and found a shank lying there, made from a sharpened piece of wood, a rag for a handle. The crudeness of the thing only made it more startling as he realized, *That was meant for me*. He kept staring at it as though it might spring to life, tell him things. He thought: Phil, you sly, untrusting fuck. That's how close we come sometimes. Shaking himself out of his daze, he settled in, lay prone, and arranged his business, nestling his elbow into the bag of kitty litter and fitting the rifle's stock snug against his shoulder as he squinted through the scope. The front doorway of Consuela Rojas's house sprang to life within the crosshairs. Two hundred thirty yards, the man had said. The scope was already zeroed in. Remember your cold shot's gonna land high right a quarter of an inch.

OSORIO AMBLED TO THE DOOR, DRESSED IN A CLEAN WHITE SHIRT, CRISP slacks. The pain in his hands was bad today—they shook, and he'd nicked himself shaving. The bloody scrap of tissue still clung to his cheek. He opened the door, expecting to greet a man. What he found instead was a jumpy, bug-eyed clown in coveralls.

Sleeper forced his way in, pushed Osorio against the wall, a hand across the old man's mouth as he stabbed his chest, over and over, a dozen times then a dozen more, his hand a blur as the blade punctured both lungs. No air, no screams. The bright white shirt was a tangle of blood by the time Sleeper was through. He pushed the old man aside and the wispy-haired fool dropped in a shudder to the floor. The look in his eyes, begging with fright, as a raspy wheeze rose faintly from his throat, the blood bubbling up. He was drowning in it.

Sleeper said, *"Saludemos la Patria, jodido."* Hail the motherland, fucker. He wiped his blade on the old man's pants.

MALVASIO FLIPPED OPEN HIS CELL. "TELL ME."

"One down," Sleeper said. "How things look up there?"

Malvasio glanced over his shoulder at the body, remembering another time Strock had looked that serene, minus the blood. He'd been sleeping off a bender in the back of his squad car, parked behind the infamous Green Bunny on the south side, of all places. Malvasio had rousted him, tapping his nightstick against the window glass, thinking it was a miracle some burner hadn't taken him out while he was lying there.

"We're good," he told Sleeper. "Ready when you are."

SIPPING COFFEE, JUDE TUGGED THE CURTAIN ASIDE TO GLANCE OUT THE dining room window. A white van he hadn't seen before sat parked in front of a house across the street, three doors down. There was lettering on the side panel, it belonged to a house painter. He called Consuela from the kitchen. "Remind me." He pointed. "Who lives there?"

Wiping her hands on a dish towel, she smiled acidly. "Ah. Osorio. The old *chambroso.*" Gossip.

"I'd like his number if you have it."

Consuela went to check while Jude dialed the number on the van. He reached an answering machine, the taped voice garbled but clearly a man's, identifying himself as Joaquín Mojica. That checked. Jude left a message asking for a quick callback, he wanted to confirm a job on Senda Numero 6 in the Villas de Miramonte.

Consuela returned with the phone book, pointing to the name and number for a Pedro Osorio. Jude dialed and the phone rang and rang, no answer. He hung up, checked the number, confirmed he'd gotten it right, and redialed. Same as before, no matter how long he let it ring.

"What's the number of the security gate up front?"

Consuela looked at him as though that were the oddest question. "I couldn't tell you. I've never—"

"It's okay," Jude said, cutting her short. Out the window he watched as the Mercedes appeared, turning the corner into the cul-de-sac. Jude had the number on speed dial and he thumbed the two-number code. Carlos picked up.

MALVASIO DREW A BEAD ON THE DRIVER'S SIDE OF THE TINTED windshield as the Mercedes passed the van outside Osorio's. Suddenly the car jerked to a stop, something was wrong and he knew he couldn't wait. He squeezed the trigger, reminding himself, a quarter-inch high right. The weapon fired, its report muffled by the silencer—a tinny, grating, hollow sound—followed by the ping of the cartridge onto the floor. The recoil felt no worse than a nudge and he almost gave in to a fleeting urge to look up, but then remembered Strock's words: Stay married to the weapon. Through the scope he watched the windshield shatter, a spiderweb pattern the size of a saucer. Not quite where I wanted, he thought. Calm down. He fired two more shots in quick succession, the windshield shattered further. The car began to drift backward.

AS SOON AS HE SAW THE WINDSHIELD FISSURE, JUDE PUSHED CONSUELA down and pulled the curtains. "Stay away from the windows!" He ran to the front door, checked the lock, and threw the chain—it wouldn't keep out a rumor. To Consuela he said, "Go upstairs with Oscar and his mother. Put the vests on and lock the door."

Axel scrambled down the stairs, stopping at the landing midway as Consuela climbed toward him. "Get the pistol I gave you," Jude said, running to his duffel to dig out the extra clips he'd loaded, stuffing one in each pocket. He told Eileen, rushing in from the back garden, "Shut the screen door and latch it. Leave the glass door open, get the shotgun. Make sure it's loaded." He pitched a box of nine-shot to her. "Here's backup."

"What's going on?"

"No more questions. Just do as I say and shoot anything coming over that wall."

He put his shoulder to the sofa and pushed it over to the sliding door for Eileen to use as a barricade. When Axel reappeared, Jude tossed him his last two spare clips and told him to stay on the stair. He could provide cover fire for Eileen from there or come down to help Jude if need be.

Jude redialed Carlos's number, whispering, "Pick up, come on, pick up." No answer. Crawling to the front window, he lifted the edge of the curtain to peek out. The Mercedes's tinted windshield was shattered, three shots, and the car was coasting slowly backward up the cul-de-sac, aiming crooked. Carlos was hurt or dead. Then four guys in white coveralls boiled out of the van near the old gossip's house, charging forward. They were armed.

As MALVASIO WATCHED THE MAGNIFIED IMAGES SCRAMBLING THROUGH his crosshairs, he felt an odd psychological bond with the weapon in his grip and suffered a fleeting impulse to shoot all four *mareros* dead: Sleeper, Chucho, Magui, Toto. The way he'd told Strock it would go. End this thing. It would be quixotic, strange, inexplicable, fun. A sudden lightness of spirit came over him, a sense that all things were possible.

Then gravity returned. Do that, he thought, what was the point of killing Phil? The question evoked an odd discomfort, which he decided was regret. Besides, he told himself, you cross the likes of

Hector Torres, Wenceslao Sola, the judge, the colonel, you better have a safe haven. He'd been slack in that regard, an unwise oversight, but the plan had been constantly in flux. More to the point, where did he honestly think he could run?

All of which was academic now, the thing was in motion, the trajectory set by laws as old as time. There is no freedom of action, he thought. Choice is an illusion. We are who we are.

JUDE PRESSED HIS PISTOL BARREL UP AGAINST THE PICTURE WINDOW and fired once to shatter the glass. The report made his eardrums throb, his hearing went muddy. He ducked against the shower of jagged shards, then regained position, braced his firing hand, and took aim at the closest of the four attackers. He fired a two-shot hammer—waiting out the split-second arc of recoil before letting the second shot go—then swung to the next nearest man and repeated, ducking as return fire shattered more glass. He screamed out to Eileen, "Down! Against the wall!" his voice sounding dull, miles off, even inside his own skull.

An even odder, more distant sound broke through the hum in his ears. A choking cry. It came from outside—he'd hit one of the men. Jude dove under the window to the other corner, rose up, spotted the man he'd apparently missed, ten yards away, and got off another two shots. The man took both rounds in his chest and promptly reached out an arm to break his fall as he sat down in the street, a dazed expression on his face as though he'd just been interrupted in the middle of a thought.

Peering over the window ledge, Jude saw the remaining two men regroup and scurry back the way they'd come. They left their two *chamacos* behind, the first—a huge guy, skinhead, tats on his face—on all fours, retching up blood, the other still sitting there with that stunned look in his eyes, trying to breathe but patting around blindly for his weapon. The two who'd run reached the van and one scrambled up behind the wheel, the other hopped in back.

Jude pulled a backup clip from his pocket, ready for reload, as the van lurched into reverse, backing up into the street.

It turned sharp in his direction.

Moving backward, the van slammed the Mercedes aside, tagging it on the rear right corner, spinning it out of the way as the taillights shattered, the van's back doors banging open and closed from the impact. The driver was aiming straight for the house now, the transmission keening as he gained speed, the van tottering as it barreled closer. He meant to ram the house, break down the whole front wall.

MALVASIO FELT ODDLY DETACHED FROM THE EVENTS BELOW — THE depersonalizing distance, the crosshatched magnification. Things would jump at the merest twitch and he'd have to settle in again, let his breath out evenly as his world narrowed down once more to its small tight circle.

He watched Magui—trailing blood, a head wound, first to go down outside the house—scramble on his knees, trying to reach safety. Why do the big ones always prove so worthless? Toto—also bloody, stunned, sitting where he'd fallen—was at least trying, however hopelessly, to shoulder his gun. It made him strangely oblivious to what was happening behind him. The van's back bumper knocked him flat, then the left rear tire crushed him as Sleeper barreled on in reverse, steering a collision course with the house.

Malvasio felt an odd pride in how gutsy the kid was proving. Chucho, too. Too bad no one would ever know.

JUDE WAS UNABLE TO GET A CLEAR SHOT AT THE VAN'S DRIVER. HE DOVE away from the front window a second before the wall exploded. The whole house rocked on its moorings amid the crash of steel against concrete and the final shattering of the window glass. He heard what he assumed were screams from upstairs and both Eileen's and Axel's voices shouted at him too, but the sounds barely registered, his hearing still mucked up from the gunfire. Looking back through the choking haze of dust and black exhaust, he saw the van's chugging tailpipe, its mangled bumper, its two rear doors—one ripped back and open, the other shut tight—where the wall used to be. The van sat crooked in the mauled gap of jagged cinder block. He wondered if the wall would hold as, through the one open door, one of the two remaining attackers resumed fire.

Jude scrambled back to the stair, took cover beyond the wall, firing around the corner till the hammer clicked. He hit the magazine release, let the spent clip drop as he pulled another from his hip pocket, and slammed the reload home.

MALVASIO WATCHED CHUCHO DIVE FROM THE PASSENGER SIDE OF THE van and run to the front door of the neighboring house, wielding a sledge to batter down the door. By now there'd be calls to the local police from everywhere in the neighborhood, but no one ventured outside. The Salvadorans were battle-savvy, they knew the price of getting too curious. Even the guards at the gate were staying put. Given the level of violence, the PNC would call for support from the local military garrison, and that would delay any response. There was time to finish this.

Chucho managed to get through the door finally and he tossed the sledge aside, pointing his rifle ahead of him as he disappeared inside the house. Meanwhile, Sleeper grabbed his weapon and took up position at the edge of the van, aiming straight at Consuela's front door, as a billowing cloud of black smoke began to emerge from inside her house.

THE FIRST MOLOTOV COCKTAIL, A FRUIT JAR STUFFED WITH A FLAMING rag, had hit the dining room table with a crash, spraying kerosene everywhere, which lit instantly. It wasn't the fire, though, or even the heat, that caused the problem. It was the smoke. The second firebomb just made that worse.

The only way out was through the front, but they'd be waiting.

Jude turned to Axel: "Grab Consuela, get the boy and his mother, haul them downstairs fast and out into the garden. If the smoke's too bad, break out the window in the bedroom and jump from there." He called to Eileen: "We're coming your way. Stay put."

But he wasn't coming her way, not yet. He scurried up the stairs and into the front bedroom, hugging the wall until he got to the window, which was cranked open. He eased up along the side, peeking out at the edge of the curtain. Down below, one of the gunmen crouched behind the van's front tire, using it for cover as he trained his rifle on the door.

Where was the other guy?

Take care of this first, Jude thought. The angle was bad. He braced himself with the wall, aiming carefully, getting the crown of the gunman's head squarely in his sight. He whistled. Sure enough, the guy looked up—a kid, actually, twenty years old tops. Jude fired and hit him square in the face. The kid toppled like he'd been punched, arms flailing as his back hit the ground. Jude fired three times more, into the kid's chest, insurance rounds, just as he heard gunfire from the back of the house, followed by a blistering scream.

Malvasio watched Sleeper get hit and realized it was up to Chucho now. Dirty Dog. The roof lines prevented him from seeing the garden behind the house, so he wouldn't know till later how the nervy little *chavo* fared.

Meanwhile, he thought, work to do.

Sighting the weapon felt natural, thanks to Strock's tutoring. He had nowhere near the skill to be able to hit something pinballing around, but given Strock's scope adjustment, fixing the proper zero point, as long as he could have a moment to relax into the shot, he could hit his target.

He trained his sight on Magui shuffling woozily up the cul-de-sac, one hand clutching his bloody head wound. Guy thinks he can simply walk away. Malvasio aimed for the high left side of his back, the heart zone, then eased his breath out, squeezing the trigger. The big man flinched, like he'd been stung, then toppled, losing his balance but not quite falling over. He put out his free hand, dropped to a knee. Malvasio fired again and once more for good measure, at which point Magui collapsed onto his side in the street.

THE SMOKE BOILED UP FROM THE DINING ROOM IN DENSE, NOXIOUS clouds. Jude couldn't make it back downstairs or even see more than a few feet into the living room, and so he scrambled back up to the second floor, ran to the rear bedroom. Looking out, he saw through the trails of smoke curling up from the doorway below that Oscar, wearing the bulky vest, lay twisted on his back in the garden, one eye pulpy with blood, another wound on the side of his face. He was convulsing. His mother screamed from inside the house, held back by Eileen and Axel and Consuela because the fourth gunman—he looked even younger than the one out front—had found a perch in the corner of the garden wall the next yard over. He stood on a table, aiming, waiting for the smoke to drive everyone out.

The kid had set the perimeter sensor off, and the alarm sounded with a throbbing shriek. Except for the smoke, he presented an easy target, but just as Jude was drawing a bead, a shotgun blast erupted from downstairs and the kid ducked down, taking cover behind the wall. Jude knew he didn't have time to wait—the smoke. He could hear through the pealing alarm the sound of choking coughs downstairs, he was starting to gag himself. But the kid with the rifle looked willing to wait till he knew he had everybody outside, gasping for air, before popping up again to take his next shot.

Meanwhile, the mother wailed: "¡Oscar, mi pobrecito, es Mamá, es Mamá!"

Jude shouted as loud as he could, "Eileen! Can you cover me?"

"She's hurt!" It was Axel, shouting over the wailing alarm and the mother's screams.

"I'm okay." Eileen's voice was labored, clenched. "It's not bad."

Jude fired off a round into the corner, to keep the kid with the rifle down. To Axel, he shouted, "Can you cover me?"

"Not for long."

Jude glanced down, saw the tip of the shotgun's barrel poke out through the punctured screen and then fire. Jude tucked his pistol into the waist of his trousers, cranked the window open as far as he could, and crawled out as a second blast came from below. He gripped the window ledge, let go with his feet, hanging, dropping to the ground, rolling with the fall, then running as soon as he had his legs beneath him, darting past Oscar who lay there, blind, trembling from shock. Jude couldn't take time to help him. With the alarm providing cover for the sound of his movements, he reached the corner of the small garden and pressed himself against the *veranera* vines torn ragged by the buckshot. Ignoring the thorns, he crouched below where he guessed the gunman would pop up to shoot once he decided to take his chance.

That was when Axel decided to improvise. Jude watched in disbelief as the older man crawled out from behind the sofa barricade, slid open what remained of the screen door, and walked out into the garden.

"I'm coming for the boy," he shouted, using Spanish—it was for the gunman's benefit, not Jude's. "I need to make sure he's okay. Whatever you want, you can have, just let me get to the boy. He's young, he means no one any harm . . ."

Watching him, Jude thought to himself in an eerie moment of calm: He gave his vest to the boy's mother.

Axel just kept jabbering, switching to English just in case, coming closer to the wall. His eyes looked spent but there was fury in them too. Jude edged up slowly, careful not to rustle the *veranera* leaves. Finally he saw the barrel of the AR-15 pop over the top of the garden wall. He rose to full height, grabbed the weapon and pulled down, lodged his pistol into the throat of the kid, then fired. The boy's jaw exploded in a hurl of blood. He toppled down into the neighboring yard. The rifle came free in Jude's hand and only then did he realize how hot the barrel was, scalding his fingers.

JUDE TURNED OFF THE PERIMETER SENSOR, AND SUDDENLY THERE WAS only the sound of the fire and Oscar's sobbing mother.

The side of Eileen's white shift was soaked with blood, her skin grimed from the smoke. She whispered between coughs, "I tried to catch him . . . Oscar . . . but I couldn't see when—"

"Hush. Come on."

Jude lifted her to her feet, wrapped her arm around his neck, and led her out from behind the couch. Greasy black clouds billowed around them as he guided her haltingly into the small garden, thick with the stench of cordite and burning kerosene. Both of them hacked, and Eileen's spittle came up dark. Consuela tried to comfort Oscar's mother, who gripped her son to her chest and rocked back and forth, mewling in grief. Axel stood dazed amid the others, unsure who needed comfort, who needed help.

Jude took a running start to scale the wall, the *veranera* thorns snagging his shirt and hands, but he got up and over in one quick move and landed in the neighboring yard, primed to take on the kid if he flashed a backup weapon. But the boy was down for good, one side of his face a gory mask, blood bubbling from his neck, the other side of his face frozen in a wide-eyed grimace. Jude patted him down, found a knife, took it away. He thought of Oscar and had to fight an impulse to shoot this kid dead, then elected to opt for triage, help the others first. By the time he got back, the thing would be decided.

He hoisted himself onto the same table in the corner the kid had used as a firing stand and waved for everyone to come toward him. "We'll get out this way," he said, gesturing to the neighbor's house. Consuela managed to get Oscar's mother to her feet and lead her to the garden wall. With tortured eyes, she handed up her son's body to Jude. It felt like nothing, the bones so slight, skin like paper, but blood came away on Jude's hands as he set the boy down gently in the grass. He climbed back up onto the table, wiped his hands clean, then held them out and the woman grabbed on and climbed over, quickly scrambling down to pick up her son again and wrap him in her arms.

Next, Consuela and Axel helped Eileen. She couldn't put weight on her left leg so they had to hoist her up to where Jude could wrap both arms around her. She bit down to fight the pain, puling in his ear as she kicked herself over with her one good leg. Jude eased her down slowly but her whole left side collapsed. Her eyes were dull, she was panting, her breath smelled like tin. They needed to get her to a hospital before she went into shock. Jude turned back to help Consuela then, and finally Axel.

Everyone eyed the wounded young gunman but no one approached. His stare seemed fixed on something else—far away or deep within, Jude didn't know or much care. Axel, wearing a look of anguished desperation, trained his pistol on the boy and nodded that he had the situation under control as Jude drew his own gun and lifted it close to his chest in a ready position, venturing inside the strange house.

He'd seen only four men charge out of the van, but there could be others, maybe one of them hidden here, a trap. But when Jude got beyond the doorway, he found only the owners, an aging couple, the Chilean missionaries, crouched in terror behind an armchair in the corner of the living room, the man's arms wrapped around his tiny wife. Jude asked if there was anyone else in the house and they said no, just the one who had run through to the garden. Still, Jude checked every room. Once he knew the place was clear, he went back out and collected everyone, telling them to move on inside. Everyone did except Oscar's mother, who remained kneeling in the garden, clutching her dead son and staring at the young man, not much older than Oscar, who had killed him.

The old woman in the house saw Eileen's blood and ran to her kitchen to fetch clean towels and soap. Her husband said he'd called *emergencia*—he'd been told the police were on their way, but that felt like ages ago. Jude looked at his watch, realizing only then that barely fifteen minutes had passed since he'd first looked out Consuela's window and seen the strange van parked down the street.

The old man's wife returned from the kitchen and, using sewing shears, cut away the bloody cotton of Eileen's dress and underwear and gently washed the wound. Once the blood was wiped away, Jude could see the bullet, lodged within the puncture it had made in the muscle of her hip. Eileen shook and gritted her teeth, looking up at Jude. "It's gonna be okay, I know it, I can feel it, it's gonna be fine. You gotta help Oscar."

The old woman glanced at Jude to suggest he leave Eileen alone for now, so she wouldn't exhaust herself with further talk. Jude leaned down, squeezed Eileen's hand, and kissed her hair, not knowing what to tell her, then went to the front door, pulled it open, and stepped outside.

His pistol still at the ready, he checked the street and found the shooter who'd hidden near the van lying where he'd fallen, dead. Nearby, another lay crushed in his own blood where the van had run over him, his back corkscrewed. Up the street, the large one lay facedown. That, plus the kid in the back garden, made four. Jude checked inside the van, ready to shoot, but found no one else. Then he remembered the van had been parked outside a house up the block, the old gossip's place. Osorio. That'd bear checking.

He turned to head that way and found Axel wandering ahead of him, toward the black Mercedes.

Jude hurried to catch up, snagged Axel's arm. "I need you to stay inside."

Axel shook him off. "I have to see Carlos."

Jude planted himself in Axel's way. "It's not safe out here, you're not wearing a vest, I need—"

"I'm not much concerned about your needs, frankly." Axel stared into Jude's eyes with a vacant, hateful intensity. "Isn't safe? Out here? Well, isn't that refreshing? In contrast to all the perfectly secure and docile places I've been of late. Why, didn't you know, just a few moments ago, I was sitting inside the home of a dear friend. We had a little fire going and—"

The bullet came silently and from nowhere and hit the side of Axel's head near the ear, the impact creating a tiny halo of blood. His expression froze, the eyes suddenly glassy and wrong. He tottered. Then a second round hit him in the throat and he buckled into Jude's arms.

PART V

FACELESS

There is always another level, another secret,
a way in which the heart breeds a deception
so mysterious and complex it can only be
taken for a deeper kind of truth.

—Don DeLillo, *Libra*

American Business Consultant
Murdered in El Salvador

SAN SALVADOR, El Salvador (Inter-American Media Agency)—An American hydrologist was slain early today in what authorities believe was a failed kidnap attempt.

Axel Odelberg, working on behalf of Horizon Project Management, was shot dead shortly after seven o'clock this morning in the eastern town of San Bartolo Oriente. A second American, anthropologist Eileen Browning, was critically wounded in the attack. Her condition has stabilized, but she is scheduled for evacuation to the United States shortly for further treatment.

Seven Salvadorans were also slain: Odelberg's driver, an eight-year-old boy, a seventy-nine-year-old neighbor, and the four would-be kidnappers. The four attackers were killed as Odelberg and Browning defended themselves with the assistance of Odelberg's bodyguard. The alleged kidnappers were identified by their tattoos as members of Mara Salvatrucha, a notoriously violent Salvadoran street gang with roots in Los Angeles and a rapidly expanding membership throughout the United States and Central America.

A regional spokesmen for ARENA, El Salvador's ruling party, stated: "This attack underscores the terrorist ambitions of these gangs and the need for La Mano Dura and even tougher laws. The voters in the recent election spoke loud and clear on this, and we will give the people the security they demand."

Odelberg's killing sent particularly severe shock waves through the American business community, since it took place in the aftermath of Teamster Gilberto Soto's murder just last week.

"Mr. Odelberg was a gifted man whose death hits all of us hard," said Robert Strickland, an executive with Torkland Overby Enterprises. Strickland was in El Salvador to confer with Odelberg regarding the expansion of a soft drink bottling facility operated by Estrella, C.A., in which Torkland has a significant equity position. "Axel believed deeply in the need for sound development throughout the region. It was his life's work." Asked if Odelberg's death would cause Torkland to rethink its commitment to Estrella, Strickland responded, "If anything, we're more committed than ever. We can't back down now. That would be a victory for the terrorists and an insult to Axel."

41

It took a second for Jude to place the man. The context was all wrong and he'd changed in ten years, a weariness of spirit, hair fading, the body still neck-bending tall but thicker from middle age. There was no mistaking the eyes, though.

The man pulled up a chair across the metal table from Jude and rested his briefcase on the floor. "You may not remember me."

"I can't place your name at the moment," Jude said. "But I remember you."

The man took out a card and slid it across the table. Special Agent John Pitney, Federal Bureau of Investigation, Chicago. "I've come a long way, obviously, and if it's all right with you I'd like to jump right in."

Jude stared into Pitney's singular green eyes. "Sure."

Jude had spent most of the previous day watching lizards scurry across the walls of the cramped, sweltering PNC garrison in San Bartolo Oriente where he was questioned by members of the infamous Directorate for Investigating Organized Crime. It had been clear almost immediately that the men working the case had bought into the botched kidnap angle—for all Jude knew, they were its masterminds. Or answered to higher-ups who were.

He elected to play along without committing himself to their interpretation, reviewing their pictures—they had hundreds, a numbing testament to the thoroughness of the cover-up—and he identified as best he could who was who and what was where. They asked nothing about the timing of the shots that killed Axel, or of the situation involving Estrella, or the abducted little girl, or why Oscar and his mother were at the house. Jude didn't volunteer, either, or even ask if Consuela was saying anything of the sort, reminding himself of the farce the investigation into the murder of Gilberto Soto had become.

He'd accepted a change of clothes at the garrison, surrendering what he'd been wearing—more pointless evidence. He ignored the food he was brought; the intense smells nearly made him retch. Then, quite late, he was driven all the way to the capital by two silent men and encamped in this small, windowless room, tucked deep within the bowels of the embassy. He'd lain awake on his cot all night, fending off the nightmares he knew sleep would bring.

Wakefulness proved just as punishing. Nothing he would hear from anyone over the coming days, regardless how damning, would approach in viciousness his own self-laceration. His epiphany of two days earlier, when he'd discerned the little machine cranking out so many of his missteps—the blind swings in temperament back and forth between shrewish self-hatred and stubborn numbness—it seemed a kind of fantasy, a moralistic fable delivered up quaintly to a wholly different person. Here and now, the guilt felt right, it felt necessary, the more eviscerating the better.

Over and over, he replayed the entire sorry history in his mind, from that first call from Malvasio to watching Axel die in his arms, getting played like somebody's fat kid brother, then all the buck-up bromides he'd fed himself to do the thing, the moral qualms he'd swept aside, the plain common sense he'd ignored, the conniving knack for covering his ass he'd developed, blinding himself to the obvious to pursue the convenient, all for the sake of what? Telling himself he could look men like Malvasio and Strock in the eye, play their game and walk away, prove himself their equal but not their kind.

Gee. That turned out well.

He realized it sounded squirrelly and not a little chickenshit, but he'd developed an almost eerie fascination with the unseen impulses at play. He envisioned himself a sleepwalker who suddenly wakes up in a strange room, finds himself before a mirror, and has the ridiculous audacity to say, "I know that guy," before laughing in his own face. Wasn't that what he'd been after—some dark, grand adventure that would tell him, finally, who he was? Well, embrace your success, he thought. You're the fool who got sucked in deeper than he could handle and then couldn't step up, come clean, the spitting image of your father—how's that for unseen impulses?

Meanwhile, he thought, Axel is dead. And given how it happened, he may as well have been killed by you. Figure out how you intend to live with that.

Come morning, Lazarek had barged in, joined by a nameless sidekick who also clearly had a military past: leathery face, savagely blond hair, big ropy hands. They spent two hours going at him, mocking him for his farcical stab at a kidnap swap that made no sense. A baffled Hector Torres had passed word on to an equally puzzled Wenceslao Sola, Sola had contacted Lazarek, and everyone concerned was still scratching his head. They'd be laughing, he added, if it hadn't ended so badly.

Lazarek tried to badger Jude into admitting he knew nothing about any involvement between Malvasio and Torres, let alone Sola or anyone else connected with Estrella. "And don't expect Waxman, the reporter, to bail you out. That pudgy fuck prints anything resembling the hoax you've been peddling, he'll walk into a buzz saw." Jude just sat there in silence through all of that, and it galled the man. The mockery escalated—What kind of loser would indulge such nitwit fantasies in the first place?—culminating with outright blame for Axel's death on Jude's getting sucked into such crap instead of focusing on his job: his real job, the one he got paid for.

Fair enough, Jude thought, for all the wrong reasons. And yet he wondered what they really knew. You tell your secrets, he thought, I'll tell mine, though it was far too late for that. Besides, why waste the truth on these two?

His next visitor followed up on the same theme, minus the venom. It was Jim Leonhard, Trenton's regional supervisor and the man who'd originally recruited Jude at Los Rinconcitos in the Zona Rosa. "You let the principal dictate the terms of his own protection," Leonhard said, explaining why Jude was fired. "I know you were fond of each other. I can only imagine the regret you must feel. But we're not in the regret business."

Lucky you, Jude thought.

BACK IN THE PRESENT, PITNEY FUMBLED WITH THE CLASP TO HIS briefcase. "The bureau has an unfortunate reputation for taking more than it gives," he said. "Well, I'm here to give a little. And I'm going to start by telling you about someone named Lolly Turpin."

Finally getting his briefcase open, he rummaged inside and produced a photograph of a woman in her late thirties, seated at a long table in an institutional dining room, wearing a faded denim shirt with FOX VALLEY ATC stenciled above the pocket. She had a pretty but dead face, spent blue eyes, ash-colored hair cut short with a center part. Her chest was generous but sliding downhill and a little lopsided, suggesting a bad silicon job, just as her clenched lips suggested meth use, her teeth rotting black or gone altogether.

"Fox Valley," Jude said, "that's the women's prison." The name was a statewide joke.

"Adult Transitional Center. It's out in the woods, nice job-training operation, an HIV peer group program."

Aha, Jude thought. "She's sick."

"I'll get to that." Pitney took a moment with the picture, as though to remind himself of something. "Almost all the information we had on your father and Bill Malvasio and Phil Strock came from Lolly. She had a thing for cops. At least seven officers got involved with her at one point or another, including—"

"My father," Jude said.

"You know this story."

"Strock told me a little about it on the flight down here. Up till then—"

"Your father was something of an exception, you know. He got serious."

"Yeah. I heard. Two years."

"He fell in love, was what I meant."

Jude sat back, thinking: Don't let this guy wind you up.

"I realize it may be discomfiting to hear a psychological profile of your father as told by a speed-freak hooker with AIDS, but bear with me. I found Lolly's take rather compelling."

"You've spoken to her recently."

"Yes. But that, again, is getting ahead of things. Lolly was fond of your dad. She said he was a good-looking man—I see a lot of him in you, actually—but, according to Lolly, he had no sense of that."

He was married to my mother, Jude thought. You need a program?

"He compensated with the bull cop routine and, like most guys of that ilk, all it took was somebody to light up the lamps, say she understood. 'I see the real you.' I'm not saying she played him for a complete fool—Lolly's pretty straight that it was mutual, at least for a while. But your dad fell fast and hard. She said he spent money on her like it was gas and they were going somewhere, and I'm not talking a big Friday night on Rush Street every now and again. He put her up in an apartment on Riverside Drive, paid the monthlies, bought her implants and a butt makeover, even a full-length mink."

Jude noted the sad breasts again, then remembered the fights, his mom and dad, the ones over money always the worst.

"We were surprised to find the twenty grand hidden in your house, actually, couldn't imagine he'd have any to spare. But he'd talked a lot about the two of them running away. He'd get a divorce, leave your mother."

Leave us all, Jude thought. It seemed oddly anticlimactic, learning that. But he was pretty hard to impress on a lot of levels at that moment.

"You want to spend money like that on a cop's salary, you need a sideline—that's right around when your dad and Strock and Malvasio started going out on their little capers. I don't mean it was your dad's idea. Malvasio had been nudging him for a while. They worked something out with the Gangster Disciples running Cabrini Green, which meant the Stones and Vice Lords were fair game, and that was who they went after.

"This went on awhile, then things with Lolly took a turn. Your dad was a talker. It started out like bragging then felt like confessing then just turned woe-is-me. Lolly got scared—a sloppy cop who hates his life and tells you way more than you ever wanted to know. That's poison.

"Being who she is, she did about as dumb a thing as she could come up with. She figured she better start saving a little of her own money, so she pawned a charm bracelet he'd bought her. He found out, of course—she'd picked his favorite thing—so he kicked her around, a bad habit he'd formed, then took the ticket, bought the bracelet out of hock, and gave it back to her to say he was sorry. That's when she got in touch with Hank Winters."

"The cop who was killed."

"She'd had a little whirlwind with Winters right before she hooked up with your dad, and he seemed the safest harbor she could hope for. She vanished from the apartment your dad had her in, and Winters put her up. But Winters was, if anything, the worst choice she could've made. Once he bled the story out of her, he started blackmailing everybody—your dad, Strock, Malvasio. He particularly hated Malvasio, it was mutual, and suddenly there was talk about killing. Lolly caught on she'd made blunder number two. Meanwhile, your dad was leaving calls with every escort service on the near north side, trying to hunt her down."

And kill her, Jude thought, wondering if he finally understood the old man.

"She got in touch with the bureau then—on the sly, not so Winters knew. Took a week just to coax her in for a sit-down. I was her handler. She wasn't all that forthcoming, at least not at first—she haggled, got weepy, played games, the whole time trying to see how much she could buy and how little I'd make her pay for it. Bit by bit, though, we began to make some headway."

"But then Winters got killed," Jude guessed. "And she disappeared."

"With Winters dead we had to move. That's why the arrests and the search at your house came down that day. But Lolly was our case and, yeah, she hit the wind. We tried to get evidence off the bangers your dad and Strock and Malvasio had chumped, but that was a dead end. We didn't believe half what they were telling us and knew the grand jury wouldn't, either. Meanwhile Malvasio was on the run. Your dad and Strock worked out deals. That ended it, more or less."

"Where'd Lolly end up?"

"Detroit. I didn't know that at the time, though."

"But somebody did."

"Your old man. Lolly didn't have two twenties to paste together, and friends in Detroit are like enemies anywhere else. When she heard your dad walked away with a deal that meant no jail time, she saw an opportunity. Winters had schooled her well. She started calling, hitting your old man up for cash. One minute she'd threaten, tell him she was going to come forward with everything she knew, then she'd turn around and say the two years with him were the best of her life, she hadn't been happy since, they could still make it work. Regardless of how it got there, the conversation always ended up in the same place: Send money. Your dad didn't have that kind of scratch anymore, had no way to get it. She wouldn't hear that. Her threats got freakier, more personal. In the last call she made to him, four days before he died, she told your dad if he didn't come up with five thousand dollars by the end of the week, she was contacting a reporter for the *Sun-Times*. She'd tell him everything, down to the kink. And she meant it."

The small room felt even smaller. "And so," Jude said, "my dad went fishing."

"Not before he sent Lolly a wire." Pitney reached down into his briefcase again, this time removing an old telegram that had been folded up for years, the paper soft as tissue, creases ready to tear. Gingerly, he spread it out on the table and turned it so Jude could read. The message consisted of two words: *Forgive me.*

"Lolly believes your old man got himself good and drunk, then dove over the side and tied himself to something underwater. It was planned, he killed himself, she has no doubt about it whatsoever."

Get in line, Jude thought. He wanted Pitney to put the telegram away. Ask your strung-out hooker squeeze to forgive you, but not your family. Of all the ways to die . . .

"She blamed herself for your dad's death, and the next ten years were a long, slow fall. Her peculiar gift for bad company took several nasty turns, but the drugs kept her moving. She ended up back on the street in Chicago, turning twists for crystal. Meanwhile, the bureau kept getting hints that Malvasio was coming across the border every year or so, staging hits for a variety of clients, then vanishing again. It was smoke and rumor, nothing could get proved, but an MO developed. We figure he's been involved in as many as thirty homicides, about a dozen of those connected to a fire a year ago in California. He hides down here in between trips north. We have pretty good ties to the PNC, but Chicago's not the only place with twisted cops. Given what they pay their people down here, it's a miracle they're not all on the take. Any event, we could never get our hands on him."

"Can I stop you for a second?" Jude felt light-headed. He'd been in this room with its ungodly light for how many hours now? But it wasn't just that. He'd heard some of this from Fitz but the thing just got worse every time it came up. "Why didn't McGuire tell me any of this? When he came to question me, I mean."

Jude sensed from Pitney's reaction that he'd struck a nerve. "When Ed called for a briefing, he reached the agent of the day and got a pretty stock response. Nobody bothered to connect him to me, and I didn't find out about his interest till a week ago. You've heard about the bureau's computer problems. Believe me, they're real. And communication between offices is a sore point, regrettably. Between regions it's worse, and between the States and here . . ." He let the rest hang.

Too bad, Jude thought. Maybe, if McGuire had been brought up to speed before he met with me, I wouldn't have stonewalled. Maybe I'd have told him the truth, Axel would still be alive. And maybe that's giving myself far too much credit.

"In any event," Pitney said, "back to Lolly. About a month ago, she contacted the bureau again. Asked for me personally. About a year ago her latest excuse for a boyfriend got popped for exposing himself to some tourists, and he handed Lolly and another street hooker up to buy himself a pass. She got sent to Dwight down south first then transferred to Fox Valley. She was a mess on intake: tweaked, broke, sick. Apparently someone or something turned her around. She got clean, made a searching and fearless moral inventory, as they say—and, among other things, decided she no longer wanted to live with being the sole witness to an unsolved murder."

"Winters," Jude guessed.

"She'd been waiting for Winters for over an hour—a man with many hats, he was her connection at that point, on top of everything else. Bit of a control freak, that Hank. She was pacing back and forth, biting her nails, smoking, near midnight. Winters turned into the alley. It was dark but there's a sodium lamp at that end. He looked up, spotted Lolly in her window. He didn't even see it coming—Malvasio slipped out of a doorway and just glided on up. Lolly saw the muzzle flash and Winters went down. Malvasio leaned over him, fired an insurance round, then turned toward her building. He was coming for her. She ran to a friend's place the next floor up, stayed there till dawn. Then left for Detroit."

Jude thought better of sharing what Strock had told him about his and Malvasio's first, botched attempt on Winters's life. Why complicate the thing? And he mentally compared this version of what had happened with Malvasio's, could almost see how two people, Bill and Lolly, could remember the thing so differently, though he had every reason to believe both of them were lying. But none of that mattered to Pitney, Jude supposed. "You've finally got a witness."

"Be nice to get him on everything, but one's a start. It's Illinois, he won't get death, not now. But maybe something will shake out once we get him under wraps."

"What does she want?" Jude asked. "Lolly. In trade, I mean, for testifying."

"She gets released soon. Medicaid funds are getting cut and she's going to need protease inhibitors. They're expensive. Plus living expenses, relocation. That's acceptable to us."

"All you have to do is find Malvasio."

"Which leads me back to you." Pitney collected the telegram and photograph and tucked them back into his briefcase. "Not every cop with the PNC buys into the kidnap-gone-wrong scenario. Not that they'll come forward—do that, might as well quit the job. Some very influential people have their hands around this thing. But a few straight cops have passed on a thing or two to Ed McGuire, and he and I have hashed it through. In particular, we find it interesting that one of the neighbors said the shots that killed Mr. Odelberg came well after the gunmen were already down. This neighbor hadn't heard gunfire in a while, so she was looking out her window, she could see the street. The *mareros* were dead. None of them fired at Mr. Odelberg, at any rate. The shots seemed to come from somewhere else, she said. And she saw you looking off, down the street, after Mr. Odelberg went down. You looked stunned. But she also wondered why you weren't shot too. You threw yourself over Mr. Odelberg's body. You were a perfect target. But nobody fired. Whoever the shooter was—my money's on Phil Strock—he didn't want to kill you."

Jude swallowed. Counted to five. Here we are, he thought. "What do you want?"

"Unfortunately, given the fact you brought Strock down here, that suggests you might have been in on the killing. You have to admit, it could be looked at that way. If I were you, I'd want to do everything in my power to dispel such a notion."

42

THEY TOOK A CAR FROM THE EMBASSY, AND TWICE WITHIN A MATTER of blocks the driver ducked into a parking lot, chose a space, and waited. Once it seemed clear no one was following—the Salvadorans and even the State Department frowned on the FBI tooling around the country at will—they headed out again for the heart of the capital.

Jude had to think hard to remember a time he'd ridden in back. Pitney, sitting beside him—rear right side, Axel's usual place—said, "The rumor mill down here's been as active as it has up north when it comes to Malvasio. Though we could never pin it down, word's trickled in over the past year he's been working as a glorified bagman for Hector Torres." A chastening glance. "The man you so boldly confronted at his restaurant."

"There was a little girl involved," Jude said. "Axel felt pretty strongly about it."

"Oh, I know the story. Lazarek over at ODIC won't shut up about it. He's incensed, the cheek. How dare you. Slandering decent men doing honest business in a dangerous place. And look where it got you."

I don't need reminding, Jude thought. Out the window, he spotted the Mercado Nacional de Artesanías and it brought Eileen to mind. Harriet Handicraft. In between interrogations and bouts of self-condemnation, she'd been on his mind almost incessantly. He'd been told about her med-evac to the naval hospital at Camp

Pendleton, where she'd been met by her parents. How odd it must have been, to have their anthropologist daughter in El Salvador, not their marine son in Iraq, flown home wounded. She was recovering well, he'd been told, no further word.

"The first time I met Lazarek," he said, picking up on Pitney's cue, "I got the feeling he and McGuire had no use for each other."

Pitney chuckled under his breath. "Ed has a very low tolerance for being lied to, not the best trait for a cop. In any event, back to Malvasio—there's always a gap between knowledge and proof, but down here it's a farce. Fish rots from the head down, as the saying goes, and Hector Torres has influential friends. Malvasio chose wisely." He paused, regarding Jude with an odd mix of pity and bewilderment. "Whatever possessed you to get involved with him, knowing what happened to your father?"

How much time do you have, Jude thought. "He came across like he'd taken a good hard look at himself and wanted to make amends. And he made it sound like I was doing Strock a good turn. He would have helped my dad if he could."

Pitney considered that, or pretended to. "There will be those who find that hopelessly naïve. And that's the kindest thing I can imagine them saying."

"Yeah, well," Jude said, "they didn't grow up with Malvasio showing up at the house damn near every day. They didn't see the sides to him I did. It's hard to explain."

They veered onto the Avenida Olímpica, heading toward the Fuente Beethoven. "He's as close to a true sociopath," Pitney said, "as anyone I've encountered in almost twenty-five years with the bureau."

Jude turned and waited till Pitney met his eye. "Gee. And I always thought he was just a kick in the pants."

THE HOUSE WAS LOCATED A BLOCK FROM THE ARGENTINE EMBASSY ON a serene tree-lined street in the Colonia Escalón. Like every other home in the area, it lay barricaded beyond a high wall topped with barbed wire and fitted with video cameras.

They found McGuire sitting in the dining room across from Consuela. She'd been secreted here for her own protection. Oscar's mother had refused the same offer, choosing instead to remain in San Bartolo Oriente to bury her son and await the unlikely return of her daughter.

The house was opulent and sprawling, and Jude wondered who the sympathetic *patrón* might be. Ironically, the place seemed far more Consuela's element than the sad, spare house in Villas de Miramonte: burnished parquet floors, tapestries, and tasteful watercolors. Beyond sliding glass doors sat a garden rimmed with *pito* trees and filled with bird-of-paradise and flowering *izote*. Butterflies skittered about in the blinding sun.

Seeing Jude enter, Consuela rose from her seat and walked toward him. As she drew close, an ugliness gathered in her eyes and without a word she slapped him viciously.

Jude resisted the urge to reach up and touch his face. "I don't know what you've been told," he said. "But you have no idea how sorry I am."

She slapped him again, harder this time, then McGuire pulled her off. Her eyes were pitched with a grief so unforgiving Jude would have looked away if he could. Pitney hustled him into a small sitting room off the entry and closed the door.

"Didn't see that coming. Sorry."

"What did you tell her—that I set Axel up to get murdered?"

Pitney gathered himself. He seemed comically tall against the closed door. "We'll straighten it out. I promise." He gestured to a writing table near the window. Sunlight flared along the edges of the drawn blinds. "I'd like to explain where we hope to go from here."

McGuire joined them shortly. Unlike Pitney, he saw no need to apologize for any misunderstandings. He sat down, staring at Jude with principled revulsion. God only knows how he'd act, Jude thought, if he realized I still haven't told them everything.

"Where's your partner?" Jude asked. "Sanborn."

Pitney stepped in to answer. "Jimmy doesn't see the problem letting this thing sit where it is. Four *salvatruchos* in a kidnap scheme involving an American, it's what he's down here for." Catching a glance from McGuire, he added, "Don't get me wrong, Jimmy's a solid cop. He just thinks that if Malvasio's in with the people we think he is, trying to nail him's a waste of time. Could just end up slamming doors Jimmy'll need open if he's going to get anything done here."

"He's got a point." McGuire chafed his hands in thought. "But—"

"Malvasio's a one-man crime wave," Pitney finished. "In particular he killed a cop in furtherance of a criminal conspiracy and we've finally got an eyewitness. True, she's damaged goods. But you don't get to pick your evidence. Regardless, we've got a green light from Quantico."

"Jimmy won't get in the way," McGuire said, more for Pitney's benefit than Jude's.

Pitney rocked on his heels. To Jude he said, "I'd like to tell you we've devised an uncanny and foolproof plan for bringing Malvasio in."

McGuire, with a cold smile, added, "But that would be lying."

"Basically," Pitney said, "it comes to this. The way you've described the attack tells me there weren't supposed to be survivors. Apparently, they underestimated you. In fact, if there hadn't been a fifth gunman, you'd have come out all right."

All right as in Oscar, Jude thought. As in Eileen. A testament to my skill.

"The fact you weren't killed with everyone else tells us something," Pitney continued.

"Assuming you weren't in on it," McGuire said.

Pitney shot him a look. Turning back to Jude: "If the point was to silence everybody, they failed, obviously. You're still a risk. As is

Señora Rojas. Which leads me to think Malvasio will get in touch. Once things settle down a little. He'll need to know what you've said."

"He already knows what I've said to the PNC. And Lazarek. I'd bet on that."

"But not to us. Or that reporter you and Axel met with, Waxman."

"I haven't had time—"

"Malvasio's gonna buddy up," McGuire said, still skeptical but coaching now. "Play along. You're the grieving bodyguard, use that."

"Then what?" Jude felt his pulse quicken. The thought of seeing Malvasio again, face-to-face. "You don't have jurisdiction here."

"It's not like the entire PNC's corrupt," Pitney offered.

McGuire said, "The hard part will be keeping a lid on it. We can't wait long. You talk to Malvasio, gain his confidence, get him to sit down somewhere. The guys we trust grab him, then bring him to us at the embassy, not the local garrison. Before anybody who's been bought off even knows what's up, we stick him on a plane."

"And what if one of these guys you trust, when he realizes the stakes, changes sides? Or what if somebody at the embassy—okay, not Sanborn, but somebody—leaks the plan to Lazarek, he tips off Sola, Sola calls Torres . . ."

Pitney worked up another mirthless smile. "As I said, the plan's not foolproof."

Jude sat back, looked at the two of them. "And these other guys, the ones who actually call the shots—Torres, Sola, Judge Regalado, Colonel Vides—they just walk away."

Pitney said, "You go with what you can prove. And, as you pointed out, there are limits to what we can do here."

"You don't like it," McGuire added, "write your congressman."

Jude nodded out toward the dining room, where Consuela sat alone. "That what you're going to tell her?"

THE AGENTS HOLED HIM UP IN A MODEST HOTEL IN THE CAPITAL near the Plaza de las Américas, spreading word far and wide—the embassy, the PNC—where he could be found.

From the patio where breakfast was served he could see the statue of El Salvador del Mundo, the Savior of the World, encircled by fast-food restaurants and airline offices. Asian businessmen predominated among the hotel guests: Taiwanese bankers, Japanese engineers. They wore business suits despite the heat, patted their brows with dazzling white handkerchiefs, and clamored in their native dialects at each other or into cell phones until Spanish was required, at which point they displayed a patient, lilting fluency. Once breakfast was over, they trooped out en masse, awaited by their drivers and bodyguards, leaving Jude alone in the quiet hotel except for the staff, who kept a courteous distance.

Sitting on his bed, he watched TV for updates concerning the investigation into Axel's killing, but they became increasingly brief and repetitious, in the end seeming almost like ads for Estrella. By local standards, the crime was solved.

He worked off his frustration with blistering calisthenics in his room or by practicing Krav Maga—hammer-fist punches, roundhouse kicks, combinations, counterattacks. Exercise became the only thing keeping him sane, and when the room grew too claustrophobic, he launched off on long runs, all the way down the Alameda Roosevelt with its choking traffic and garish billboards to the Mercado Ex-Cuartel.

His second day out—Holy Thursday—as he skirted the edges of the market, three *mareros* swaggered out from within the catacomb of vendor stalls, one wagging a gun. Jude's only valuables were his watch and cell phone, but handing them up never crossed his mind. Nothing much at all crossed his mind, actually. He deflected the pistol with a quick hand strike, drove a kick into the gunman's groin, moved in, elbowed him across the jaw, kneed him in the stomach, and twisted the gun from his hand, taking him to the ground and finishing him off with fierce stomp kicks, driving his heel down into the man's throat and solar plexus.

The punishment induced a kind of clarity. For the first time in a long while, Jude felt awake.

The other two *mareros* fled, leaving their disarmed pal curled up in the street, sucking air through blood. Jude left the scene before a crowd could form, jogging back the way he'd come, now the dubious owner of a Walther 9mm that, back in his room, he tucked deep beneath the mattress.

The week concluded with Easter Sunday and its nationwide orgy of candlelight *desfiles,* with glass coffins containing wood-carved Christs held aloft by the devout in traditional robes, urged on by devils with whips. Still, no contact from Malvasio. Jude considered slipping out on his own, taking the initiative, tracking the man down. He knew him well enough, though, to stay put. Let him come to you, he thought. He's too smart and too connected not to see you coming.

It was why Jude had lied to Pitney and McGuire about where he'd actually met with Malvasio. He figured they'd respond by putting the restaurant in San Marcelino or the *rancho* on the beach under surveillance. Malvasio would make their guys or get tipped off by his own contacts within the PNC and that would be it, game over. Jude couldn't abide that. One way or another, he intended to hook up one last time, and if that meant wait, he'd wait. If it meant move, he'd know when the time was right.

THE WEDNESDAY AFTER EASTER THE FIRST OF THE SCATTERED RAINS presaging *invierno* hit the capital, the muggy sheet of rain falling straight down and flooding the streets while thunder rumbled over the hills surrounding the city. Jude was standing at the window screen, watching the overflow tumble from the hotel's clogged rain gutters, when a knock came at his door. He expected it was maintenance, checking for leaks. Or maybe someone from the front desk letting him know the bed of his pickup had turned into a dog bath.

When he opened the door, though, he found a boy about Oscar's age. It took him aback. The boy had sunken cheeks and ghostly eyes and he stood there drenched, holding a knotted plastic bag. Wordlessly, he handed the bag to Jude, then turned away and disappeared down the hallway to the stair, his footfalls leaving puddles on the smooth brown tiles.

Jude tore the bag open and found a cell phone inside. He set it on the bedside table. Ten minutes later the call came in.

"I know you think I had something to do with what happened in San Bartolo Oriente," Malvasio said. "But I didn't. I think Strock—"

"Whoa, back the fuck up. Don't even—"

"The guy I told you about, Ovidio, the PNC cop who was supposed to connect with Strock? Well, he did. He came by the *rancho,* the day after you dropped Strock off. Clara told me they both trekked off with the rifle and ammo and haven't come back since. These people—"

Jude cut him off. "You abducted a little girl. For Hector Torres. You were seen."

"I didn't do it for him. Christ. He wasn't even supposed to know. You almost got me killed, going to Torres with that."

"Poor you. Okay, I'll bite—why'd you snatch the girl, then?"

"I fucked up. I thought . . . Christ, I don't know what I thought. Look, I made no bones about the kind of people I work for down here. I was totally up front about that. Doesn't mean I had any idea they were planning to waste your guy. Or all those other people."

Jude felt as though his head were turning inside out. "You have the gall to talk to me like this?"

"Listen to me, damn it, I didn't—"

"You insult me?"

The static crackled. Interference from the storm.

"Look, Jude—believe what you want. That's not why I called.

You told Torres you wanted the little girl returned to her mother. Am I right?"

Jude tasted a faint trace of copper. Blood—he'd bitten his lip open. "Tell me where."

"You can't fuck me on this, Jude. I'm already behind the eight ball with Torres because I lied to him and you can't fuck me on this. You've seen how these people operate. You've got to come alone. I'll tell you where but you come alone and no one knows but you. Otherwise I can't make promises about this girl."

JUDE WALKED OUTSIDE, LOOKED UP AND DOWN THE BLOCK, AND spotted the car parked near the corner bus stop. It contained a bureau underling, the same man who'd driven Jude to the house in the Colonia Escalón. He'd been stationed there by McGuire and Pitney. Jude had seen him around all last week—the same face each day, keep the number of people in the loop to a minimum. He'd been embarrassingly easy to lose on Jude's runs downtown.

The guy seemed more the junior foreign service type than an agent—wonky, trim, neat but not too. He dropped his copy of *El Diario de Hoy* as Jude gestured for him to crank down his window.

"I'm going batty cooped up inside. Think I'll take a drive up to Puerta del Diablo." The Devil's Gate: a volcanic rock formation above the city. "See what the world looks like after the rain. Figured it'd be a good idea to give you a heads-up."

"Thanks. I appreciate that." The guy started up the car, cleared the windshield with his wipers. He looked relieved.

"I'm Jude, by the way."

"I know. Tony Lamm."

They shook hands. Jude said, "I didn't mean to make you look bad the times I've gone running." He cracked a smile. "Well, okay, maybe I did."

"It's all right. This wasn't supposed to be . . ." He couldn't find a way to finish.

"We're on the same side," Jude guessed.

The guy had to think about it. "Exactly."

"Great. I'll drive out the Paseo General Escalón, just follow me up the mountain."

"Sure thing. By the way—you know why they call it Puerta del Diablo, right?"

Be nice, Jude thought. Humor him. "No. Tell me."

"It used to be called Puerta de los Angeles. But then the locals discovered tourists preferred something named after the devil. Weird, huh."

Jude smiled. "Human nature. Go figure." He turned to head back toward the hotel.

Lamm called out after him. "Wait. Forgot. There's something else. It showed up at the embassy." He rummaged around, came up with an envelope. "Got it yesterday. Private courier. Maybe the day before."

Jude recognized the handwriting. "You waited to give me this why?"

Lamm shrugged, frowned, did a little I-dunno bob and weave with his head and shoulders, the whole fuck-if-I-know-don't-get-mad routine. Jude sighed his disgust and walked back to his truck. Once he was behind the wheel, he cracked open the envelope and found a greeting card inside, the kind you found in any hospital gift shop.

Dear Jude:

I don't have a lot of energy and I'm woozy from meds so I'll keep this short.

I'm okay. Seriously.

I know you. I know how you think. Don't blame yourself for what happened. Every person in that house chose to be there. We all knew there were risks. Don't do anything stupid or put this on yourself. Please.

I still feel terrible about Oscar, so I know the deal. Strange,

how both my brother and I now have a dead boy on our con-
sciences, but I'll tell you what—if you forgive me, I'll forgive
you. How's that?

I only hear the network news about what's going on down
there. My God, it's maddening, the lies. If you get the chance,
write, tell me what's happening. Better yet, come see me. My old
man would like to meet you. I mean, he'd like to kill you too, but
I think I talked him out of that. And in a weaker moment he told
me a story about when he was in Vietnam. A wrong turn, they
got lost on patrol, four of his men died. So he may understand
better than anybody.

Come see me, I mean it. If you don't, once I'm up and
around again, I'll come down hunting for you. That's a promise.

I have to stop now. I miss you.

Eileen

He read it through twice, took heart from "I'm okay" and "I miss
you," her devotion to reconnecting, her gutsy attempt to absolve him.
But she'd left out the key thing: Nobody who'd chosen to be there, as
she put it, owed quite the explanation he did. He could imagine what
she'd say: You couldn't have foreseen what those men would do, can't
be blamed for it. But he doubted even she'd settle for that in the long
run. And who could blame her? Besides, there was this other thing
to deal with now, the "anything stupid" Eileen so wisely foretold. If
that turned out okay, if he pulled this off, maybe then he could visit
that hospital, sit by her bedside, and not secretly wish her ex-marine
old man would put his own buried guilt to good use.

And yet what if she really could forgive him? She said it herself:
I know you. The girl who was raised by wolves. If anyone could redeem him, she was the one. Could he live with that?

He took the Walther out from under his shirt and stuffed it into
the glove compartment, then backed out of the hotel parking lot. He
let Lamm catch up and then pulled out into the traffic circling the
redondel at the Plaza de las Américas, heading west.

You learned quickly in San Salvador that defensive driving can get you killed. The uniform standard of aggression kept everybody safe, the invisible hand of the highway, and Jude maintained speed with the surging flow of traffic, always making sure that Lamm remained in his rearview. They negotiated the next *redondel,* at Fuente Beethoven, without a hitch, the traffic in and out of the roundabout never breaking speed. When they reached the next *redondel,* at Plaza Masferrer, Jude signaled that he'd be exiting right. Once he saw Lamm commit to follow, Jude broke left, throttling to cut off the driver in the next lane. He floored the pedal, burst ahead of the chain reaction of collisions behind him, then cut off two more irate drivers and left more wreckage in his wake as he sped south. He checked his mirror for signs of Lamm, then turned off at the Calle La Mascota, pulled a U-turn, and waited, out of sight of the main drag. It took less than a minute, but then Lamm barreled through the intersection, charging south toward the Pan-American Highway. Jude put the truck in gear, crossed the avenue, and headed east.

He wished there were some way to follow through with Pitney, make Malvasio suffer, make all of them suffer, hold everyone to account for everything, straight down the line. But he had this one chance to save the girl and he intended to see it through. He owed that to Oscar's mother. Owed it to Axel.

He reached La Puntilla just before dusk, the shirtless boys chasing his pickup down the sandy lane as always with their shouts of, "*¡Parqueo! ¡Barato! ¡Parqueo!*" As before, he pulled into the vast thatched parking structure where the same old man in the skipper's cap and blue shorts waited, this time in a circle of fellow boatmen, gathered about a trash fire. Jude opened his glove compartment to collect the Walther, stuck it in his waistband, slid out from behind the wheel, and locked up his truck.

43

USING DUCT TAPE, MALVASIO FASTENED THE HOLSTER TO THE UNDER-side of the table in the dining room, then slipped his pistol in. Hopefully, it wouldn't come to that, but he'd given up predicting which way things would go. Clara watched him, sitting on the floor in the corner and clutching the little girl to her chest. She stared at him hatefully, fearfully. He'd lashed out, backhanding her once when she wouldn't stop nagging him about the child. He regretted that, but she'd been quiet since and he needed to think.

The day of the shootings, he'd dumped Strock's body out in the mangrove swamp near the abandoned soccer field. Given the heat, the body was no doubt black and bloated beyond recognition by now, not to mention crawling with bugs and getting picked apart by the buzzards. He'd tossed Strock's belongings and the AR-15 into the estuary and that was that, the perfect crime, though you'd hardly know it the way Sola and the rest of the prissy little gangsters involved were whining.

Malvasio had learned of their discontent from Hector over lunch at El Arriero. The news reports were everything they'd hoped for—there was even the extra bonus of the boy, Oscar, dying in the attack, something Malvasio hadn't foreseen. He hadn't known the kid and his mother had holed up with Consuela, and you can't buy luck like that. Malvasio was primed for an attaboy. But there was the issue of the four survivors.

"We aren't too much concerned with Consuela Rojas," Hector had said. "Her ex shares family ties with Wenceslao, and if he can't prevail upon her to keep quiet for her own good, she'll be reminded she has children. True, they're adults, but that doesn't mean bad things can't happen to them. The woman whose boy was killed is a raving mess, we hear. By the way—have you heard anything about her little girl, the one she says was kidnapped?"

Malvasio, his mind elsewhere, hadn't caught his reaction in time. "There a reason I should?"

"Relax. Just inquiring."

"I said it already, she hid the girl to protect her."

"We'll see. If she did, she'll be quiet about it now that her boy is dead. No sense attracting attention—she could end up losing them both. But if she didn't have anything to do with the girl's disappearance, my guess is we'll hear about it once she regains her tongue. The NGOs and human rights crowd, they'll prop her up in front of as many TV cameras as they can find."

Malvasio hadn't known what to say, so he'd just kept quiet. He'd hired four guys he thought could handle the job. It didn't turn out that way. Jude sniffed out the attack before it got started and things took their fated course. Look at the bright side, he'd wanted to say. *Listen to the news.*

"The young American woman who was wounded presents a similar problem. She's out of the picture for now but nothing guarantees that will last. She was hanging around with that reporter. Even so, none of that is as bad as the bodyguard."

"He hasn't said anything."

"That hardly means he won't. He can make himself out to be the hero."

"Heroes don't get fired. And we can always cloud the water by bringing up his role in bringing Strock down here. Clara will confirm he dropped Strock off at the *rancho*, she saw the weapon, the ammunition. He'll be too busy trying to prove he hadn't been in on his own guy's murder to point the blame at you."

"That just confuses things. We don't want a second scenario suggested for the killing. That would just open the thing up again. People would start asking all the wrong questions. Right now guilt lands right where we want it, on the *maras*. It serves more than one purpose. You're missing the bigger picture by not seeing that. The Americans are already talking about additional aid. CAFTA's been given a new boost—fight crime through jobs, just what the *efemelenistas* are always bitching about. And the way it stands now, nobody will bat an eye if the government not only renews La Mano Dura but makes it more severe. You get it? All that benefit provides protection. Take away the gang angle on the killing, it disappears."

"Like I said, if it turns bad, tie him to Strock, you can dig up the clippings from Chicago. Plenty of talk about gangs in those. Beyond that, let's get serious. Only a fool hands out guarantees in a thing like this."

"Do yourself a favor, my friend—don't say that again. At the very least, the bodyguard should have died. Why wasn't he shot at the same time as the hydrologist? We hear it would have been easy, they were standing right there together in the street. But no one fired. Why is that?"

"It was too late. There were already people nosing out of their houses into the street. The hydrologist dies, that's a quirk. The bodyguard dies right after, that's a pattern. People would see, they'd remember, they'd make a point of telling what they saw, and then the cover-up goes to hell and, like you said, that's the whole point of the thing."

Malvasio knew at the time he'd come up with that ruse that he couldn't keep it alive forever. A part of him knew he hadn't killed Jude because he couldn't bring himself to do it. He'd watched the kid grow from a scrawny mope to a young man, muscle up, play ball. Ray had always said he'd never come to much, too inward, too cautious, but Ray had been wrong. Pop Gun had given up on his own kid—no surprise, he'd given up on himself. And so it was Malvasio who'd seen what Jude was truly made of—a far better enemy than anyone would've guessed. It created a kind of bond. Malvasio felt proud for him. But that wasn't why he'd spared his life.

Looking through the scope, he'd watched the thing go bad like a drunken scrum, and in its unraveling symmetry he'd recognized a simple truth: His luck had run out. It had been turning by degrees the past few years, but he'd always believed that you don't step away from the game when that happens, you ride out your streaks. He couldn't afford to live that fiction anymore. Time to find a way out. He'd need Jude for that.

The bell at the gate rang out. That would be the boy from the *pueblito*. Malvasio had told him to come running when he saw the old man's *lancha* pull up at the dock on the estuary. It meant they had five minutes.

He went over to Clara, who remained hunched on the floor against the wall. The infant was sleeping in her arms. Clara kissed the little girl's head and stroked her hair. Malvasio extended his arms. *"Dámela."* Give her to me.

JUDE RECOILED WHEN CLARA OPENED THE WOOD DOOR AT THE *RANCHO* gate. Her left eye was swollen shut and the skin was darkening. Fresh blood glistened from a cut on her cheek.

"Lo siento, señor," she whispered. She came toward him and with the gentlest of hands patted him down, finding the Walther tucked into his waistband. She glanced up into his face, eyes pleading. *"Con permiso."* Everything in her eyes let him know he'd lost the advantage long before he'd even shown up. He pulled out the gun and handed it to her. If it came down to a fight, he'd use his hands. She held the pistol awkwardly but with her fingers clear of the trigger. Turning back toward the door, she gestured for him to follow her inside.

Jude found Malvasio seated at the dining room table, cradling a little girl in his lap. Oscar's sister, Jude supposed. The child seemed alert, even startled, but not upset. Clara showed Malvasio the Walther and he nodded.

"I can understand why you brought it," Malvasio said. "But you won't need it." He nodded to Clara and she went to the doorway, stepped out onto the patio, and pitched the gun over the wall, onto the windy beach beyond. Jude considered asking Malvasio if he was armed but realized he wouldn't believe him if he said no.

"Have a seat. We've got a lot to talk over."

Jude took a chair across the table from Malvasio. Clara found a spot against the wall and slid down to the floor, holding her skirt modestly so it didn't flare out, the whole time never once taking her eyes off the little girl.

"You look well," Malvasio said. "All things considered."

Jude mentally judged the rough-hewn table's weight, wondering what it would take to flip it. He didn't want to hurt the child, though. He nodded toward Clara. "What happened?"

Malvasio adjusted the infant on his lap. "I told her the little girl belongs to her mother. Clara, she's grown fond. Too fond." He sighed. "It's a story." He shot her a look that seemed both scolding and contrite. "Any event, she wouldn't let go."

Jude leaned forward and reached across the table. "Why not hand her to me now?"

Malvasio responded with an oddly sunny smile. "Not yet. There's a few things to talk through. I'm going to need your help."

Jude felt a sudden jolt of rage. Or guilt. "That's a lot to ask, all things considered."

"You still think I had something to do with what happened. I didn't. I swear."

"I get it. That's your story. Help you how?"

"It's not a story."

"Help you how?"

"I want to come in."

Jude sat back and cocked his head. "And you think—"

"You can help. I try to connect on my own, or, God forbid, show up at the embassy, I just end up in prison. That's not a place you want to be when you've been a cop." He resettled the child in his lap again, clearly awkward holding her. "I've got information. I told you about the people I worked for. Well, you've figured out they may have had a hand in killing your guy—"

"Axel."

"Okay. Axel. Like I said, I wouldn't be surprised if Strock got dragged into it somehow, and I suppose that's my fault but my point is I'm tired. I'm done. I want to make you a deal. I'll hand this little girl over so you can get her back where she belongs. In return you bring me in."

"To who?"

"There's a guy, an American, on the edges of this. His name is Lazarek."

Jude couldn't help it, he laughed. "You don't say."

"You know him?"

"He works for ODIC. Or says he does."

"He's got a lot to lose, word slips out what his people down here have been up to."

"He knows?"

"I can't tell you that. I never met him. I just heard his name used. But I wouldn't be surprised. He knows but he doesn't know—understand what I'm saying?"

"What would he want from you?"

"I'm insurance. He has me in his pocket, he knows everybody's secrets. That's power. The upper hand."

Jude leaned forward again. "Bill, I don't know how to say this—"

"Jude, you don't know how this end of the world works. I do. Guys like Sola, the judge, the colonel, even Hector, they're never gonna pay—not here. You want them to suffer, you've got to find a way to drag them into court in the States. Or at least have that hanging over them."

"I thought you didn't know they were involved in Axel's murder."

"I don't. Not for sure. But I know something else."

"Like what?"

"No. Come on. That's Lazarek's deal to negotiate, not yours."

Beggars can't be cheaters, Jude thought, one of the old man's favorite cracks. "You want me to front for you, but I have no clue what it is you've got to hand up. Or if it's even real."

"Lazarek will know. He'll have an idea. And it's real."

Jude realized he was right. It explained things. Lazarek had gone to bat for some dubious men and they'd fucked him. It happened all the time in the third world, but that didn't mean he wouldn't want to make an example: Ask Noriega. Ask Saddam. Today's amigo, tomorrow's abomination—one must remember who swings the bat. That kind of thing was as old as empire. Lazarek and the men he answered to would make it look like they cared about the rot at the top, intended to kick ass and assemble dossiers, but soon enough everything would fall back into place the way it had been. Normalcy. Order. Progress.

But what was all that to Jude?

"You said you were tired, Bill. Me too. I came out here thinking I could do a good thing. But that little girl's mother? She was half out of her mind before her boy was killed, and I'd be amazed if she could even function now. She's dirt-poor besides. Maybe the little girl's better off here, with Clara, after all. Regardless, it's not my problem. I'm with you, I'm done." He rose from his chair. "Work out whatever you have to. But leave me out."

Malvasio regarded him with his head cocked back. Smiling. "You're bluffing."

Here we go again, Jude thought. "Suit yourself."

He turned and walked through the kitchen, then down the narrow hallway to the door. He noticed the bullet holes in the wall this time, wondering why they hadn't registered on the way in, then remembering he'd been focused on Clara holding his weapon. He didn't see blood on the wall but, even so, he quickened his step to get out.

He was through the door and halfway to the gate when Malvasio called out from behind: "I can tie all these people to a child prostitution ring that leads to Houston and Phoenix. That means they can be indicted in the States. Understand what that means?"

Jude turned. Malvasio stood in the doorway, still clutching the child. She was writhing in his hold and whimpering but not crying. Not yet.

"How do you know this?"

"It's run from the judge's plantation. The colonel gets the kids across the borders, deals with the police and hands out bribes. He also manages the security with help from Hector. That's Hector's expertise, muscle. I know, I help collect his taxes. Sola's the one with connections in the States, plus he and a handful of other men in his circle run the brothels around the country. It's insanely easy to do here. Wiretaps are illegal so you're never going to convict anyone in a conspiracy case, it's a joke. And the PNC's supposed to handle alien smuggling, but the clowns over at the Municipal Guard have jurisdiction over child prostitution, and neither side's known to break much of a sweat trying to coordinate. Meanwhile, tricking itself isn't even illegal and, when it's kids, the government just considers it a social service problem and hands it off to the NGOs. Seriously, you could grow old, die, and spend some quality time in purgatory before anybody but the usual handwringers said so much as boo about it here."

"Were you involved?"

Malvasio looked off, thinking that one through. "You know what's funny, Jude? You think I don't know what's going on in your head, but you're wrong. You're hoping this is some kind of test. Like a puzzle. If you can just frame the thing right, visualize the pieces, it'll all fall together and you'll see it. A way out. But you crossed a line, you did it that first day, when I said let's get together and you said sure. A whole lot of bridges went up in smoke that day. You can't go back. They won't let you. And you know that, you've felt it—you know what I'm saying. You may not want to admit it, you may hate yourself—and I'm sure you hate me—but you under-stand, deep down, this is right where you belong. You're going to help me. Don't bother with why, because why is a snake pit. I mean, you think it through and you realize all this work, this fucked-up misery, this trouble—Christ, I don't know what to call it—it's all about what: Kids? Water? Money? Why go there—it doesn't solve anything, knowing that answer. Just help me get to Lazarek so he can cover his own ass making these fat-cat fuckers pay to the extent they're ever going to, and be glad for that and stop trying to find someone or something to blame."

Jude had trouble putting the voice, which he'd known most of his life, with the increasingly addled words he was hearing. "Sound a little loose on deck there, Bill."

Malvasio chuckled drily. "Don't change the subject."

"I'm serious, Bill. You sound like you could use some sleep."

"Now that's observant. You should've been a cop—anybody ever tell you that?"

"Yeah," Jude said, feeling tired himself suddenly. Everything around him seemed liquid in the hot, windy moonlight. "You did, among others. A long time ago."

Malvasio switched the little girl from one arm to the other. "You wisely ignored me."

"I saw what happened."

"There you go, blaming again."

"I just meant—"

"Nobody's who you think they are, Jude. Nobody. Not me, not your dad. Not you. And that's no great tragedy, either. The ones who don't get that, they're the real animals. Slit your throat on principle. Do it for your own good."

The fatigue turned into a mild sort of vertigo, then Jude realized it wasn't fatigue at all. It was confusion, tinged with fear, and the fear had a rancid whiff of the very old to it. I should have a name for this, he thought. But where the name should be, he sensed an emptiness instead, and the bitchy voices of self-loathing he'd heard in his head for as long as he could remember echoed through that emptiness like crow caws. The effort of deafening himself to that sound, day after day, hour after hour, it was wearing him out. He resented it. He'd been doing it for years, it was no one's fault but his own, still . . .

"The thing that changed for me?" Malvasio's smile spoke of luck, his eyes of treachery. "I'll tell you what it was. I stopped pretending. I stopped fighting and just said, hey. This is it. People know they can't trust me, but that's exactly what makes me reliable. It's who I am. I'm the guy certain men turn to when they've run out of better options. And know what? So are you. Now."

Jude supposed he should feel insulted or at least pissed off, but he couldn't muster the will. Instead he glanced past Malvasio toward the moonlit window just beyond him, and suffered a freakish illusion as he caught his own reflection in the flawed glass. *Stop worrying*, the reflection said. *Just one more favor, everybody wins. Who knows you better?*

"I know who that is," Jude murmured.

Malvasio ignored him. "The weird thing? It's not how I pictured ending up, and that's probably true for you, too, but in a funny kind of way it's gratifying. We're very good at what we do, you and me. Better than your father ever was at anything." He turned to go back into the house.

Jude, as though drawn by something he couldn't see, followed him in. Given his state of mind, the hallway seemed twice as long this direction as it had coming out, Malvasio farther away than he really was. The trippy distortion held as they veered through the kitchen and Clara, a look of sudden panic on her face, leapt from her spot on the floor in the far room and scrambled toward the table. It puzzled Jude till he saw her pull the pistol out. He realized then Malvasio had set him up, might have meant to kill him all along, but then the rest happened faster than he could piece it together. Malvasio held the child tight to his body, shielding himself with her, shouting at Clara, telling her to give him the gun. But Clara just kept waving it at him, screaming for him to give her the child. It seemed to go on forever—their voices at a keening pitch, the little girl wailing now and the bare room echoing the sounds like a howl. Jude felt a painful dizziness even as, for the first time since arriving, he knew exactly what to do. It felt like sleepwalking. Stepping forward, he placed his weight on his left foot as he swung his right fist forward, turning his hip and shoulder into the blow, hitting Malvasio right where the spine and skull meet. He felt a vertebra crack beneath the punch and Malvasio's head snapped back. His knees crumbled, his arms flew out, and the child slipped free before he hit the floor. Clara scrambled forward to grab the girl as Jude stomp-kicked Malvasio in the kidneys then reached down, pulled him over, drove his knee hard into the solar plexus. He tightened his right fist and began to pound as fast and hard as he could, driving every punch from the shoulder, using his whole body for leverage and feeling the bones surrender as the room around him gradually dissolved into a grainy shimmer that filled up everything. By the time he heard Clara's voice again—she was screaming, *"¡Pare!"* Stop!— he was drenched in sweat and his lungs were heaving. He glanced up, saw her near the wall. She took form in pieces—gripping the child to her body, her face slack, her eyes hollow. She was staring at his hand.

PART VI

CLARA

Shall our blood fail? Or shall it come to be
The blood of paradise?

—WALLACE STEVENS, "Sunday Morning"

44

I HAVE WITNESSED MANY WRONGS IN MY LIFE, SUFFERED THEM myself like anyone, even when I was a little girl. But not until I watched the young American, the one named Jude, kill with his bare hands the older one, the one we called Duende, did I feel myself in the presence of a great sin. And by that I do not mean a terrible evil so much as an aching, endless sorrow—our exile from God.

I knew I was part of that terrible sin. The *evangélicos* say wanting more than you have is an insult to God. I don't know. But I can say this—it can turn into a kind of madness. Wanting Constancia made me crazy that way. I would have killed Duende myself with that gun. Certainly the wish was in my heart. And so I was not blameless. And I could not turn away from Jude, who did no more than what, only a moment before, I had wanted to do.

I watched as, little by little, he awoke to what had happened, seeing the blood, looking at his ruined hand as though it belonged to someone else, then looking down to see the monstrous thing he'd done. I have seen animals crushed by cars, and this is what came to my mind. You could no longer see a face. And then Jude began to weep. He crawled into the corner of the room and buried his head and wept so long, so horribly, I thought of the words the sisters taught me as a girl: *We send up our sighs, mourning and weeping in this vale of tears . . .*

As I said, I knew this sin was not just his but mine, and we needed, together, to make ourselves right with God. I knelt beside him and touched him and told him I could not keep Constancia. It was wrong of me and that wish had brought about this terrible thing.

I took his hand still sticky with blood and felt his splintered bones beneath the skin. He did not cry out in pain, but just looked at me as though he had forgotten who I was. I said, "Get up. Please. Lead me to this little girl's mother. We will go together and make this thing right." And with that beautiful child bundled in my arms I helped him to his feet, led him out of that house, and we walked beneath the moon and stars together and I told him it would be all right, even as my heart broke. For I loved Constancia. I always will.

AUTHOR'S NOTE

Although El Salvador obviously exists and many of its locales are represented in this book, some—such as San Bartolo Oriente and the Río Conacastal—are the author's inventions. Even existing cities and places have been changed and shaped to suit the author's sense of story and dramatic purpose, and thus the narrative should be seen as taking place entirely within a fictive world.

As with places, so with incidents and people. Some of the events recounted herein did indeed take place—the election of 2004, the CAFTA protests, the riot at La Esperanza, the murder of Gilberto Soto—but they have been compressed into an imaginary time line to suit the narrative and thus must be seen as parts of an imaginary, rather than factual, whole. The principal characters herein are entirely the products of the author's imagination and should not be confused with real individuals, living or dead. Although some persons named within the story do or did indeed exist—President Antonio Saca, assassinated Archbishop Oscar Romero, the murdered Teamster Gilberto Soto, and other persons of historical note—their roles in the story are minor and have again been shaped or changed to suit the author's dramatic designs, and they should not be conflated with real persons.

ACKNOWLEDGMENTS

The author owes a debt of gratitude to a number of people, without whose assistance this book would not exist. First and foremost are his editor, Mark Tavani, and his agent, Laurie Fox, who provided guidance and support throughout several drafts of the manuscript. The author's profoundest thanks are also due to: Paul Hartford, M.D., and D. P. Lyle, M.D., for their assistance with medical details; Jay Pirouznia, Tempe P.D. (Ret.), for his guidance on executive protection matters and the details of sniper tactics, with additional assistance from the Tempe SWAT Unit sniper detail; Joaquin Aragon of Punta Mango (www.puntamango.com) and Dionisio Mejia of Guacamaya Eco Tours (www.guacamayaecotours.com.sv) for serving as the author's guides in El Salvador, patiently explaining its culture, flora, and fauna; Ana and Mark Ramirez for aiding the author with Salvadoran slang; Eileen Beall for assistance with Spanish phrasing; Katherine Baylor, P.G., Jon Fenske, P.E., and CPT Michael J. Fuller, USAR, hydrogeologist, for their help on groundwater issues, with CPT Fuller especially helpful with information specific to El Salvador; Carlos Vasquez for educating the author on gang matters (and a word of thanks to Claire Marshall, BBC, for steering me to Carlos); Special Agent George Fong, FBI, for details concerning Mara Salvatrucha and FBI procedure outside the United States; and Michelle and Chelsea Gonsalves for their help in understanding hypothyroidism. These informed and generous individuals are in no way responsible for the thematic material of this book, nor can they be held accountable for its content. The author is solely to blame for any errors or misstatements in the text.

The author also relied on numerous written sources, specifically: *From Madness to Hope: The 12-year War in El Salvador: Report of the Commission on the Truth in El Salvador,* by the UN Commission on the Truth in El Salvador, Belisario Betancur, chairman (1993); *Our Own Backyard: The United States in Central America, 1977–1992,* by William M. LeoGrande (University of North Carolina Press, 1998); "Window on the Past: A Declassified History of Death Squads in El Salvador," by Cynthia J. Arnson, from *Death Squads in Global Perspective: Murder with Deniability,* edited by Bruce B. Campbell and Arthur D. Brenner (St. Martin's Press, 2000); *El Salvador, A Country Study,* edited by Richard A. Haggerty (Federal Research Division, Library of Congress, 1990); *Culture and Customs of El Salvador,* by Roy C. Boland (Greenwood Press, 2001); *Empire's Workshop: Latin America, the United States, and the Rise of the New Imperialism,* by Greg Grandin (Metropolitan Books/Henry Holt, 2006); *Understanding Central America* (third edition), by John A. Booth and Thomas W. Walker (Boulder: Westview Press, 1999); *Inside El Salvador: The Essential Guide to Its Politics, Economy, Society and Environment,* by Kevin Murray and Tom Barry (Albuquerque: Resource Center Press, 1995); *Inevitable Revolutions: The United States in Central America,* by Walter LaFeber (W. W. Norton & Company, 1983); *On Your Own in El Salvador,* by Hank and Bea Weiss (On Your Own Publications, 2001); *The Art of Executive Protection,* by Robert L. Oatman (Noble House, 2000); *Indian Crafts of Guatemala and El Salvador,* by Lilly de Jongh Osborne (University of Oklahoma Press, 1995); *The Blood Bankers: Tales from the Global Underground Economy,* by James S. Henry (Four Walls Eight Windows, 2003); *Water Wars: Drought, Flood, Folly, and the Politics of Thirst,* by Diane Raines Ward (Riverhead Books, 2002); *Water: The Fate of Our Most Precious Resource,* by Marq de Villiers (Houghton Mifflin, 2000); *Field Hydrology in Tropical Countries, A Practical Introduction,* by Henry Gunston (Intermediate Technology Publications, 1998); "Water Resources Assessment of El Salvador," October 1998, US Army Corps of Engineers, Mobile District and Topographic Engineering

Center; *Basic Ground-Water Hydrology,* by Ralph C. Heath, United States Geological Survey Water-Supply Paper 2220 (prepared in cooperation with the North Carolina Department of Natural Resources and Community Development, Eighth Printing, 1995); "The Way of the Commandos," by Peter Maass, *The New York Times Magazine,* May 1, 2005; "The Girls Next Door," by Peter Landsman, *The New York Times Magazine,* January 25, 2004; "Gangs in the US: A Multipart Report," by Ann Scott Tyson, *The Christian Science Monitor,* February 27, 1996, through May 12, 1997; *Gangs and Their Tattoos,* by Bill Valentine (Paladin Press, 2000); *Street Gang Awareness,* by Steven L. Sachs (Fairview Press, 1997).

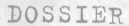

DOSSIER

Blood of Paradise

DAVID CORBETT

MORTALIS

FROM TROY TO BAGHDAD
(VIA EL SALVADOR)

By David Corbett

THE STORY'S GENESIS

I conceived *Blood of Paradise* after reading *Philoctetes,* a spare and relatively obscure drama by Sophocles. In the original, an oracle advises the Greeks that victory over the Trojans is impossible without the bow of Herakles. Unfortunately, it's in the hands of Philoctetes, whom the Greeks abandoned on a barren island ten years earlier, when he was bitten by a venomous snake while the Achaean fleet harbored briefly on its way to Troy.

Odysseus, architect of the desertion scheme, must now return, reclaim the bow, and bring both the weapon and its owner to Troy. For a companion, he chooses Neoptolemus, the son of his slain archrival, Achilles.

Neoptolemus, being young, still holds fast to the heroic virtues embodied by his dead father, and believes they can appeal to Philoctetes as a warrior. But Odysseus—knowing Philoctetes will want revenge against all the Greeks, himself in particular—convinces Neoptolemus that trickery and deceit will serve their purposes far better. In essence, he corrupts Neoptolemus, who subsequently deceives Philoctetes into relinquishing his bitterness to reenlist in the cause against Troy.

The tale has an intriguing postscript: It turns out to be the corrupted Neoptolemus who, by killing King Priam at his altar during the sack of Troy, brings down a curse upon the Greeks even as they are perfecting their victory.

This story suggested several themes, which I then molded to my own purposes: the role of corruption in our concept of expedience, the need of young men to prove themselves worthy in the eyes of even morally suspect elders (or especially them), and the curse of a hard-won ambition.

WHY EL SALVADOR?

I saw in the Greek situation a presentiment of America's dilemma at the close of the Cold War: finally achieving unrivaled leadership of the globe, but at the same time being cursed with the hatred of millions. Though we have showered the world with aid, too often we have done so through conspicuously corrupt, repressive, even murderous regimes, where the elites in charge predictably siphoned off much of that aid into their own pockets. Why did we look the other way during the violence and thievery? The regimes in question were reliably anticommunist, crucial to our need for cheap oil, or otherwise amenable to American strategic or commercial interests.

We live in a dangerous world, we are told. Hard, often unpleasant choices have to be made.

It's a difficult argument for those who have suffered under such regimes to swallow. They would consider it madness to suggest that it is envy of our preeminence, or contempt for our freedom, that causes them to view America so resentfully. Rather, they would try to get us to remember that while their hopes for self-determination, freedom, and prosperity were being crushed, America looked on with a strangely principled indifference, often accompanied by a fiercely patriotic self-congratulation, not to mention blatant hypocrisy.

Not only have we failed to admit this to ourselves, but the New Right has embraced a resurgent American exceptionalism as the antidote to such moral visitations, which such conservatives consider weak and defeatist. Instead, they see a revanchist America marching boldly into the new century with unapologetic military power, uninhibited free-market capitalism, and evangelical fervor—most immediately to bring freedom to the Middle East.

The New Right's historical template for this proposed transformation is Central America—specifically El Salvador, trumpeted as "the final battleground of the Cold War," and championed as one of our greatest foreign policy successes: the crucible in which American greatness was re-forged, banishing the ghosts of Vietnam forever.

There's a serious problem with the New Right's formulation, however: It requires an almost hallucinatory misreading of history.

Misremembering the Past

In their ongoing public campaign to justify the Iraq war, many supporters and members of the Bush Administration—including both Vice President Dick Cheney and former defense secretary Donald Rumsfeld—have singled out El Salvador as a shining example of where the "forward-leaning" policy they champion has succeeded.

Mr. Cheney did so during the vice presidential debates, contending that Iraq could expect the same bright future enjoyed by El Salvador, which, he claimed, is "a whale of a lot better because we held free elections."

What Mr. Cheney neglected to mention:

- At the time the elections were held (1982), death squads linked to the Salvadoran security forces were murdering on average three to five hundred civilians a month.
- The death squads targeted not just guerrilla supporters but priests, social workers, teachers, journalists, even members of the centrist Christian Democrats—the party that Congress forced the Reagan Administration to back, since it was the only party capable of solidifying the Salvadoran middle.
- The CIA funneled money to the Christian Democrats to ensure they gained control of the constituent assembly.
- Roberto D'Aubuisson, a known death squad leader, opposed the Christian Democrats as "Communists," and

launched his own bid to lead the constituent assembly,
forming ARENA as the political wing of his death squad
network. His bid was funded and supported by exiled
oligarchs and reactionary military leaders, and managed
by a prominent American public relations firm.

- "Anti-fraud measures" proved intimidating. For example:
  ballots were cast in glass jars. Many voters, who had to
  provide identification, and who suspected the government
  was monitoring their choices, feared violent reprisal if
  they were observed voting "improperly."

- ARENA won thirty-six of sixty seats in the assembly, and
  D'Aubuisson was elected its leader.

- This was perceived by all concerned as a disastrous
  failure for American policy. When D'Aubuisson tried
  to appoint one of his colleagues as assembly president,
  U.S. officials went to the military and threatened to cut
  off aid. D'Aubuisson relented, but it was the only
  concession he made to American demands.

In short, there was American influence, money, and manipula-
tion throughout the process, putting the lie to the whole notion the
elections were "free"—though Mr. Cheney was arguably correct
when he stated that "we" held them. Unfortunately, all that effort
came to naught, as what America wanted from the elections lay in
shambles. Even when, in the following year's election, a great deal
more money and arm-twisting resulted in Washington's candidate
being elected president, he remained powerless to reform the military, curtail the death squads, or revive the economy, measures
Washington knew to be crucial to its counter-insurgency strategy.
By 1987, the Reaganites decided to abandon the decimated Christian Democrats for ARENA—the party it had spent five years and
millions of dollars trying to keep from power.

As for Mr. Rumsfeld's remarks, he made them in the course of a
brief stopover in El Salvador to thank the government for its support

in the Iraq war. The defense secretary trumpeted the just nature of the cause in Iraq, noting that the Middle Eastern country had once been ruled by "a dictatorship that killed tens of thousands of human beings . . . A regime that cut off the heads and hands of people. A regime that threw people off the tops of six-story buildings with their hands and legs tied."

The irony of these remarks, which bordered on the macabre, was not lost on the locals: The Salvadoran military—which we funded, trained, and expanded tenfold—achieved a similar body count, employing similar if not identical methods in its bloody suppression of the internal opposition. The Salvadoran air force, for example, typically threw its bound captives not off rooftops but out of helicopters and airplanes (the so-called "night free-fall training"), and the practice of cutting off the head and hands of death squad victims was so common it earned the sobriquet "a haircut and a manicure."

These mischaracterizations, however, are merely part of a much larger deceit. In truth, America's claim to victory in El Salvador is delusional. As late as 1988, military and policy analysts of every political stripe were admitting that despite huge infusions of American cash, the government was in a stalemate with the Marxist guerrillas. Although six strike brigades were arguably up to the task of actually engaging the guerrillas, Salvadoran field tactics were often derided by Green Beret advisors as "search and avoid," and the government's propensity to slaughter its critics desisted only when it felt unthreatened.

Then, in 1989, the Soviet Union collapsed, and the Salvadoran oligarchy's main bargaining chip with Washington, its staunch opposition to a Communist takeover, became moot—but not before the guerrillas staged one final offensive, in response to which the military reverted to form, strafing and bombing whole neighborhoods, reviving the death squads, and murdering six Jesuit priests, their housekeeper, and her fifteen-year-old daughter.

International outrage over the murdered Jesuits finally brought matters to a head. The time had come to consider a truce, which the

UN, not the Americans, stepped in to broker. In 1992, the final Peace Accords were signed.

Thus, after over a billion dollars in military aid and three billion in non-lethal aid (most of it spent rebuilding infrastructure destroyed by the fighting) plus more than seventy thousand Salvadorans killed, over forty thousand of them civilians (and more than 90 percent of them murdered by their own government), the U.S. obtained a result it could have achieved over ten years earlier, in 1981, when the guerrillas first proposed a negotiated settlement—a prospect that the Reagan hard-liners, many of whom now serve in the Bush Administration, flatly and repeatedly rejected. Only victory would do for them, a victory that proved utterly elusive until the distortions of political memory took over.

MISCHARACTERIZING THE PRESENT

But even if the Reaganites didn't "win" El Salvador, isn't it true the situation there has improved dramatically? With peace and stability, internationally monitored free elections, and a demilitarized judicial apparatus, cannot El Salvador be credibly described as "a whale of a lot better" now?

Consider the following:

- Impunity from the country's civil and criminal laws continues, particularly for the politically, economically, or institutionally well-connected.
- The concentration of economic power remains in the hands of a few. In fact, in the 1990s wealth became even more concentrated as a result of neoliberal reforms introduced by ARENA.
- Land transfer provisions dictated by the Peace Accords have suffered endless delays.
- Child labor remains endemic.
- El Salvador is a source, transit, and destination country for women and children trafficked for sexual exploitation.

- Civil society is under siege due to the availability of weapons left behind by the war, the formation of shadowy crime syndicates by ex-military officers now turned businessmen, and the presence of transnational youth gangs founded by Salvadoran immigrants in the U.S.
- Death squads have returned, to conduct "social cleansing."
- The highest levels of the the Policía Nacional Civil (PNC) are controlled by former military men with dubious pasts. Corruption is widespread, and there are many ties between the police and organized crime. An attorney with the Human Rights Ombudsman stated: "When we go to the [police] Directorate for Investigating Organized Crime, we never go alone. There always has to be at least two of us, because they might do something to harm us."

The old political system was based on corruption, privilege, and brutality, and such things do not just evaporate, even in the welcome light of peace and free elections. As we know from worldwide example—Serbia, Ulster, Palestine, Thailand, Somalia, Afghanistan, and, yes, El Salvador and Iraq—today's paramilitary force is tomorrow's Mafia. And so-called free elections can often mask extreme imbalances of power, which voters feel helpless to change.

Meanwhile, almost a third of the population of El Salvador has emigrated to other countries, primarily the United States. The migration wave continues today, estimated by some observers at seven hundred persons per day. These expatriates now send back to their less fortunate family members remittances (*remesas*) of nearly three billion dollars per year. If the country were reliably secure and prosperous, with wealth distributed reasonably among its people, it would no longer need this foreign cash machine. But the most significant form of voting in El Salvador is done with one's feet: If one can leave, one does.

Those who have stayed behind have become increasingly frustrated. The unwavering grip that ARENA has on power—with conspicuous assistance from Washington—reminds many of the oligarchy's brutal control prior to the civil war. Organized protests have turned increasingly violent, and many fear the country is once again coming apart at the seams.

On July 5, 2006, student protests against bus fare increases resulted in gunfire, with two police officers killed and ten wounded. President Tony Saca blamed the FMLN before any credible evidence was available (and subsequently retreated from this position). The FMLN responded by condemning the violence. As it turned out, a gunman caught on tape was identified as an expelled party member, now belonging to a splinter group calling itself the Limon Brigade.

Beatrice Alamanni de Carillo, the Human Rights Ombudsman, remarked, "We have to admit that a new revolutionary fringe is forming. It's an open secret."

Gregorio Rosa Chávez, the auxiliary bishop of San Salvador, stated, "We signed the treaty but we never lived the peace. Reconciliation is not just based on healing wounds, but healing them well. . . . People are losing faith in the institutions."

THE "SALVADOR OPTION"

If we described honestly the real state of affairs in El Salvador, would ordinary Iraqis truly wish that for their future? Would Americans consider the cost in human life, not to mention billions of dollars per day, worthwhile? Forget all the blunders along the way (or the more jaundiced view that democracy was never the issue)—is this truly a sane model for a stable state?

It's too late to pose the question, of course. The New Right's distorted understanding of the past and present in El Salvador has created an almost eerie simulacrum in Iraq, with even ghastlier results. Taking one particularly ominous example: In the summer of 2004, as American efforts to stem the Iraqi insurgency foundered, U.S.

officials decided to employ what came to be known as "the Salvador Option." American advisers oversaw the establishment of commando units composed of former Baathists. The commandos began to exert themselves in the field, enjoying successes the Americans envied, but also employing methods American troops shunned, especially in the aftermath of the Abu Ghraib scandal. The American advisers overseeing the commandos—who had extensive backgrounds in Latin America and specifically El Salvador—adamantly stated they in no way gave a green light to death squads, torture, or other human rights violations; they may well have been sincere. But matters spiraled murderously out of control when Shiites dominated the elections of January 2005 and took over for the Interim Government: Shiite death squads, linked to the Badr militia but acting under the aegis of the Ministry of Interior, soon began systematically hunting and killing Sunni men, creating a sectarian bloodbath that continues to tear the country apart. American calls for transparent investigations of the murders have netted little in the way of results.

Regardless of what the future holds for Iraq, these commandos, along with the paramilitary units and the other sectarian militias operating in Iraq, will not melt away into nothingness. Many of their members are tomorrow's gangsters (whose rackets will predictably fund terrorist organizations).

Meanwhile, the escalating bloodshed has caused, among countless other troubles, the dislocation of millions of refugees, and the flight from the country of large portions of Iraq's professional class, who like ordinary Salvadorans realize the future lies elsewhere.

Given all this, it's difficult not to revisit the notion of a curse. In achieving sole superpower status, we have relied on false notions of ourselves and others, excused atrocity under the guise of expedience, sought our own national interest over all other considerations (with at times a cavalier appreciation of whether short-term successes might in fact poison long-term ones)—all the while proclaiming, not without some merit, all the best intentions in the world. To think this wouldn't come back to haunt us is to believe in notions of power and innocence too fatuous for an adult mind to entertain.

One last example should make the case conclusive. Consider our support for the Contras, a makeshift band of mercenaries assembled for the sole purpose of causing as much havoc as possible for the Sandinista government in Nicaragua, whom we accused of supporting the Salvadoran guerrillas. While President Reagan steadfastly proclaimed the Contras to be the "moral equivalent of our Founding Fathers," an adviser to the Joint Chiefs of Staff called them "just a bunch of killers." By 1985, the Contras had murdered at least four thousand civilians, wounded an equal number, and kidnapped perhaps five thousand more. Even the CIA admitted the Contras steadfastly refused to engage the Sandinista military and instead preferred to execute civic officials, heads of cooperatives, nurses, judges, and doctors, while showing a stubborn propensity for abducting and raping teenage girls. The strategy: not to seize power or even prevail militarily, but simply to terrorize average Nicaraguans, and demonstrate that their government could not protect them or provide even basic services.

And who has steadfastly imitated this strategy?

The jihadists and insurgents in Iraq.

Like the victims of, yes, a curse, we find ourselves trapped in the exact same position in which we put our previous enemies. Not even Sophocles could have devised it more neatly.

The Murder of Gilberto Soto

The historically suspect pronouncements of Messrs. Cheney and Rumsfeld and their camp followers were not the only topical incidents of relevance to occur during the writing of this book. Another, far more chilling event also took place, an event that not only underscored the deterioration of civil society in El Salvador, but eerily echoed elements of the novel's plot: the murder of an American—a Teamster named Gilberto Soto.

He was visiting family in El Salvador—and also hoped to meet

with port drivers to discuss possible plans to unionize—when gunmen shot him dead outside his mother's house in Usulután. Many of
the trucking companies that would have been affected by
unionization are run by ex-military officers, but the police investigation never pursued this. Instead, two gang members were pressed
and possibly tortured into confessing that the victim's mother-in-
law, who had less than a hundred dollars to her name, hired them to
kill Soto out of some vague, illogical family rancor.

Two of the three defendants, Soto's mother-in-law and the alleged triggerman, were acquitted in February 2006. The man alleged to have supplied the murder weapon was convicted, despite
the fact the Human Rights Ombudsman, in her scathing critique of
the investigation—an investigation which was not conducted by the
local prosecutor, but the PNC's notoriously corrupt Directorate for
Investigating Organized Crime—specifically noted that no chain
of evidence existed concerning the gun and bullets.

This murder took place during the American debate over ratification of the Central American Free Trade Agreement (CAFTA),
and only by considerable arm-twisting was the Bush administration
able to secure the necessary votes for passage. (CAFTA passed the
House by a mere two votes.) How can there be free trade, opponents
argued, if men and women seeking a just wage can be murdered
with impunity? But such arguments did not prevail.

A Final Note on *Blood of Paradise*

All of which leads to a brief summarizing glance at two of my characters, Jude and Clara.

Like Neoptolemus, Jude allows himself to be seduced by a
morally questionable elder into a reckless scheme. In a sense, he
stands for all of us: an everyman who wants to do good in a world
he knows needs plenty of it, but who also suspects that to accomplish
that end a few nefarious deeds must be indulged. He wants to believe
as well that one can withstand such evil, rise above it, even as one does
its bidding: Good intentions, sound character, and professional skill

will prevail over necessary compromises with immorality. Who knows, it might even be fun—kick ass, take names, shake hands with the devil but don't let him hold your wallet. We're Americans after all, blessed by God and history. How can we not prevail?

Clara—Salvadoran war orphan, rape victim—sees the matter differently. She ultimately understands that only through real sacrifice can the future possibly redeem the past. Being deeply religious, like many Salvadorans, she sees this call for renunciation as the challenge of the crucifixion. And so, in the end, she finds the heart to act upon her conviction—not in an empowering act of violence, but in a selfless, agonizing act of love.

DAVID CORBETT is a poet and screenwriter and the author of numerous short stories and articles, as well as the novels *The Devil's Redhead* and *Done for a Dime,* the latter a *New York Times* Notable Book. For fifteen years, he was a senior operative with a prominent San Francisco private investigation firm, working on a number of high-profile criminal and civil litigations—including the Lincoln Savings & Loan scandal and the People's Temple trial—after which he joined his late wife in a small law practice in northern California, where he continues to reside. Visit his website at www.davidcorbett.com.

ABOUT THE TYPE

This book was set in Granjon, a modern recutting of a type-face produced under the direction of George W. Jones, who based Granjon's design upon the letter forms of Claude Gara-mond (1480–1561). The name was given to the typeface as a tribute to the typographic designer Robert Granjon.

2

rc 3.9.09 (hf hoes)
   ba 12.17 (2)

NNS

NC

Core Author